By a Spider's Thread

By a Spider's Thread

LAURA LIPPMAN

ORION

First published in Great Britain in 2004 by Orion,
an imprint of the Orion Publishing Group Ltd.

Copyright © Laura Lippman 2004

The moral right of Laura Lippman to be identified as the author
of this work has been asserted in accordance with
the Copyright, Designs and Patents Act of 1988.

A CIP catalogue record for this book is available
from the British Library.

ISBN 0 75285 987 0 hardback

ISBN 0 75286 662 1 trade paperback

**Printed in Great Britain by
Clays Ltd, St Ives plc**

F123.161
E16

The Orion Publishing Group Ltd
Orion House
5 Upper Saint Martin's Lane
London, WC2H 9EA

www.orionbooks.co.uk

By a Spider's Thread

For David and Ethan,

with gratitude for the crash course in fathers and sons,

not to mention the Advanced Mission Battleship strategy

If God lived on earth,
people would knock out all His windows.

—YIDDISH PROVERB

Evil inclination is at first as slender as a spider's thread,
and then strong as a rope.

—TALMUDIC PROVERB

Acknowledgments

The research for this book was often the result of chance encounters and serendipity, beginning with Donald Worden's memories of transporting furs as an off-duty police officer. My former colleague Bill Salganik provided an introduction by proxy to Michael Miller, who shared his knowledge of the fur industry and let me try on quite a few coats. Scott Shane was generous with his insights into Baltimore's Russian Jewish community; Carole Epstein solved one of the book's knottier problems poolside in Las Vegas.

Quite a few folks did their best to help Tess and me grasp the finer points of Orthodox Judaism as it might be practiced by the characters in this book. These included Bernard Simon, Suzanne Balaban, Rafael Alvarez, and Sarah Weinman. I also relied on a wide range of reference books, such as *This Is My God*, Herman Wouk; *The Jewish Book of Why*, Alfred J. Kolatch; *Fables of a Jewish Aesop*, translated by Moses Hadas; *A Guide to Jewish Prayer*, Rabbi Adin Steinsaltz; and *Essential Judaism*, George Robinson. Any errors are my own. But I also invoke the novelist's prerogative to make stuff up, especially when it comes to the ever-changing social-services bureaucracy.

Much of this book was written on the premises of Spoons, so thank you to Karen, Mike, Neil, Morgan, and everyone else at that lovely oasis.

It should be noted that this story was inspired very loosely by the real-life experiences of the late Victor Persico. I met and interviewed Victor in the early 1990s while working for the Baltimore *Sun*, but the article was spiked for complicated reasons. Victor was a gentle soul, and I wish that the world had had a chance to know the full story of his devotion to his three sons, a devotion that transcended anything I could ever invent. This is much too little, much too late.

September

They were in one of the "I" states when Zeke told Isaac he had to ride in the trunk for a little while. Zeke announced this new plan in what Isaac thought of as his fakey voice, big and hollow, with too much air in it. This was the voice Zeke used whenever Isaac's mother was nearby. He used a very different one when she couldn't hear.

"You brought this on yourself, buckaroo," Zeke said, securing the suitcases to the roof of the car, then making a nest in the center of the trunk. When Isaac just stared at the space that had been created, not sure what Zeke wanted him to do, Zeke picked him up under the arms, swinging him into the hole as if Isaac weighed nothing at all. "See, plenty of room."

"Put down a blanket," Isaac's mother said, but she didn't object to the trunk idea, didn't say it was wrong or that she wouldn't allow it. She didn't even mind that Zeke had stolen the blanket from the motel room. She just stood there with Penina and Efraim huddled close to her, looking disappointed. That was the last thing Isaac saw before Zeke closed the trunk: his mother's face, sad and stern, as if Isaac were the bad one, as if he had caused all the trouble. So unfair. He was the one who was trying to do the right thing.

The trunk was bigger than Isaac expected, and he was not as frightened as he thought he would be. It was too bad it was such an old car. A new one, like his father's, might have an emergency light inside, or even a way to spring the lock. His father had shown him these features in his car after he found Isaac playing with the buttons on his key ring—popping the trunk, locking and unlocking the Cadillac's doors. Isaac's mother had yelled, saying the key ring wasn't a toy, that he would break it or burn out the batteries, but Isaac's father had shown Isaac everything about his new car, even under the hood. That was his father's way. "Curiosity didn't kill the cat," his father said. "Not getting answers to his questions was what got the cat in trouble." His father had even shut himself in the trunk and shown Isaac how to get out again.

But this car was old, very old, the oldest car Isaac had ever known, probably older than Isaac. It didn't have airbags, or enough seat belts in the backseat. Isaac kept hoping a policeman might pull them over one day because of the seat belts. Or maybe a toll taker would report his mother for holding one of the twins in her lap in the front seat, which she did when they fussed. But there were no tolls here, not on the roads that Zeke drove. Isaac was trying so hard to keep track—they had started out in Indiana, and then they went to Illinois, but Isaac was pretty sure that they had come back to Indiana in the past week. Or they could still be in Illinois, or even as far west as Iowa. It was hard to see differences here in the middle of the country, where everything was yellow and the towns had strange names that were hard to pronounce.

It was hard to tell time, too, without school marking the days off, without a calendar on the kitchen wall, without Shabbat reminding you that another week had ended. Would God understand about missing Shabbat? If God knew everything, did he know it wasn't Isaac's fault that he wasn't going to yeshiva? Or was it up to Isaac to find a way to pray no matter what, the way his father did when he traveled for business? Now, this was the kind of conversation his father loved. He would have started pulling books from the shelves in his study, looking for various rabbis' opinions. And, whatever the answer was, his father would have made Isaac feel okay, would have assured him that he was doing his best, which was all God expected. That was his father's way, to answer Isaac's questions and make him feel better.

His father knew everything, or close enough. He knew history and the Torah, math and science. He knew lots of terrific old war movies and westerns, and the names of all the Orioles, past and present. Best of all, he could talk about the night sky as if it were a story in a book, telling the stories that the Greeks and Indians had told themselves when they looked at the same stars.

"Does Orion ever catch the bull?" Isaac had asked his father once. Of course, that had been when he was little, six or seven. He was nine now, going into the fourth grade, or supposed to be. He wouldn't ask such a question now.

"Not yet," his father had said, "but you never know. After all, if the universe is really shrinking, he may catch up with him still."

That had scared Isaac, the part about the universe shrinking, but his father had said it wasn't something he needed to worry about. But Isaac worried about everything, especially now. He worried about Lyme disease and West Nile virus and whether Washington, D.C., would get a baseball team, which his dad said might not be so good for the Orioles. He worried about the twins, who had started talking this weird not-quite-English to each other.

Mostly, though, he worried about Zeke and how to get away from him.

Despite being locked in the trunk, bouncing and bumping down the road, Isaac wasn't sorry that he had tried to talk to the guard man. His only mistake was letting his mother see him do it. If the line in the bank had been longer, if it hadn't moved so fast, he might have had time to explain himself. Why did lines move fast only when you didn't want them to?

The guard was in a corner. He was old, really old, and he didn't look very strong, but he had a gun. Glancing around, Isaac had sidled over to him and tugged at the man's sleeve. But when the man looked at him, Isaac's mind went blank. He had no idea what to say. It was complicated, what had happened. He wasn't even sure exactly what had happened. His mother said it was okay, to trust her, that everything was going to be wonderful pretty soon. She had a reason for doing what she did. He was just too young to understand. He had to trust her, he had to be patient. She said this over and over and over again.

Zeke said Isaac should just be quiet and do what he was told.

"Mister . . ."

"Yeah?" The guard's eyes met Isaac's only for a second, then returned to studying the bank lobby.

"My mother . . . the woman in the blue scarf?"

"Uh-huh."

He was not sure what the guard was agreeing to—that he had a mother, that she wore a blue scarf—so he plunged ahead, his words coming fast, probably too fast. "She took us. She stole us. We don't live here. We live at 341 Cedar Court in Pikesville, Maryland, near the Suburban Club golf course, 212—"

"But she's your mother?"

"Yes."

"That's your mother?"

"Yes."

"And she's married to your father?"

This question tripped Isaac up, because he was no longer sure of the answer and he liked to be correct whenever possible. It had been two weeks, maybe more, maybe less, since his mother had told Isaac to pack his bag for a weekend trip. He had not seen his father or talked to him since that day. Did that make his parents divorced? No, divorce was much more complicated, he was sure of that much. It didn't happen just because somebody left. His father went on business trips all the time, and that hadn't made them divorced, so his mother's packing up suitcases and taking them away couldn't make them divorced either.

"Yes, we're a family, the Rubin family, but my father is back in Baltimore—"

"Are you telling stories, little boy? Have you ever heard about the little boy who cried wolf?"

His mother had gotten to the head of the line faster than Isaac thought she would. She was going to be the next one called. When she saw Isaac talking to the guard, she let out a screechy sound, gave up her place, and ran over, the twins stumbling as they tried to keep up with her.

"I'm sorry if he was bothering you," she said to the guard, finding her usual voice, which wasn't at all like her screaming one. Men always smiled when Isaac's mother spoke, and sometimes even when she didn't. Something about his mother made men act weird, which Isaac didn't understand. She wasn't clever, like his father, she didn't know lots of interesting things. But just by smiling and looking at men, nodding at anything they said, she got whatever she wanted. Something about her made people anxious to see her happy. Even Isaac felt that way. At least he had felt like that back in Baltimore, back when his mother and he had agreed on what happy was.

"Not at all, ma'am. But he was saying that you had left his father—"

"Oh, Isaac," she said with a sigh, hugging him close to her, her arms hard across his back. She stroked his hair but pulled it a little, too, a warning to be quiet and still, a reminder that Zeke was not far away even if Isaac couldn't see him. Zeke was never far away. "How often have I told you that you mustn't tease people like this? Telling stories to strangers is just as bad as making jokes at an airport. You know that."

5

Isaac's mom looked into the guard's face. "We're on our way to see my family, outside Chicago. But this is a busy season in my husband's business, and he couldn't come with us. We're traveling with my cousin." She tilted her head toward the old green car parked in front of the bank, although Isaac knew that Zeke wasn't in it, and he definitely wasn't a cousin, no matter where he was. He better not be a cousin. Isaac didn't want to be related to Zeke at all. And there was no family in Chicago, not that he had ever heard of, and although his father's business picked up in September, it didn't really get busy until later in the fall. Lie, lie, lie. A mother shouldn't tell so many lies.

"I know how it is," the guard said. He pointed his finger at Isaac, placing it on the tip of Isaac's nose and bouncing it for emphasis, which made Isaac want to scratch and rub, as if a mosquito had landed there. "Now, you be good. No more stories."

"No more stories," Isaac repeated, and he knew what it meant when books said someone's heart was heavy. His heart felt as if it had fallen to the bottom of his stomach and kept going, ending up in his shoes. He was so sad that being put in the trunk by Zeke seemed a small thing, almost. What did it matter if they put him in a trunk? No one would ever believe a little kid over a grown-up. His dad had told him it was silly to say the world was unfair, but it was, it definitely was.

"I have enough to worry about, doing my job, without a wild card like you," Zeke had said. What job? Zeke never went to work that Isaac could see. That was the problem: Zeke never went away at all. If he went away, then Isaac could run away, or call home on the phone.

Isaac counted backward in his head. He had talked to the guard two days ago, a Friday or maybe even a Saturday. Were banks open on the Sabbath? Was going to a bank work? But Zeke didn't worry about such things. One of the first things he had done, upon meeting Isaac and Efraim in the motel room, was take the yarmulkes from their heads and hand them to their mother, instructing her to pack them away for good. "One less thing to notice," he had said.

That had been almost two weeks ago, and Isaac could not get used to the feel of his crown being exposed. The yarmulke was there to remind him that God was above, always, and now it was gone. Did that mean God was gone? Would God understand that the missing yarmulke, too, was beyond his control? His bare head, the unkosher meals. Efraim had eaten bacon at breakfast the other day, even after Isaac told him not to, and Zeke had laughed and laughed, as if it were all a joke. "It's so good, isn't it, little man?" Zeke had said, giving Efraim another piece. "Once you've had bacon, you'll never go back. Maybe I'll get you a lobster when our ship comes in."

Isaac had filed this piece of information away: Lobsters were from Maine. Ships sailed on big oceans, and they needed ports if they were going to come in, although maybe some of the Great Lakes were big enough, too. Still, he was pretty sure that the ships that carried people were all on the oceans. Did this mean they were going east, which was where they had started? Wherever they were going, they weren't going very fast. They were in the car all day, it seemed, yet the countryside never changed and the towns all looked alike.

The car stopped, and he heard the doors slam. He counted in his head, because Zeke had taken his watch from him, too. One, one thousand, two, one thousand—all the way up to two hundred, one thousand, more than three minutes. And then they were off again, the tires making a great squealing noise, the car surging, then settling down. He wondered how long Zeke would drive before he let Isaac out. What if Zeke forgot? But his mother would never forget that he was back here. She would make Zeke take him out as soon as possible.

He touched his head, found that it was still covered by a thick mat of bristly hair, then reached his arm up to the lid of the trunk and pressed on it, as if he might be able to pop it through sheer will.

7

He decided to pretend the trunk was the sky, placing the stars that he knew best. Sirius, Orion. The North Star. If you can find the North Star, his father had told him, you can navigate by night, find your way. You will never be lost if you can find the North Star. Or, better yet, Isaac could be Jonah, in the belly of the whale. Which may not have been a whale, according to Isaac's dad, but just a very big fish instead.

Only Isaac's situation was not the same as Jonah's. Jonah got swallowed by the whale because he didn't want to do God's will. Isaac was in the trunk because he was trying to do what God wanted. At least, he was pretty sure that God wanted his family to go back to their old life. The story of Jonah was told at Yom Kippur—which was no more than a month away, Isaac realized. There was something about a plant, which Jonah loved, and the worm that God sent to kill it, which made Jonah angry at God. Of course, God had sent the worm, so it was really God who'd made the plant die, to teach Jonah a lesson. Perhaps Zeke was the worm in Isaac's life, and there was a lesson to be learned here, too. Well, Isaac was good at lessons. He'd figure out what God wanted him to do, and he'd do it. His family would be home again, and everything would be the way it was before Zeke-the-worm came along.

Wednesday

1

Tess Monaghan had been a high school senior when her father had bestowed his single life lesson, the one piece of advice that was supposed to open all doors and allow his only child to hurdle every obstacle: He showed her how to shake a man's hand.

He demonstrated by making firm, confident contact at the V between her thumb and index finger, then gave her arm one adamant shake. "Don't wag it like a garden hose," Patrick Monaghan had said, and that was that. His daughter was ready to go forth into the world, or at least the world her father knew, where a handshake still counted for something.

Patrick Monaghan had neglected, however, to tell his daughter what to do when the intended recipient of her firm, manly handshake looked at her palm as if it were contaminated.

"I'm so sorry," she said, remembering a beat too late. "But I thought—"

"Your uncle told me your mother's family was Conservative," her prospective client said, hands clasped behind his back, just in case she made another lunge for his digits.

"Well, I think what my grandfather always said was 'The temple my family does *not* attend must be Conservative.' The Weinsteins are not a particularly observant bunch."

Mark Rubin didn't laugh at the old family joke. Several inches taller than Tess, which put him well over six feet, he was stocky in a robust, attractive way, and he wore a beautifully tailored suit that emphasized his broad chest and shoulders. He had glossy dark hair, black-brown eyes, a trim black beard, and the kind of blue-black hair that teenage girls tried to emulate when they went through a Goth phase, only with a shine that marked it as natural. The over-all effect reminded Tess of a stuffed-sealskin otter she had been given as a child, back when such a gift would not have been re-garded as a gauche act of political incorrectness.

Or perhaps she had that old toy on her brain because she knew this man sold furs for a living, and the otter had been fashioned from the leftovers of an aunt's jacket. She wondered if Rubin wore a fur coat himself, when winter came. This September day was al-most too warm for his lightweight wool suit.

"Your uncle," he said, his voice stiff as his collar, "is quite active in Jewish causes. That's how we met and how he came to recom-mend you when he found out I needed the services of someone in your line of work."

"My Uncle Donald is active in Jewish causes? Was it court-ordered?"

Rubin frowned, although this wasn't an attempt at humor on Tess's part. Her Uncle Donald had had a short-lived association with a sleazy state senator that haunted him to this day.

"I'm not sure when he started volunteering, but I met him over ten years ago, so it's been quite some time. He's a very good man, your uncle."

"Oh," she said, annoyed and flustered by the hint of reproof in his voice, the implication that her uncle had not prepared her well for this meeting. Uncle Donald had, in fact, briefed her thoroughly. He had told her he had an acquaintance, that the acquaintance was a wealthy furrier, an Orthodox Jew in need of a discreet private detective. Modern Orthodox, Uncle Donald had clarified, not Hasidic, which was why Tess had thought herself on safe ground offering Rubin her hand.

Really, the only thing that Uncle Donald had neglected to mention was the large pole permanently inserted in Mark Rubin's sphincter.

"Would you like a seat? Something to drink? I keep Coca-Cola and bottled water in my fridge, and . . . well, that's kosher, right? If it's done under supervision. We could check the label for . . . what? A little *k* in a circle . . . ?"

"I'm fine," Mark Rubin said, taking the wooden chair opposite her desk. His dark eyes scanned the room, absorbing his surroundings without comment. Tess had decorated the one-room office with whimsical artifacts to provide conversational fodder for the ill at ease, but these photographs and strange objets d'art didn't seem to be having much effect on Rubin. He didn't even raise his eyes to the "Time for a Haircut" clock, a barbershop find of which Tess was particularly proud.

Although it smarted a little now, sitting beneath that glowing clock, given the untimely circumstances of Tess's most recent haircut. Self-consciously, she reached for her hair, a stubby ponytail where a long braid had once hung. Her friend Whitney said the style made Tess look like one of the original signers of the Declaration of Independence. It was, like most of Whitney's tactless assessments, all too true, but Tess didn't care. She wanted her braid back, and she was prepared to live through all the growing-out stages.

The furrier did take notice of the greyhound and the Doberman vying for control of the sofa. The greyhound, Esskay, was winning, but only because she fought dirty, rabbiting her legs so her untrimmed toenails scraped the tender-skinned Miata, who whimpered piteously. Esskay always triumphed over Miata, the world's most docile Doberman.

"Are the dogs for protection?"

"More for companionship. The neighborhood's not that bad."

"Times change. My grandfather couldn't wait to get out of East Baltimore. Of course, we lived closer to Lombard Street, just off Central."

"Near the old synagogue."

"There were several synagogues in the neighborhood then."

He had a funny way of holding his neck, as if that pole in his butt ran all the way up his backbone, and Tess wondered if his rigid posture came from years of balancing a yarmulke on the crown. There was no sign of a bobby pin or a clip. Did Mark Rubin consider bobby pins cheating? Were bobby pins unorthodox? Up to five minutes ago, Theresa Esther Weinstein Monaghan had considered herself well versed in the religion practiced by her mother's side of the family. She knew a little Yiddish, could fake her way through a seder as long as the Haggadah included an English translation. But now she felt 100 percent goyish. To her visitor she probably looked like some field-hockey player from Notre Dame Prep.

"Did Donald tell you anything of my situation?"

"Only that it was a missing-person case, an unusual one that the police won't handle. He said you would prefer to fill me in on the details."

"Persons," he said. "Missing persons. Four, in fact. My entire family."

"Divorce?" She suppressed a sigh. Until recently Tess had disdained divorce work, picking and choosing her jobs. But she had lost several weeks of work this summer and could no longer afford to be fussy.

"No, nothing like that. I came home one day and they were gone."

"Voluntarily?"

"Excuse me?"

"I assume your wife's flight was legal and not suspicious, or this would be a police case."

"The police agree it's not their case," he said, his voice so low as to be almost inaudible, and Tess realized that what she had taken for coolness was an attempt to keep strong emotions in check. "Me, I'm not so sure. I went to work, I had a family. I came home, I didn't. I certainly feel as if something has been stolen from me."

"Was there talk of a separation? Had you been quarreling? It's just hard to imagine such a thing happening out of the blue."

"But that's *exactly* what did happen. My wife left with my children, with no warning, no explanation. She simply disappeared the Friday before Labor Day, right before school started and just as my business was picking up."

"Early September is your busy season?"

"No, but many of my customers get their furs out of storage in the month before the high holidays, just in case."

"Would the Orthodox wear fur to shul on Yom Kippur?" Tess had no idea where her mind had dredged up this odd fact, but she felt as if she had just pulled off a sophisticated thought in a foreign language. Score one for her.

"Not all my customers are Orthodox. They're not even all Jewish."

Point lost. Tess had envisioned a sea of glossy hats in a synagogue, but maybe she was thinking of some long-ago church service her grandfather had dragged her to. Or perhaps she wasn't having a memory so much as she was replaying a movie version of someone else's memories. Probably Barry Levinson's. A lot of people in Baltimore had Barry Levinson's life lodged in their heads and had begun to mistake it for their own.

"It's never cool enough to wear a fur in September, not in Baltimore."

"Yes, but hope springs eternal." He offered Tess a crooked smile. "I guess that's why I'm here."

She bent her head over her desk, focusing on the lines of the legal pad in front of her, counting on Rubin to get his emotions under control if she didn't look straight at him. Tess was sure he didn't want her to see him cry. She was even surer that *she* didn't want to see him cry. Men crying creeped her out.

"If your wife took your children without your permission, isn't that a kidnapping? Can't the police go at it from that angle? Don't get me wrong, I'd love to have the work, but the police have far more resources than I do."

"I know, and that's why I started with them. But . . . it's amazing. If you're married and your spouse leaves you, taking your children, you have no real rights. I've been told that I have to get divorced in absentia and petition for custody. Only then will I have any rights to assert. And that could take up to a year."

"Oh, there has to be some way to expedite a divorce in this case. I can't imagine the state would hold to the one-year rule in such a case." Maryland did have odd marital laws, Tess knew. It was all too easy to get married here—it was one of the few states that didn't require a blood test, which years ago had made Elkton a destination for impatient New Yorkers—but relatively difficult to get divorced. A legacy, she had always assumed, from its Catholic founders. Marry in haste, live in purgatory.

"You don't understand. Even if I divorced my wife under Maryland law, it wouldn't count, not to me."

"Why not?"

"I would need a *get* from a rabbinic court as well. Divorce may be granted easily in the world at large, but my faith insists that a couple make every attempt at mediation and reconciliation before giving up on a marriage."

"But I assume your wife's actions would satisfy even a—what did you call it?—rabbinic court." Tess had an image of an appeals court, only in slightly different robes and with the bushy beards, side curls, and large-brimmed hats of the Hasidim.

"Perhaps, but it would not satisfy *me*. How can I give up on my marriage when I don't know what went wrong? You have to understand she gave no sign, absolutely no sign, that she was unhappy in any way. How could she be on the verge of something so drastic and provide no clue?"

She probably gave you a million clues, Tess thought, but kept the observation to herself. In her experience, men were capable of going to great lengths to ignore the evidence of women's unhappiness. It was how men survived, by not inquiring too closely about the melancholy some women carried with them. If they ignored it, maybe it would go away.

Sometimes it was the woman who went away instead.

"Mr. Rubin . . ." She paused, but he did not invite her to call him Mark, so she forged ahead. "The very nature of my work requires me to ask rude, intrusive questions, not unlike the kind that doctors and lawyers ask, so I'll beg your forgiveness in advance. Did you have a good marriage?"

"We had a *wonderful* marriage."

"No disagreements, no tensions?"

"Nothing out of the ordinary. There was a slight age difference. . . ."

So that's where the dog was buried, as her Grandma Weinstein might say. "How much?"

"Twelve years. I married relatively late, at thirty-one."

Funny, Tess was thirty-three, and she considered that a damn early age for matrimony.

"You're . . . what?" She checked her notes. "Forty-one. So she was only nineteen when you married?"

A slight defensiveness crept into his tone. "Yes, but Natalie was an unusual woman, more mature at nineteen than most women are in their thirties." Was it Tess's imagination, or did he glance at her neon HUMAN HAIR sign just then? A gift from her boyfriend two Christmases ago, it complemented the "Time for a Haircut" clock nicely.

"How old are the children?"

"Isaac is nine, the twins are going on five. We wanted more, but it was not to be. I had hoped to have a houseful of children."

"And your wife?"

"Of course I want my wife in my house. That's why I'm here."

"No, I meant . . . did your wife want a lot of children, too?"

"Absolutely. It's our way. It's what God wants."

Mark Rubin's very certitude seemed a bad sign to Tess. It was bad enough to claim you knew your wife's mind, another to assume you knew God's as well.

"She had absolutely no reason to leave?"

"*None.*" The reply was too firm, too automatic. He wasn't allowing anyone to question this fact, beginning with himself.

"What about addictions? I'm not talking just about drugs or alcohol, but gambling or other compulsive behaviors, such as eating disorders. Even shopping."

"No, nothing like that."

"Does she spend a lot of time on the Internet?" A new wrinkle in divorce cases, stealth adultery, which didn't reveal itself until the person ran off to be with his or her virtual love. Installing spyware was one of Tess's first steps in any case where a spouse suspected another spouse of fooling around.

"She barely knows how to use a computer. Our oldest son had to set up her e-mail account."

"And there was no"—she took a breath and plunged ahead—"no violence in the household?"

"*No.*" Here, at least, he was utterly convincing.

"It's just that it's very unusual for a woman to up and leave, taking her three children. Does she have a job?"

"No matter my circumstances, I would never allow—I mean, I would never expect my wife to work outside the home."

"Then how would she support them? Does she have her own money? Family?"

A slight hesitation here. "Not one that she can rely on. Her mother is still here in Baltimore, but she and Natalie have been estranged since her parents' divorce, back when she was a young teenager. Her father's completely out of the picture now, has no contact with her at all."

Tess wondered if Rubin's marriage had been an arranged one, then wondered if the Orthodox still used arranged marriages. Her upbringing had been bicultural primarily in the culinary details. The Weinsteins went out for Chinese and held backyard crab feasts, rationalizing that anything eaten outside wasn't really *treyf*. The Monaghans had lesser palates, but they loved the Sour Beef dinner put on by the ladies of Good Counsel every autumn. On St. Patrick's Day, they drove for lean corned beef to what Tess's paternal grandfather called Jewtown. Pop-Pop Monaghan had called the neighborhood that to the day he died, literally. In his bed in the old house on Wilkens Avenue, he had reached for Tess's hand, mistaking her for his only daughter, Kitty, the youngest and best loved of his seven children.

"Well," he had said, "Patrick married a Jew. What do you know about that, Kitty? A Jewess from Jewtown."

There was no meanness in his tone, no censure. He was just calling a spade a spade, a Jew a Jewess. As for Jewtown—well, that designation had appeared on some local maps well into the 1930s, and Pop-Pop Monaghan's worldview had pretty much jelled by then.

"I know," Tess had replied, trying to find something that would be neither rebuke nor agreement, "that he loves her."

"Love," her grandfather scoffed.

Some men might have been smart enough to exit on a line like that, but Brian Monaghan, a belligerent Irishman to the end, wore out his welcome, coming back from death several times in that last day. Finally life seemed to tire of *him* and shuttered itself against his return, like a tavern giving someone the bum's rush.

But her Monaghan side was of no use here. Today Tess needed to rely on her Weinstein genes if she was going to find any affinity with this prickly man who clearly had the wherewithal to help her out of her financial slump.

"Do you have any leads at all? A vehicle, a name she might use, a place, a friend she might reach out to, a list of long-distance phone calls from before she left?"

"All our cars are in our garage, untouched. My guess is she'd revert to her maiden name, or some form of it. Natalie Peters." Tess idly wondered what the surname was before it was changed. Her grandfather had been too stubborn to consider such a thing, and he was proud of having the Weinstein name on his stores until the day they sank into bankruptcy. "As for family or friends, it's only her mother, and, as I said, they have no relationship. I think she lives up on Labyrinth Road. Vera Peters."

"Still, it's a place to start. Now, has Natalie drawn on any accounts—checking or savings—since she's been gone? Used a credit card?"

"No, nothing like that."

"And the police didn't find that suspicious? That's usually a sign of . . . well, it's certainly something they look at."

She had not wanted to say, *It's usually a sign that a person is dead.*

"They know what you know, and they still don't think this is a matter for them. They have these, too."

He took a folder from his briefcase and brought out three photographs. The first could have been a miniature Mark Rubin, a boy with the same dark eyes and hair, although not the somber expression. He beamed at the camera, a little self-conscious, but clearly happy at whatever moment he had been captured. He was holding a plaque, so perhaps it was an awards ceremony.

"Isaac, my oldest."

The next photo showed a boy and girl of the same height. Their hair was several shades lighter than the older boy's and their features sharper—narrow eyes with a hint of a tilt, prominent cheekbones that gave them a foxy look. They must favor their mother.

"The twins, Penina and Efraim."

He was shy about sliding the last photograph to Tess, or perhaps just reluctant to surrender it. The woman in the picture was gorgeous, an absolute knockout, with the lush lips and heavy-lidded eyes of a movie star. Not just any movie star but a specific one, although Tess couldn't pull up the memory. Ava Gardner? Elizabeth Taylor? One of those smoldering brunettes from the studio days. The dark hair was perfect, cut and shaped into curls that looked too natural to be anything but labor-intensive, and the makeup had the same deceptively simple aspect. She had taken less care with her clothing, content with a simple cardigan that was buttoned to the top, the wings of a white collar visible above the dark wool.

She also was the unhappiest-looking woman Tess had ever seen, a woman whose very expression—the dark eyes, the set mouth, which really was the shape of a Cupid's bow—bespoke a secret burden. But Mark Rubin looked at the photo as if all he could see was the beauty.

"Your wife—did she have a history of psychiatric problems?"

"Of course not."

"Why 'of course not'? There's no shame in having emotional problems." Tess didn't bother to tell Rubin that she had just finished her own course of court-ordered therapy. It was simply too long a story. "It's all chemicals, just another organ in your body having problems."

"I know *that*." Still too sharp, too defensive. "But chemicals are not the issue here."

"What about organs?"

"Excuse me?"

But that was as close as Tess would get to asking Mark Rubin if he and his wife had a fulfilling sex life.

"So there were no problems, and you don't have a clue why your wife left, and you're not even sure she wanted to leave, yet you don't think there's foul play involved?"

"Sometimes—I mean, I have no evidence of this—but sometimes I think maybe she left to protect me from something."

"Such as?"

"Nothing that I know of. But I can think of no other reason she would leave. Whatever she does, she always puts her family first."

"Is there anything to support this, um, idea?"

"No, not really." His shoulders, which he had been holding so straight and square, sagged. "I honestly don't know what is going on."

Tess looked at the photos in front of her. If there had been only one, and it had been the wife, she would have advised him to save his money and go home. She might have even recited the dorm-wall-poster wisdom of letting something go if you really loved it. But there were the children to consider. They were entitled to their father. He was right, even admirable, in his desire not to let them go.

"I'm going to scan these pictures into my computer, so you don't have to leave them with me. Besides, then I can print them out as necessary, show them to people, create flyers."

"And then?" he asked.

"I never promise results in any case, and I'm not starting with a lot of leads. But I have some ideas about how to proceed. Meanwhile, I'll need you to sign a letter of agreement and pay the equivalent of . . . eighty hours up front, as my retainer."

Tess had an unofficial sliding scale for her work. She didn't gouge anyone, but a man like Rubin could subsidize some of the less prosperous clients who found their way to the detective agency officially known as Keyes Investigations. She had been having a run of such clients lately, down-on-their-luck types and flat-out deadbeats. After making a quick calculation, she tossed off a figure that seemed fair to her, only to watch in amazement as Rubin pulled out a wallet and paid in cash.

"Maybe I'll remember more, or come up with some other leads for you," he said, counting off the ATM-crisp bills. "I'm still a little . . . numb. My only comfort is knowing that Natalie is a good mother. She's a good wife, too. I don't know why she decided to stop being one. If I failed her—if I worked too hard or was too inflexible in my ways—I'm willing to change. But I have to find them first, right? Without my family I'm nothing, just a man who sells coats."

Tess didn't have the heart to tell him that the best she could do was find his family. In a case like this, Tess was all the king's horses and all the king's men, picking up the broken pieces at the foot of the castle wall.

Mark Rubin stood, then reached for Tess almost as if to tuck a loose strand of hair behind one ear. She recoiled instinctively, nervous about allowing any strange man too close to her, confused at how Rubin could attempt this kind of contact when he had made such a point about refusing her hand. But his hand quickly retreated, holding a quarter he had pretended to pluck from behind her ear.

"I used to do this for my oldest son," he said. "You see, I'm actually a funny guy. I make people laugh. I was a joyous man—it's one of the tenets of Hasidism I happen to embrace as a Modern Orthodox, the idea that one honors God by being full of joy. But you'll just have to take my word for that for now."

2

Tess found a toehold on a metal handle jutting from the side of the Dumpster, scrambled to the top, and swung her legs so she was perched on the lip. She was now staring down into, if not the abyss, a reasonable and pungent facsimile. Even in hip waders and the decontamination suit she had acquired from a friend in city Homicide, she was less than eager to take the plunge.

"*Baruch ata Adenoid*, Mark Rubin," she said, pronouncing the blessing as she had misheard it in her childhood, when she believed her Aunt Sylvie was offering a prayer to cure her cousin Deborah of her allergies. "If working for you means no more Dumpsters for a while, I won't complain about what a deluded tight-ass you are."

Meanwhile, a girl had to eat, although at this exact moment it seemed unlikely that food would ever interest Tess again. The

Dumpster was one of three behind a popular Fell's Point bar, and it smelled strongly of stale beer, processed cheese, and rancid meat. As a bonus there were bright yellow and blue newspaper wrappers tucked among the dark green garbage bags, knotted in a way that any responsible dog owner would recognize.

Feeling only mildly ridiculous, Tess secured a surgical mask over her face and scooted down the interior wall in her best Spiderwoman fashion, landing as softly as possible. The garbage bags were packed closely, and the effect was not unlike a Moonwalk ride at a small-time carnival, albeit one with occasional crunchy sounds underfoot that she tried not to ponder. Bottles? Crack vials? She took small, tentative steps, hoping to feel something relatively solid beneath her. She walked the perimeter, circling toward the center. No, her quarry was definitely not here.

On to the next Dumpster, which smelled more like secondhand margaritas under the late-afternoon sun.

"Divorce," Tess said, speaking out loud to keep herself company, "makes people do some weird shit. Or hire those who will do it for them."

To think she had been cocky enough to imagine matrimonial work was behind her forever. But a string of clients, stung by this strange hit-or-miss economy, had told her to line up behind their other empty-handed creditors. So Tess found herself with no choice but to take on the soon-to-be-ex of a city official, a harridan who swore that her husband had ordered sanitation workers under him to remove incriminating files from his office and leave them in these Dumpsters.

Like most novice criminals, the public-works boss had been a little too in love with his cloak-and-dagger maneuvers. Because these Dumpsters were privately owned, their debris should have ended up in a private landfill. He must have figured that no one could tie the king of public waste to trash serviced by private contractors. But he had chosen a bar that had a habit of stiffing hauling companies, so the garbage tended to sit for a few days. Hard on the nose, unfortunate for the neighborhood, but very good for Tess and the soon-to-be-ex-wife.

Assuming that the documents were actually here. The wife could be wrong. Divorcing spouses were often clueless about each other. Hence the impending divorce. Tess was almost to the center of the third Dumpster before her foot hit an unusually solid bag that neither cracked nor oozed. Crouching down, she made a slight tear in the plastic with her gloved hands and saw reams of documents on Baltimore City letterhead. *Score.*

The bag was heavy enough that the seams might pop if Tess heaved it over the side. Resignedly, she ripped it open and ferried the papers out an armful at a time, which took almost a dozen trips but allowed her to skim some of the documents as she worked. They did make for interesting reading.

It was all here, just as the wife had promised, a history of bribes and kickbacks that helped explain how a midlevel city bureaucrat had come to own a vacation home in Rehoboth Beach and a time-share in Steamboat Springs. Sure it was graft, but even graft was marital property under Maryland law. If the IRS could tax ill-gotten gains, the wife's slicky-boy lawyer was going to argue, then a spouse could claim half of it, too. The argument was a bluff, but one her husband would never dare to call. A settlement would be reached quickly and quietly once Mr. Public Works knew that his wife had these documents in her possession.

The bottom of the bag yielded an unexpected bonus, a memo that was small potatoes for the divorce but a big find in the annals of city folklore—the official plowing list. Here was the shifting hierarchy of city power brokers, with names crossed off and reinstated according to how the political winds blew in any given year. There was even an enemies list, stipulating which streets should *not* be plowed, such as the cul-de-sac of a former mayor.

Tess put that aside, reserving it for her one friend left at the *Beacon-Light*, Kevin Feeney, a throwback who still cared about good old-fashioned politics. She loaded the rest in the trunk of her ancient Toyota, while the dogs, who had been tied to a nearby utility pole, began panting and pulling at their leashes, anxious to leave.

"Good girls," she cooed as they sniffed her legs, intrigued by the smells that clung to her. No anthropomorphizing here—dogs really did grin. Better yet, they loved you when you stank of garbage, loved you just for coming through the door at the end of the day or putting down a dish of food, which made it easy to love them back. "Just let me scald myself in the office shower, and we'll convene to the branch office for our coffee break."

" 'My appetite comes to me while eating,' " Tess announced upon taking one of the outdoor tables at Pearl's, dogs still in tow. Her apt quotation of Montaigne did not seem to impress the sullen waitress, much less the dogs. The attitudinal blonde simply disappeared inside to place Tess's usual order—a chocolate-pumpkin muffin, a latte, and two large bowls of water. Tess's usual orders were known all over Baltimore, from the mozzarella *en carozza* at the Brass Elephant to the lamb lawand at the Helmand and the veal scallopine at Pazza Luna. Ruts weren't ruts if you varied them, Tess had reasoned.

Pearl's was new to Baltimore, and Tess had been prepared to object to it on principle, the principle being that three-dollar muffins might be the final straw in a wave of gentrification that would price her out of her Butchers Hill office. But the small café, which was as cheerful as its waitstaff was sullen, was simply too convenient to ignore. And it wasn't a franchise, Tess reminded herself every time she dropped six dollars for her afternoon snack. She was supporting a local merchant, a dog-friendly one who served bird-friendly coffee and appeared to have a thing for shorthaired German pointers. How else to explain the small bookshelf that held nothing but Robert B. Parker novels?

She spooned up a bit of frothed milk, then held her face up to the sun, trying to be mindful of her good luck. She was outside, unlike Baltimore's office-bound drones. She was her own boss. She was alive, and she had learned the hard way not to take that for granted. Persuaded, she turned on the clam-shaped plastic monster that ran her life and, through a technology she couldn't begin to understand, grabbed an open line from thin air and jumped into cyberspace via WiFi.

Her e-mail was the usual mix of spam and people eager to grant her the privilege of doing things for free. Today it was an invitation to teach a course in self-defense, something about which Tess knew nothing—and she had the scar to prove it, a purple-red checkmark on her left knee. She sent a form-letter reply from her "assistant," S. K. Chien, which stated Miss Monaghan's fee structure—five thousand dollars for public speaking, five dollars per word for articles (minimum fee of one thousand dollars), and first-class travel arrangements for out-of-town gigs. That usually ended the queries, although some of the pushier types asked if the fee could be waived. S. K. Chien, however, was never moved by such pleas; she simply sent the same form letter until these supplicants gave up. Greyhounds are stubborn that way.

Her mailbox culled, Tess settled down to the messages from people who actually knew her. There was a political petition from Whitney, who had awakened one morning and decided she actually cared about the world. And an oddly formal invitation to lunch from Tyner Gray, a lawyer who had helped her get started as a PI and still threw her work. He had, in fact, vetted Rubin and hooked Tess up with Mrs. Public Works, so Tess probably owed him a lunch. She typed back her RSVP.

She saved for last the daily SnoopSisters Digest, a networking service for female private investigators that was fast becoming the highlight of Tess's working day.

Dear Sisters, the first entry read. **Weather fine and clear in St. Louis this a.m., almost too warm to my way of thinking. I am trying to figure out where a prominent local man may have stashed assets prior to wife's divorce filing. Usual trails all dead-ended. Any thoughts? Letha in St. Louis.**

Dear SS'ers: There's a good seminar on computer-related investigation in Houston in January. I'm enclosing a link to the program sked. I'll put you up if you don't want to spring for a hotel room. By the way, here's a link to one of those quiz sites that helps you figure out whether you're a hobbit, an elf, or a troll. I'm an elf. JR, your Texas Tornado.

The digest was the brainchild of Tess's onetime partner, Gretchen O'Brien. Baltimore born and bred, Gretchen had slipped on the ice last winter and suddenly decided she wanted to live in . . . Chicago. "They do winter right there," Gretchen had said with her usual conviction. "If you're going to have winter, you might as well have it in a city that can cope." Tess suspected there was a man involved in this western trek, but closemouthed Gretchen seldom yielded such personal information.

Soon after she returned to work in late August, Tess had scored a lead on an identity thief she was pursuing. The guy was in Naperville, Illinois, but moving fast. Tess's client, already facing bankruptcy because of her former fiancé's credit-card shenanigans, couldn't afford for Tess to buy the pricey last-minute plane fare. (She was one of the clients who ended up stiffing Tess, but ever so apologetically.) The guy was such a small-timer that the Naperville police couldn't be bothered to pick him up in a timely fashion. Enter Gretchen, who had already made contacts with several Chicago-area bounty hunters. She had the guy hog-tied on his own motel-room bed within three hours of Tess's e-mail, and DuPage County was happy to extradite him once he was caught.

Where Tess saw a fortuitous coincidence, Gretchen had seen the future of the small businesswoman.

"The thing is, independents like us could save money if we had a network operating in key hub cities," Gretchen had decreed. "Not so much with collars, but with paperwork, the various bureaucracies. Everything's still a long way from being online, and there's always stuff you can only get in person, with a little persuasion. Why not have a cooperative, with women working out of key cities, exchanging work on a barter basis?"

And so the SnoopSisters Digest was born. Tess loathed the name. "Why not Miss Marple's Tea Party?" she had suggested. "Or the Redheaded League?" The literal but never literary Gretchen had pointed out that their only flame-haired member was Letha in St. Louis.

Even with the unfortunate name, the network was an unqualified success. There were still some wide-open places to be filled—they had no one to cover the vast swath west of the Mississippi and east of the Rockies, and an Atlanta connection would have been helpful. But they were otherwise solid along the eastern seaboard and could do most of Texas and the Pacific Coast in a pinch. They shared information, brainstormed tough problems, and, as they got to know one another, divulged more and more details about their private lives—boyfriends, husbands, teething children, rambunctious dogs, garden pests (except for Gretchen, who got very impatient with what she called the "damn chitchat"). A typical digest might contain information about a handy new database followed by a recipe for those overwhelmed by the summer bounty of tomatoes and zucchini.

And Tess loved it, somewhat to her amazement. The digest was a virtual kaffeeklatsch, with all the chummy camaraderie of an office and none of the backstabbing politics. The group was also genuinely helpful—no one-upmanship, no macho posturing, no disdain for simple questions.

Dear S-Sisters, she wrote that morning, refusing to use the full name on principle and eschewing "SS" because of its unkind historic associations. **I have scanned three photos into the shared files, part of a missing-persons case. To say that the information is sketchy would be generous. Natalie Rubin, nee Peters, disappeared three weeks ago with three children—a boy, Isaac, 9, and boy-girl twins, Efraim and Penina, 5. Police have ruled out foul play, but husband insists he never saw it coming and thinks—hopes—her flight may have actually been done for his benefit. What's the emoticon for skepticism? I'll enter DOBs for all four into the shared files. No known aliases. No**

known anything, really. Assumption is they're traveling together, but who knows?

It pained Tess a little, adding this cynical bit of doubt, but, out of Rubin's sight, she had to be tough-minded, entertain the possibilities he could not. There was the notorious Pennsylvania case of almost two decades ago, where a woman and two children had disappeared. The woman's body was found within forty-eight hours, the victim of a bizarre plot by her charismatic lover; the children had never been found. And if everyone was alive . . . well, it was hard to travel with one child, much less three. Harder still when there was no money and no vehicle. Whatever Natalie was running from or to, she'd run faster alone, to paraphrase Kipling. **Would appreciate any ideas about how to proceed.**

Tess then added a few lines about Baltimore's glorious Indian summer, described the muffin she was eating, and asked, almost as an afterthought, **Anyone here know much about Orthodox Judaism? I'm curious because my client—Modern Orthodox, not Hasidic—refused to shake my hand. I knew, but forgot, about the prohibition against men touching women who are not their wives. Still, shouldn't the religion have evolved beyond this concept by now? What's the point in this day and age?**

Tess disconnected and tilted her face back to the sun, trying to convince herself that she felt like Goldilocks. Everything was *almost* just right—the weather, her work. Rubin's job alone would make her fourth quarter, and now there was a possibility that Tyner was going to throw something lucrative her way. Why else would he summon her to lunch at Petit Louis? Meanwhile, she would start the Rubin case tomorrow by visiting Vera Peters, Natalie's mother. She imagined a Pikesville matron, a more devout version of Tess's Weinstein aunts. Perfect nails, perfect hair, shining house. Really, how estranged could any Jewish mother be from her daughter?

Then again, perhaps the reason that Natalie Rubin had exploded, taking her whole family with her, was that she had kept everything from everyone. Tess could see that happening. She had been accused of doing the same thing, but the way she saw it, a girl just couldn't win. You either talked too much or too little. There was denial, that old river in Egypt, but there also was a place called Laconia, the aptly named land that had once contained Sparta. Tess was determined to live in Laconia for a while, a place where there wasn't so much yakking about feelings and emotions.

And, yes, she knew all about the little Spartan boy who had let the pilfered fox nibble his internal organs rather than cry out in pain, but she wasn't worried. All you had to do to avoid that fate, Tess figured, was not steal any foxes.

3

Natalie enjoyed picking out new names for the children once Zeke explained why the change was necessary. Zeke was good that way, making sure she understood the *why* of everything they had to do. Moshe had only pretended to make her an equal partner in decisions, but he always got his way in the end. All along, Natalie had wanted to give her children American names, pretty names, names that meant something to her, not God. She knew better than anyone how a name could change a child's life. Hadn't she chosen "Natalie" for herself, keen to fit in, to erase the awkward foreign girl who was teased and belittled? And it had worked, too, worked like a charm. Besides, Moshe used "Mark" in the outside world. Even his store had a fake name, so who was he to lecture her on what was real?

But when she'd made that point, he said the store's name was a business decision, one made by his father. Robbins & Sons Furriers was too well known, too successful to change its name at this late date. It would be silly to forfeit the brand over this small point, yet pigheaded to perpetuate the self-destructive practice of cultural assimilation generation after generation. Those were his exact words, for this was how Moshe spoke when intent on winning an argument—and he was never not intent on winning. He strung together self-important phrases, as if the words could make him right. Natalie thought he sounded like an old man, and a boring one at that. They were Jews, Mark kept repeating, their children were Jews, and they must work hard to preserve their identity in a world that attempted to substitute the secular for the spiritual. Blah, blah, blah. When Mark started talking like this, Natalie left the room, at least in her own head.

"I'm not going to repeat my father's mistakes," he often said when making his big points, and Natalie longed to fling back at him the news that he had committed a far larger one. But Moshe didn't know that, of course. So she held her tongue. She ended up holding her tongue for ten years, a third of her life. Really all her life, for her father had been quick with a hand when she dared to question him. "Whore," he might say, for no crime greater than her having an opinion. "Thief," she'd countered once, just once, and he had struck her so hard that he had not allowed Natalie to sleep for two days, in case she had a concussion. He had been kind to her for those forty-eight hours, bringing her soup, hovering by her bed. He never hit her again, and he was never quite as nice to her again either.

Zeke, however, always treated Natalie as a partner, an equal. So when he suggested that the children should have new names—she, after all, was traveling under a new one, she had arranged that in advance—he had left the decision up to her.

"We should have done this earlier, before the first time, back in Terre Haute," he said. "They need new names—and new birthdays, too, while you're at it."

"That's a lot to remember," Natalie had said. She wasn't good with numbers, whether dollars or dates.

"Give 'em easy ones, then. Fourth of July, New Year's Day. Look, a blind man could see those are your kids. No one's going to ask a lot of questions."

Except Isaac, of course, who didn't want a new name. Isaac always had questions.

"Warren?" he said, making a face. They were at a rest stop, an old one that was not particularly inviting, even on a bright, almost fall-like morning. "Warren is a stupid name. Why do I have to be Warren?"

The twins, younger and more docile, accepted that they were Robert and Daisy, although they could not remember the names from one moment to the next, and stared blankly when Natalie tried to get them to respond, until she ended up using them together, as in, "Penina-Daisy, take your thumb out of your mouth and listen to me." Or, "Efraim-Robert Rubin, are you eating dirt?" Even then their little faces looked blank, as if she were speaking to them in a foreign language.

"I want to be Sandy," Isaac persisted. "Or Hank."

"Why? What's so special about those names?"

"Dad would know." What was wrong with him? Isaac had never been so sassy at home. But then he was growing up. It was just the natural order of things for a boy to get more combative as he grew older.

"Well, your father's not here," she said, stubborn as any Rubin man, perhaps more so. "So you will do as I say. And as Zeke says."

Zeke, who had been sitting on the next picnic table over, enjoying a smoke, looked up warily. He threw the cigarette down and ground it beneath his heel.

"You shouldn't litter," Isaac admonished. Zeke walked over and crouched in front of Isaac, forcing him to meet his gaze.

"You know what I always say, *Warren*?"

Isaac glared at Zeke for using the new name but didn't try to correct him.

"Call me whatever you like—just don't call me late for supper."

With that he had ruffled Isaac's hair, enveloped him in a bear hug—and then popped him into the trunk. "Got to make money today," Zeke said to Natalie, "because we sure didn't make any yesterday or the day before. Isaac may have saved us from making a bad mistake back in Mount Carmel, but we're scraping bottom now."

Natalie's stomach clutched when she saw her son's face in the split second before the trunk closed. It was so stony and unforgiving, pinched with the effort of not crying. He never looked more like his father than at such moments. He was her son, her oldest boy, and she loved him with a ferocity that rivaled any emotion she had ever known. But while Zeke and others saw Natalie in her children, the only face Natalie could see in Isaac's was Moshe's, and she didn't want to see Moshe's face anymore, because it made her feel guilty and sad. She didn't hate him. She just didn't love him, not really, and no woman should have to spend a life with a man she didn't love, when the man she did love was finally in a position to claim her.

With Isaac stowed away for now, out of sight if not out of mind, Natalie settled into the front seat. The twins began to sob, asking for Isaac—they had already forgotten all about the new names—but she told them it was okay, that he wanted to ride in the trunk because it was like a little bed, so soft, so luxurious. All this accomplished was changing the tenor of the twins' sobs. Now they wanted a turn, riding in the trunk, in Isaac's cozy little bed.

"Nice job, Nat," Zeke said. "Don't try to explain everything to them. They're children. They're not our equals. We tell them what they need to know, when they need to know it."

"But I thought that's what you hated about the way you were raised."

"When I was in high school, yeah. But not when I was fuckin' five." She shot him a look for using profanity in front of the children, and he put his hand over his mouth. "Sorry."

"Okay," she said, not wanting to fight. She snaked her hand

across the seat and let it brush his thigh. She didn't dare touch him when Isaac was around, and even the twins would find it confusing if she showed Zeke too much physical affection. They needed more time to get used to the new ways. She had suggested they call him "Uncle Zeke," but he had quickly vetoed that. "That's not what I am to them," he had said, and he was right, of course. Zeke was going to be their father, more of a father to them than Moshe, who was never home, who worked all the time.

True, he had spent time with Isaac, talking and reading to him late in the evenings. But Natalie had always felt that was because Mark found Isaac better company than she was. They liked the same dull things, history and baseball, things found in books. During the day Isaac was obedient and loving, interested in the things she cared about. They had a standing date at 4:00 P.M. to watch that decorating show, the one where the neighbors changed houses. But when Moshe came through the door, it was as if Natalie didn't exist anymore. They ganged up on her, made fun of her. She was the butt of all their private jokes.

"Do you think," she asked Zeke, "that we should aim a little bigger? At least on your end? There's not much I can do to bring more money in. But if you don't change up, we're going to be working almost every other day. We burn through money so fast, what with motels and eating in restaurants."

"A man has to know his capabilities," he said. "Look at your father if you ever doubt the wisdom of that."

Natalie didn't have much affection for her father, but hearing him criticized caused the usual defensive reflex. "My father lost his temper at a bad moment, that's all. He was good at what he did."

"Yeah, but he got in over his head, didn't he? That's all I'm saying. He tried to be a big shot and ended up crossways with the wrong guy. Look, I learned how to do this. I paid attention, I listened. Small is the way to go. Small towns, small places, as close to state lines as possible. Just be patient."

As if she hadn't already waited forever, as if she hadn't proved she was more patient than almost any woman on the planet. She was beginning to think Zeke was a person who loved the planning, the buildup, just a little too much. She always did everything he told her to do, only to find there was still one more thing required of her.

There was a legend in Natalie's family about a relative, a great-uncle or something like that, who had hidden himself in a cupboard at the end of World War II and stayed there for two weeks without moving. He was the only person in his family to survive the destruction of his village. He was fourteen at the time, small for his age, and he never grew another inch after he came out of that cupboard. Natalie's mother said he was forever known as the "Little Uncle." But there were no photos of him, and Natalie's persistent questions threatened to unravel the story. (Where was the village? What year was this? Weren't the Germans in retreat by then?) Her mother finally made it clear that the Little Uncle was an article of faith in her family and Natalie was a bad sport for trying to undermine the tale. "This is what happens, when you come to America," her mother had complained at last, throwing up her hands. "Your children become Americans."

"Where are we going?" Natalie asked Zeke.

"Not Indianapolis," he said. "Too big."

"I didn't ask where we *weren't* going."

He gave her a look, but he liked that she had spirit, that she talked back to him.

"An-ti-ci-pation," he sang. "You'll know where we are when we get there."

"But how long?" She couldn't help thinking of Isaac, back in the trunk.

"Not long. Not long at all. Get your game face on."

The Plymouth hit a bump just then, and Natalie wondered if Zeke had done it on purpose, hoping she might cry at the thought of Isaac in his little nest. It helped if she cried, they had found that out the first time, when he had hit her. Well, not hit her, because Zeke would never hit her, just pushed her a little, shook her, when she had balked. At first she hadn't wanted to do her part, didn't see why they couldn't get by on his efforts alone. Moshe had never expected her to work. But this was a partnership, a one-two system, and Zeke couldn't do his part unless she did hers. The near miss back in Mount Carmel had convinced her of the brilliance of his plan.

But what if the story of the Little Uncle were true? What if Isaac, already small for his age, never grew into his height because Natalie let Zeke put him in the trunk? No, it was for his own safety, for his own good. Isaac was as stubborn as his father and his mother combined. He would keep trying to call attention to them, and the one thing they could not risk was being noticed. Zeke had been pounding on that point from the moment he met the children.

"Act like normal and you'll pass for normal," he kept saying. "If anyone's looking for you, they're looking just for you and the kids. They don't expect to see you with a man."

They jolted over another bump. But Isaac had those blankets and a pillow, and it was such a big trunk, and it wouldn't be for more than an hour, maybe less. An hour couldn't possibly stunt his growth. But the fear must have registered in her face, for Zeke glanced over and frowned at her, and the twins began to cry as if on cue.

"Jesus, pull it together, Nat." Zeke then called over his shoulder to the twins, "I'm going to teach you a song, a song my dad taught me when I was your age and we took trips. I'll sing a line and you sing it back to me, okay? Okay?"

The twins stammered between their tears, but the noises they made sounded like agreement.

" 'We're hitting the road'—come on, sing it back. 'We're hitting the road.' "

Natalie sang, providing cover for the twins' small, garbled voices.

" 'Without a single care!' " Zeke's voice was booming, almost too loud, and Natalie knew that his song was scaring the twins more than it was cheering them up. But she didn't want to criticize him when he was trying so hard.

" 'Without a single care,' " Natalie and the twins echoed.

" 'Cuz we're going, and we'll know where we are when we're there.' Wait—don't sing that one. But then you come in again: 'We haven't got a dime.' "

" 'Haven't got a dime,' " the twins lisped dutifully after a confused pause.

" 'But we're going, and we're going to have a wonderful time, yes, sir, we're going to have a wonderful time!' " Zeke slapped the dashboard as if they were having a wonderful time, but it all fell a bit flat in Natalie's opinion. The twins went back to crying, although not quite as loudly, and Zeke looked hopeless, his scariest look of all.

"You know," he said to Natalie, "there weren't supposed to be any kids. I told you—no kids."

"But there are." She tried a light, careless laugh, as if Zeke were complaining about something at once trivial and beyond anyone's control, like the weather.

"There weren't supposed to be."

She let it drop, knowing him well enough by now to pick her battles. He was just being obstinate. The children couldn't have stayed with Mark. Children needed their mother. Besides, Zeke would soon love them as much as she did. Natalie had no doubt of that. Zeke would come to love them as he loved her, and they would be a real family at last.

Thursday

4

Tess had never doubted she was a highly suggestible person. So it was only natural that Vera Peters, living on Labyrinth Road, would remind her of a Minotaur.

Or perhaps thoughts of Minotaurs were unavoidable no matter where Vera Peters lived, given her enormous head, snoutlike nose, and the two tufts of white-blond hair sticking up like little horns. The short, stocky woman also was about as welcoming as a Minotaur in its lair, yanking open the door of her modest row house and bellowing "WHAT?" only after Tess had depressed the doorbell for twenty long seconds.

Or, more accurately, "VAT?" The woman's accent was thick, another surprise in a morning of surprises, the first of which was this modest, lower-middle-class neighborhood deep inside the city, as opposed to the upscale suburban home Tess had imagined for Natalie's family. Given Mark Rubin's appearance and business, not to mention Natalie's well-groomed beauty, she had assumed that the runaway wife was . . . well, a JAP. Tess didn't think of the Jewish-American Princess as a negative stereotype, more of an exotic species that happened to occur in Northwest Baltimore, like some butterfly found in a particular rain forest. JAPs were seldom glimpsed this far inside the Baltimore Beltway.

"Vy do you keep ringing my bell?" demanded the woman, presumably Vera Peters, although maybe she was a deranged housekeeper. If so, she was falling down on the job, judging from the dark, cluttered interior Tess glimpsed through the narrow space between door and frame. "I don't vant to buy anything—or talk about God, if that's vat you do. I have my own God, not that he does me any good. Go away, go bother someone else."

"I'm a private detective, and I'm looking for Vera Peters."

"Vy?" Tess loved this reply because, nine times out of ten, it meant she had found the right person. "Why" was the ultimate hedge, asked just in case she might be from Publishers Clearing House and the van was looking for a parking spot.

"I work for your son-in-law."

"Mark Rubin?"

"You have another one?"

"I don't have him, you ask me. I am not in his life, and he is not in mine."

"And your daughter? Do you have much contact with her?" Rubin had said she didn't, but Tess had to work from the assumption that Rubin didn't know everything about his wife, not even close.

"She made her choices long ago. She is not my concern."

"Three weeks ago she made a choice to walk out on her husband, taking their three children with them. Is that a decision you support?"

The woman eyed Tess thoughtfully, fishing a pack of cigarettes from her sweatpants and tapping one out. "Show me your ID."

Tess produced her private investigator's license and her driver's license, on which she looked insanely cheerful. It was an old photo.

"Vat does this prove?" the woman asked after squinting at the two cards. "I know men who can make these in their basements."

"You're the one who asked to see it. At the very least, it establishes who I am and that I live on East Lane, and I was thirty-three as of August."

"My daughter's thirty." Said as if an important point had been made, although Tess wasn't sure what it was. That the Minotaur's daughter was younger? Or that people born in different years couldn't possibly know one another?

"I know. Born March seventh."

"How do you know this?"

"I told you, I'm working for your son-in-law. I know quite a bit about your daughter already."

"Quite a bit" was an exaggeration, if not an outright lie. The only thing Tess knew about Natalie Rubin was that she was thirty, a wife and a mother, and she was gone. Oh, and somehow her dark, almost exotic beauty had been formed by this stooped-over woman, whose thin hair showed an inch of dark gray roots before changing over into the startling white-blond shade. Mrs. Peters wore a pink sweatshirt, dark blue sweatpants, and yellow slippers, open at the front and back. Her feet were painful to behold—raw, red, and chapped at the heels, with knobby anklebones. The gnarled toes, with yellowish nails several shades darker than the slippers, looked more like talons. A Minotaur crossed with a phoenix.

"Vy you want to talk to me?" Mrs. Peters said at last, coming out on the porch and closing the storm door behind her. That was fine with Tess. She avoided going into strangers' houses when possible. It was a selective claustrophobia, and a new one.

"I thought you might have some idea where your daughter is."

Mrs. Peters puffed hard on her cigarette but had no comment.

"I've been hired by her husband to find her and the children."

The bent-over woman bent over a little farther, clutching her midsection, although her thin, scratchy giggle did not seem particularly gut-busting. Eventually her laughter turned into a sharp wheeze, then a phlegmy coughing fit.

"So he sent you to find her? He never learns, does he?"

"I'm not sure what you mean."

"I mean if you have a dog who bites, you should be glad when it runs avay, not spend money trying to bring it back. He's a very stupid man, Mark Rubin. Which has its advantages. But he needs to get over it."

"Get over being stupid, or get over Natalie?"

"Natalie left my house years ago, and I didn't send anyone to get her back. Mark should do the same."

"She took their three children."

"Luckier still. Vat vould a man who vorks as much as Mark Rubin do with three little children? He'd just have to find another voman to marry. Or hire someone to do it. But he's cheap about those things, things that he thinks a voman can do. He's a cheap Jew."

"Excuse me?" It was not unheard of for Jews to be anti-Semitic. Tess's Weinstein relatives sometimes made cutting remarks about the Orthodox families coming into Baltimore from New York, drawn by the real-estate prices. But that was all in the family. No one she knew would ever speak to a stranger that way.

"Oh, he never minded paying for things. Have you seen the house?"

"Have you?"

"No, but I've heard. It's huge, with every kind of"—she fumbled for a word—"machine that anyone could vant. It's an automatic house; it can run itself and it does, every veekend, when the Sabbath comes. Lights come on and off, heat and air-conditioning, stoves and televisions and stereos. He's religious, right, but a religious man who likes to have things his vay. I'm not religious, but if I were, I don't think I vould spend so much time trying to get around things, you know? To me this is not devotion. It's a game, like children play."

"Still, it sounds as if he gave Natalie a nice life."

Vera Peters balanced herself on the arm of an old plastic chair, grimy from seasons of dirt, and picked at the cracked skin on her heel with an amazingly pristine fingernail, well shaped, with a fresh coat of a delicate pink shade.

"As I said, I don't talk to Natalie, but I hear about her from others. Mark Rubin liked buying things. But he didn't like paying for things he thought his vife should do—cleaning, cooking, vashing. Natalie was like a slave. A vell-dressed slave, who ate and drank good things, but still a slave."

Something finally clicked for Tess—the accent, the neighborhood.

"You're Russian," Tess said.

Vera Peters rolled her eyes. "No, I'm from Ukraine."

"How long have you lived here?"

"Twenty-some years."

"Natalie was born in Russia?" Perhaps it wasn't relevant, but it seemed an odd detail for Rubin to omit. Everything Tess had projected on Natalie was wrong, inferred from the image Rubin had put forth. Had he intended that? Or did he, like most people, simply not realize what others might find odd or unusual about his life? Perhaps he thought it was normal for a thirty-something Orthodox Jew to marry a nineteen-year-old Russian beauty with virtually no religious training.

"In *Ukraine*. But she's an American girl, through and through. I don't know vy she married a Jew. That face could have had anyone."

"But you're Jewish. If you came over in the 1980s, that would have been during glasnost—"

"Um-hum," the woman murmured, making the sort of polite agreement that a person uses when it's too complicated to contradict. "Yeah, sure, ve're Jewish. But ve're not *Jewish*. You couldn't be, vhere ve lived. So ve came here and now, bam, ve're Jewish, and people are saying ve should give Natalie a bat mitzvah and go to services. But it's the land of the free, right? So ve don't have to do nothing."

She ended defiantly, as if daring Tess to contradict her.

"Mrs. Peters, I work for your son-in-law, but it's in your daughter's best interest to be found. If this drags on, if she doesn't come home or make contact, he's eventually going to get frustrated and divorce her in absentia, getting custody of his children."

The last was a lie, but a harmless one, and it would test Vera Peters's ignorance of her son-in-law. When the woman didn't protest, Tess prompted, "Is that what you want? A daughter who's wanted by the law?"

"None of this," she said, shrugging, "is vat I vant."

The shrug seemed to encompass her home, her life, Baltimore, the United States. She had lived here for two decades, close to half her life assuming she was a haggard fifty-something. By almost any standard, it was probably better than the place she had left behind. But it wasn't home and never would be.

"I need any lead, no matter how slender. Has she called you or written to you? Does she have friends in the area she might have contacted? Do you have a hunch where she might have gone or how she's supporting herself?"

The woman craned her neck in order to stare into Tess's face.

"Monaghan," she said, giving the name a hard *g*. "What kind of name is that?"

"Irish. But my mother's family was Weinstein. They came to Baltimore from a small town somewhere in Eastern Europe, before World War I. It was a Russian town when they came, I think, but I'm not sure where it ended up."

Actually, she believed that it was a German town, but the borders of that time were so porous that Tess didn't see any harm in trying to establish a small kinship with the Peterses.

The woman looked puzzled at this attempt to find common ground. "So you're a Jew?"

"I'm a mutt. Like everyone, right? We're all mutts in this country."

The woman frowned, pulling her head back into her round shoulders as if she had been insulted. "You vant information? I don't have much. But vat I have, I'll give you—for a price."

Tess paid for information all the time, so she was hardly surprised to be asked for money. She just hadn't expected a man's mother-in-law to pad his per diem costs.

"How much?"

"One hundred dollars."

Tess counted five twenties out of her wallet.

"Per piece."

"Excuse me?"

"It's one hundred dollars for every name or fact I give you. Cash."

"I only have two hundred dollars on me."

"Then you only get two things."

"How much do you have to sell?"

"Ve'll see. Vat vould you like first?"

"I'd like to know if Natalie has contacted you in any way since she left."

"No." The woman took a hundred dollars from Tess's hand.

"Wait a minute. You didn't tell me anything."

"You asked a question, I answered. That's one hundred. There's an ATM on Reisterstown Road if you need more."

A serious case of caveat emptor, Tess decided. She wasn't going to pay for any more of these so-called leads until she had road-tested at least one of them.

"No, that's okay. I'll ask you just one more question. If it's a bum tip, I won't be back, and you'll never get another hundred dollars from me, all right? And by the way, that doesn't count as my question."

The woman nodded. "You may ask one more thing."

"Did Natalie have a friend, someone in whom she confided? If so, I'd like a name and number—a simple yes doesn't count as the full answer." She held her money above her head, well out of Mrs. Peters's stubby reach.

"Natalie didn't care for friends, especially girlfriends."

Tess continued to hold the money above her head, and Vera Peters studied it the way Esskay the greyhound stared down an out-of-reach dog treat.

"But she had one, a girl from this neighborhood. They went to school together, vorked together before Natalie got married."

"Worked together? Mark told me his wife never had a job."

The woman smiled. She had gorgeous teeth for a smoker, big and white and probably fake. "*Him*. Between vat he doesn't know and vat he won't tell, you have your vork cut out for you."

5

The numbers Vera Peters had for Lana Wishnia proved to be a cell phone and a work phone. Unfortunately, there was no landline listed with directory assistance. Tess was running into this new world order more and more, and it was frustrating, because crisscross directories were rendered virtually useless. Of course, Tess used two cell phones, one for outgoing, the other for incoming. This meant that others' caller ID functions wouldn't get her real number, just the outgoing phone. And she never answered that phone when it rang, simply took note of the number that showed up on *her* caller ID. It was all part of the communications arms race, an ongoing battle to safeguard her privacy while raiding others'.

She tried Lana's cell but got voice mail, an electronic voice curtly instructing the caller to leave a message. Tess disconnected, then punched in the work number.

"Adrian's," trilled a woman's velvety voice, with just a hint of supercilious challenge.

"Is Lana Wishnia there today?"

"She's with a client. Are you a client?" The voice indicated Tess should be. "Do you have an appointment?"

"No—yes—I mean—does she have anything open today?"

"I'll see if she has had a cancellation, although I doubt it." The voice was cool with disapproval. The Velvet Frost, Tess thought. "Perhaps if you could come in at four."

The voice made it clear that coming in at four was terribly gauche.

"Sure, I'll take that."

"And this would be for . . ."

"For, you know, that thing Lana does." Tess assumed that a place called Adrian's had to be a beauty salon or spa, although there was an outside risk that she was signing up for an MRI or a high colonic.

"We offer a full range of services at Adrian's. But, given Lana's schedule, you must choose."

"Choose . . ." Tess had found that repeating a word when lost in a conversation sometimes prompted the other person to provide enough information for her to continue whatever deception she was working.

"Feet or hands, pedicure or manicure. But there won't be time for any special treatments—massage or a wrap for your hands, reflexology. We cannot offer such accommodations at the last minute."

"Hands. A simple manicure."

"Very well. We will see you at four, Miss . . ."

"Theresa Weinstein," Tess said, not sure why she was lying, even less sure why she had chosen her mother's maiden name. But Adrian's was probably somewhere in Pikesville, so the Weinstein name might thaw the frost.

"At four, Miss Weinstein. Have you been here before?"

"No, it was recommended by a friend. I'll be coming from North Baltimore after a late lunch. What's the best way to get there?"

"Take the Beltway around to the Reisterstown Road exit. We're in the old Bibelot, the bookstore that folded."

Lose a bookstore, gain a spa. No wonder Baltimore was no longer known as "The City That Reads." But it did have great hair. Baltimore had even taken Broadway by storm with an entire musical devoted to the joys of teased coiffures.

Tess had said at least one true thing in her exchange with the Velvet Frost: She was due in North Baltimore for a late lunch. Such a journey, no more than eight or ten miles, should have been easy enough at midday. But perhaps Vera Peters had placed a gypsy curse on Tess, for she encountered an obstacle in every mile of her trip—a series of inexplicable traffic jams on the expressway, which she abandoned only to find herself caught in a tangle created by a road-construction project. She was blocked on her alternate route by a moving van, which didn't see why it shouldn't close two lanes of traffic to unload furniture, and finally by a beer truck, whose need to deliver four cases of Bud and Bud Lite was being treated like a presidential visit at the small corner deli.

And Tess would have been happy to offer these details as apologetic explanation to most dining companions, but the moment she saw Tyner Gray's scowling face and heard him bark, "You're late," she just shrugged.

"Sorry. I was working. Got here as soon as I could."

The restaurant Tyner had chosen was an oh-so-chic French bistro, Petit Louis, which had hit Baltimore's foodies like a Gallic love affair. Even the *New York Times* had anointed its kitchen, but Tess liked it anyway, especially during rowing season, when she had the metabolism of a cheetah. Tyner preferred it for a different reason: By one-thirty, when the ladies-who-lunch crowd cleared out, Petit Louis was fairly amenable to a man in a wheelchair. No steps, no carpets, just smooth wood and tile floors.

"So," Tess said, expecting Tyner to get down to business as he usually did.

"So?" he echoed, fiddling with the menu, picking it up and putting it down, as if he wasn't sure what to order. Tess selected the smoked duck for an appetizer and the steak frites for lunch, and she put in for the crème caramel at the same time, lest the kitchen run out at this late hour.

"What she's having," Tyner told the waitress, as if he couldn't be bothered to make a decision. The young woman seemed a little disappointed that she didn't get to perform her full spiel of specials.

"I haven't seen you at the boathouse much this fall," Tess said, making conversation as Tyner fumbled with his flatware and napkin. An Olympic rower before the car accident that had left him paralyzed below the waist, Tyner was a harsh but effective coach. It was hard for rowers to complain about sore leg muscles to a man who couldn't walk.

"I'm out on the water before you get there," he said. "In fact, it seems to me I've seen you going out as late as six-thirty."

"I'm self-employed. I'm not in college with eight A.M. classes. If I want to row at the disgracefully late hour of six-thirty, I'm entitled."

Funny, Tess's father seldom riled her this way. Patrick Monaghan was a quiet man, and although he had his frustrations with Tess, his aversion to conflict was stronger than his need to change his only child.

"It's a matter of safety," Tyner said. "A single-sculler such as yourself, with no coxswain to see what's coming, is better off when the traffic is lightest."

"You know, I don't think you invited me to one of Baltimore's nicest restaurants to talk about my rowing habits. You could just hang out at the boathouse and yell at me there. So what do you really want to discuss?"

If it wasn't a job, maybe it was retirement. She was fuzzy on Tyner's age, but reasonably sure he qualified for the senior-citizen discount at the dry cleaners. Tess wondered if he was going to ease someone new into his practice, a young lawyer who would take care of Tyner's regulars while building up a new roster of clients. That would probably mean less work for Tess. More worrisome, it would mean no more cheap legal assistance, which Tyner swapped out hour for hour, despite the stark difference in their billing rates. Maybe she could just get arrested less often in the future.

Tyner cleared his throat, a noise as dry and scratchy as two pieces of sandpaper rubbing together, then placed a small velvet box on the table. It was an old one, judging by the greenish cast and worn spots. He popped the box open, displaying a band of silver—well, probably white gold or platinum—with a single diamond at its heart.

"My mother's," he said.

"You had a mother?" Inane, but Tess was not prepared for where this was heading.

"Of course I had a mother," Tyner snapped, sounding like himself for the first time today. "Do you think I was suckled by a wolf? She gave this to me years ago, decades ago. I never thought I would have any use for it, but, well . . . I'm going to marry your Aunt Kitty."

Tess was still too overwhelmed to make sense. "Does she know?"

"Of course she knows!" Tyner's voice was so loud this time that even the blasé waitstaff of Petit Louis twitched in their crisp white shirts. "I asked her last weekend. For God's sake, we've been living together for almost two years now."

"I guess I thought you were asking my permission or something like that. Although I suppose you should really ask Dad, or one of his brothers, since Pop-Pop Monaghan is no longer around—"

"Your aunt is in her forties—she hardly needs permission from her brothers to marry. I just wanted to show you the ring and see if you think Kitty would ever wear anything like this. It's awfully old-fashioned."

"She likes old-fashioned things." Tess balanced the box warily on her fingertips, as if it held a poisonous insect given to impulsive attacks. "She'd prefer this to a big old solitaire on a gold band or one of those encrusted things you see on some ladies."

"It's not . . . well, insulting, to present her a ring rather than give her the option of picking it out?"

"Not at all. It's a romantic gesture. Or would have been if you had given it to her during the proposal instead of waiting for a second opinion, you doofus. Hey, how does a guy in a wheelchair propose? You can't go down on one knee, so you do you go down on one elbow?"

"Don't be tacky," Tyner said, hugely pleased. He enjoyed Tess's company because she was one of the few people who didn't treat his wheelchair like a bad smell, something to be politely ignored under any and all circumstances. "There is one thing I do want to ask you, however."

"Yes?"

"Given that Kitty's and my combined ages top one hundred, we don't want to get too silly, even though this is a first wedding for both of us."

"Good plan. Vegas? Elkton?"

"So instead of having bridesmaids and best men and all that folderol, we want only one attendant—you."

Tess, who had managed at this point in her life to avoid any and all manner of responsibility in the nuptial process, was not thrilled. Tyner, misunderstanding her silence, plowed ahead.

"I know you're probably wondering why we didn't ask you and Crow to do it as a couple."

"No, that's not it. That's not it at all—"

"But the fact is, I'm not close to him, and he couldn't very well be Kitty's attendant. And you told Kitty the other day you're not sure when he's going to be back from Charlottesville, so he can't really be involved in the planning, right?"

"Right." Crow had moved home to care for his mother, who was undergoing chemo for breast cancer, and Tess didn't know when he would be back.

"Besides, you're the one who brought Kitty and me together."

"Don't remind me."

"Anyway, it will be simpler. How carried away can she get if there's only one attendant?"

Tess began to see some advantages in the situation. "Okay, sure. Crow won't mind, given that he's been staying with his parents in Charlottesville. And if I'm standing up for the bride *and* the groom, I could wear, like, a really sharp Armani pantsuit, or at least a skirt-and-jacket thing, instead of some god-awful bridesmaid's dress."

"Well, actually, I'm not so sure about that." Tyner was suddenly manifesting all the nervous confusion of a young groom. "Kitty seems to have . . . a lot of ideas. I mean, she keeps saying it's just going to be a party where two people get married, but she's been making a lot of phone calls and appointments. I think she even has a color scheme."

"What is it?"

"It changes almost hourly."

"Uh-oh."

"But she's leaning toward black for your dress. At least, as of yesterday, she said she liked the idea of you in black."

"Well, I can pick out a black dress on my own," Tess said with glad relief.

"Of course you can. Except Kitty wants to . . . um, help." He pushed a card across the table. "She has an appointment for the both of you at this boutique in Towson. To start. She also mentioned some other places, like Vassari and Octavia and maybe the Neiman Marcus in the Washington suburbs if she can't find the right dress in Baltimore."

The card for the Towson dress shop was white with discreet silver letters in a curvy font, a whisper of pink blossoms scattered across its face. Just touching it made Tess's palms itch.

"So this lunch is really a bribe, right? You lured me here not to get my approval of the marriage, or even to ask my opinion of the ring, but to break the news that I have to go buy a dress in a *bridal* store. I can just see it. You know it's going to have some huge bow over the ass."

"I was hoping you'd think of this lunch as a celebration. I thought we might even splurge, have a good bottle of wine with lunch. On me, of course. This is all on me."

"Wine for lunch is fine, but I'm going to need a g-pack of crack to survive dress shopping. Be straight with me—is Kitty losing her mind? Is she getting all giddy and nuts? Just how bad is this going to be?"

Tyner just smiled ruefully and summoned the waitress, ordering a $150 bottle of Châteauneuf-du-Pape.

6

A half bottle of Châteauneuf-du-Pape turned out to be excellent preparation for Tess's appointment with Lana Wishnia at Adrian's.

The spa had done much to obscure the bookstore Tess had so loved before it sank beneath the weight of one of the more curious bankruptcy cases in Baltimore history. From the outside it was now just another door in another suburban strip center. But that frosted glass door opened into a foreign world, a butterscotch-colored anteroom with fabric-swathed walls and two more frosted-glass doors marked SALON and SPA. Tess felt as if she had fallen into the bottom of a caramel sundae, or one of the more perverse compartments in Alice's rabbit hole. Come to think of it, Adrian's was probably full of potions that commanded "Drink Me" and "Eat Me," although with less immediate results than their Wonderland counterparts.

"You are Lana's four o'clock?"

The voice was unmistakably the Velvet Frost, but its owner was far from the style maven that Tess had envisioned. She was dumpy and middle-aged, with a large part between her front teeth. She did, however, sport acrylic nails, winged eyebrows, and fiercely streaked hair.

"Yes."

"She is running late." Was Tess paranoid, or was the woman blaming her for Lana's tardiness? "I would have called you, but you did not leave a contact number. May I get you anything while you wait?"

Tess looked at the magazines arrayed fan style on a low, maple-and-glass table in front of a chenille sofa in the same maple hue. They were not real magazines, just handbooks designed to create impossible dreams in the women who were forced to wait here because Lana—or Tatiana or Esme or Jean-Paul or Horatio Horn-blower—was running late. Tess wanted to ask for a magazine with articles, or even a newspaper, but she felt as if she had already acquired too many demerits.

"No, I'm fine, just fine."

"Tea? Coffee?" Even the easy questions sounded quizlike here.

"No thank you."

"Mineral water? Wine?"

"Wine would definitely be redundant."

The receptionist narrowed her eyes as if she thought Tess might be trying to slide a rude word past her. "You are new to us, yes? Then you must fill out a client card."

She handed Tess a clipboard with a questionnaire as long as anything a doctor's office would require. Tess perched gingerly on the edge of the backless sofa, one of those low-slung pieces of modern furniture that seemed to be designed for *Candid Camera* stunts. Only a person with steel thighs could rise from it with a shred of grace intact. Dutifully, she checked off a series of "no" boxes—pregnancy, medications, chronic pain—pausing only when she reached the lengthy portion on plastic surgery. She had not even heard of some of the procedures named.

Tess seldom gave much thought to what she wore or how she looked, but the checklist and the Velvet Frost's curled-lip inspection were making her self-conscious. Covertly, she glanced at one of the many mirrors in the room. She had a few freckles, souvenirs of a summer spent mainly outdoors, but her face was otherwise clear and unlined. Her hair was at an unruly length, neither long nor short, but that was the price of growing it out. Her makeup routine consisted of darkening her lashes and penciling a narrow line beneath her eyes to keep them from disappearing into her face.

True, her clothes were not particularly distinguished, not by Adrian's standards. She wore black trousers and a black T-shirt beneath a man's vintage shirt, a butter yellow Banlon with black stitching. Her one concession to adulthood was a newfound preference for expensive shoes and boots, but only because she had learned they were a good value, sturdier and more comfortable than cheap ones. Today she had on a pair of black cowboy boots, whose two-inch heels put her within shouting distance of six feet.

I yam what I yam, she decided, glancing toward the salon side of Adrian's, presumably full of women trying to be anything but. Meanwhile, white-uniformed men kept leading women out of the "Spa" door, holding their charges by the elbow of their terry-cloth robes as if they were recovering from major surgery.

"Salmon and asparagus," one attendant whispered to his client, whose face was covered with a pale green goo that made her look as if she had just been smacked with a key lime pie. "All you want, but nothing else. Your . . . uh, urine will smell, but your skin will look fabulous. But only asparagus and salmon, nothing else for seven days, or it won't work. It's all about the salmon."

"Belly or Nova?" the woman asked, and Tess's head shot up at the familiar voice issuing from the green cream.

"Deborah?"

"Tesser!" her cousin crowed with pleasure, and Tess remembered too late that she was here under a semifalse name and thoroughly false pretenses. At least the old family nickname didn't give her away. "Since when do you come to Adrian's?"

"Oh, I thought I'd start paying a little more attention to my appearance, get a manicure."

"Well, it's a start."

There was no malice in Deborah, although Tess had not always understood this. Her cousin simply lacked the usual filters: If a thought passed through her brain, it headed straight to her mouth. Tess had come to think of Deborah as sort of a walking James Joyce novel, albeit one narrated by a preternaturally self-satisfied matron. They had been competitive as girls, and even as adults, until they finally stopped to wonder what, exactly, they were competing for. They had chosen different paths, but not as a rebuke to each other. And they had the foxhole of family in common, a powerful bond.

Deborah peered into Tess's face. "Isn't this awfully far off the beaten track for you? I thought you never went outside the Beltway if you could help it."

"Yes, but everyone says this place is the best."

Her cousin smiled, happy to be complimented for her taste in spas. "It is, and it's convenient to Sutton Place Gourmet, not to mention a Starbucks."

"No caffeine," her attendant practically squealed. "Are you trying to undo everything we've done?"

Deborah giggled. She was not a stupid woman, and it was doubtful she believed that this young man had any interest in her beyond her lavish tips. Yet she clearly was enjoying their flirtatious shtick.

"Not even one mocha?" she wheedled.

"Decaf, no whipped cream," he decreed, and she nodded, as if his word were law, but Tess knew that her cousin would be clutching a venti with the works when she roared out of the parking lot. The Weinstein side of the family did not run toward sacrifice. "Now let's go make sure that Carlos does a fabulous job on your hair. Not so red this time. Something softer, a shade that sneaks up on a person. I didn't do all this work on your face just to have the Castilian wonder screw up the presentation."

"Have fun," Deborah called to Tess over her shoulder as she headed into the salon. "You ought to think about getting a seaweed wrap next time. Or a kosher salt scrub."

"Does that come with belly or Nova?"

But Deborah had sailed out of earshot, so all Tess's flippancy earned was a frown from the Velvet Frost.

"I believe Lana is ready now. You were lucky to get this appointment. She is our most popular girl." The voice thawed perhaps one degree. "I did not realize you were one of *the* Weinsteins. Is Deborah your sister?"

"Cousin," Tess said, feeling the lack of challenge occasioned by telling the unadulterated truth. "First cousin."

"Ah," the Velvet Frost said, and Tess could see her calculating: not one of the Weinsteins of Weinsteins Jewelers, just an impoverished twig from another part of the family tree. Tess's advantage was lost as quickly as it had been gained.

7

Lana Wishnia balanced Tess's hands on her fingertips, clearly unimpressed. No rower has pretty palms, but even the tops of Tess's hands were unattractive, with short, nicked nails, ragged cuticles, and a few random cuts that she couldn't recall inflicting on herself. After a few moments of stony inspection, Lana took Tess's left hand and flipped it over, touching it the way one might handle a dead animal brought home by a faithful cat. Here the damage was far worse—a corporal's stripes of hard yellow calluses. Still, Lana said nothing, her face impassive.

The only consolation was that Lana's hands, while nowhere near as damaged as Tess's, were not spectacular. Her nails were blunt cut and unpolished, her fingers stubby and plump. *Manicurist, file yourself.*

"What do you do?" she asked, dropping Tess's hands into warm, soapy water. They were the first words she had spoken since they were introduced. Her accent was quirky—American, with a hard, aggressive edge, more New York than Baltimore. She had a broad, unsmiling face, and her heavy makeup made her look older than she was, assuming she was Natalie's contemporary. A single pockmark on her forehead indicated a poor complexion or a bad case of chickenpox, but heavy foundation covered any other telltale marks.

"Do?" Tess echoed. She preferred not to lie outright, but she also wasn't ready to tell Lana that she was a private detective, not just yet.

"To your hands. What do you do, that they're so beat up?"

"I row."

"What?"

"Row. On the water—I row a single scull." Tess couldn't use her hands, as Lana was now holding them both in the water, pushing them down as if they were a pair of kittens she hoped to drown. She rolled her shoulders and jerked her elbows, attempting to mime the movement, and succeeded only in looking as if she were having a convulsion.

"For exercise?"

"Yeah." It was easier to agree than try to explain that rowing was more for her head than her body or heart. There were a dozen activities Tess could do for endurance and strength training, but rowing was the only thing that brought her close to the kind of Zen-like state that others claimed to find in yoga and meditation. She had never loved it more than this summer, when she'd had to give it up for a few weeks. Sidelined after cutting open her knee, she had needed it more than ever.

"Weird. I oughta do something." Lana's complacent voice made clear that she had no intention of doing anything. Was she married? She didn't wear any rings, but perhaps a ring would interfere with her work. "I should tell you—if you go out and row again, it's not going to last. Just so you know."

Tess nodded, but the judgment stung a little. She didn't go in much for beautifying routines, but she liked to think that she wasn't beyond hope.

Lana removed the shallow basin of water and began massaging Tess's hands. This felt heavenly. Tess thought about Deborah, wrapped in seaweed, abraded with kosher salt, covered with pale green cream. Did she really think she needed all these treatments, or did she come just for the touching, to be massaged and rubbed?

"There's a reason I asked for you today," Tess said, deciding they were far enough along in the process that Lana couldn't abort, or walk away.

"Yeah, I was in *Baltimore* magazine's 'best of' issue three years ago, and people still call."

She nodded toward the wall behind her station, where a framed certificate attested to her honor. Invited to look, Tess also took in the photographs and personal mementoes that Lana had put up there. There was a stuffed bear in a T-shirt that said MARDI GRAS, and a photograph of Lana with a dark-haired woman, the Inner Harbor in the background. It was small and a little blurry, but Tess recognized Natalie. Younger and more tarted up than in the photo Mark Rubin had given her, but definitely Natalie.

"I heard about you from someone else—Natalie Rubin's mother."

Lana didn't miss a beat in her ministrations to Tess's hand, and if there was a change in her expression, Tess couldn't see it. "That was nice of Vera, to send me a customer. She's a nice lady."

"When did your family come over?"

Lana looked up, squinting at Tess as if it were impolite to mention that someone was not a native. Perhaps it was, in these paranoid times.

"Twenty-eight years ago. I was a year old." So she was twenty-nine, a year younger than Natalie.

"Where are your parents from?"

"Sheepshead Bay." She gave Tess a crooked smile. "Now, I mean. They were originally from Belarus. They moved to New York, but they sent me down here to live with my aunt because . . . well, because they hoped I'd be more *dutiful* in Baltimore. Also, they thought Baltimore was more American. They figured they had come all this way, so I should live in a real American place. You could walk down our block sometimes and not hear a single word in English."

"Do you ever think about going back, to see where you came from?" The question was born of simple curiosity. Tess had no experience with exile. If she wanted to visit her roots, she could walk from her office to the old East Side Democratic Club, where her parents had met. But as soon as Tess spoke, she saw a horrible possibility: If Natalie had gone back to her homeland, she and her children were beyond the reach of Keyes Investigations, the SnoopSisters Digest, and even most legal authorities.

"There's no one there to see," Lana said. "Maybe some distant cousins, but I never knew them."

"How do you know Natalie?"

"The usual way."

"The usual way?"

"School, the neighborhood. You know, you need to push back your cuticles."

Tess knew what a cuticle was, but she had never understood what was meant by pushing one back. With what? The flat of her hand, a stern word?

"When did you come to Baltimore?"

"They sent me here when I was in junior high. How do *you* know Natalie?"

"I don't. I know her mother." Tess waited a beat. "And her husband."

Lana didn't respond.

"In fact, her husband hired me to find Natalie and their children. They've disappeared."

Still no comment, as Lana concentrated on shaping Tess's nails, which should not have required so much attention. There wasn't much there to file.

"Has she been in touch with you?"

"If she has, I wouldn't tell you."

"But you know she's gone, because you don't seem at all surprised by the information."

Lana was good at skipping past comments she didn't want to address. "She's my friend. Whatever she's done, I'm for her, not for her husband. I never liked him much."

"Do you even know him?" It was hard to imagine that Mark Rubin would withhold information about his wife's friend.

"No, but Natalie tells me things. He's not right for her."

"Why would you say that?"

"Do I have to have a reason?"

"Yes, and it must be a pretty profound reason if you're willing to keep a man from finding his children."

Lana paused, her emery board poised over Tess's nail. "He's full of himself," she said at last.

"Because he's rich?"

"No, not so much because he has money, although that's part of it. He's just so . . . well, Jewish."

That odd prejudice again. "*You're* Jewish."

"It was just what we were, not what we did." Lana's parents may have succeeded in creating an American girl, but her shrugs were Old Country through and through. Put her in a head scarf and Lana would have looked at home in a *New York Times* photo of Russian women, circa the year of her birth, lined up for bread and toilet paper.

"What about Natalie?"

"What about her?" Lana turned her back on Tess, taking a long time with her wall of nail polishes, as if there were dozens of variations on the shade of "clear" that Tess had chosen when they first sat down.

"Was she also indifferent to Judaism? I mean, before she married Mark?"

"She didn't go to synagogue, if that's what you mean. Most of the Russian families around here didn't, not regular."

"So why did she marry an Orthodox man and agree to lead an Orthodox life?"

"Love," Lana said, her back still to Tess. "Women have done weirder things for love. And it's not as if—" She stopped herself. Tess waited to see if she would finish the thought, but she didn't.

"Still, Natalie knew she was marrying an Orthodox man. Mark Rubin didn't convert one morning and make Natalie go along with him. I'm sure he was very clear about what he expected from his wife."

"Oh, yeah, Mark Rubin was always very clear about everything." Lana seemed to be smothering a laugh. "But I have to say, boring as he was, he was at least a little fun, before. You know? I was married once, for all of six months. But the marriage wasn't as good as what came before. Things change. It's like, before I came to Baltimore to live, it was a place I visited and had fun. Then it was the place I lived and went to school, and now it's the place I work. It's not all going out to eat and the aquarium anymore."

Tess had to admit that Lana's definition of marriage matched her own views. It transformed love into work, and who needed another job?

"So Natalie decided to take a vacation?"

"I'm saying she had reasons. They're hers, and they're private, but they make sense to her, so who are you to get involved?"

Lana was now applying polish to Tess's fingers with quick, easy strokes, always the right amount of fluid on the brush, a perfect drop of translucent lacquer. The talents of Baltimore's best manicurist were obviously wasted on this mundane assignment.

"She doesn't have any money, though."

Lana stroked, face impassive.

"And then there are kids, kids who should be in school."

"Only Isaac," Lana said. "The twins would have started kindergarten this year, but no one learns anything in kindergarten. Isaac is smart. He'll catch up—" She caught herself.

"When? When will Isaac catch up? How?"

"When he goes back to school, of course. I mean, I just assume Natalie won't keep him out forever."

"She has a plan, doesn't she, a plan she shared with you? She's going to settle somewhere, raise her children. Has she called you from the road? Do you have any idea where she might be?"

Lana started on the next hand, her movements now a little less precise.

"A woman has no right to keep a loving father from his children. Whatever problems Natalie and her husband have, what she's doing is wrong."

Stroke, stroke, stroke.

"If she tries to get in touch with you, I'll know."

But it was too big a bluff, she couldn't carry it, and Lana was already on her pinkie. "She has no reason to get in touch with me."

Tess glanced back at the photo: Lana and Natalie, on some sunny, long-ago day at the harbor, big, overdone hair blowing in the breeze. They had their arms around each other, and their mutual affection was unmistakable. While Natalie looked straight into the camera, eyes sparkling, Cupid's bow mouth stretched into a huge smile, Lana was looking at Natalie, mesmerized by her pretty friend, basking in her happiness.

"You must miss her," Tess tried.

Lana placed Tess's hands beneath an air dryer. "Wait at least five minutes, or you'll smudge," she said, setting a timer. "Ten is better. When you leave, your check will be up front. Our tip envelopes are up there, too. You'll excuse me, but I have another appointment."

She opened her drawer wide, ostensibly to put something away, but also so Tess could see the fives and tens stacked there. She then all but ran away, and Tess couldn't follow her—not unless she was willing to smear the clear polish on what the slip would claim was a twenty-five-dollar French manicure.

She tipped lavishly despite Lana's rip-off. There was nothing to lose in overtipping. Come to think of it, that was another life lesson from her father, a little Irish karma: *Be generous with your tips when you are flush, because they are returned to you in ways you didn't expect when you go bust.* Tess wasn't flush these days, but Mark Rubin was. Besides, she suspected that he could use a little help in the karma department, too.

Lana Wishnia emerged from Adrian's about an hour later, finished for the day. Squinting at the light, she made her way to a bright green Dodge Neon at the far end of the parking lot, then pulled out onto Reisterstown Road, heading north.

Tess was right behind her. Following Lana had been a last-minute impulse, inspired by a quick stop at Sutton Place Gourmet. The sheer novelty of a different grocery store had seduced her into silly purchases—coconut macaroons, a kiwi, a slab of tomato-rosemary focaccia. These spur-of-the-moment choices reminded Tess that all humans were creatures of impulse. If Lana was upset or disturbed by Tess's visit, she might feel compelled to act as quickly as possible. If she had a coconspirator, she could seek his or her counsel.

And if Natalie were actually in the Baltimore area—a long shot, but not entirely implausible—Lana would take Tess straight to her.

Instead Lana left one strip mall only to lead Tess to another, about two miles up the road, a shopping center with a Giant grocery and several smaller shops. Okay, so Tess's hunch was off. The manicurist was just stopping to pick up some food on her way home, and she didn't make Sutton Place Gourmet wages.

But Lana walked into a Mail Boxes Etc. store. She was inside for perhaps two or three minutes, nowhere near enough time to send a package or a fax, and came out empty-handed.

At least she was empty-handed as far as Tess could tell. Lana's purse, a bulging shoulder bag of dirty beige leather, was so big that it could easily conceal a sheaf of letters, or even a box. Tess made a note of the address and continued to follow Lana north.

Lana's next stop was a town-house complex called Camelot

Hills. It was fairly new, yet already careworn. Even the banner advertising move-in specials was limp and bedraggled. Lana parked and went into one of the middle units on Lancelot's Way, and Tess decided to wait awhile to see if she would head out again. The flow of people returning home from work was frenetic enough for her to sit in her car without drawing attention to herself, the setting sun bright enough to excuse the sunglasses that covered much of her face.

She had assumed that Lana would choose to live among other single folks, but there were plenty of families scattered throughout the complex, and the children were out in force on this crisp evening, riding bikes, playing the eternal games, such as four-square and hopscotch. Most, however, were caught up in a sport of their own invention. It appeared to be called "jump out," and it was a combination of hide-and-seek and capture the flag.

The two smallest boys, pretending to be police officers, walked up and down until they would suddenly leap at a clutch of children loitering on a corner. The goal was to arrest as many kids as possible, while the others fled to a safe house on the steps of the sliding board. Those who were caught were placed in the jungle gym, clearly the jail. The larger girls and boys ran away over and over again, squealing in delight, while the two little boys demonstrated a heartbreaking familiarity with the gray-area brutality common to such police actions, flailing at their captives with fists and makeshift batons.

Ah, well, Tess had once played Mugger in the shadows of Ten Hills, and she had turned out to be a decent enough citizen. Such games were all about having a reason to run and squeal, night air filling your lungs, adrenaline soaring through your body. She studied the children carefully, but there was no miniature Mark Rubin among them, no fox-faced boy-and-girl twins. When the darkness became so complete that parents started calling children to homework and bed, Tess headed for her own.

8

The twins sat on the edge of one of the double beds, backs ramrod straight, hands folded in their laps, although Efraim absentmindedly put his left thumb in his mouth from time to time. Television had been rationed in their old life, by their father's insistence, and the twins still treated it with a kind of nervous awe. They didn't laugh, or even smile much, just stared at the cartoon channel with unblinking attention. Perhaps they thought if they showed no sign of enjoying it, no one would think to take it away from them.

Isaac, too, had liked the unlimited cartoons at first, especially *Jimmy Neutron, Boy Genius*. But now he was getting bored. He wished he had a book, a new one. His mother had allowed him to pack only one, *From the Mixed-Up Files of Mrs. Basil E. Frankweiler*, and he hadn't argued because he thought they were going away for a long weekend, not forever. He had finished it the first two days on the road, before they met Zeke. He could reread it, but the book made him sad. If you were going to run away from home, you should have an adventure, do something important and thrilling, like the brother and sister in the book. You shouldn't just drive from town to town, sitting in motel rooms that looked alike and watching the same television shows you could have watched back home. That is, if you were allowed to watch all the cartoons you wanted back home.

Teachers were always saying Isaac had a vivid imagination, but it certainly had never occurred to him that he might have a life without books. In his "before" life—his *real* life was how Isaac thought of it—his father never said no to anything involving a book. Whether it was buying one, staying up late to read one, or even trying to read what everyone else said was a grown-up book, Isaac's father always said it was okay. It would have been easier to imagine a world without food, or a house. Even if a person was very poor, there were always libraries. But you couldn't have a library card when you drove to a new town almost every night, because how would you take the books back on time?

Isaac would like to ask his mother if they were poor now, but not in Zeke's hearing. Because if they had lost all their money, that would be a private thing. His father wouldn't want other people to know about it. His father was very proud. But it would explain a lot, if they were poor. It might even explain why they had left. In the story of Hansel and Gretel, the father and the stepmother took the children to the forest because they didn't have enough to eat. Maybe his mother had been planning to let them go in the forest, then decided she couldn't do it. Or maybe that was Zeke's plan, although he wasn't a stepparent. He was mean enough to be a stepparent.

Certainly Isaac's mother and Zeke talked about money all the time, about the cost of everything, in a way his father never had. "Down by thirty-seven dollars," Zeke might say, after paying for breakfast. "Up by three hundred dollars," he had announced yesterday as he helped Isaac out of the trunk last time. Down was bad, no matter how small, up was good. But it was never good enough, judging by Zeke's face, which always looked as if he were adding and subtracting.

They had started out with a thick envelope of money, but his mother had given much of it to the big, hairy man who gave her the car, the papers, and the shoe box. Isaac's mother had cried, accusing the man of taking too much of her money. The man had said the car was cheap, but the things she needed to drive the car came a little dearer. Isaac remembered the exact phrase, for it was new to him. *Came a little dearer.* His mom had handed over the money and gotten the crummy green car in return. She should have been willing to walk away. That was important in making a deal, his father had told him. You always had to be ready to walk away.

That had been in the mountains, the Appalachians—he had learned about them in geography. His mother's friend, the woman with the fuzzy hair and the sad eyes, had driven them to a farm. On the way his mother kept talking about what a great weekend they were going to have, picking fresh fruit at orchards, maybe swimming. The signs promised a lake—Deep Creek—and cabins. They had gone west, west, west, past Frederick and Hagerstown, past Cumberland. They may have even left Maryland before they were done. Isaac wasn't sure. He was thinking about the lake and wondering if his father would teach him how to fish. Did Jews fish? They weren't allowed to hunt, he knew that, not the Orthodox. But fishing was different for some reason, maybe because fish were kosher and bears were not.

But when they got to the old farm, his mother's friend had unloaded their bags and taken off, hugging Isaac's mother and wishing her well. His mother had put them in the new car—well, the old car that was new to them—and driven them to a motel, one with a pool. That had been the last motel with a pool, at least a working one. The next day they had been in the car forever, driving into the night, passing motel after motel, only to pick one that looked like all the others. The next morning his mother had put Isaac in charge and left for an hour. When she came back, she was with a man who had the palest face that Isaac had ever seen. "Meet your Uncle Zeke." Even then Isaac had thought his father would be joining them soon. It was only later, when his mother told him to stop asking, that he understood they weren't going home.

Tonight his mother and Zeke had gone to talk in the car. They were always going to share secrets in the car, which was rude. Isaac's father didn't believe in having so many secrets. The car was parked right outside the door of their motel room, so Isaac didn't dare sneak away. He looked longingly at the phone, but Zeke had taken the talking part with him, just so Isaac couldn't try to use it. He would have, too. He wished now that he had been fake with Zeke, pretended to like him, because then Zeke might trust him more. And if Zeke trusted him, his guard would drop, and Isaac would find a way to make a phone call.

Not to the police, though, not after his experience with that guard man. If the guard man, a man who wore a gun, didn't believe Isaac, then a police officer probably wouldn't believe him either. Maybe it wasn't a crime what his mother was doing? Besides, she would just convince everyone that Isaac was a liar. He would be the boy who cried wolf, even though he hadn't—he was screaming for people to look at the wolf that only he could see. No, he had to get to his father, tell him where they were. Only his father would believe him, right away, and not waste time asking for other sides.

Penina leaned over to Efraim and whispered something, making him laugh. Her voice was a low mumble, but Isaac wasn't sure he would know what she was saying even if she spoke up. When the twins spoke their made-up language, just for them, it made Isaac lonely and nervous. When Zeke was around, they barely spoke at all.

His mother and Zeke came in, their cheeks flushed as if the night had turned cold. Zeke made a big show of attaching the talking part back to the phone—the handset, that's what it was called—looking at Isaac as if daring him to say anything. It was as if Zeke wanted to say, *I'm smarter than you!* Isaac wanted to shout back, *So what? You're a grown-up, you're supposed to be smarter.* Instead they just looked at each other, like two men in a western about to have a gunfight, and Isaac's resolve to make Zeke like him fell away. He would never in his life be that good a pretender.

But you didn't always have to be the smartest one to win. His dad had taught him that, when Isaac was learning to play Advanced Mission Battleship, the new improved version with missiles and lots of sound effects, so when you sank someone's ship, it made a really satisfying *kaboom* sound, with splashing, and when you finally won, the woman's voice announced in a pleased way, "Con-grat-u-la-tions, Admiral." Isaac almost never, ever beat his father at Battleship—only twice so far, and both times had been luck. His father had pressed the wrong buttons, firing his Tomahawks in the wrong pattern, even though he knew where Isaac's PT boat was. So Isaac didn't think his wins really counted.

But his father had said, "Don't scorn luck. A lot of my success in life has been luck. Ditto my father's, and his father before him. If I could wish just one thing for you, Isaac, I think I would wish you to be lucky."

"Really?" Isaac thought his father might at least wish he had a ninety-mile-per-hour fastball or early admission to a really good college.

His father had taken him into his lap. (How Isaac missed that lap, which was big and warm and safe, although he was really getting too big for such things.) "Well, I guess I would wish first and foremost that you would be a virtuous man."

"What does that mean?"

"To be good, to have . . . well, virtues. To be honest and kind and modest. You know, the Christians take credit for the Golden Rule—love your neighbor as you love yourself—but the Jews have their own version, and it is much older. And, I think, a little wiser. We say, 'Do not do to your neighbor what you would not want done to yourself.' That makes more sense to me. I don't think it's possible to love others as we love ourselves and our families, but we can avoid doing anything to them that we would not want done to ourselves."

"What if someone is really mean to you? Can you be mean back? Since they started it?"

"It depends. Is someone being mean to you?"

Actually, someone had been mean to him, a boy at school, calling him teacher's pet and Rubin the Nose-Rubber, which made no sense, but everyone laughed as if it were extremely funny. It had been terribly important at the time, but Isaac no longer remembered why that boy disliked him so, or even why it bothered him. It was so long ago, so far away, back in the second grade. The things that once made him cry—another boy's insults, a reprimand from his father, a scary dream—would never make him cry now. He was determined that nothing would make him cry, not in front of Zeke.

He cried only in the privacy of the trunk. Or, sometimes, late at night, long after everyone was asleep. Even then he had learned the trick of crying silently, without even a snuffle, so it was barely like crying at all.

Friday

9

Tess—I know it's commonly believed that Jewish dietary law was nothing more than a series of sensible precautions developed in response to
foods that carried risks—trichinosis in pork, for example. But Jewish law
is more subtle than that, Tess, and trying to reduce its tenets to mere
pragmatic considerations robs it of its deep philosophical underpin-
nings.

Take the tradition of the *mikveh,* which has gone by the wayside even
in some Orthodox families. It is not the misogynistic, female-phobic
practice some would have you believe. The rationale for abstinence is
not that women are "unclean" but that the days following the prohibition
is when they're at their most *fertile.* For further insight into your new
client, I strongly recommend you read Herman Wouk's *This Is My God.*

Ask a question, get an answer. So far the SnoopSisters had few
concrete ideas about how to find Natalie Rubin and her children.

But Tess's casual question about Mark Rubin's refusal to shake her hand had started a lively thread, with posts from Susan Friend in Omaha, who could always be counted on to provide the historic and intellectual overview of any topic, and Jessie Ray in Houston, who reminded the SnoopSisters that Texas husbands once had carte blanche to execute men who trespassed on their land or their women. And now this gently chiding missive from Margie Lynn in Southern California.

I read *Marjorie Morningstar* as a teenager, Tess typed back. Do I get half credit for that?

The sun was barely up, and Tess was in bed, her laptop balanced on her knees, the greyhound stretched across the foot of the bed like a lumpy quilt, the Doberman on the floor. Since Crow had left for Virginia to help his mother through her chemo and recovery, Tess had allowed the dog to take his place, but Esskay was a poor substitute for a number of reasons. She didn't give back rubs, and she wouldn't spoon. And her breath remained as vile as the day Tess had met her, despite changes to her diet and a tooth-cleaning regimen that required Tess to don a rubber fingertip and scrub each fang individually.

No wonder Tess didn't get manicures more often. Using one's fingers as a greyhound's toothbrush did not keep nails in tip-top shape. She wondered if Kitty's growing obsession with her wedding would lead her to a keener interest in Tess's grooming. Almost without thinking, she shared these thoughts with the SnoopSisters. This morning check-in had become a ritual of sorts, making her feel as if she had human company while sipping her first cup of coffee.

A first yesterday, interview-by-manicure. Makes it hard to take notes, but it also makes it difficult for the person you're questioning to walk away. Riddle me this: Why do Baltimore's manicurists tend to be Russian, when they're Korean almost everywhere else? No, never mind, I'm sure I'm showing my cultural/ethnic ignorance all over again, possibly being racist.

At any rate, I'm lucky I could focus on the interview at all. Tyner Gray, the lawyer for whom I've worked off and on, dropped a bombshell over lunch. He's going to marry my aunt. They've lived together for almost two years, but I find this discombobulating for some reason. Perhaps because I've been instructed to wear a dress and warned that my aunt, a once-sensible woman, is now a giddy bride-to-be with visions of bows and peplums and handkerchief hems. I'm not even sure what a peplum is, but I know one of you will enlighten me.

She stopped to admire her hands. Well, hand. Lana had done a superb job on the left; the right one bore the marks of the rush job that it had become once Tess's questions grew sharper. She sent the e-mail off, feeling extremely productive. How many people went through their in-box at sunrise, then spent an hour rowing?

Almost as soon as her e-mail vanished, her computer trilled back at her, and an instant message popped up on her screen. No-nonsense Gretchen, up even earlier in Chicago, had some on-topic advice:

Sorry, just saw your request to the digest. (I get it as individual e-mails.) When I was a city cop, there was a woman coming up behind me, Nancy Porter, very good police, who ended up leaving the department about the same time I did. She's out in the county, in Homicide. Call her, use my name. If there's something hubby isn't telling you, she'll share.

You're a gem, Gretchen, Tess typed, making a note of the office and pager numbers that Gretchen had enclosed for the detective.

Tell me something I don't know.

Tess promptly disconnected from the Internet and dialed the work number, assuming she would get voice mail. But the detective had just arrived at her desk, showing up early for the seven-to-three shift. Tess thought such a seemingly ambitious county Homicide cop, who saw perhaps one case for every thirty the city worked, would be up for any distraction, but Detective Nancy Porter was reticent to the point of rudeness until Tess dropped Gretchen's name. Then she was just reticent.

"Yeah, I know about the Rubin family," she said. She had a high, clear voice, almost little-girlish. "Family Crimes worked it, but the detective ran a lot of the stuff by me because I've done some missing-kid work. It's interesting, a stone-cold whydunit. It's just not a criminal case."

"I'm curious to know why the department is so sure of that."

Nancy didn't answer right away. She didn't answer any questions right away, and while her cautious manner made Tess impatient, it also struck her as admirable. She should try it herself sometime, thinking before she spoke.

"At the risk of sounding paranoid, I don't like talking on the phone with people I don't really know," the detective said at last. "I've got to go down to Northern District in the city this morning, so I'll grab a late breakfast with you in Hampden. That's near your house, right?"

"How do you know where I live?"

"Caller ID. I can match almost every prefix in the city with the neighborhood. I'm guessing you're north of Cold Spring but west of Charles."

Tess was impressed. This was a geek after her own heart.

"So if you're meeting with me, you've got something to tell me."

"I know a little bit. I'm not sure it will help you find the Rubin family, but it will give you some perspective you'll need if you're going to work for this guy."

Tess's mind raced. "Is Mark Rubin concealing something from me? Did Natalie Rubin have to disappear for a reason? Was she—"

"Later." The girlish voice was surprisingly firm. "I'll answer all your questions the best I can when we meet."

10

Tess stopped off at the Hampden Post Office before her late-breakfast meeting with Nancy Porter, sending three certified letters to the Mail Boxes Etc. store that Lana had visited. Each one contained a card with a typed message, one for Lana and two for Natalie, addressed to both Rubin and Peters: *I know what you're doing. Call me.* She used her second cell-phone number, the one that couldn't be traced to her. But just getting either of the Natalie letters accepted at the address would be a key piece of information.

The morning was bright and breezy, and Nancy Porter had taken one of the two porch tables at the Golden West, a restaurant carved out of a row house on Thirty-sixth Street, aka the Avenue. Long the main business artery in the working-class neighborhood of Hampden, the Avenue had become hip in spite of itself, bringing in the usual mix of cafés, galleries, and shops. Tess's personal favorite was Ma Petite Shoe, an establishment that sold only chocolate and shoes. That pretty much met all her needs, although most of the shoes tended to be on the girly side.

"I'm glad you were okay with meeting here," Nancy said, rising to shake Tess's hand. "I'm on a low-carb diet, and they have the best huevos rancheros, which almost make up for the fact that I can't have the tortillas."

Tess sized up the detective. She appeared a year or two younger than Tess and only a few pounds heavier, although those pounds were packed on a shorter, finer-boned frame. Men probably didn't mind Nancy's weight as much as she did. She had an all-American-girl cuteness, and the wedding band on her left hand would seem to indicate she didn't lack for companionship.

"Well, we're the perfect dining companions, then," Tess said.

"You're doing low carb, too?"

"No, but I love huevos rancheros, and I'll happily eat your tortillas along with mine."

Nancy favored her with a crooked grin. "I hate women like you. You can probably eat anything you want and not worry about it."

"Oh, I could worry about it, but what's the point? I accept my height and shoe size, my eye color and my hair color. I might as well live in the body I was born with, too."

"You can change your hair and your eyes, though."

"Would you?" Tess challenged the blue-eyed blonde.

Nancy laughed, shaking her head. "Gretchen said you were funny. Said you'd talk my ear off about nonessential stuff, too, but she swears you're a good investigator when you aren't being all philosophical."

"You talked to Gretchen?"

The blue eyes in that baby face had a knowing spark. "Oh, yeah, as soon as I hung with you. Woke her up, too. Sorry, but there was no way I was going to take your word for anything. I've gotten burned a time or two, talking to people I shouldn't. For all I knew, you were a reporter. In fact, Gretchen said you used to be."

"I've been a private investigator almost as long as I worked as a reporter." Tess paused, surprised by her own stat. She double-checked her arithmetic. Three years at the *Star* before it folded, now going on three years as a licensed PI. "And I wasn't much of a reporter. I was so far down the fourth-estate food chain that I was plankton."

"If you say so. Anyway, Gretchen vouched for you, and she's as tough on people as I am. So here I am. What can I tell you?"

"Did you work the Rubin case?"

"There is no Rubin case, as far as the department is concerned. And I hope he's not trying to say there is. Family Crimes checked it very thoroughly. His wife walked out, taking their kids. No sign of foul play. And until he gets a custody order, which he says he doesn't want to do, no laws broken."

"That's pretty much how he tells it. But I was curious about the fact that her credit cards have been dormant since she left. Isn't that suggestive of foul play? How can she be on the run without any money?"

"Didn't he tell you?"

"Tell me what?"

Another knowing smile. Nancy might be younger than Tess, but she had more experience listening to people's lies.

"Mark Rubin kept his wife on a short, tight leash when it came to money. She had credit cards for everything she needed, and an ATM-Visa card, but he didn't let her have more than a hundred dollars in cash. Plus, he made her account for her cash day by day. Withdrawals, too. At the end of the month, he went over everything again, item by item."

"I don't get it. That would make her more likely to use the credit cards, right?"

"Not if she doesn't want him to know where she is. So she figured out a way to get around his system, get enough cash to hit the road."

"How?"

"Oh, she's shrewd. Rubin withdrew his cash for the week every Monday, and he seldom went to the machine again before the week was out. So she figured she had five days before he would notice that the balances were off. All she had to do was lie to him, not show him the slips at night. Starting the Monday before she left, she went to the ATM every day and withdrew five hundred dollars. That gave her twenty-five hundred."

"Decent seed money, but it won't take you far, not with three kids."

"She wasn't done. She bought some high-end electronics on one of the credit cards, stuff that Rubin can't find in his house. Probably sold it for twenty cents on the dollar through a friend, or a fence. We figure she got at least another thousand pulling that scam. And then, the day before she left, she deposited a check for twenty-five hundred dollars, to cover what she had taken. I guess she was worried he could come after her for theft, even though it was a joint account."

"Where'd she get the check?"

"It was a personal check signed by Lana Wishnia."

"She's a manicurist. Where does a manicurist get twenty-five hundred bucks to lend?"

Nancy nodded approvingly. "You are good. Rubin didn't know about her at all, and he thinks Natalie was just her client, but I think different. Lana told detectives the check was to repay some loans Natalie gave her over the years. My hunch is that Lana Wishnia was the fence, but it's legal, right? No law against buying electronics and selling them cheap."

"Why didn't Natalie just write herself a big check on the joint account, wipe out the whole thing?"

Nancy cocked an eyebrow, a trick that Tess had never mastered.

"Because the bank had instructions to call Mr. Rubin if Natalie wrote a check for cash for any amount over five hundred dollars."

"Did anyone ask Rubin about his, um, strict household bookkeeping?"

"Absolutely. You see behavior that controlling, and you have to wonder—how else is this guy controlling his wife? Detectives checked 911 logs to see if the Rubin residence was known for calling in domestics. It came up clean, but in that community that's not unusual."

"What do you mean, 'that community'?" Tess's tone was sharp, her Irish roots forgotten. She was suddenly 100 percent Weinstein, and the girl on the other side of the table was just another bigoted shiksa. Never mind that Tess herself had basically asked Rubin when he stopped beating his wife. That was different.

"Look, I was posted to Northwest in the city before I came to the county. I know that the Orthodox like to take care of their problems when possible, whether it's the elderly or drugs or domestic abuse."

"All communities should do as good a job of caring for their own," Tess said, still feeling self-righteous.

"No question. But the downside to keeping problems all in the family is that there's no paper trail when a situation gets out of hand. If you don't get the batterers in the system when they start, then sometimes you can't clamp down on them when their behavior becomes truly life-threatening."

"I don't see Mark Rubin as an abuser."

"Neither do I. But I can be definite on this point because we looked into it. We also checked to see if there had been any accusations of sex abuse, if the school had noticed anything in the oldest kid's behavior. Look, we even had to consider if Mark Rubin was some criminal mastermind who'd murdered his whole family, then played the part of the grieving husband. The fact that he hired you is only further proof that he's in the clear."

"Or an expensive bluff."

Tess was thinking of the pregnant woman who had become a national sensation a while back. Her husband hadn't been the most persuasive grieving spouse in the world, though, given that he was an adulterer who put their house on the market and sold the family car within a month of her disappearance. Rubin was much more convincing in his agony.

"You said you know the detective in Family Crimes who worked this. What's her take on it?"

"Maria says if Mark Rubin had anything to do with this, he's the biggest, two-faced Bluebeard ever. No one has a bad word to say about the guy. Employees, people in his congregation, neighbors. Even ex-employees, and you know what they're like. Everyone agrees he's a great guy. Although they say it as if it were a little bit of a surprise."

"Really?"

"Yeah, the older ladies at his synagogue, the ones who had known him since he was kid, kept telling Maria he was such a nice man, 'considering everything.' And when Maria asked, 'Considering what?' they'd just smile or pat her hand. Again, it's a close-knit community. They're not going to tell us all the gossip."

"What about Natalie?"

"Maria says no one knows her—and no one seems to want to know her. In fact, she's probably the 'everything' that all those women find so objectionable." Tess, knowing Natalie's background and youth, saw Nancy's point. "And then there's Lana Wishnia, but she's not saying anything."

"She stonewalled me, too, but I like to think that Baltimore County Police can be a little more persuasive."

"We can—if we have a charge on you." Again Nancy raised a single eyebrow. "But you have to remember, no law has been broken, and Mark Rubin didn't want to pursue custody through the system, so . . . sayonara. Not our case, not our stat. The major only expended as much energy as he did because he thought the community might get up in arms, bring all this pressure to bear if we didn't make every effort to establish there was no crime. The last thing he wanted was to turn on the news and see some little old ladies marching around the Public Safety Building, picketing the department."

Tess was transformed back into Teresa Esther, defender of the faith. "Are you saying Jews are pushy when they want something?"

"I'm saying *people* are pushy. But some communities are better organized than others, always have been."

"What are you, anyway? You look WASP, you have a WASP name, but you sure don't have the attitude." *Or the bone structure.* Nancy Porter's round face was pleasant, but she would never pass as one of Baltimore's moneyed bluebloods.

"Porter is my married name. I was born Potrcurzski. We're pretty burned out, us Poles, just as left behind as your people, Monaghan. We're never going to run this city or state again."

"Baltimore has an Irish mayor now. He even plays in his own Irish band."

"You know, that's one of the few things makes me glad I'm working in the county these days. My sergeant says we live in an era where the politicians want to be rock stars and the rock stars want to be politicians—but only one of those jobs actually takes talent."

Tess laughed. "I have a feeling I'd like your sergeant. Is there anything else I should know about Rubin?"

"His business is sound, and there's no life insurance on his wife or the children. Just on him, which is what you'd expect. Oh, and he's pretty well fixed. Not so much from the business, but from an inheritance. His dad died a few years ago, left him everything, and everything was quite a pile."

"So why did she leave? Why run away from a rich man who adores you and gives you everything you want, if not all the cash you can carry?"

"I'm sorry, but it's not the kind of thing we do at my shop," Nancy said. "We do more concrete stuff. Dead body, who did it, let's lock 'em up. Motives are a luxury I can't afford."

"Still, you must trip over them from time to time. You can't be a cop without learning a lot about human nature."

"Yeah." The single syllable carried a world of memory and meaning. "But when I do find out why someone did something—I usually wish I hadn't."

11

Like an old lady who didn't trust banks, Baltimore sometimes hid its money in odd places. Robbins & Sons, a white stucco building that resembled a bunker, was tucked away on Smith Avenue, a quiet street just northwest of the city limits. Yet its nearest neighbor, a shoe store, sold high heels that even Tess's inexpert eye put at three hundred dollars and beyond, while a dress store in the same strip center was advertising a trunk show for a designer who was surely famous among those who paid attention to such things. These one-named stores—Evelyn's, Soigné—had been built in a different era, when shoppers still expected to brave the elements to go door to door and had to enter stores to get a sense of their wares. The small, narrow displays offered only one or two items for a window-shopper to contemplate.

The stores also provided an interesting contrast to the men

strolling along the street here in northwest Baltimore, strictly observant Jews in beards and brimmed hats. It struck Tess for the first time how funny it was that one of the major streets through the heart of this middle-class Jewish neighborhood was named Smith. Did even streets assimilate?

Robbins & Sons had no windows at all, just glass double doors and a sign so discreet that it was unlikely anyone ever stumbled on the furrier by accident. Was that intentional? Tess assumed that furriers were besieged these days, quivering inside their stores while picketers circled with cans of red paint. A few years back, her mother had stopped wearing the raccoon coat that Tess's father had given her on their twentieth anniversary, proclaiming herself much too nervous. She then bought a faux fur, but it was such a convincing fake that she was scared to wear it. Instead she wore a good cloth coat. "Like Pat Nixon," joked Tess's Uncle Donald, which angered his sister. Any comparison to any Nixon was considered harsh rhetoric in the Monaghan-Weinstein families.

But there were no protesters here on this bright fall morning, and no evidence that they had been here anytime recently—no splashes of red on the pavement, no leaflets proclaiming "Fur Is Murder." There was nothing here but cars, expensive ones, with women of all ages coming and going as if it were the most normal thing in the world to shop for a fur coat on a day when the temperature would probably reach eighty degrees. Tess pushed through the doors and entered a place as hushed as a temple—and as cold as a meat locker. She wondered if the overly chilled air was for the furs or the menopausal customers.

"May I help you, miss?"

If the salesman thought Tess, in black trousers and white T-shirt, an unlikely customer, nothing in his manner betrayed this fact. He clasped his hands behind his back, his tone polite and helpful, yet not in the over-the-top style of a salesperson who hopes to drive someone away.

Tess decided to test his mien before asking to see Mark Rubin.

"Well, I don't know," she said, giving her voice a Valley Girl whine. Greenspring Valley, that is, or perhaps Worthington, a place where Baltimore's rich WASPs and Jews lived in an uneasy truce. "I've always thought of fur coats as being something my mother and grandmother wear, but after the last couple of winters, I can't help wondering if it might be a good idea."

"A fur is a wonderful investment," the salesman said, sizing her up. She eyed him back. Tall and slim, with thinning hair, he could have been anywhere from forty to sixty, married or single, straight or gay. "I don't see you as the mink type—"

"Why not?" Did she look poor? Movie stars shopped in T-shirts, after all, and her loafers were Cole Haans. Not as expensive as some designer brands, but not inconsequential.

"I'm not talking about price," he said, remaining smooth and un-ruffled. Oh, he was a salesman through and through, but a salesman suited to luxury goods, a man who understood that moving minks and Mercedes-Benzes and Bose stereo systems meant long, drawn-out courtships—and much higher commissions. "But if your clothes today are indicative of your preferred look—what I like to call the casual sophisticate—a mink would probably be too formal. Have you thought about beaver?"

Tess figured she could keep a straight face if he could.

"Not really," she said. "I have to admit, I'm so overwhelmed by the process that I don't know where to begin. How can I know if I'm getting my money's worth?"

"Trust your sense of touch." He pulled a jacket from a nearby rack and held its sleeve toward Tess, which she stroked dutifully. "We call the top hairs 'guard hairs.' These should be silky, while the underfur beneath should be even in texture. Now, how does this feel to you?"

"Nice," Tess said. It felt like a dog, although a better-cared-for one than either of hers, whose short coats shed alarmingly.

"Try this." He brought out another jacket, which felt a little softer and seemed to shine with more subtle variations. It was like switching to a top-line colorist after relying on Nice 'n Easy.

"What's the difference?"

"About two thousand dollars." The salesman smiled. He was onto her, he had to be, but the charade seemed to be as amusing to him as it was to Tess. "The second one was made from female pelts, which requires more pieces, and comes from a name designer. All those things add to the price, although not necessarily the quality. Try it on."

"No," Tess demurred, but the salesman was already shrugging it up over her left arm, as if she were a balky toddler who didn't want to put on her snowsuit.

"There," he said. "Look how nice you look—although with your hair I think you'd want to go with ranch instead of wild."

Tess turned reluctantly toward the full-length mirror behind her. She had worried she would look like a furry butterball, but he had picked out a sleek coat with the furs placed in a gently curving pattern that flattered the figure. She looked pretty, glamorous even, not that she had ever aspired to glamour.

Yet her image disturbed her, too. It was so matronly, so grown-up. The vision in the mirror was the woman she might have been if she had taken a few different turns in life. More accurately, this would be the Tess who had taken no turns at all, just embarked on that greased chute of marriage and motherhood. For while most of her friends had started out on a gung ho career path, Tess noticed something odd happened when the babies started coming. Female friends who never would have dreamed of leaving their jobs at their husbands' insistence had clamored for the stay-at-home-mommy gig when it became a kind of status symbol.

It was, of course, undeniably good for the kids to have a parent at home. Tess didn't even like to put her dogs in a kennel, so she understood women who were nervous about day care. Still, it was creepy, this voluntary army of Stepford wives who didn't look quite as happy as they insisted they were. Tess had a theory that Botox had soared because so many thirty-something women were frowning. What was the source of their anxiety? They had money, as evidenced by their cars, shoes, and purses, and they clearly spent time on their appearance. Hair, nails, skin—all just so. They were the women she had glimpsed at Adrian's, the ladies who lunch, only these days it was the ladies who *didn't* lunch, who dutifully followed the diet of the moment and trudged to the gym, then came home to drive the SUV around in the going-nowhere circles necessitated by car pools and soccer matches and gymnastic classes.

A sudden wheeze gripped Tess, and she felt a horrible, messy sneeze coming on, which she decided to stifle rather than risk spraying across a twelve-thousand-dollar coat.

"Fox might be good for you, too," the salesman said thoughtfully. "Or shearling."

"What about the . . . issues?"

"What issues?" he asked sharply. One thing to be a shopping dilettante, Tess supposed, another to be a PETA activist scoping the place out.

"Well, you know, the humane issues."

"Oh." His expression couldn't have been blander. "I suppose that is a consideration for some people. Certainly I would never recommend a fur to someone who couldn't reconcile her personal beliefs with the industry's practices, any more than I would serve a vegetarian friend a steak. Here at Robbins & Sons, we don't *proselytize* for fur. But what I've found is that most people realize that nature is hierarchical, and while we try to coexist peacefully with other living things, we have created a world where people come first. At least I hope we have. We eat animals—you do eat them, right? I couldn't help noticing you were wearing leather shoes."

"Yes, I eat meat and wear leather. I kill cockroaches, too, but I always give them a shout-out before I go into the kitchen at night, so they have a sporting chance to flee."

"Hmmm. So, really, for you, the question isn't whether this should be done but how others might react to you?" He let his voice scale up, but Tess sensed he wasn't really asking a question. "You care what people think."

He was good, in some ways better than the psychiatrist that the state of Maryland had forced Tess to see up until recently. "I guess I do."

"Consider this. What do we tell older women about avoiding street crime? We tell them to walk with confidence, heads held high, purses clutched firmly under their arms. Well, I tell my customers the same thing, especially women such as yourself, who buy their own furs. Walk with your head high. You have purchased a fine garment, a timeless garment, an investment that enhances your beauty. You walk like that, you don't have to worry about other people."

Tess looked in the mirror again. She did look pretty. And, really, she couldn't argue against the fur business on principle. The image still bothered her, but it wasn't the source of the coat's materials, more its message, an announcement of consumption and self-indulgence. Tess could happily blow hundreds of dollars buying a piece of outsider art that her mother assumed she trash-picked, or thousands on a new computer just to go a few seconds faster on the Internet. But she could not make peace with any adornment, any object, that invited others to envy her relative comfort. It was an invitation to the evil eye, and the Weinstein side of her never wanted to provoke the evil eye. Crow had never gotten that, but then Crow had the cheerful optimism that came from being born into money and comfort.

A soft chime sounded, indicating that the front door had opened, and Mark Rubin entered the store. He did not seem impressed by the sight of Tess in mink.

"You find Mrs. Gordon's lynx?" the salesman asked.

"Yes, Paul, I've handled the 'emergency' as I've handled it every year for the past decade when Mrs. Gordon has scheduled one of these trips and forgotten to call ahead to get her coats out of storage. This year it's a Scandinavian cruise."

"She's such a—" Conscientious Paul remembered he was standing next to a potential customer. "She's such a sweet lady, but a little forgetful."

"Well, that's why we have our own storage vault. I can always get a coat for a valued customer, as long as it's not on the Sabbath."

"You have your own storage facility?" Tess was trying to cover up the awkwardness she felt, as if she had been caught at something.

Mark nodded curtly. "The other locals use a warehouse in northern Virginia. I'll take over from here, Paul. Miss Monaghan came to see me."

"Certainly, Mr. Rubin." The salesman disappeared with the practiced discretion of a man who knows how to make himself invisible.

"He's good at his job," Tess said as soon as Paul was out of earshot.

"He's excellent. So why were you wasting his time? Not to mention bringing my personal business into my workplace. I hope you don't squander your own time as carelessly as you used my salesman's. After all, I'm paying for it."

"I was curious about your business," she said, taking off the coat and returning it to the rack. Rubin reached out and gave it a few smoothing strokes, as if Tess had defiled the mink in some way. "Right now I'm curious about everything you do. Somewhere in your life, there's got to be a clue, a hint, as to where your wife might have gone, and why. For example, is there anyone else in your life who disappeared about the same time?"

"What do you mean?"

"An employee, for example. Someone from your street. The guy who delivers your newspaper. Natalie had to have some help. She only had a few thousand dollars, right? At least that's what I just learned from the Baltimore County cops. You didn't trust your wife with cash, so she had to figure out a way to sneak it. But she was scared enough to pay most of it back, with a check written by a manicurist who happens to be her oldest friend. But for some reason you didn't think to tell me about your household accounting or

99

to give me Lana Wishnia's name as a lead. I had to pay Natalie's mother a hundred dollars just to find out she existed."

Mark Rubin looked around the store. "Let's go back to my office. I'd prefer not to have this conversation out here, on the floor, where customers come and go."

———

His office was utilitarian, a windowless room with a messy desk stacked with catalogs. The only personal touch was a bright red shelf filled with photographs of his children and his wife. This long mantel was mounted to the wall behind Rubin's desk, almost like a credenza, so Tess ended up facing all those photos when she sat opposite him. The photos made her feel guilty, as if the children's faces were pleading with her to bring them back to a place where they had smiled and laughed as they did in these photos. Their mother, however, was somber—lips together, eyes downcast. But there was a kind of calculation in the look, too, a sense that Natalie Rubin was striking a pose, her eyes sliding away from the camera's lens lest it glimpse her secrets.

"I never knew this little shopping center existed," Tess said, making conversation. "Have you always been here?"

"My father opened the store in this location about thirty-five years ago. Like most merchants, he started off downtown, but he was quick to figure out that the customers were moving farther and farther away and that the stores needed to follow them. He was already making plans to relocate when the riots came. But we always lived out here in Pikesville. We had to."

"Why? It's not like those old real-estate covenants barring Jews were still in effect in the other neighborhoods."

"I have to live within walking distance of my shul," he said, his voice patient, yet a little patronizing. It was becoming a familiar tone to Tess. Had he spoken to his wife with these same inflections? That would explain a lot.

"Right. So where's the other son?"

"What do you mean? Have you learned something about Isaac and Efraim?"

"No, no—the store is called Robbins & *Sons*. I figured out that Robbins is simply Rubin, anglicized. But you're the only son here. Did you have a brother?"

"Oh." He shrugged. "The name goes back to my father. The other furriers in town—Mano Swartz, Miller Brothers—had such impressive-sounding names. And he had a partner in the beginning, when he was downtown, but they went their separate ways. So Robbins & Sons, two lies for the price of one. Only one son, and the name is Rubin. But if my boys . . . if my boys . . . well, perhaps we'll make the name true yet."

Tess completed his thought in her head: If his boys were found, if they were okay. Apparently, Mark Rubin had his own reservations about tempting the evil eye.

"Did you feel obligated to go into the family business?"

"Not at all. I considered it a privilege. My father made it clear, early on, that our partnership was to be a two-way street—I could say no, but he could, too. If I wanted to do something else, there would be no hard feelings. And if he decided I didn't have the brains to run it, then no hard feelings on my part either. Some people found my father rather . . . rigid. Strict, at least in business."

"What do you mean, 'at least in business'?"

"He wasn't strict about religion at all. My father considered himself Orthodox, but he did things I would never do. Dance with a woman who was not his wife, for example. Eat in nonkosher restaurants. Such looseness was more common before the Conservative movement gathered strength. I decided I wanted to follow a more traditional Orthodox lifestyle. It's all relative. There are Hasidim who consider me unspeakably liberal."

"Was there a reason you embraced a stricter version of the religion than the one practiced in your family?" The question was asked out of nothing more than sheer curiosity. One of the perks of being a private detective was that one was allowed to pursue topics considered outrageously rude in everyday life. Tess could ask people about their income, their sex lives, and even about religion, the most forbidden topic of all in some ways.

"Reasons, I'd say. But they all fall under the general heading of growing up, moving on. My father died ten years ago. Heart attack. Died, in fact, carrying an armload of furs into the vault. The last thing he said to me was, 'Mark—grab the coats.' He didn't want them to fall. He was dead when he hit the ground."

"This was just before you married, right?"

The shrug again. Rubin was an eloquent shrugger. "My father was fifty-five when I was born, yet he outlived my mother, who was twenty years younger and died before my fifth birthday. He also outlived my stepmother, who died when I was a teenager. I was in no hurry to marry, and my father seemed to enjoy my companionship. Besides, I was waiting for a love match, a true one."

"I guess a good-looking Orthodox furrier doesn't want for prospective wives."

He stroked his beard, amused. "How nice to know you think I'm good-looking."

Tess pretended to be flustered, but the compliment had been calculated. She had wanted to soften him up before she began asking the ruder questions. "So . . . about Lana Wishnia."

"I didn't know her." Said quickly, as if that would make the subject go away. "And the police told me she was Natalie's manicurist. You say they were friends, but this is the first I've heard of that."

"I'm more curious about the check Lana wrote to Natalie—and your little bookkeeping system, which made it necessary. Why didn't Natalie have money of her own?"

"She had credit cards, an ATM card, accounts at all the stores where she shopped. She never wanted for anything."

"C'mon, it was pretty medieval, and not even in keeping with your own beliefs. Jewish women have always been given a lot of control over their homes, allowed to have their own money. Was it a bone of contention in the marriage? Did Natalie want things set

up differently? Maybe this whole disappearing act is a walkout intended to get you to change some things."

"No," he said, an edge to his voice. "No, you have the wrong idea."

"Really? Then would you point me in the direction of the right
idea? Again, I have to ask you if Natalie had an addiction of some
sort. Because that's the usual reason not to entrust a family member
with cash."

"I don't want . . . You shouldn't ask such questions. This is the
mother of my children, my wife. You're being disrespectful."

The phone rang just then, and Rubin flicked on the speakerphone. A man's voice, high and reedy through the distortion of the
voice box, started out tentatively: "This is Jack Reid, up in Montreal, and there's a small problem with the knitwear you ordered for
this fall."

"There are no small problems, Jack." Mark Rubin's voice took
on a cold, ruthless quality that Tess had not heard before. *I wouldn't
want to go up against him in a business deal*, she thought. Then she realized she already had, and he had acquiesced readily at the price
she named. She must have underbid the job.

The voice on the speaker continued, clearly nervous. "The per-
unit cost quoted you . . . my assistant . . . well, he's new, and he didn't
figure in some ancillary costs. There are some complicated tariffs
and shipping fees, at least in order to make the October date we
agreed to. You see, we get the pieces from New York, but still have
to assemble them here, so you're talking a really fast turnaround."

"That's your problem."

"But I'm going to lose money if you hold me to that price."

"No you're not. You may not make as *much* as you counted on
making this fall, but you won't lose money, not in the long run. The
way you'll lose money is by trying to renegotiate the price or delay
delivery. Then you'll lose a lot of money, because I'll never buy
from you again, and I'll persuade other merchants in my area to
blackball you, too, tell them how unreliable you are. You'll never
make another sale in the Mid-Atlantic region."

"But, Mark—"

"No, Jack. Do it for the agreed-on price, delivery on the con-tracted date, or we're through. *You're* through."

"If you could just split the difference in the shipping?"

"I can, but I won't. Fob it off on one of your stupider clients, who doesn't read every line on his bill. But don't try to play me for a fool."

"Mark, if you could just see your way clear . . ."

"Jack, hang up now, or I'm going to insist you deliver a week ear-lier. At your expense."

"Pleasure doing business with you," the disembodied Jack said, allowing himself a small measure of sarcasm in his defeat.

"The pleasure," Rubin said, "is all mine." He punched a button, disconnecting the line.

Tess sat in stunned silence, half admiring, half appalled.

"In business," Rubin said, "you have to remember who works for whom. He needs me more than I need him. So I win."

"Well, by that logic I work for you, but you need me and you need to heed my advice. You can't keep everything decorous, Mr. Rubin." Funny, she was closer to him in age than his own wife was, but she just couldn't call him by his first name, and he never invited her to. "You can't mark areas of your life 'keep out,' especially if they might hold the key to where your wife and children went."

"I want to find my wife, but I don't want to violate her, or ex-pose her."

"Expose her to what?"

"Nothing," he said, backpedaling. "It's just that I've come to you with a problem of what I would call location. I want to know *where* my wife is. Why she left isn't so important to me. We'll deal with that when she comes home, between us."

"But I may not be able to find her unless I know the *why*. So if there's anything you're not telling me . . ."

The phone rang again, and Rubin punched the speakerphone with great enthusiasm, as if happy for the interruption.

"That better not be you, Jack," he warned the phone. But the voice that came back was mechanical and unhearing.

"This is a collect call from 1-800-CALL-ATT. If you wish to accept this call, please press '1' on your TouchTone phone. The message is from—"

A pause, then another voice, a human one, small but determined: "Isaac."

Rubin almost broke the phone's plastic surface in his effort to punch the 1, but his voice was controlled when he spoke. "Isaac? Isaac? Are you there?"

A rush of words, boyish and high, filled the room, for Rubin had left the phone in speaker mode. "Daddy, this is Isaac. I'm in a McDonald's, but I'm not sure where. I tried to call you earlier, when we first got here, but I got your voice mail and I used up the money that I told Mama I wanted for a salad. Now everyone is playing in the ball room, and they think I'm going to the bathroom. Don't worry, I didn't eat anything, although I guess a salad would be okay. I'm not supposed to call you, but I don't care, because I want to come home and be with you, in our house, and go to school and— Daddy! *DADDEE!*"

And the call ended on that long-drawn-out syllable, a shriek that faded away, followed by a vague scuffling noise.

"Isaac? Isaac? Isaac, are you there?" But there was no reply, just a click. The line had definitely gone dead.

Rubin grabbed at his hair, as if he might tear it out, then pushed the phone off the desk as if it were responsible for whatever was happening on the other end of the line. He then began throwing every sheet of paper from his desk, showering Tess, who was on her hands and knees, trying to retrieve the phone even as paper rained down on her.

"I'm calling AT&T back," she said, trying to stay calm in the face of Rubin's amazing rage and grief. "They should be able to tell us the number he called from."

"He said he tried to call earlier and I wasn't here. Why wasn't I here? Because of that *behayma*, Mrs. Gordon, and her stupid lynx. She should fall off the *Norwegian Princess* and drown for what she's cost me."

The phone had caller ID, and the number was on the LED display. Tess found a phone book beneath a pile of glossy catalogs showing young women in furs of not-in-nature colors—lilac, moss green, peacock blue. "Area code 313 is southwestern Indiana."

"We should go, we should call the police, we should—"

"You call the police," Tess said, "while I dial this number back."

But it rang busy. It rang busy every time they tried it for the next hour.

12

W hat the *fuck* are you doing?"

Zeke seized Isaac by his collar and arm, yanking him so hard that the pay phone, loosed from Isaac's grasp, bounced on its metallic tail like an enraged cobra, hitting the white-tiled wall and caroming off, catching Isaac hard enough across the face to raise a welt. Good. It was almost as good a release as hitting the goddamn kid himself. Which he would never do, and not just because Natalie wouldn't stand for it. Zeke had known the end of a belt as a boy and had sworn to himself never to inflict such pain on a child. It hadn't been the beatings so much. It was the *ritual* of the beatings—the weary trudge to the closet for the correct belt, the chair in the kitchen, the way the belt was looped just so over the right hand. And, more than anything else, it was the mournful resignation, the insistence that he had brought the punishment on himself.

"I said, *'What are you doing?'*" Zeke depressed the hang-up switch but let the receiver swing free. He then turned the boy around, pressed him against the wall—okay, pushed him against it—and dug his fingers into his neck and shoulders just hard enough to let Isaac know that he meant business. But his voice was low. He had learned this, too, in childhood. As long as you kept your voice low, you could get away with a lot. It was tones, the shrill and the sharp, that made people look up. You could practically kill a person and not draw a crowd, as long as you never raised your voice.

Isaac kept his eyes on the floor. "I was making a phone call."

"To who? To who?" Zeke might have started shaking him then, but a woman came out of the restroom and gave them a curious look. He threw an arm around Isaac's neck, trying to make their interaction look like good-natured roughhousing.

"To *whom*," the boy corrected, and Zeke really wanted to slap him then. What nine-year-old knew the difference between "who" and "whom," much less cared? The stupid kid should be grateful for his rescue from that tight-ass upbringing, not spending every moment scheming about how to return.

"You didn't call 911, did you, Isaac?" Even Zeke lost the new names when his emotions ran high. "We're all going to be in some deep shit, you try that. You know what they're going to do? They're going to take you away from your mom. But they won't give you back to your dad—oh, no. They'll split you and Efraim and Penina up, put you in foster homes. Is that what you want?"

Isaac's lip quivered, but he didn't break easy, this kid. Spoiled as he was, he was a tough number.

"You called your dad, didn't you? I heard you say 'Daddy,' don't deny it. Look, I can pick up the phone right now, call the operator, and ask her where the last call went from this phone, so you might as well tell me."

"'1-800-CALL-ATT,'" Isaac said in a mockingbird's singsong voice. "'Free for you and cheap for them.'"

"Ike, you want to spend more time in the trunk? Because that can be arranged. You can ride back there all the time, take your meals there, spend the nights there if that's what you want."

Isaac stared back, yielding no ground. God, he was tough. Those had to be his grandfather's genes, not his father's. But the boy couldn't hold it together very long, and he finally whispered, "I called my dad, at the store. I miss him."

"Did you get him?"

"I'm not sure. He never . . . The machine didn't pick up, but I'm not sure he was there."

Softened by his victory, Zeke bent down next to Isaac, examining the red mark the phone had left. Not good, a kid with a bruised eye. People noticed things like that. They had to avoid attracting any attention, at least for the next few weeks. That's why they had been on the move since Natalie had refused to take the kids home. Her stupid impulse had forced Zeke to risk much, more than he wanted, but what could he do? He couldn't convince her to leave without telling her everything, and Natalie couldn't be trusted with what Zeke thought of as the global overview. Her ignorance of certain details was key to the success of his plan.

"We'll want to put something on that. I'd ask for a raw steak, but I'm pretty sure they don't have real steak here. Hey, maybe I could ask for a McRib, but the barbecue sauce would stick to your face."

The boy didn't smile. "All the food here is crummy. I wouldn't want to eat it even if it were kosher."

"It's good food—you don't know what you're missing. Other kids love it, would eat it every day if they could."

Isaac just shook his head, his lips pressed together as if someone might try to sneak in an outlaw french fry. Zeke was actually worried about how little the kid ate, holding out as much as possible. Today he had agreed to drink a strawberry milk shake, on the grounds that it wasn't made from real milk, then asked for the money for a salad. He loaded up on salad bars when they went to places like Ruby Tuesday, sometimes asking the waitress for a Styrofoam to-go box and plastic utensils. He was rigid, a little chip off the old-before-his-time block. But there was something defiant in his behavior, too, a thumb-in-the-eye slyness that drove Zeke mad.

"I know about keeping kosher, but it's bullshit, my man, just old superstitions that don't make any sense. You think God cares what kind of plates you eat from or whether you have a lobster now and then? Why would God make something as delicious as lobster if he didn't mean for man to eat it? Think about it."

"It didn't look good, when we went to that Red Lobster place. The twins left it on their plates. They said it tasted like butter-flavored rubber."

Zeke decided to try a different tack. "You miss your dad, don't you, partner?"

The boy nodded miserably.

"Look, I know what it's like to miss someone, buddy, but you have to understand. This is for the best. Your dad was good to you, but he wasn't good to your mom. Your mom was very, very un-happy, living like she did. And your dad knew it, but he didn't want to do anything about it. So she had to leave."

"She could have left me with Dad. I wasn't unhappy."

"Is that what you wanted, a life without your mother?"

The question was cruel, almost worse than a smack, asking a child to choose between two parents. Zeke could see that Isaac was floored by the impossibility. Like every kid since time began, he wanted his mother *and* his father. Yeah, well, four out of five den-tists pick Trident, and one out of two marriages folds. Get used to it, kid. One parent is better than nothing. Zeke had two, then he had one, then none. It was all survivable.

"Was my mom really unhappy?" the boy asked. "I never saw her cry."

"She didn't want you to know, but yeah, she was really unhappy."

"But my dad was happy, and I was happy, and the twins were happy."

"I suppose so. You thought you were, which is as good as. But now that you know how unhappy your mom was, maybe it was all an illusion."

Isaac shook his head, defiant now. "No, I was definitely happy. So you're saying that for my mom to be happy, it's okay to make us all unhappy—me and my dad and the twins."

"The twins are like puppies, my man. They're fine as long as they're warm and their bellies are full."

"Still," Isaac said, "two against one, me and my dad."

"What?"

"Majority rule. If we were happy, she should have tried to be happy."

Oh, man, the apple really don't fall far from the tree. Another little selfish shit, courtesy of Orthodox Judaism, arguing every point as if it were straight from the Talmud. *What about my happiness?* Zeke wanted to ask this smug brat, but he knew that Isaac didn't consider Zeke a factor. As someone outside the Rubin golden circle, he didn't matter at all.

"Look, partner, there's some stuff kids just can't understand. If we go back to Baltimore, they're not going to let you live with your dad."

"Why?"

"You wouldn't understand."

"I could if you pick the right words. My father tries to explain everything to me, no matter how complicated."

"I'm not your father," Zeke said, straightening up. "Thank fuckin' God."

He assumed that Isaac would have a smart-ass retort, but Natalie appeared in the corridor just then, the twins in tow, her lovely face flushed and on the verge of tears.

"Penina—I mean, Daisy—made . . ." She gestured helplessly at the girl, red-faced and damp, either at the end of a crying jag or about to begin one.

"Made what?" Zeke asked, although Isaac was nodding as if he understood.

"*Made*. In her pants, in the ball room, and they're all out there screaming at me, saying the sign says no children who aren't toilet trained. Only she is, she was, for over three years now—never even wet the bed in all this time. I don't know what's gotten into her."

The girl babbled something, and the boy twin babbled back, comforting her, or so Zeke assumed. He couldn't understand a word these two said, even when it was allegedly in English. Natalie said they used to talk like normal kids, but you couldn't prove it by Zeke.

"Take her in the ladies' room and clean her up the best you can," Zeke said. "I'll take the boys out to the car and wait for you there. And if we have to, we'll start strapping diapers on the two of them. If I'm all but living in a car, I don't want it to smell like crap."

He left the receiver dangling on its silver cord, catching Isaac's longing looks toward it. Zeke was going to have to watch this one like a hawk. Watch him or put him in the trunk more often. He had no choice.

You'll be sorry, he thought, then wondered who the words were for, Isaac or some long-vanquished foe. Was the boy his enemy or simply a reminder of others who had wronged him? Oh, things would be so much simpler if Natalie hadn't shown up with the children, if she'd never had them in the first place. *There weren't supposed to be any children.* But there were, and Zeke prided himself on his ability to improvise. The key to a truly genius plan was its flexibility, the planner's ability to modify, to roll with the punches.

Natalie had always been good at keeping secrets. That was a big part of her attraction. It occurred to Zeke for the first time that perhaps she had grown too good at staying mum, that there could be other surprises in store for him as well. He might have to think this all through again, change his plan one more time. He had to figure out just what he was going to do about the kids.

13

Tess sat in Rubin's office chair for the next hour, hitting the redial button with her index finger until she began to feel a twinge from wrist to elbow. Finally the unsympathetic buzz of the busy signal gave way to a ring, which turned into a puzzled "Hello?" on the twelfth ring.

"Could you please tell me where I'm calling? I know it's a McDonald's in Indiana, in the 313 area code." Caller ID and Isaac had combined to give her that much information. "But I need the town name and the location of this phone."

"You're calling McDonald's but you don't know why or where it is?" The voice was pleasant if foggy, a young man blissed out on Happy Meals or some other substance that had led to the sudden need for a cheeseburger.

"Long story," Tess said. "Boring one, too. But I sure would like to know where you are."

"Well, according to conventional cartography, I am at the forty-second latitude and seventy-fifth longitude, aka French Lick, Indiana, you'll pardon the expression."

"Is that really the latitude and longitude for French Lick?" Tess asked, curious in spite of herself.

"No, I just made it up, but it sounds plausible, doesn't it? Where are you calling from?"

"Baltimore."

"Oh, I don't think so," the young man said, hanging up. Tess felt like one of the errant knights in a Monty Python film, denied permission to cross a bridge because she'd waffled on her favorite color. She had already struck out with the state police once they heard that Mark's son had confirmed he was with his mother and there was no custody order for the father to enforce. No laws broken there, the police said, compassionate but firm. If only Isaac had spoken of kidnapping or said he feared for his life.

Tess called directory assistance and asked to be connected to the only McDonald's in French Lick, but the manager refused to answer any of her questions, saying she had just gotten on and couldn't possibly know who had passed through the restaurant even an hour ago.

"Is there someone else—" Tess began.

"Have you seen the sign? Over a billion served? Well, about half of 'em were here today already, and I don't have time for this. You should see my restrooms."

The manager ended the call by slamming down the phone with a bang hard so hard and an epithet so coarse that it shattered any stereotype Tess harbored about kindly, salt-of-the-earth midwesterners.

"French Lick, Indiana," Tess said to Mark, who had been pacing his office like a caged animal, literally pulling at his hair. "That mean anything to you? Do you or Natalie know people there, or anywhere nearby?"

He had the desperate look of a kid in a spelling bee asked to tackle a word he had never heard of, sounding it out as if stalling for time. "French Lick, French Lick, French Lick, French Lick."

"Just go," said Paul the salesman. Apprised of the afternoon's events, he had been keeping vigil with his boss, scurrying back into the store whenever the chime announced arriving customers. "Get in your car and go, boss. I can take care of things here."

"Maybe I should. How far could it be. Ten hours? Twelve hours? If I started driving right now . . ."

"You wouldn't be doing anyone any good," Tess said. Her bluntness seemed to offend the two men, but she didn't have the patience for the rhetorical curlicues—the "I think"s and "perhaps"es that women were supposed to use when giving orders. "Look, I know you want to *do* something. But I can get someone there faster, and learn a lot more, without ever leaving this chair."

"How can that be?" Rubin asked.

Tess patted the side of the IBM ThinkPad lying open on his desk. "Good old-fashioned networking. Just tell me how to connect to your ISP, and I can guarantee results in less than two hours."

———————

She had them in one. Gretchen used the instant message function to link all the online SnoopSisters via a spontaneous chat, even as she was assuring Tess that (a) she could take the gig and (b) yes, Chicago was closer to French Lick than anyone else in the network and (c) Tess was a total idiot when it came to geography outside Maryland. Letha in St. Louis jumped in and said French Lick was, in fact, closer to her, but her son had a soccer game Saturday afternoon, so let Gretchen take it. Gretchen said the whole point would be moot in a few days, when the newest SnoopSister, a documents whiz from Columbus, Ohio, signed on. She also said she rather liked McDonald's and felt that the company had taken a bad rap in the infamous coffee lawsuit. Perhaps that was the real reason the manager had been so rude to Tess.

This prompted Jessie Ray in Texas to point out that the McDonald's lawsuit was not at all frivolous but one involving real injury to an elderly woman, possibly second-degree burns, and that the rumored settlement was not some pie-in-the-sky amount but a sum correlated to McDonald's coffee profits. Plus, the restaurant had been warned about overheating its coffee, so punitive damages were not without warrant. Susan in Omaha countered that people who drank McDonald's coffee had already suffered enough.

STAY ON TOPIC, PLEASE, Tess typed. And get on the road, Gretchen.

Rubin watched all this furious typing with skepticism, as if activity that didn't produce a tangible product couldn't possibly accomplish anything.

"Trust me, this will work better in the long run," Tess assured him after signing off. "Gretchen will be there tonight, with photographs of your children and wife to show people she interviews. She'll go back to the restaurant tomorrow, too, visiting about the same time of day as the calls were made. That way she has a shot of getting the right manager, the right shift workers, who might be more responsive to a visitor than they were to my phone call. If your family is still in town, she'll find them."

"And if they're not?" Rubin bowed his head and pinched the bridge of his nose, but this couldn't stem the tears coursing down his face. He didn't seem the least bit embarrassed about crying in front of Tess. She, on the other hand, was mortified.

"Let's not get ahead of ourselves. Gretchen is really dogged. Give her a chance. She's swapping the work out against future work from me, so it doesn't cost you any extra."

"I still think I should go myself."

"Earlier today you said you hoped I was judicious with my time. I am. That's why I know this is the smart way to go. Meanwhile, at the risk of repeating myself, can you think of any reason your wife would be in French Lick, Indiana, or passing through there? Family, friends, any kind of connection?"

"No. What little family she has is . . . here. I mean, I suppose there are relatives back in Russia, but in this country it's always been just Natalie and her parents."

"I've met her mother. Where's her father?"

"I'm not sure. But I'm pretty sure it's not Indiana."

"What's his name?" Tess tore a piece of paper from a memo pad on the desk: ROBBINS & SONS—SINCE 1946.

"Why do you want his name? He moved away long ago. He and Natalie don't even talk."

"Databases. I'll run it through all sorts of databases, and he could pop out. Maybe in French Lick. You never know."

"It's such a common name, Peters, I don't think you'd be able to do much with it."

"Let me worry about that."

"Come to think of it, I'm not sure the surname was ever adopted legally. I think her father might be using his Russian name."

"I can narrow the results down with age and any other information you have for him, like past addresses. I assume he lived in the row house on Labyrinth at some point."

"I think Vera got that place after they separated."

"Could I just have a full name? And an approximate age?"

"Boris Pasternak."

"Author of *Doctor Zhivago*?"

"I'm sorry. I meant Petrovich, Boris Petrovich. And I guess he's about fifty."

"So your father-in-law is closer to you in age than your wife is?"

"Not by so much. I'm twelve years older than Natalie, he's eight years older than I am."

Tess willed herself to have no reaction. "How did you meet anyway?"

"Who?"

"You and Natalie."

"Oh. Well, I had seen her around—Baltimore is small that way, northwest Baltimore smaller still." This was true, Tess knew. Baltimore wasn't so much a metro area of 1 million–plus as it was a dozen small towns that overlapped in various places. "The first time we spoke was in the old Carvel's on Reisterstown Road. She worked behind the counter. I stopped in for a cone, and we got to talking."

"I thought you said she never worked."

"Did I? I mean that she never had a career. She had summer jobs, like any other teenager. Carvel's, babysitting." He shook his head, as if burdened by his memories. "Isaac loved that story. He'd ask us to tell it again and again. I thought that was odd, because boys don't usually care for that kind of detail. But he was very aware of the fact that he would not exist if it weren't for the chance encounter of his parents. It was almost like a suspense story for him. What if we hadn't met? What if we hadn't spoken?"

"Why do you think," Tess said, "that she took them with her? The children, I mean?"

"She's their mother. She loves them."

It was what he had said before, and while it was perfectly reasonable, Tess was not yet convinced it was a complete answer. "Is that the only reason?" He looked bewildered. "Is she trying to get at you? Did she take the children because she knew it would hurt you?"

"Why would she want to hurt me?"

"I don't know." Tess wished she could plug him into the virtual world of the SnoopSisters, whose members would have been happy to enlighten Rubin about the many reasons women want to hurt, or at the very least startle, the men with whom they shared their lives. So many women in relationships had bouts of feeling they had been more colonized than courted, subsumed by a larger, more powerful entity. And when they rebelled, it was nothing short of the Boston Tea Party. Everything—everybody—went overboard.

"You should go home," she said. "Nothing's going to happen, not here, not tonight. I'm going to go toodle around on my laptop, see if I can find a match for Boris Petrovich in the Indiana phone book."

"You won't." Even in his frenzied grief, Mark Rubin retained his irritating, know-it-all quality.

"Well, we'll find out by this time tomorrow if your family is still in French Lick, and maybe that's all we need. I'll call you—" She caught herself. "I'll call you as soon as the Sabbath ends."

"You could call earlier. I think I would be allowed to answer the phone under such circumstances."

"Do you have caller ID?"

"No."

"Then how will you know it's me who's calling? Wait until sundown. Gretchen probably won't get to me much sooner than that anyway."

"And what if my family has left French Lick?"

"Then we're where we were this morning, no different."

"No, it will be worse, because I've had this moment of hope. If I had been here the first time he called . . ."

"We have a lead. If Gretchen finds out anything significant, she'll stay throughout the weekend, keep digging. That will cost you, though. Her extra expenses are on top of my per diem."

"I told you, money's not an issue."

"Yeah, people always say that—and yet it always is somehow."

———

Her laptop open on the dining-room table, Tess checked the clock in the upper-right-hand corner—7:15. The dogs looked at her with mournful patience. She could take them for a quick one around the block, then return to work, or finish up and then give them the nice long saunter they had earned after being cooped up all day. It was a beautiful night, dry and cool since the sun had gone down. And it was a clear night, so the stars would be visible overhead.

She started to close her laptop. The search for Petrovich could wait a few hours, although Rubin would probably writhe in anxiety if he knew she was postponing any task, even for a few minutes.

Except . . . for all his impatience about everything else, Rubin had been so certain she wouldn't find Boris Petrovich/Peters that he didn't care if she tracked him down at all. He had, in fact, seem determined to keep her from following that one lead, using that fake name. If she hadn't been an English major, Boris Pasternak might have slid right by her.

She sat back down, ignoring the dogs' profound disappointment, and began dropping the two variations of the name into every database she had. Rubin was right about one thing: Petrovich was a common surname. There were a surprising number of Boris Peterses on the planet, too. But by working backward from the property records for Labyrinth Road—for Boris had been on the deed before the divorce, according to the city tax rolls—she was able to find an MVA record, which led to his date of birth.

Bit by bit the information accrued—name, age, last residence, which appeared to be not far from Labyrinth Road, although that house had been sold as well, about thirteen years earlier, and there was no new address and no phone. But he wasn't on the Social Security database, so he was either still alive or not in their system at all. Dead end—until Tess thought of one last search, a place where a man might live without generating much of a paper trail. It wasn't a record that civilians could access easily, but Tess had a back door, thanks to the systems manager at the *Beacon-Light*.

Tess had paid dearly for this dummy account that allowed her to skim the wide array of online information available to *Beacon-Light* reporters. The trick was to be judicious with her access, for each search cost money, and profligate users were sometimes flagged in random audits. Tess typed in her user name—Jimmy Cain—and the password, "Indemnity." Given how rapidly management changed at the *Beacon-Light*, it was entirely plausible that this familiar version of the novelist's name would escape notice even in the event of a wide-scale audit that kicked out everyone. But he had been a Baltimore journalist before he headed out to Hollywood. Tess liked to imagine an assistant city editor staring worriedly at a staff roster and asking his boss, "Hey, who's this Jimmy Cain kid? I don't remember seeing his byline lately."

Yes, here was Boris Petrovich at last, with an all-too-permanent address—the Maryland Correctional Institute in Jessup, where he was serving a twenty-year sentence for second-degree murder.

Saturday

14

Tess's Uncle Donald winced when he entered the Kibbitz Room at Attman's Delicatessen. The pained expression puzzled Tess. He normally doted on the restaurant, one of two holdouts on the once-thriving block known as Corned Beef Row, and he loved the food. "More than it loves me," he often said, for his doctor despaired when Donald indulged in things like corned beef and *Matjes* herring.

"Why the long face?" she asked. "It's a beautiful day, you have a pastrami sandwich and a Dr. Brown's celery soda. What more could you want?"

"I feel like I'm visiting a ghost town when I come here," he said, unloading his tray. "Thirty years ago you couldn't move three paces down the sidewalks here on a Saturday. Now you could drive your car along them and not hit anything, except the occasional rat.

Corned Beef Row indeed. Don't you need more than two places to make a row? It all just makes me feel old and sad and tired."

"Still, the food is good." Whenever Tess came to Attman's, she wondered why she wasn't there at least once a week. "Best deli in Baltimore, by my lights."

"Which is great if you're a healthy bundle of metabolism like yourself. My blood pressure goes up just looking at this food." He took a mournful bite of pickle.

"Do you really have to worry?" Tess was still of an age where high blood pressure, cholesterol, and bifocals were no more than rumors from a distant country, one she honestly thought she could avoid visiting.

"We live in a world of measurement, where everything is judged by whether it's going up or down. The stock market goes up, that's good. Your blood pressure goes up, that's bad. The stock market goes down, and that's bad. So your blood pressure goes higher, and that's bad, too."

Tess laughed. "I've noticed that whatever state agency you're posted to seems to shape your latest theories on life. When you were at Human Resources, you were talking a lot about the safety net, the social fabric, and the myth of empowerment. Now you're at the Department of Licensing and Regulation, and suddenly it's all about measurement."

"Well, given that I never have to think much about what I do at work, is it so wrong for me to think about it in a wider sense, to try and find meaning in the meaningless?"

"Damn, Uncle Donald." Tess gave the no-longer-profane profanity the full Baltimore pronunciation, so it had two syllables and a distinctive twang. "Are you angling for a transfer to some newly formed Department of Existentialism and Despair?"

"I'd like that," Donald said, chewing hard. The sandwiches here required huge, snapping bites, like those seen in nature documentaries about lions. One had to open jaws wide, stretching the hinge, and then chomp down with determined ferocity as if to break the spine of a small beast. "We have a state folklorist. Why not a state philosopher? If the new governor weren't a Republican, I bet I could get a job like that, maybe even use it to promote the case for slot machines. But it would probably be an at-will position, and I don't want to give up my PIN."

While most people associate PINs with ATMs, the Monaghan-Weinstein clans, steeped in generations of civil service, used it as shorthand for the Personal Identification Numbers in the state civil service. Keep your PIN, keep your job. Not necessarily the same job, as Uncle Donald's career illustrated, but some kind of post. Thirty years ago, when his state-senator boss had gone away for mail fraud, Donald's consolation prize had been a lifetime of full employment, moving from state agency to state agency as needs and budgets dictated. Wherever he went, the two constants were his clipboard and his frown. With those two, Uncle Donald said, anyone could survive in a bureaucracy.

"Anyway, what's your agenda this morning? It's a cinch you didn't call your uncle for his company, excellent though it is."

Uncle Donald's tone was light, but it made Tess squirm. She did have a bad habit of reaching out to her family only when she needed something. And she had been especially scarce in recent weeks, ducking dinners and get-togethers, citing the extra work she had taken on to make up for her layoff. She just hadn't been in the mood for family gatherings and the interrogations they inspired.

"This is a thank-you lunch. I really appreciate you steering the Rubin case to me."

"I find myself waiting for the 'but.' "

"No 'but.' Maybe a 'however,' or a 'yet.' Mark Rubin seemed to go out of his way to keep me from learning something. Did you know that Rubin's father-in-law is in prison for second-degree murder?"

"Sure. That's how we met."

"Because you know his father-in-law?"

"Because we visited prisons together. Rubin and I were in the same Jewish men's club, and we organized an outreach program for Jews in Maryland prisons. It was his idea, in fact."

Your uncle, Rubin had told her, *is quite active in Jewish causes.* She had assumed he was talking about B'nai B'rith.

"Jews in prison? What, for accounting crimes?"

"You know, you may qualify for citizenship in Israel, but I'm not sure a girl named Monaghan should traffic in those stereotypes. Someone who didn't know you so well could take offense."

"Would you feel better if I assumed everyone you visited was a murderer?"

"We've always had some very tough Jews, you know, for good and bad, throughout history. Gangsters, of course, but there's also the story of the Warsaw ghetto—"

"I'm sorry, Uncle Donald," she said, hoping a quick apology would derail him, but he was too wound up.

"Not to mention Sandy Koufax."

"How did we get on the subject of Sandy Koufax?"

"I'm just saying, he was a Jew, one of the greatest baseball players that ever lived, and when he didn't play in the World Series on Yom Kippur, he showed the world a little something. People talk about Jews being money grubbers, but it wasn't Sandy Koufax who was pushing Mr. Coffee, was it? No, he retired with some dignity, although he hardly made a tenth, a hundredth, of what a player like him would make today."

Uncle Donald normally spoke with a slight Baltimore accent, an almost Cockney-like inflection distinguished by its odd-shaped *o* sounds. But as he warmed to this topic, he began to sound more and more like his immigrant forebears. It was only a matter of time before Yiddish broke out. Tess decided to mollify him.

"What did your men's group do?"

"We visited Jewish inmates once a month and led them in an informal service. And we observed major holidays. Passover was my favorite."

"How do you do Passover in prison?"

"Well, they can't leave the door open for Elijah and there's no wine, but they chant 'Next year outside' instead of 'Next year in Jerusalem.' Very touching, actually."

"I didn't know you cared about religion. You never talk about it."

"Jews don't proselytize," Donald said. "Your parents decided to raise you with virtually no religious education, so who was I to interfere? Besides, I'd be suspicious of anyone who did so-called good works, then ran around talking about it. Sort of misses the point."

"I wouldn't say I was raised *without* a religious education. Dad told me his version, Mom told me hers, and I was free to make my own decisions. I opted for being a nonobservant Jewish Catholic who believes in Santa Claus and the Easter Bunny but can hang with the bitter-herb crowd at a seder. Remember last year? I kept the horseradish in my mouth longer than anyone except Crow, and he has an asbestos tongue from his time in Texas."

"He's a nice boy. How's his mother doing?"

"Fine, all things considered. They're Episcopalians, by the way. I mean, as long as we're taking inventory of who believes what."

"Do you believe in God, Tesser?"

Tess squirmed on the molded plastic chair, which had probably been in the Kibbitz Room since President Jimmy Carter's visit, which was featured on the wall above her in a series of newspaper articles, some framed, some shellacked to pieces of wood. She didn't want to talk with her uncle about her love life, but she was even more reluctant to discuss religion.

"Sure," she said. "Why not? So did Rubin get involved in this group because his father-in-law was in prison?"

"Oh, no. He met Natalie at the prison because her father was one of the men in our group. You see, she sought Mark out, very keen that her father embrace his faith, eager to know what she could do to help. She had found great comfort in Judaism after her father's arrest. But Boris Petrovich . . . well, Boris couldn't have been less interested in the program. I think he signed up because it was a nice diversion and we brought in good food. The man knew nothing about his own religion."

"Not unusual for a Soviet Jew. In fact, I'd say Natalie's the odd one, from what I know, choosing to live an observant life after almost twenty years of being wholly ignorant of Judaism."

"True, but Boris always seemed to be working some angle." Uncle Donald frowned at the memory. "It's a funny thing, charitable work. You might not go in expecting people to be overwhelmed with gratitude, but you think they'll be polite at least. Petrovich was a bit of a jerk, a schemer through and through, whether he was asking for an extra macaroon or wheedling one of us to write a letter to get some privilege reinstated. But the daughter—the daughter was nothing but lovely."

"She wasn't part of the group, though? Rubin met her through the prison connection?" So there went the touching little story about the Carvel stand, a lie through and through.

"Yes. I admit I thought it was one of Petrovich's schemes at first. He may not have known how rich Mark was, but he had him pegged as a mark, a prosperous prospect. Hey—try saying that three times fast. Prosperous prospect, prosperous prospect, prosperous—"

"You're the king of the tongue twisters," Tess agreed.

"Anyway, Natalie contacted Mark about her father, and they ended up getting married. Then Mark dropped out of the program, saying he didn't have time for it anymore. That was at least eight, nine years ago, so maybe that's why he didn't mention it to you."

Tess rescued a few pieces of fallen corned beef from her plate.

"Only here's the part that's bothering me, Uncle Donald. Rubin's the one who keeps saying he thinks his wife disappeared for some reason she can't tell him. So why withhold the information that her daddy is a convict who killed a man?"

"Well, for one thing, people sometimes forget that others don't know what they know about themselves. Maybe he thought I'd tell you about Natalie's father. Besides, Mark's always been . . . an elliptical man. Formal and reserved. I think it comes from spending a lifetime of telling overweight women that they don't look fatter in a fur coat."

"His mother-in-law suggested he's not always truthful."

"Really?" Donald picked up a pickle from his plate and sucked on it before taking a bite. "I never had that sense. He's extremely reticent with most people, but he's charming when you get to know him, funny even."

"Rubin?"

"Not a jokester. No lamp shades on the head. But a very—I don't know—dry wit. Like Mort Sahl."

"More salt?"

"No, Mort Sahl. He was a Jewish comedian—"

Tess patted her uncle's forearm. "I'm teasing you. I'm much better on the details of our cultural history than I am on the religious stuff. Why did Mark come to you when he needed a private detective? Are you two close?"

Uncle Donald shook his head. "Not particularly. He's a wealthy businessman, living up in the county in some *Architectural Digest* house, with a wife and kids. I'm a state employee, with my little rental in Mount Washington. He says his prayers three times a day. I go to shul on Rosh Hashanah, fast on Yom Kippur, and try to find a relative to take me in on Passover."

"So why did Mark Rubin come to you with this very delicate matter?"

But now she had offended him. "Your uncle is still known as a man who can get things done, Tesser. Maybe I can't do things directly, but I know who to call."

"He didn't know I was a private investigator, then, he just asked for your help in finding a PI?"

"When he came to me, he wasn't even talking about private investigators. He thought the police were putting him off, not taking him seriously, because . . . well, because, you know . . ." He made a strange, helpless gesture with his hand.

"I don't know."

"Because he's Jewish. I mean, Jewish-Jewish, really Jewish, not just Jewish-surname-Jewish. *Different*-Jewish."

"Oh, Uncle Donald, that's paranoid beyond belief." Tess had already forgotten how quick she had been to take the other side of this argument with Nancy Porter.

"Yeah? One detective even asked him if this was an arranged marriage or a mail-order bride."

"So? There are still arranged marriages of sorts among the Orthodox, and there are mail-order brides from Russia, where Natalie was born. They were just doing their jobs, asking those questions."

"Oh." He chewed with intense concentration, as if the act of grinding his molars also helped his brain to work. "At any rate, when I determined that the police weren't being obstinate, that they really couldn't help him, I told him he needed a private investigator—and I knew just the person. The idea of a female investigator was a bit of an obstacle for him, but I persuaded him that you were more discreet than anyone else he could hire." He wiggled his eyebrows in best Groucho fashion.

"Thanks, Uncle Donald. It's nice for a family member to steer me toward a wealthy client for once. But if he doesn't start being more forthcoming with me, I'm not sure how much I can help him."

"Are there other things he's not telling you?"

"I don't know. Something. Maybe it's just, you know . . ." She shrugged, unsure how to broach this topic with her uncle. "Maybe his wife wasn't, um . . . fulfilled in their relationship."

"Fulfilled? Oh, you mean sex. No, I never got that impression that was the issue."

"So there *was* an issue?"

"I'm just assuming. She left, so something must have been wrong. Right? No one walks out on a perfect relationship."

"One person's perfect could be another person's hell." Tess took out a pad and pen. "What about the other men you visited, particularly in Jessup where Petrovich was held? Do you have a list of their names?"

"I don't, but the organization might keep such records. I'm sure we had correspondence with the Department of Corrections, to get clearances and the like. Why?"

"A man's wife and children disappeared. Now, I'm still betting she just took off, for whatever reason, but he's adamant that there's something more sinister involved. Looking at known criminals in his past makes sense. I also need to find out who his father-in-law killed, don't I?"

"Oh." He furrowed his brow. "You're not mad at me, Tesser, for making this referral? It's good money, isn't it?"

"It's great money. But one of the stinky things about my line of work is that the longer it takes me to solve a problem, the more money I make. Doesn't that seem a little backward to you?"

"So you asked me here today to talk about Mark, this case?"

"Well, yeah. But to see you, too," she added. "And to gossip about Kitty's wedding."

"But mainly to talk about work?" He seemed adamant about scoring this point, which was not Uncle Donald's way. He was one of the few relatives who never tried to make her feel guilty.

"Yes, okay? Yes, I asked you here to talk about the Rubin case."

He pushed his check across the table. "Then you pay for me and put it on your expenses, *mameleh*. I would hope you should know that by now."

15

"G ood news, bad news," Gretchen said over the unreliable line of a cell phone. It was 4:00 P.M., and she had already seen and conquered French Lick.

"They were here. In fact, they made quite an impression. One of the employees remembered the mother because her little girl had an accident in the playground—you know, in one of those ball rooms—and it got a little ugly. They yelled at the woman for letting her daughter go in there, knowing she wasn't toilet trained, the mother said the girl was, that it must be diarrhea from the food, and it went downhill from there. They roared out of there, leaving no forwarding address and, its being McDonald's and all, no telltale credit-card slip. Not that this woman ever uses a credit card. But it was definitely her."

"If it was Natalie, she was telling the truth about Penina's being toilet trained. The twins are five."

"Okay, great, I'm glad to know who was telling the truth in the great poopie-diaper debate. Anyway, the manager told me they were clearly passing through. They were in some big old car."

"And the car was . . . ?"

"Green. Old. Didn't notice the tag, just that it wasn't local. One worker thought they had suitcases on the luggage rack when they pulled in, but another was adamant that the car didn't have anything on the roof when it pulled out. So big, green, and old, not from Indiana. Think we can get state police to give us a roadblock based on that information?"

"Funny, Gretchen."

"I'm sorry, but it *kills* me how unobservant people are. You know, our government's been telling us since 9/11 that we gotta pay attention, that we're their eyes and ears on the front lines of the war against terrorism. Meanwhile, the average Joe wouldn't notice someone building a dirty bomb at the corner table in Starbucks."

"But they were sure it was Natalie?"

"What? Oh, yeah. Apparently men remember that face. Which brings me to the most important piece of news—"

Gretchen's cell phone picked this moment to go out. Tess waited a few seconds to see if Gretchen would wander back into a good cell, then hung up, knowing she would call again.

"Sorry. Anyway, I did learn something else, but it's not going to make your client happy."

"Yeah?"

"Natalie's traveling with a man."

Tess wished she were more surprised. "Description?"

"About as helpful as old and green. Thirties or forties, tall, blue eyes, dark hair, cropped short. Muscular, but not muscle-bound. No facial hair. Dressed in what the cashier called a cowboy kind of way, which apparently translates to jeans, boots, and a denim jacket in this part of the world. She said he was good-looking, but I'm not sure the McDonald's cashier and I have the same taste in men."

"Anything else?"

"No, it's pretty much the land of generic one-syllable adjectives. Although Natalie probably would have been noticed even if her daughter hadn't flamed out in the ball room."

"Because she's so pretty?"

"And she has dark hair. You don't see a lot of brunettes in this part of the world."

Tess hung up the phone and got out an atlas, an old one, but its version of the world was good enough for her purposes as long as she wasn't tracking someone through Natalie Rubin's country of origin, still listed here as the USSR.

French Lick was in southern Indiana, and it wasn't on a major interstate. It was—Tess worked backward, using the mileage charts for Evansville and Louisville—almost seven hundred miles from Baltimore. The Internet provided the helpful information that it had a golf resort and something called the Antique Hair Museum.

But on what route did it lie, why would someone pass through there? That's what had Tess stumped. If Natalie was heading west, why was she traveling so far from the interstate, and why had she made so little progress? Gone three weeks, she could have reached the opposite coast by now. Tess knew that movies often showed people trying to hide out in small towns, but it was a ludicrous plan in practice. A strange family would be more noticeable in a small town, not less. French Lick had only two thousand people, the nearby county seat of Paoli a mere twenty thousand. It was no place to hide, and no place to go, unless Natalie was a fervent Larry Bird fan paying homage to the basketball legend's hometown.

This was one drawback to the SnoopSisters network. Gretchen had swept in and done exactly what was requested, with concrete results. She had gotten there faster and cheaper than Tess ever could. But this job-share arrangement was no substitute for seeing a place with your own eyes, for walking the streets, for getting lost and then found again. Tess often made her best discoveries as the results of wrong turns and tangents.

She had promised Rubin to call as soon as the Sabbath ended.

But such news would have to be delivered in person. It would be too coldhearted to drop it on him in a phone call, to pretend the news was anything less than devastating. Natalie was traveling with a man. He probably paid the bills. That answered one question, but it raised a lot more.

The September sun was strong, and Tess decided to sit on the deck and watch it go down, dropping in and out of a novel as her attention span allowed. Too keyed up to read something new, she chose to reread, picking the guiltiest of guilty pleasures, *Peyton Place*. She considered pulling *Marjorie Morningstar* off the shelf but decided she'd rather hang out with Metalious's repressed New Englanders, who did such shocking things when they thought they were unobserved. Marjorie, on the other hand, was just a tiresome virgin who had to learn the hard way to give up on rascals and settle down with a nice Jewish boy.

In Wouk's worldview this left Marjorie with a minor deformity, not unlike the crippled arm of the man who had despoiled her. For Tess, Marjorie's mistake was the only quality that made her bearable. Choosing the wrong man was an essential step on the road to finding the right one. Or so Tess had heard.

16

Natalie leaned against a table in the automatic laundry in Valparaiso, watching their clothes tumble through the dryer. Her entire wardrobe was a single dryer load now, and the children's made up another, only slightly larger one. Back in Baltimore she had a laundry room larger than her childhood bedroom, outfitted with not only an extra-capacity washer and dryer but a special sink for hand washing, built-in cedar closets for out-of-season storage, and a pine table where she folded and stacked the endless, fragrant loads. She had been embarrassed when Lana had pointed out that her folding table was nicer than the Ikea one from which Lana ate her meals. "Take it, then," Natalie had urged. But Lana refused, probably out of pride. "It's too big for my place, and the style is different."

Lord, how Natalie had hated Moshe's house, if only because she could never make it hers. It had so many constant, unending needs—even more than Moshe. The Sabbath was supposed to provide a day of rest, but Natalie spent her Saturdays thinking of the tasks that the next week would bring, and the week beyond that. She had never dreamed she could miss such a burden, but life on the road had made her wistful for the things she had taken for granted, for the very things that had held her captive. For that laundry room, for bathrooms that never smelled of mildew, for gleaming copper pots, for cool lavender-scented sheets on a king-size bed in a room that belonged just to her. And Moshe, of course.

Today's trip to the launderette marked the first time Natalie had been alone in days, apart from when she was in the bathroom, and she wouldn't have been given this brief reprieve if Zeke hadn't agreed to watch the children in the room, rather than try to control them here. Plus, this way they could strip the kids down to nothing and wrap them in towels, giving Natalie a chance to clean all the clothes at once. "We're outnumbered when we take them out," Zeke had agreed. "Besides, no one's going anywhere wearing just a towel."

Isaac's head had swung up sharply, as if he wanted to disagree, and Natalie knew her oldest son would forgo modesty if he saw a chance to get away from Zeke or make another phone call. It would take more than a towel wrapped around his skinny body to keep him in his place. If his spirit weren't so wearing, she might have been proud of him. He was tough. Those were her genes, her family, the Tseltsins.

That was their name back in Russia, their real name, before her father had helped himself to the identity of Boris Petrovich in order to immigrate to the United States as a Soviet Jew.

"We're Jews?" Natalie had asked her mother, not even sure what the word meant, yet certain that it was at odds with whatever she imagined herself to be.

"Sure, why not?" her mother replied.

Her father changed the name again, after they settled in Baltimore. The reason for that second change was unclear to Natalie, like much her father and mother did. The truth was, she wasn't particularly interested in her parents. "Is your father *affiliated?*" Lana had asked in a tone of hushed respect the first time she had visited the house on Labyrinth Road and seen the evidence of his so-called job—the boxes of electronic equipment stacked in the kitchen, the new clothes that he would sell without letting Natalie pick even one outfit. "I don't know. I don't care," Natalie said. She wasn't ashamed that her father was a criminal. She was embarrassed because he was a bad one, as Zeke never stopped reminding her.

But it was her parents' foreignness that Natalie resented. She couldn't help feeling they were holding her back, that an American girl with her looks would have had dozens of ways to make her mark on the world. The Russian girls who became famous in the United States tended to do athletic things, figure skating and gymnastics and tennis. Natalie had no talent for sports. She was too short to model, according to all of Lana's magazines, and acting did not appeal to her because she didn't want to be anyone but herself. Still, whenever she looked in the mirror, she just knew that destiny had special plans for her.

She was fourteen when she saw the movie with the improbable name *Inside Daisy Clover.* It was old and strange, and she probably would not have lingered on the channel were it not for the fact that the television had become a mirror. "You look like her," Lana had said, and she did, she really did. Natalie tracked down other movies with Natalie Wood—the *other* Natalie, as she thought of her—even went to the library and checked out books about her. That was amazing enough that someone might have noticed, if anyone had been paying attention to her at the time. Natalie, who never read, filling out reserve cards at the branch library, even taking the bus downtown to find the one old video that wasn't at Blockbuster, *This Property Is Condemned.*

Here was the amazing thing: Natalie Wood had been born Natasha, just like her, and changed her name to Natalie, just like her. She was Russian, too. And she had died in a strange accident not long after Natasha came to the United States and became Natalie. So no, she couldn't say she was reincarnated, but perhaps the actress's spirit was lodged in her body. Natalie submitted herself to Lana, her sights already on cosmetology school, and the results were surprisingly good. Lana shaped her brows into those perfect arches, showed Natalie how to paint her lips and fix her hair. The resemblance was amazing.

Yet somehow no one else seemed to see it. They saw her beauty, and it greased her way through the world, making most things easier and a few things harder. But no one else made the connection.

Until Zeke. She still remembered the feel of his eyes on her the first time she went to visit her father, just after her eighteenth birthday. She was used to stares, but this gaze was different. Intense, about something more than sex. Then he pursed his lips and let out a soft, lingering whistle, five distinct notes. "Somewhere." He was Tony, singing to Maria. Except, thank God, he was a million times better-looking than the actor who had played that part in the movie. He was better-looking than James Dean, too, in Natalie's opinion, better-looking even than Warren Beatty, with that coal-black hair and those shocking blue eyes.

And he had been so courtly. He did not want what the others wanted. He had asked her father permission to write to her—acting as if Boris were the accomplished man he wanted to be, instead of just another prisoner. Zeke's letters had been amazing, better than anything she had read in books or even seen in the movies. He said theirs was a true love, a once-in-a-lifetime love, and the obstacles to it only made it more precious. His sentence was two years. She would be a mere twenty when he got out, a baby still. She promised to wait for him. Months went by before he told her about the federal time that awaited him after he did his state stretch. She was furious with him, but by then she would have done anything he asked, absolutely anything.

Even marry a man she didn't love, because a loveless marriage was, in its own way, the best way to stay faithful to Zeke. True, she hadn't seen it that way, not at first. But between their visits and his letters, Zeke had convinced her. She was so young. She knew about sex, but she knew nothing about love. Committed to Zeke in her heart, she was still susceptible to false love, to falling under a man's spell, only to find that it was a pale imitation of the real thing. She should marry a man who could provide for her, a man whose embraces would never move her—a man who would never threaten her loyalty to Zeke. It wasn't really wrong. She was like an artist, back in the Renaissance, Zeke explained, and her husband would be her patron. Lots of marriages ended, for all sorts of reasons. She would give a man ten years of her life and then leave, asking for no more than was her due. It was more than many women gave their husbands.

Zeke had chosen Mark Rubin. He was rigid in his ways, older than his years, but basically decent. Natalie didn't mind him too much. And once the children came, her affection for him increased. He had given her the greatest gift she could imagine, a gift that doctors had claimed was beyond Natalie, because of a disease she never knew she had—a disease you couldn't see, or even feel, until you tried to conceive. And it had taken quite a bit of talking, trying to explain to Mark how she had come to have this thing called chlamydia. She had told him it was too painful to speak of to him, and let him draw his own conclusions.

True, children were not part of Zeke's plan, but even Zeke had to yield to God's wishes. Besides, Zeke knew about the other men, and he had never minded that. He also knew she had to sleep with Moshe and that he would never allow her to use birth control, given his beliefs. Besides, she had needs, too, and ten years was a long, long time. Mark was not her dream lover, but he wanted to make her happy. If she closed her eyes and thought of Zeke, which one was she really betraying? Both? Neither?

The dryer ended with a shudder and a sigh. Like most of life's obligations, like the children themselves, laundry seemed to multiply in mass when it had to be carried anywhere. Look at the mounds of clothes on the table—you would think it would last them a month, yet Natalie would be back in another laundry, in some other town, within a week. She had packed very little, because she had thought they would be on the road no more than five days. Now it was going on three weeks, and nothing made sense to her. She had thought Zeke would be happy to see her in Terre Haute, that they would go to Chicago as he had promised. Actually, he had seemed kind of mad.

And now they were traveling in odd, directionless circles through ugly little towns. She did not like the way Zeke had chosen to make money, especially her part in it, but he said his counted-on windfall, a trust or something, had been delayed by a few weeks. He pointed out that they harmed no one, unless fooling people was a kind of harm. For his part, he said, he was giving something in exchange for what he got, a great story, an anecdote. "I'm the single most exciting thing that ever happened to these people."

The phrase lingered in her head—*the single most exciting thing that ever happened.* Zeke had been that for her, a secret treasure, her double life. Driving her minivan, waiting in line at Seven Mile Lane Grocery, enduring the long services every Friday and Saturday, fumbling her way through the prayers she had learned so late in life—the knowledge of Zeke had been like a secret drug that made her heart race, filling her days with soaring expectations.

And yet here she was in a coin laundry in Indiana, reduced to five pairs of underwear, three T-shirts, and two blouses. Zeke had allowed her to buy three pairs of blue jeans with their scant funds, a wonderful treat after years of wearing the wool slacks Mark insisted on. Still, she couldn't help thinking about the clothes she had left behind. Conservative, true, but beautiful and well made. She missed those, too.

Catching her reflection in the porthole of the dryer, she saw a young man sneaking a look at her behind. Too bad for him, his girlfriend caught the look, too, and gave him a nice flat-handed smack across the back of his head. Natalie approved. She would have done the same, or worse. Maybe not for looking, but if she ever caught Zeke doing anything else—well, just say that she would make sure he'd never cheat on her again. In the end it was up to women to take a stand, stake out their men, keep them in check. Zeke may have been afraid of losing her, but she had been just as afraid of losing him, that he would disappear, leaving her in the cold, sad lie of her marriage. Even now that they were together, the fear hadn't subsided. Not for her, and not for Zeke. Something gnawed at him, late at night, made him whimper and fret in his sleep like a small boy. Yet when she asked, he said he never dreamed, that he had willed himself to stop dreaming long ago.

She carried the clothes to the car, taking two trips. She would have liked to stop at the Dairy Queen for a shake, or even a hot dog, but Zeke would make her account for the money she spent. Not because, like Moshe, he didn't trust her, but because they had so little. For now. He swore they would have plenty of money soon.

She checked under the front seat and made sure the box that Amos had given her was still there. Funny, but Zeke wouldn't use it. Even when working, he wanted no part of it. He had a knife, but he never unsheathed it. He said she was a fool, using up precious dollars for something they didn't need, but it made her feel safer. She tied the string back around the box, making sure it was knotted tight. It would be a tragedy for the twins to find it, or even Isaac, prudent as he was. She knew from her own father how the mere fact of having a gun at hand could wreck so many lives.

Although, in the long run, it had saved hers. She wouldn't be where she was now, on the verge of finally being happy, if it weren't for her father's mistakes, if he hadn't killed a man and ended up in prison, where he met Zeke, and then Zeke found her. You could even say a man had sacrificed his life so Natalie might realize her destiny. More proof, as if she needed any, that she and Zeke were special, God's favorites, living by different rules from everybody else.

17

Mark Rubin's house was a starkly modern box of glass and stucco on a country-club street given to more traditional Tudor-style homes. Not the sort of place that Tess would choose, but she realized it was a good example of mid-twentieth-century architecture. Its design, within the context of its simply landscaped lot, had balance and dignity. But it was a discordant note on this suburban street, a prickly outsider.

Not unlike the man who lived inside.

"Bad news on my doorstep," he said when he saw Tess, and it was hard not to paraphrase "American Pie" back to him. *Yes, and I don't want to take one more step.*

"Neutral," she said, knowing that her information was anything but. "They were there, but they appeared to be passing through. The manager at the McDonald's remembered Natalie and the children. They're in an old green car, a sedan of some sort. At least one employee thought they had luggage on the roof when they pulled in."

"Where did she get an old green car? And why would they tie the luggage to the roof?" Tess understood why Rubin was seizing on these details, which were easier to grasp and dissect than the larger issues. "They can't have that much luggage. They hardly took anything, three suitcases total."

"There's more—"

"Luggage on the roof of a green car—this is all you found out? This is what you consider a result?"

It was hard trying to be solicitous of someone's feelings when the other person was not so considerate. But Tess was determined to break the news about the mystery man as gently as possible.

"There is more, but before I tell you everything Gretchen learned, I want to tell you something I found out from my Uncle Donald. He told me the true story of how you and Natalie met."

"And?"

"As I understand it, no Carvel stand was involved, not unless Jessup had a franchise."

Rubin looked angry and relieved at the same time, as if embarrassed by the lie but also glad to give it up. "Why don't you come in? We have much to talk about."

———

"I didn't tell you that story to mislead you," he said. "I told it out of habit, quite forgetting that your uncle knew the true circumstances."

"And how did you get in the habit of lying?" They were sitting in his office, a cozy, cluttered refuge from the sterile perfection of the other rooms she had seen, open expanses decorated in a minimalist style, with lots of birch-pale hardwoods, pastel upholstery, and modern art. Tess wondered how someone with three children could keep a house this pristine. Then she realized that Mark Rubin hadn't—Natalie Rubin had. Another reason to head for the hills. Tess could tell by the way Rubin used a coaster for his wineglass that his standards for housekeeping were exacting.

"Natalie and I agreed when we became engaged that we would have an official version of how we met and courted. It's easier, with a story, to always tell the same one."

"Yes, that is a good rule for liars." She didn't want to let him off the hook too easily.

"I won't argue semantics with you," Rubin said. His tone made it clear that he wouldn't argue only because it would slow him down, not because he wouldn't win. "There were already so many obstacles to Natalie's being accepted in my community. She was young, with only a high-school education. She had not been raised in the faith, although that is hardly her fault. And because she was vague about her family's background, she even agreed to be dunked."

"Dunked?"

"She went for instruction with the rabbi and did the mikveh. In some ways, her passion for our religion seemed stronger than that of some lifelong Jews I knew."

"Converts making the best adherents, et cetera, et cetera."

"Well, not strictly a convert, but I know what you mean. Her zeal was exceptional. At the risk of sounding egotistical, I thought it was bound up with her love for me. When we met, Natalie seemed to think of nothing but pleasing me. She was . . . uncannily perfect, everything I wanted in a woman."

"Right down to the eighteen-year-old part?"

He blushed. "Matches between older men and younger women do make sense, biologically. I'm sorry if that fact offends you, but an eighteen-year-old woman is ready to marry and have children. Culture may have changed. Our bodies did not."

"Well, Sarah had a baby at ninety or something like that. Should I interpret that biblical story as evidence of the first surrogate, or did God do some in vitro?"

"An apt biblical reference. I admit to being surprised."

"I'm agnostic, not ignorant."

Pleased with herself, Tess took a sip of the kosher wine that Rubin had poured for her. The wine was quite good, a red blend from Chile. She was beginning to get a glimpse of the man her Uncle Donald had described. Rubin might be a pain as a client and a terror as a businessman, but he probably was excellent company in social situations. The books on his shelves indicated a worldly man, with a wide range of interests, and he clearly had a talent for the kind of verbal sparring Tess enjoyed.

Then again, how would Tess and Rubin have ever met under different circumstances? Ten miles apart in physical distance, they might as well have been in different galaxies. Their Baltimores barely intersected.

"You're not the first person, male or female, to snigger at my choice of a bride. And there was some animosity toward Natalie among the women in my congregation, women who have known me all my life, who took a special interest in me after my mother died. So you can see why I didn't want to give them additional ammunition. Yes, Natalie's father was in prison, and that's how I met her."

"My Uncle Donald said she sought you out to discuss her father's refusal to embrace his faith. But he also told me that Boris gave the impression of someone who was always running a game."

"Your uncle is astute. Boris was running a game—but on his daughter, not me. When Boris became aware of my relationship with Natalie, he attempted to blackmail her. Soon after we married, he coerced her into making deposits into an account in his name, a nest egg for when he's finally released from prison."

"Blackmail her? Over what?"

"I don't know, and I don't care. I'm sure Natalie had her share of youthful indiscretions. She was a high-spirited girl who knew almost no parental supervision after her parents divorced. When I found out what her father was doing, I told her she must break off all contact with Boris." Rubin swirled the wine in his glass, studying it with an oenophile's critical eye. "That's the reason behind our financial system. I don't know what hold Boris had over Natalie, but she was clearly terrified of what he might tell me. I didn't want her to succumb to his extortion again."

"I'm surprised he gave up so quickly."

"A man in prison is easy enough to ignore. You refuse the collect calls, you don't open mail with a certain postmark. Besides, when I told Boris I didn't care what he knew about Natalie, he lost all power over us. Blackmail isn't that different from other luxury goods. The pool of customers is smaller, so the salesman has to be sharper. Boris had only one customer for what he was selling, and I shut that down."

"But now that Natalie's gone—"

"I vowed to her ten years ago that I would not listen to her father's lies about her. A promise is a promise."

"She promised to love, honor, and cherish until death do you part, so I think you can go back on your word in this instance."

"Whatever he wants to tell me, it's probably not true. So what's the point of listening?"

Mark Rubin's face seemed to be hardening as she pressed him. But Tess saw more than stubbornness in his features. She also saw fear and desperation. He was terrified of hearing whatever his father-in-law had to say.

"Because it's a lead, the best one we have. You're the one who suggested Natalie left because she wanted to protect you from some secret in her past. Boris may know what it is."

"*No.* He's a liar. And a thief. Not to mention a killer. Trust me, there's no reason to talk to him."

"The thing is"—she hated herself for what she was about to do—"maybe Boris could help us figure out the identity of the man who was with Natalie in French Lick."

Tess might as well have vomited on Rubin's desktop, given the way he recoiled. She tried to pretend the gaffe was more accidental than it was.

"I'm so sorry. Does kosher wine have a higher alcohol content than the regular stuff? Because that's not how I intended to tell you that one detail."

"I'm not sure anyone would know how to break such news. When you say 'with' . . ."

"That's all I know. With. The people at the McDonald's said Natalie left with a man. The description was vague—six feet, dark hair, slender. Not a lot to go on, but does it mean anything to you?"

"She was with a *man*?"

It had never occurred to him. Which was amazing, because the likelihood had been in the back of Tess's mind from the outset.

"It helps to explain the strange car, and maybe even how she's getting by financially. But it doesn't explain why she's in French Lick, Indiana. And it doesn't mean she's *with* him. I mean, if she wants to leave you for someone else, she could have done it in a more traditional way."

"More traditional?"

"Served you with papers and asked for half of everything you have."

"She wouldn't get it. The divorce, I mean. I would fight her on that."

"You could, but all she has to do is wait you out two years. After a two-year separation, even an involuntary one, Maryland courts will grant a divorce, no matter what rabbis do or don't do. Of course, the custody and the financial details would still have to be arranged. But it's pretty hard to make someone stay married to you these days."

"Our rabbi would talk to her, make her see common sense. Besides, there isn't that much money."

Tess rolled her eyes. "You mean, besides this million-dollar house and everything in it, and the business, and your investments? Not to mention the child support you'd have to pay."

"The business's value has been flat, and even this house has increased only marginally in value. I bought right before the market slumped a decade ago, and I'm just beginning to catch up. Most of my money comes from an inheritance. Spouses have no right to inherited funds—and that's true under state *and* religious law."

"You know a lot about Maryland's marital-assets law," Tess said, "for a man who has never contemplated divorce."

Rubin swirled his wine again, watching the dregs slide down the interior of the glass. "A few years back, Natalie had a strange episode of depression and talked about leaving. I . . . outlined the financial realities of such a decision. I also told her I would fight for custody of Isaac."

"You *said* there was no marital strife, that you had never discussed separation or divorce." Tess, usually tolerant of clients' lies and evasions, was beginning to lose patience with Rubin.

"We hadn't, except that one time, and it was six years ago. We're talking about a week or two, one bad patch in an otherwise strong and happy marriage. It turned out she was pregnant with the twins at the time, and we both decided it was just hormones."

You decided, Tess thought, and Natalie acquiesced. What other options did she have after you told her you'd give her no money? But she let it go. There were more pressing matters to explore.

"So any ideas about our mystery man?"

He winced, pained just by the mention. "None. As far as I know, the only men in Natalie's life were the merchants at the local stores, some teachers at Isaac's school."

"Does she have a friend, or a male relative, who might help her leave for whatever reason?"

"Not to my knowledge."

"Was there any man she came into contact with on a regular basis?"

"I don't see how."

"This man was tall and slender, with dark hair and blue eyes. Clean-shaven. Sound familiar?"

"No."

"Don't be so quick and emphatic. Think about it. Everyone

knows someone who looks like that. My boyfriend looks like that, okay? Hey, maybe he's in Indiana with Natalie, not in Virginia with his family."

Rubin frowned and waved Tess away, as if he wanted her to leave, or disappear. *Abracadabra, make all bad news go away.*

"Okay, I just thought you should know what Gretchen found out, and I thought I should deliver the news face-to-face. Now I have. Please call me if you think of anything, anything at all. Because we're at a dead end unless your phone rings again. You should get caller ID at home, by the way. If your office phone hadn't shown us that number, we wouldn't know anything right now. Star 69 is okay, but more stuff gets through on caller ID."

Rubin opened his mouth as if to speak, then thought better of it.

"I've been cheated on," Tess said. "It sucks. I cheated, too, and that sucks even more, believe it or not. And I still didn't learn from that. I did a Jimmy Carter cheat on my boyfriend a few years ago—I was guilty only in my mind, but it was just a matter of time before my body followed. He knew me so well he saw it coming, and he left. I had to follow him all the way to Texas to get him back."

"Why are you telling me this? Take my advice, these are not the sort of confidences that a businesswoman imparts to someone who has hired her. I don't wish to know anything about your private life."

"I'm confiding in you because I'm human, and I know how this feels. Okay, you say your wife would never cheat on you, that you'd know, in your bones, if she had slept with another man. And maybe you're right. But in my line of work, I see people who do things primarily for two reasons—sex and money."

"Surely there are other reasons, other secrets."

Tess nodded. "Yes, there's shame, the need to cover up a past transgression. Is that involved here? Is there anything else you're not telling me?"

Rubin shook his head.

"Your wife left you, forgoing money. She's driving around in the

Midwest in some old clunker of a car and eating at McDonald's, which wasn't kosher last time I checked. Did she want to get away from you and your life that badly? Or did she want someone else that much? It's one or the other, and it could be both."

She thought her harsh words might make the always-emotional Rubin dissolve into tears, but he just stared into the distance, shaking his head. He truly seemed overwhelmed by everything she had told him, which surprised Tess. Typically, the revelation of an affair was an *aha* moment that shed light on many smaller mysteries in a person's life. It was like living in a house where plaster cracked and faucets leaked and wind whistled around the window frames, then finding out the foundation was sliding off the slab.

"I believed in my marriage," he said at last. "I would never be so blasphemous as to compare it to a religion, but I counted on it and assumed it would always be there for me."

"People make mistakes," Tess said. "They do stupid things. I don't know if your wife will ever come back to you once I find her. But if that's what you want, you're going to have to forgive her and be open to understanding why she did what she did."

"*When* you find her. Why are you suddenly so confident, when you've just told me you have no leads?"

"Because we have someone helping us out."

"That friend of yours? With all due respect, I don't see anything extraordinary in her efforts so far."

"Gretchen did okay with what we gave her. But the accomplice I'm really counting on is your son Isaac. He tried to call you twice yesterday. And he's quite the little schemer—hustling money for the first call, calling collect the second time."

"He's a smart boy, at the top of his class," Rubin said, allowing himself a moment of fatherly pride.

"So we've got someone working for us on the inside. But we can't put everything on him, and we can't give up. I'd like your permission to visit Natalie's father, ask him the secret he's been sitting on all these years."

"No."

"I won't tell you what it is. That way you won't break your promise to Natalie. And if it has no bearing on her disappearance, we'll never speak of it again. Deal?"

She would have liked to offer her hand, but she knew better. Instead she tipped her glass close to Rubin's. He hesitated, then clinked hers. They were good glasses, Riedel, a single goblet worth more than Tess's entire set of mismatched glassware.

They also had to be hand-washed. Another reason, in Tess's opinion, to run away. A sixty-dollar glass was a luxury only if you didn't have to wash it yourself.

Sunday

18

I thought you said I could wear black," Tess said, standing on a footstool in a huge dressing room and tugging miserably at a tube of crimson silk. Clearly intended for a beanpole without freckles on her shoulders, the dress had one zipper, two seams, an elasticized band around the top, and a fourteen-hundred-dollar price tag. There was more workmanship in the apron that Tess had made in home ec at Rock Glen Junior High. The apron had *pockets*.

"Black would be fine, but it's so boring and safe," Kitty said, studying Tess and then Tess's reflection, as if the mirror might yield a more pleasing verdict. "I wanted to see you in some colors for a change."

"It's appalling to pay this much for a dress like this."

"I don't care for it much either. Your hair and skin are going to fight that shade of red every step of the way."

"No, I don't mean *this* dress, I mean any dress that's all label and

Third World workmanship. Jesus, Kitty, let's go to C-Mart when the next truck rolls in, buy a marked-down gown from Saks, and give the rest of what you were planning to spend to one of the local soup kitchens. Besides, who knows? You might find another Prada bag marked down to seventy-five dollars."

Kitty had indeed unearthed a Prada bag at C-Mart five years ago, and it was the stuff of family legend. Tess's mother, Judith, had driven the thirty-plus miles out to the Belair warehouse several times with her Weinstein sisters-in-law, hoping to repeat Kitty's good luck. Prada proved elusive, but Judith had ended up with an out-of-season Kate Spade, a pair of Stuart Weitzman pumps, and several cashmere twinsets for twenty dollars apiece.

But Kitty was a Monaghan. She didn't mind paying retail to get what she wanted—or even asking these bridal boutiques to open on Sunday, just for her, so she didn't have to miss a day of work in her own store. Kitty's Karma, the family called it.

"I told you, this is my gift to you." Kitty kept circling Tess, poking and prodding, as if her persuasive hands could make the dress behave. "I'm exercising my bridal prerogative to boss you around, but instead of forcing you into some hideous lavender tulle concoction to match an insane color scheme, I want to pick out your dress and mine, then work backward, base everything on that. Just once I want you to have a perfect dress, the kind of thing you would never buy yourself."

"But it's such a waste."

"Far from it. Trust me, Tess. One day you'll regret not making more of the time in your life when all you needed was a little eyeliner to be dazzling. Does Crow have a tux?"

"I have no idea."

"Well, it's black tie optional, and I know he doesn't have money to spring for a new one, and rentals never fit right. But I wouldn't be surprised if his father had one he could wear. Mention that the next time you talk to him."

"Sure."

"Was he surprised? I hope he doesn't mind that we're going to go with a little jazz combo instead of one of the more avant-garde local bands he champions."

" 'I knew the bride,' " Tess said ruefully, " 'when she used to rock and roll.' "

She had quoted the old song title just to change the subject, but as soon as she spoke, Tess had a vivid image of Kitty as a young college student, throwing herself around the Monaghan living room to some cutting-edge punk band, showing a young Tess how to pogo. She had been a most satisfactory aunt all these years. She was entitled to a little bridal madness.

The saleslady appeared with a tray of tea, sandwiches, and cheese puffs, and Tess looked at them with longing. But she wouldn't dare eat a crumb while surrounded by ten thousand dollars' worth of dry-clean-only duds.

"No luck with the red?" the woman asked a little too brightly. She was extremely thin, perhaps even a size zero, but a tad old to carry the youthful fashions she wore.

"Do I look like I'm having any luck with the red?" Tess asked.

"What about the salmon?"

"The color was okay, but the style was wrong," Kitty said. "Too fussy."

"Ah. Now, if it were you—"

"But it's not for me. We're shopping for my niece today."

This was the third store of the afternoon, and they had heard this same wistful refrain before. *If it were you* . . . Kitty, with her petite figure, peachy skin, and red-blond curls, was a saleswoman's dream, even if she didn't have the height to carry true couture. Tess, clomping behind her in boots and jeans and sweater, had felt like one of Cinderella's stepsisters.

"What are you going to do with the hair?" the saleslady asked, as if it were a stray pet Tess had adopted, not part of her body.

"Shave it," Kitty said. "Mine, too. Everyone at the wedding is going to be bald. I saw it in *InStyle* magazine. Very chic, and it saves a fortune on hairdressers."

The saleslady backed away with a nervous smile, and Tess was reassured that her aunt had not completely lost her sense of humor.

"Can we break for lunch?"

"Just one more stop," Kitty said, using the soft, wheedling tone that had sold so many books and won so many men before she decided she could live with just one. "There's a place in Towson that carries Vera Wang."

"Vera Wang doesn't really do hips, which I have in abundance."

"But she does do cleavage, which you also have in abundance."

"I've never gone for that bosomy swell where you end up on nipple patrol the whole evening, worrying that an entire breast might pop out of the top of your dress and hit someone in the face."

"Good point," Kitty said, studying Tess's décolletage, which was fighting the red dress even harder than her hair and her skin. "We couldn't afford the liability insurance if those things got loose at the reception. High neck it is."

Gratefully, Tess jumped down from the footstool, knocking over her bag, which sent her gun skittering across the floor. Kitty lifted the hem of her ankle-length skirt, as if the Beretta were a rodent.

"Do you always carry that now?"

"Everywhere it's legal."

"Will you insist on bringing it to the wedding?" Kitty was striving for a light tone, but Tess could tell she was upset. She didn't like guns, and she didn't like being reminded that Tess would now be dead without one. Her aunt simply could not reconcile those two facts. Tess understood. She wasn't particularly fond of this reality either, but she was getting used to it. She tried to think of the Beretta as a paradoxical talisman: As long as she had it, she would never need it.

"Depends on whether the dress has a belt, so I can holster it. Of course, I also have a shoulder holster. Or maybe that fancy handbag designer, the one who does all those one-of-a-kind bags for Oscar night, could whip up something for an armed and dangerous bridesmaid."

"You know, I think we should break for lunch after all."

19

The little boy was looking for his father.

He went from room to room in the old house, only vaguely aware of the flames in the windows, the heat building up around him. He was not scared. He is never scared. From somewhere outside the house, his mother screamed, telling him to turn around, to come back, to flee to safety, but he paid no heed. He knew that his father was in the house somewhere, and he would not leave without his father. He walked from the third floor to the second, from the second to the first. The house was his family's, the only house he had ever known. Yet it was unfamiliar-looking, with strange furniture he had never seen before. And the basement was still unfinished, not the playroom he used in the day-time, filled with toys and games and gadgets. This was a dark, creepy place with a cold stone floor, no furniture, and no electricity. Upstairs the fire crackled happily, making a sound like Jiffy Pop. He still was not afraid. Jiffy Pop was nothing to be afraid of. Maybe his father was making it for him. Only his father could make it right, so every kernel popped, just like it said on the bag.

And then he saw his father lying on the basement floor, dressed as if for work, his gray suit surrounded by a burgundy stain. Had Poppa spilled something? Cranberry juice or Hawaiian Punch? Would Mama be mad at Poppa for making a mess? There was a gun, his father's gun, which he had to carry for work. But the gun was in Poppa's right hand, and his father was left-handed, like him. Why was the gun in his right hand? Someone else must have killed him and tried to make it look like his father did it to himself.

The boy took the gun away and put it in his toy chest, which had suddenly materialized, and now the basement was the rec room he remembered, with the cast-off sofa and pine paneling and the old black-and-white RCA in the corner, because his father just bought a big color television for the den. Would they have to give the color television back, now that his father was dead?

———————

Zeke willed himself awake, an essential trick to master for those prone to nightmares. He had thought the dream was the by-product of his old life and assumed it would end when he finally got out. But here it was again, more or less the same. Some details varied, but the fiery house remained constant. It always started off as a surreal approximation of the shingled Forest Park home his family had owned before his father's death, then reclaimed itself at the end, taking on its true contours in case Zeke ever made the mistake of thinking his father's suicide could be confined within the boundaries of a bad dream.

And the young Zeke always had some petty thought upon finding his father's body. *Would they get to keep the color television? The new Cadillac?* Strange, the one question the dreamworld Zeke never asked was the one Zeke had asked in real life: *Did this mean they weren't going to the Orioles game?* Zeke didn't beat himself up too much over that. He was only five when his father died—in the basement of what was left of his business, as a matter of fact, not at home. And he was discovered by an employee, not his son, so the event had seemed unreal to the little boy. After all the rabbi's vague talk about journeys and God's fate and being summoned by the Angel of Death, Zeke came to believe that his father had gone to a place from which he might return. So he had asked what a five-year-old boy would have asked in those years, the glory years of Mc-Nally and Palmer and Brooks: "Does this mean we're not going to the Orioles game?"

The rabbi took their tickets. Or so Zeke always assumed. At any rate, Zeke didn't go to the game that night.

He stared at the ceiling, taking in the sounds around him. Life on the outside was at once louder and quieter than he remembered, the sounds more varied and less predictable. Natalie didn't exactly snore, but she whistled a bit as she slept, curled into his side like a kitten. The children, who shared the other double bed, were mouth-breathers and snufflers. The twins slept in a tangled jumble, while Isaac hugged a narrow strip along the side. Once or twice so far, Zeke had awakened in the night and found Isaac's brown-black eyes boring into him in the dark, full of hate. The boy slept so far on the side of the bed that it was amazing to Zeke he didn't end up falling every night, but he had an unnatural rigidity. Again, just like his father. The Rubins were very rigid men.

Spoiled, too. At every stop Isaac asked if he could have a rollaway bed, but Zeke had said a motel double was big enough for three kids. The truth was that he just didn't want to draw attention to the fact that they were traveling with three kids. Bad enough that they sometimes drove with the luggage on the roof, although that sometimes worked as an optical illusion. Now you see it, now you don't.

"What makes you think motels even have rollaways?" he had asked Isaac once.

"The Waldorf-Astoria did," he said. "We had a suite, and I slept on the rollaway in the living room part, and the twins shared the other double bed."

"The Waldorf, huh?" Even when Zeke's father was alive and the business was thriving, Zeke had never taken material things for granted, never assumed the world was his oyster, never even understood that puzzling expression. If the world was your oyster, what were you? A grain of sand being pounded into a pearl? "You stay at the Waldorf a lot, Lord Fauntleroy?"

"Just once. Daddy had business in New York, and we went up for the weekend. He took me to the museum with the dinosaurs and the big planetarium. He said he finally understood black holes after going there. Do you know what a black hole is?"

"Of course." If he said no, Isaac would launch into a long, tedious explanation. The kid was in love with the sound of his own voice. It was an unexpected bonus of locking him into the trunk, not having to listen to him yak. *You*, he wanted to say. *You're a goddamn black hole, a motherfuckin' maw, demanding attention.*

Too bad the boy didn't take after his mother, a woman with the rare ability to keep still. Natalie's beauty was remarkable, but it was her composure, her need not to fill silences, that Zeke prized above all. Most women were so busy, never at rest. They puttered, they frittered, they fussed. The spark between Zeke and Natalie hadn't been so much love at first sight as it was the thrill of recognition, two aliens trapped on an unfriendly planet, the only members of their species. Natalie, like Zeke, knew she deserved whatever she could wring out of this world.

Granted, he found himself wishing that she had been a little more communicative when she showed up in Terre Haute. *Surprise! I've left Mark, I didn't want to wait anymore, not even a month or two. Oh, and I have three kids. Guess I forgot to mention that in all the letters.* Zeke had never even suspected the kids existed, although it struck him in hindsight that Lana had dropped a spiteful hint or two over the years. He wasn't an idiot, he knew Natalie had to have sex with Mark, but she had told him she couldn't have kids. Truthfully, he hadn't minded the idea of Mark's being denied the children that an Orthodox man would consider his due. He had even hoped it might make Mark question his faith, or God's love. He yearned for that prig to question something, anything, but that was the Rubin secret to survival: Never look too closely at the source of all that good luck.

Even as Zeke processed the inconvenient fact of the children's presence—in Terre Haute in particular, on the planet in general—he understood why it never would have occurred to Natalie to leave them behind when she bolted. What was hers was hers; Natalie was almost crazed on this point. It had killed her, having to leave so many of her possessions back in Mark Rubin's house. But the children were hers, and hers alone, according to Natalie's bizarre logic. Motherhood had gotten under Natalie's skin in a way Zeke never could have predicted. She still put him first, above all others, but she didn't see why she couldn't do that while tending to the children she had conceived with another man. If only Zeke's own mother had been committed to such a paradoxical idea. But Zeke's mom had always put her happiness above his.

He had tried to convince Natalie to go home, to wait just a month or two more, although her disappearance and reappearance would make Mark inconveniently suspicious. Failing that, he urged her to put the children on a bus before they had seen too much and knew too much, although he didn't phrase it quite that way. "Don't you see he's going to do a full-court press to find you? A wife runs away, a man might come to accept it. But when she takes his kids, it's like throwing down a gauntlet. He has to hunt for you now."

Natalie had just stared at Zeke blankly, not getting it. Her English was flawless, unaccented, yet riddled with holes of willful incomprehension. She knew twenty-seven different ways to describe red lipstick, but she wouldn't know a gauntlet, whether thrown down or run down.

"With or without the children, he was going to look for me," she said. "He loves me. You told me to make sure of it, and I did. He adores me."

"Yeah, but . . ." Useless to explain. Although generally pliable, Natalie could be thick when it suited her. By leaving early and taking the kids, she had screwed up everything, forced him to improvise. Zeke preferred not to improvise. Then again, Natalie didn't know the particulars of his plan—he had needed her to be plausibly bewildered when the payoff came—so she could almost be excused for throwing a goddamn monkey wrench into the works. Natalie didn't have the benefit of ten years of planning, thinking, dreaming. She had gone about her reasonable facsimile of an Orthodox mama's life, driving her kids to school and Gymboree, shopping at the kosher markets, marking time until the day that Zeke would summon her and their real life would begin.

And then, with only a few weeks to go, she had bolted, no longer able to wait. He was still trying to process the mere fact of *her* presence when she led him into that motel room and showed him the three solemn-faced children waiting there, three little Rubins, three goddamn contingencies to be dealt with.

Short term, Zeke had figured out how they could use the kids to their advantage, make them pay their way. So they drove from town to town, masquerading as a family, telling a lie, getting a check, using the check to case the banks, which allowed them to get even more money if the security proved to be as nonexistent as Zeke had heard. Amazing how many places skimped on things like cameras and guards, content to let Plexiglas carry the day. But then, that's what he had learned, back in Terre Haute. It may be a federal charge, but it didn't have to be that risky, not if you were careful. The feds had bigger things on their minds these days. Too bad it was such a small score, but what could a man do? He'd get his big payoff soon enough, and he'd be hundreds of miles away when it all came down.

Because here was something else that Zeke had figured out in Terre Haute: The best schemes weren't in the minds of other inmates out on the yard but in the prison library, and in the novels at that. The nonfiction books were written from the point of view of the cops or the losers, but the novelists were a larcenous lot at heart, devising criminal enterprises that they themselves then foiled. Elmore Leonard, James M. Cain, Donald Westlake—Zeke might have been the first person to read these men for their plots, making careful notes. In Zeke's view there was no reason that Walter Neff and Phyllis Nirdlinger shouldn't live happily ever after on the largesse provided by Mr. Nirdlinger. The trick was not to get greedy and go for the double-indemnity clause. And to roll with the punches when necessary. That's what Zeke had done when Natalie showed up with those damn kids, and so far it was working.

Besides, Zeke's scheme might have been born of necessity, but it had a certain serendipity. The lies that Natalie told would become the truth, as lies often did. There was even a pleasing symmetry. His father's name had been smeared, and he had taken his life out of despair over the unfair accusations against him.

Now Mark Rubin's life would be destroyed—figuratively, with the loss of his wife and children, and then literally, by one of the poor souls he had deigned to help. The self-righteous prig. Zeke almost wished Mark could be alive when his widow returned to town to bury his body and claim the life insurance, not to mention his sizable estate. Those who consoled her would be treated to her whispered confidences: Mark Rubin had beat her, that's why she had run away. Look, she had the welfare handouts to prove it, emergency checks given by trusting social workers, appalled by the old-fashioned patriarchy of Orthodox life. Another bit of luck from Terre Haute—Natalie couldn't have pulled this act in, say, Chicago, where Zeke had planned to settle short-term. But in the rural hamlets of Indiana, Illinois, and Ohio, sympathetic souls couldn't wait to raid their emergency funds for the abused Orthodox wife on the run. So yeah, he had made it all work for him this far, rolled with the punches, handled every unplanned contingency.

Except, of course, for the children. But he'd figure out what to do with them, too, and sooner rather than later. Zeke wasn't going to raise Mark Rubin's bastards. As he fell back to sleep, he found himself wondering if Mark was the kind of man who insured his children. Possibly. Probably. He was that tight-assed—and that clueless. Mark Rubin thought he could anticipate every contingency, but he would never see what Zeke had planned for him.

Monday

20

By Monday morning Tess was on the road, her breasts safely stowed beneath her usual turtleneck and a perfectly acceptable cocktail dress parked in her closet—black, halter-necked, and sleeveless, showcasing the shoulders and deltoids instead of the pectorals. Meanwhile, Uncle Donald had spent the weekend pulling strings, old and frayed as they were. Tess was now on the visiting list for Boris Petrovich, a process that normally required weeks of back-and-forth with the Department of Corrections.

"Who else is on the list?" she asked her uncle's DOC contact, curious to see if Natalie had gone behind Mark Rubin's back and continued to visit her father all these years.

"His lawyer, his wife, and someone named Lana Wishnia."

"*Really?*"

"Yes, but she hasn't been to see him since he was moved to the Eastern Shore six months ago. Probably too far for her to go."

"I guess inmates learn who really cares about them when they end up on the Eastern Shore."

Petrovich had been transferred to Eastern Correctional Institution in Somerset County. It was a long trip, made longer by the lack of an interstate past Annapolis. And because it was an autumn weekday, as opposed to a summer weekend, Tess didn't even have the consolation of grabbing a barbecue sandwich or buying fresh produce from a roadside stand. Not that she had much appetite this morning. Her stomach had clutched while crossing the Chesapeake, but she reminded herself that neither the bridge, the bay, nor the islands it contained were the source of her troubles last spring, just the routes she had taken to find them.

The orange DOC jumpsuit is unkind to most Caucasian complexions, but Boris Petrovich looked particularly yellow, as if he had liver trouble. Uncle Donald's state contact said Petrovich had been transferred here after abusing the privileges granted those inmates in a special program for older prisoners at Jessup, which fit with what Tess knew about the man. His foxlike face even looked shifty, with its flat cheekbones and narrowed eyes. Most likely he had agreed to meet with Tess because he was curious to see how he might manipulate her toward some end, even if he hadn't figured out what that end might be.

"So my daughter has run away and my son-in-law suddenly wishes my help. Interesting."

"He doesn't want your help," Tess said. "He didn't even want me to meet with you, but I insisted. He said everything you say is a lie, so it's useless to speak to you."

"Well, not *everything*. What would be the point in that? If you always lie, it's the same as always telling the truth. You have to mix it up to be effective."

Although Petrovich was serving a twenty-year sentence for second-degree murder, he was not in a maximum-security cell block, and he was allowed to meet visitors in an open area, sitting across a table instead of on the other side of a glass. So he was able to lean forward and place a finger on Tess's nose, the way a man might playfully chide a curious child. She tried not to flinch, but it was hard for her to succumb to a stranger's touch, especially a man. Especially a man with this sour, tainted smell.

"You're not just a liar, you're a would-be blackmailer, too."

He wasn't an easy man to insult. "I didn't see it that way. All I was trying to do is make sure my daughter didn't forget me, that she put some money away for me when I get out of here. After all, she made this wonderful match because of me, right? You think she would be grateful. Right? Or at least willing to pay a finder's fee? *Right?*"

The question was mocking in a way that Tess couldn't quite analyze. The repeated "right"s suggested the opposite, that something was quite wrong.

"Do you want to tell me what it was that Natalie was so desperate to keep from her husband?"

"No."

"What if I offered to pay you? Put money in that account that means so much to you? Plus, my uncle has pull with the state. I might even be able to get you back to Jessup."

"No."

"*No?*"

He grinned at Tess's surprise, showing teeth as yellow as his skin. "Everyone thinks I'm so crooked. But I have ethics, too, you know. I can't sell you what you want to buy because I've already promised it to another buyer."

"Is it Natalie?" Tess asked, thinking of the flurry of withdrawals Natalie had made in the week before she left.

He shook his head, pleased with himself.

It was Tess's turn to score a point, however small. "Lana Wishnia?"

"You know Lana?"

"Oh, yes. I know she's on your visitors' list, and I've spoken to her at length."

"But not at such length that you found out what you want to know. Or maybe not at all. Maybe you lie, too, to get what you want?" The last was asked with admiration, as if Petrovich could not respect someone who told the truth all the time.

"Sometimes. Lying's the only way to level the playing field with liars. But I do know Lana, and I believe she's a link to Natalie's disappearance. Does she know Natalie's secret as well?"

"I'll tell you this much: The person who bought my silence did it on a promise. I haven't been paid yet. And if the money doesn't come soon, maybe I will put that information back on the market, and you and I could still make a deal."

"Does this have anything to do with the man you killed?"

"That one? No. Trust me on this, no one's ever missed that man, not even his own mother." This matched what Tess had been able to learn. Boris Petrovich's victim had apparently been an unsavory type, a small-time criminal who had quarreled with Petrovich.

"I can always go back to Lana, ask her what's going on."

"She's tough, tougher than any American girl. She won't answer your questions."

Tess had a moment of wanting to impress Petrovich with just how tough this particular American girl was. She couldn't show him her gun—the prison had been quite adamant about holding that for her—but she could yank up her pant leg and display the scar on her left knee, still purplish and a little swollen three months after she fell on that broken bottle, the night she was almost killed. She could tell him what she had found the will to do, when she had to choose between her life and someone else's, the reserves of strength and violence she had discovered in herself. The nightmarish memory had faded somewhat over the past three months, so it was now bearably surreal—a flash of silver finding its target, her victim almost robotic in his agony, like a machine run amok. But the image was never far away when she was angry or upset.

Instead of saying or doing any of these things, however, Tess willed her adrenaline to ebb. Her instinct had always been to run straight at things, but her instincts were far from reliable. That, too, she had learned the hard way. She needed to be quiet, still, disengaged. Direct questions wouldn't work with Petrovich.

"Hey, do you miss the other men?"

"What other men?"

"The ones from the group."

"I wouldn't call them friends."

"Still, they're back in Jessup right, and now you're here. That's kind of a burn."

He shrugged, indifferent to the topic, seeing no profit in it and therefore no point. "Most of them are gone from Jessup anyway, their time served."

"Right. I hadn't considered that fact. After all, there were only five or six."

"Eight to begin with."

"Right, eight. And you're the only one still inside."

"Me and Yitzhak. The others are all long gone."

"Yes," Tess said. "The others. Remind me of their names. There was you, and Yitzhak, of course, and Abraham."

"Amos, you mean."

"Amos and . . . Andy?"

Petrovich scowled, furious that she had tricked him into yielding any information for free. "I won't tell you the others' names."

"I don't need you to. Someone—the DOC or the Associated— has to have a record because Mark Rubin and my Uncle Donald were put on a visitors' list, just as I was with you today. Or Mark will remember their names. It simply never occurred to him to connect anyone in the program to Natalie's disappearance—and it didn't occur to me until you said you had another buyer. Thanks a lot, Boris. You've been a huge help."

"You don't know anything. You haven't learned anything. You're on the wrong track."

Perhaps because he was frustrated and angry, Petrovich stood abruptly, and the guards stationed throughout the room took notice. Tess was reminded that the man before her had committed a crime of passion, killing another man in a quarrel. But she wasn't scared.

She wasn't scared. The realization was akin to noticing that a toothache had disappeared, or that one's head had finally cleared after a long, miserable cold. She stood, too, feeling as if she had reclaimed a piece of herself—the chunk of skin carved from her knee, the long braid sliced from the nape of her neck the same night. Her "noive," as the Cowardly Lion would have it. There was no reason to have recovered those things here, in the drab visiting room at ECI, yet she had. Seeing through Petrovich had reminded Tess how much of the world was run on bluff and bluster. She might not be as strong as everyone she met, or as fast, or even as smart. But she could *bullshit* with the best of them. Combine that quality with a license to carry, and a girl could more than get by in this life.

"It's been a pleasure *not* doing business with you, Mr. Petrovich."

"You know nothing," he called after her. But Tess knew enough.

21

Stereotypes persist for a reason, Tess decided on her way back to Baltimore, and it wasn't wrong to rely on them when they were helpful. On her cell phone, she called the Associated, a nonprofit umbrella group of Jewish charities, assuming it was far more likely to keep complete, accessible records than the state Department of Corrections was. Perhaps this was unfair to state government workers, but her generalization paid off in this case. The names and addresses Tess wanted were arriving at her office via fax machine before she crossed the Bay Bridge.

Eight men had been given permission to participate in the prison outreach program when it started twelve years ago, and—give Boris credit for telling the truth here—he and Yitzhak were the only ones who were still guests of the state. Of the remaining six, four had Baltimore addresses, while one was in Grantsville, and the sixth,

Nathaniel Rubenstein, had no address at all listed with parole and probation. Still, it was the Grantsville address for Amos Greif that puzzled Tess. The town in far-western Maryland was best known for its model Amish village and the blueberry pancakes at the local restaurant. It seemed a strange choice of residence for a Jewish ex-con who specialized in grand theft auto.

"Amos was from Cumberland," Mark Rubin said, studying the list. He had come straight to Tess's office from work, so he was wearing his usual dark suit, although the days continued almost Indian-summer warm. Tess recalled he had been wearing a crisp white shirt and khakis with a knife-sharp crease while hanging around the house Saturday night. She wondered if he even owned a pair of blue jeans. Was his formal dress the result of his religion or his work? Could God really care what anyone wore? Adam and Eve had started out naked.

"Cumberland, Grantsville, it's still more West Virginia than Maryland. And it's not a place you expect to find a Jewish car thief."

"Cumberland had a . . . I wouldn't say *thriving*, but important, close-knit Jewish community going back to the nineteenth century. The local department store, Rosenbaum Brothers, was the biggest store of its kind between Baltimore and Pittsburgh."

"You're kidding me."

"We didn't all live in crowded ghettos, Tess. The joke about Jews in small-town Maryland is that they settled wherever the mule died. Remember Louis Goldstein, the former comptroller? When Louis was born in Prince Frederick, the mohel had to travel to the bris by ferry from Baltimore."

"Point taken," she said, trying not to yawn. "You can find Jews anywhere in Maryland. In small towns and big cities. In prisons and the state's highest political office. Hey, thanks to Marvin Mandel, we know that Jews can achieve both in the same lifetime."

"Marvin was pardoned," Rubin said, a slight defensiveness creeping into his tone. "And he was no more a crook than the governor before him, that Greek Agnew."

"Well, maybe someone will get around to pardoning these gents one day, and then they, too, can find new careers as lobbyists and lawmakers. Meanwhile, I'm more curious to know if you think there's one man on this list that I should be focusing on for any reason."

Rubin perched on the corner of the office sofa that Esskay was willing to allot him. The dogs had begun to warm to him, a somewhat reliable assessment of a person's character. Of course Esskay was a biscuit slut, falling for anyone who gave her a treat, but even the more reserved Miata perked up when Rubin came around.

"Amos was an interesting case. He was born to Jewish parents but orphaned as a teenager and raised by a local farmer. No religious education whatsoever, but a real head for business. If he had applied his corporate model to more legal forms of revenue, he'd probably be running a Fortune 500 company today."

"You talked about business?"

Rubin shrugged. "It's a great commonality for men. That and baseball. Now, Larry Kirsch was a drug addict who ended up dealing. Another guy with a head for the wrong kind of business. Very shrewd, always working an angle. Mickey Harvey—that was a sad one. He was a civil engineer, rear-ended another car, killing a child in the backseat. He left the scene in a panic—he had been drinking at the baseball game—and the judge decided to make an example of him. Just a normal guy otherwise."

"A normal guy with a drinking problem." Despite her affection for a nice glass of wine and the occasional martini—or perhaps because of it—Tess was sanctimonious when it came to drinking and driving.

"Now who sounds all Old Testament?" Rubin's tone was light, almost teasing. "I felt bad for the guy. He wasn't a drunk, he probably wasn't even legally intoxicated when he had the accident. He drove an SUV, and the car he hit was one of those flimsy sedans with virtually no rear end. Change a single variable in the scenario— one less beer, a longer game, different vehicles, a different route home—and he may have gone the rest of his life without hurting anyone. Every time I saw Mickey Harvey, I was reminded how life can change in a single moment."

Rubin broke off, perhaps remembering how quickly his own life had changed because of variables that no one could identify.

"What about the others?" Tess pressed him, if only to distract him.

"They're less vivid to me. Scott Russell ran one of those fly-by-night home improvement companies, specialized in ripping off little old ladies. This generation's version of a tin man, a run-of-the-mill gonif. Danny Katzen was a burglar who beat up an old woman who had the bad luck to be at home when he broke in. An unrepentant thug, just a waste of space and protoplasm. I liked him the least."

"And Rubenstein?"

"Doesn't matter."

"How so?"

"He's in federal prison. That's why there's no address listed. He served a state sentence for receiving stolen goods, then ended up with federal time for a sophisticated fraud operation. Besides, although he signed up for the group, he never participated." Rubin allowed himself an exasperated sigh, shaking his head at the memory of Nathaniel Rubenstein. "A bright man, too. If only he had been a patient one."

"What does patience have to do with it?"

"He ran a small chain of clothing stores. It was a great idea, although a little ahead of its time. You know those Scandinavian stores that sell trendy clothing at low prices?"

Tess didn't, but nodded anyway, so Rubin would finish his story and get back to the subject at hand. The guy was clearly queer for the retail business in all its forms.

"Nat tried something similar fifteen years ago, but he was undercapitalized and he expanded too quickly. He took shortcuts, taking some shipments he knew were of dubious provenance. And when he had cash-flow problems, he used his access to credit records to scam people with bad credit. He'd tell them he could get them a card with a thousand dollars limit for a service fee of a hundred and fifty dollars. Then he mailed them an application and some coupons and pocketed the fee. That's how he ended up doing federal time."

"How do you know so much about him if he didn't participate in the group?"

"Baltimore's Jews live in a small village, especially those of us in the clothing business. There's lots of gossip we keep to ourselves, so people in the city at large won't cluck their tongues. It was shocking, seeing Nat go to prison."

"Did you know him before he went in?"

"After a fashion." Rubin gave her a lopsided smile. "The pun was unintended."

"Only it wasn't really a pun," Tess said.

"Excuse me?"

"It was a play on words, but it wasn't a pun, which involves changing a word in some way so it takes on a double meaning." It was fun, correcting Rubin for once. "You know, Mexican weather report—chili today—"

"Hot tamale. Groucho Marx." He moved his eyebrows up and down, wiggling an imaginary stogie. "I'm a huge fan. I tried to get Isaac to watch the films with me, but they didn't seem to resonate with him. He has trouble relating to black-and-white films. He asked me once if the world used to be black and white."

His voice caught then, as it always seemed to do when he spoke of his children.

"Anyway, this list gives me something concrete to do," Tess said. "Your father-in-law was clearly upset when I suggested that one of these men might be an important link."

A consistent man—the word "rigid" came to mind—Rubin had not yet asked Tess a single question about her interview with his father-in-law.

"So you'll find them, talk to them—and then what?"

"You always want to be told the future, but I won't pretend to know what I can't know." Tess hesitated, reluctant to put Rubin on the offensive. "The men on the list—do any of them resemble the man with Natalie in French Lick?"

The question clearly pained him. "Yes and no. Truth is, they all resemble one another. Except for Amos, who was huge. Not fat, just enormous, built on a different scale. The others are neither tall nor short, neither fat nor skinny, and they all had darkish hair. It's been almost ten years since I've seen them. Who knows what they look like now? Who knows what I looked like then?"

"Why did you stop volunteering in the prison anyway? I know you were on the outs with Boris, but what about the other men? Wasn't there a way you could have continued with them?"

"Natalie asked me to stop going. Once she was pregnant with Isaac, she was adamant that I must not visit the prison anymore. She said it worried her, that it was a dangerous place. Funny, she had been there all those times, as a beautiful young girl, and yet she worried about me. I have to admit, I was charmed. I was so young when my mother died. My father was wonderful, but he always treated me like a little man. No one had ever worried about me before."

Tess resisted the urge to raise her own eyebrows Groucho style, or wiggle her own cigar. When it came to Natalie, shrewd Mark Rubin was fatally thick.

22

Isaac was lying in the trunk, thinking about Anne Frank. He had given up being Jonah. After all, Jonah got out of the whale after a little bit and went to Nineveh, but Isaac was still in the trunk. Anne Frank had to stay in the attic, day in and day out, hiding from Nazis. Isaac's teacher had told the class the story of the brave girl this past year, and Isaac had been quite impressed. He did not see how anyone could live under such circumstances, especially when there was no television and, even worse, no new books to read, just a book you were writing to yourself. Which seemed kind of boring, because you would always know what happened next.

But Anne, it occurred to him now, had it better than he did in some ways. Of course, she was up against the Nazis, and that was pretty bad, about as bad as things get. But she had an entire attic and her whole family around her. She had her journal, which became almost like a friend to her. Here in the trunk, Isaac couldn't even see, much less read or write. True, he was seldom in here more than twenty minutes or so, while Anne never got out of the attic. Lately, however, Zeke had begun to put him in the trunk more and more, for all sorts of infractions. That was Zeke's word, and it was new to Isaac. Infractions. He was still trying to figure out what it had to do with math. Maybe it meant Isaac misbehaved in parts, sort of like one-third or three-fourths.

Today, for example, the trouble began because Isaac had refused to eat anything at lunch. He wasn't being stubborn. He just wasn't hungry. His mother had nagged him to eat, which made him feel contrary and mean, and he had crossed his arms against his chest, refusing to take a single bite of anything. His mother had hissed at him, threatening one minute, pleading the next, almost in tears from frustration, and people began looking at them. That was the one thing Zeke would never tolerate—people looking.

So Zeke took Isaac outside to give him a lecture, but Isaac just stared at the sky, as if he were in a place far, far away, where Zeke's words couldn't be heard.

"Listen to me," Zeke had commanded, grabbing his arm, only to drop it when he noticed the two waitresses sharing a cigarette nearby. "Man, you are a stubborn little bas—*pisher*."

"I'm not the *pisher*," Isaac had said. "Penina is."

Zeke smiled, giving him credit for the joke. "Daisy," he corrected. "Your sister's Daisy now."

"She's Penina."

Zeke gave him his meanest look, which was pretty scary, but Isaac knew he wouldn't do anything as long as those girls were around. Isaac and Zeke sat next to each other on the curb, enjoying their dislike of each other, the freedom not to pretend. Of course, Isaac never pretended to like Zeke, but Zeke put on an act when Isaac's mom was around, ruffling his hair, giving him play punches on the arm that were just a little too hard.

"So," one smoking girl said to the other, "I love your earrings."

"These earrings?"

What other earrings would she be talking about, stupid? Isaac's father said Isaac would like girls one day, but he couldn't see it. These girls had big, fluffy heads of yellow hair, and their makeup was as bright and vivid as the kind of markings that Isaac had seen on people in *National Geographic.*

"Yeah. They're adorable. Where'd you get 'em?"

"At the flea market over on Wabash. The Sunday one? Guy wanted twenty dollars, but I jewed him down."

"Ex-cell-ent." The girls tossed down their cigarettes and ground them beneath their feet. One girl wore sensible flat shoes, but the other was tottering around in high heels that looked to be almost four inches tall. How could she walk in those? Isaac had tried on a pair of his mother's high heels once, just to see how she did it, but his father had said he really shouldn't do that.

"What did they mean?" he asked Zeke when the girls were gone.

"What?"

" 'Jewed him down.' Does that mean she made him a Jew?"

Zeke laughed, an unpleasant sound to Isaac's ears. Zeke laughed only when he was laughing at someone.

"It means she drove a hard bargain."

"I don't get it."

"Jews are known for being good businessmen, Isaac. Maybe a little too good. A lot of folks think Jews are cheats, who will do anything for a buck."

"But we're not."

"Some are. Enough to give Gentiles that impression." Zeke stared off into the distance, although there was nothing to see but highway and a large truck stop across the parking lot, a huge complex of silver and chrome where enormous trucks stood idling. "Your grandfather was like that."

"How do you know my grandfather? He died before I was born."

"Well, he was famous, right? Ran a big fur store, made a lot of money, married into even more. But no one in Baltimore who knew him ever said he made his money fair."

"My grandfather was not a cheat." Said with more conviction than he felt, because he had never known his Grandfather Rubin. But his father was a good man, so his grandfather must be a good man, too.

"Suit yourself." Zeke's laugh this time was short and bitter, more like a cough.

"You said Baltimore."

"What?"

"You said no one in Baltimore said my grandfather made his money fair. Are you from there, too?"

"Let's go to that convenience store over there," Zeke said. "See what kind of newspapers they carry in this hick town."

The convenience store at the truck stop was grand, almost as big as a real store, with all sorts of unexpected merchandise—clothing, toys, cassette tapes, even a rack of paperback books. A neon sign pointed the way toward restrooms with showers, while another sign advertised something called a chapel.

"Why showers?" Isaac asked Zeke.

"For long-haul truckers, my man. They can get pretty smelly, driving all day and night. They come in here to wash up and pray."

"Is the chapel only for Christians?"

"Don't worry, Isaac. I'm sure all the Jewish truckers find a way to pray, too. Your dad prays, doesn't he? Even in the middle of making all his money, he finds time to pray, right?"

Isaac refused to answer that question, spinning the rack of books while Zeke waited in line to pay for his newspaper. They looked like adult books for the most part, but there was a copy of something called *The Amber Spyglass*. Isaac had seen older boys at school with this book. He picked it up and opened to a page. Although the type was really small, he could read most of the words. Tests at school said Isaac read at the sixth-grade level, even though he was only going into the fourth grade. He was filled with longing for this book, any book. If his mother were here, he would beg her to buy it for him. But he hated to ask Zeke for anything, and not just because Zeke almost always said no.

Back home he had a savings account and a bank shaped like an Orioles cap. He could easily buy this book for himself. Of course, if he were back home, he wouldn't have to. His father would buy it for him.

Sighing, he started to return *The Amber Spyglass* to the rack, then saw the store's security camera focused on him, beneath a sign that promised SHOPLIFTERS WILL BE PROSECUTED TO THE FULL EXTENT OF THE LAW. He stared back into the camera's eye, then made a show of shoving the book down the front of his pants, smoothing his shirt over it.

"You ready to go, buckaroo?"

"Yes. Yes, I am."

Isaac and Zeke were almost back to the side of the highway before a woman began shouting after him. "Sir? Sir?" Zeke didn't turn around right away. He never did if he could help it. "Sir—I think your little boy has something of ours."

The woman caught up with them, pink-cheeked and a little out of breath. "I'm sorry, but one of the girls thinks she saw your son put something under his shirt."

"He's not—" Zeke caught himself before he denied he was Isaac's father. "He's not a bad kid. I can't believe he would do something like that."

Isaac shook his head. He didn't have much experience with breaking rules, but he was pretty sure a thief would pretend, at first, that he wasn't one. He clutched his middle, so the book wouldn't slip out.

"There—" The woman pointed to his stomach, and Zeke bent down, pulling the book from Isaac's grasp the way he might yank a hair from his head, hard and fast.

"I'm so sorry, ma'am. I apologize for . . . my son."

Isaac's cheeks burned, and he wanted to scream, *He's not my fa-*

ther. But he didn't want to distract the woman from calling the police, or have Zeke call him a liar.

"It happens," she said. "Not so much with the books, though."

"Are you going to persecute me?" Isaac asked.

"Perse— Oh, prosecute. I don't think that's necessary. Next time, though, you should ask your daddy if you want something, or save your money so you can buy it yourself."

"The sign said you always"—he paused, making sure to get the word right this time—"prosecute."

"That's for grown-ups," she said, winking at Zeke. Women were always winking at Zeke when Isaac's mom wasn't around. Winking or patting their hair. "Little boys get second chances."

"Yes they do," Zeke said, placing a hand on Isaac's shoulder and squeezing hard enough to make him squirm. "Sometimes."

They returned to the car, and Zeke said Isaac had to ride in the trunk for the next hour, maybe the foreseeable future, a phrase that seemed weird to Isaac. How much of the future could anyone see? Isaac's mother started to argue, but Zeke told her what Isaac had done, how he had tried to attract attention, perhaps even the police. "If you show that you can be trusted, you'll get your car privileges back, buckaroo."

So he was in the dark again. For the foreseeable future. He almost wished he hadn't gotten caught, given that his plan hadn't worked. If the woman wasn't going to call the police, he might as well have gotten away with stealing and had a new book to read. It was so unfair. When people made promises on signs, they should keep them. For some reason this made Isaac think of the time he was driving somewhere with his father and they saw a huge sign that said JESUS SAVES. And his father had pointed to it and said, "But Moses invests." He had laughed, and Isaac had laughed, too, once his father explained it.

He moved his hands along the trunk's lid above him, then felt along the sides. It was such a crummy old car that parts were always falling off. The spotty holes in the fenders, like little bits of lace, let air in, but also fumes. Did his mother realize what those fumes could do? The carpeted bit beneath his blanket was almost completely gone, and you could see through to the rear lights, which rattled, loose in their casings. Bored, Isaac placed a hand where he thought the lights might be and began to poke around, just to see what might happen.

Tuesday

23

Tess made a game of tracking down the four local felons that Mark Rubin had met through his volunteer work, deriving a peculiarly Baltimorean pleasure in structuring the most efficient route through the chaotic city. Uncle Donald, glorying in his ability to get confidential information, had procured the men's workplaces from Parole and Probation, which simplified things. Katzen was on the edge of downtown, Russell in downtown proper. She would then swing into SoWeBo, the southwest Baltimore neighborhood whose dilapidated row houses were more likely to evoke Soweto than SoHo, and end the day in southeast Baltimore, close to her own office. If she timed it right, she'd make Cross Street Market for lunch, pick up some fresh Utz potato chips, hot from the fryer, and still have time for a late-afternoon dog walk and coffee break.

"Good-bye," she called to the dogs, as she headed out. "I'm off on the Jewish-losers tour of Baltimore."

She would come to regret that joke, private as it was, before the morning was through.

———

Daniel Katzen—burglar and beater of old ladies—had found gainful employment as a security guard, at no less a place than the *Beacon-Light*. If such a man worked for any other employer, it probably would have sparked a five-part investigative series on the *Blight*'s front pages. But in the newspaper's own lobby, an ex-felon with a gun was no cause for alarm. Tess wondered if Katzen had lied about his background or if the newspaper's management reasoned that Katzen's willingness to hit women in moments of stress would come in handy should its unions strike.

"You need a pass to go upstairs," Katzen informed Tess before she even had a chance to introduce herself and state her business.

"I don't want to go upstairs," she said, not bothering to tell him that she had been sneaking in and out of the *Beacon-Light* for years, using a former employee's swipe card. "I'm here to see you. Do you remember a man named Mark Rubin?"

"No."

"Let me provide some context. Seder dinners, monthly prayer sessions, *baruch ata Adonai*."

"Hebrew school? There mighta been a Rubin in my class."

"Bars, electronic fences, guard towers—"

"*Hey*." Katzen glanced around the lobby, although there was no one there to overhear. "No need to screw with me like that. Okay, yeah, I remember Mark Rubin from you-know-where. So what?"

"What about Rubin's wife? Or his father-in-law, Boris Petrovich?"

"Boris was his father-in-law?" If Katzen was playing dumb, he was exceptionally good at it. "That dirty old Russian? Man, I hope his daughter had money. Because if she looked like her old man, she was definitely a two-bagger."

"She's not a two-bagger," Tess assured him. "She's gorgeous. And missing."

"Yeah?" He patted his pockets. "Well, I'm clean. Gorgeous, huh? Go figure. But then, Rubin was rich. A rich guy can always get a girl. Women are all about money. Like you, I bet you wouldn't go out with a guy like me because I'm a security guard."

"I wouldn't go out with a guy like you because you break into houses and beat up old women."

"That's what I *used* to do," Katzen said, wounded. "I'm a changed man. I even got a pardon."

Assuming he was telling the truth—a tricky assumption—then Katzen had come by his right to carry a firearm legitimately. But Tess wasn't convinced that Katzen knew the difference between a pardon and the mere end of parole.

"No thanks. What about Natalie Rubin?"

"Who?"

"Rubin's wife."

"The dirty Russian's daughter?"

"Never mind." Katzen's mind seemed to be on a loop, and a very short one at that. Tess left the newspaper building, convinced that Katzen was far too dumb to play dumb so effectively.

———

Scott Russell wasn't dumb, far from it. But the wiry forty-something man she met for coffee was simply another dead end, using Tess's time to try to pressure her into buying stocks. He was a junior executive at a discount brokerage house, working on commission, and he spoke of the market as if it were a kind of religion, a mystical force that would transform one's life if one surrendered to it completely. Tess was sure he had once spoken of aluminum siding with the same fervent certitude, and that he would probably find other gods and goods to worship throughout his working life. She bade him good-bye as quickly as possible, taking a card and promising to give serious thought to pharmaceutical stocks.

By 11:30 A.M., when Tess rang the doorbell at a converted garage on Poppleton Street, her heart was harder than the pharaoh's. The ring went unanswered at first. She checked the address for Mickey Harvey, then leaned on the bell again.

"Coming," a man's soft voice finally answered, followed by slow, careful footsteps. "Sorry, I couldn't hear you over the sander."

Mickey Harvey looked more like a living ghost than an actual man—gray eyes, gray hair, and gray complexion.

"I'm Tess Monaghan," she said. "I work for a man named Mark Rubin."

He smiled, the first man to show instant recognition at the name. "How is Mark? I haven't thought about him in years. He was very helpful to me, during my time . . . inside."

Inside. They all said "inside." It was more truism than euphemism, Tess decided. Serving time was something that most people could never understand, so these former inmates used a word that rendered the experience at once vague and definitive.

"You're not an engineer anymore."

He laughed, a rusty chuckle that sounded as if it didn't get out much. "What was your first clue? No, I've had this woodworking business for five years now. I do custom-builts. Money's not as good as it was when everybody was rich on paper, but I'm making ends meet."

"It's nice," Tess said, "when your avocation can become your business."

"Avocation? I'm not sure I'd call it that. Time was, I couldn't hammer a nail in straight. My ex is shocked. She always says, 'I couldn't get you to change a lightbulb when we were married, and now look at you, building armoires.' You know that old joke, right? How many Jewish boys does it take to change a lightbulb?"

"How many?" Tess responded dutifully.

Mickey Harvey made an incredulous face. "They have to be changed?"

Tess didn't have to fake her laugh, but she juiced it a little.

"So how did you end up being a Jewish carpenter?"

"I entered a vocational program while I was in a halfway house, began wood-shop courses more as occupational therapy than anything else. I don't drink anymore."

The last was offered almost as a reflexive confession. Society might be through punishing Mickey Harvey, but he was a long way from being ready to stop punishing himself.

"I'm talking to men who knew Mark through the Jessup program because his wife has disappeared, taking his children with her. Her father, who was in the program, claims to have some damaging information about her, but he won't tell us what it is. I'm just looking for any lead I can find."

He shook his head. "I wish I knew something, but I didn't even know Mark had a wife. Who was her dad?"

"Petrovich."

"Oh, yeah. I guess I knew he had a daughter, but he never told me that she was married to Mark. I was in a different cell block, though. I only saw those guys when the Tribe got together." Another twisted smile, another rusty laugh. "That's what I called it. The Tribe. And even the Tribe, small as it was, had cliques."

Tess wasn't surprised. The need to divide and subdivide was instinctive to humans, and there was no stratum of society it didn't affect. "How did the Tribe"—she used the word gingerly, not sure if she had a right to do so—"divide itself?"

"Russell and Kirsch were two peas in a pod. Katzen hung with this old dude, Yitzhak Wasserstein, who was doing a long sentence for killing a woman. Boris and Amos were buddy-buddy. Thick as thieves, as the saying goes."

"So you were the odd man out."

"Yeah, I guess I was."

"Did the men like Mark?"

"They didn't like anybody. But they didn't have any reason to dislike him. The volunteers were just another fact of life. I thought Mark was a good guy. I'm sorry his wife left him."

"I didn't say she *left*. I said she disappeared."

She thought the slip might be significant, but Mickey Harvey just waved the distinction away with a swipe of his hand. "But that's what women do, right? They leave. Yeah, I knew guys who cracked up their marriages, had affairs, bullied their wives. I even knew guys who convinced themselves that they wanted some other woman, only to find out that marriage is marriage is marriage. But usually it's the women who leave."

"Men leave, too, you know." Tess's heat surprised even her.

"At any rate, my wife left me. And the thing is, she left after I got out. You see, she could take being married to a guy inside. That was theoretical. Plus, she got lots of points for that. *Oh, Wendy, you're so brave. Oh, Wendy, you're so good.* But when I came home, I was a reality again, a guy who had killed a child and run away, destroyed every chance I had in life, and my family's along with it. That she couldn't take."

"You probably changed, too, more than either one of you could anticipate. Even change for the good can disrupt a relationship."

"Yeah, I changed. I got better. I got sober. But the big change was, I stopped making sixty thousand a year. She was remarried within a year, to some attorney. So I guess I know what my wife really loved about me."

"I'm . . . sorry." She thought it was what he wanted to hear.

"Me, too. I'm sorry. I'm sorry I can't help Mark Rubin out. I'm sorry I can't help myself. I'm sorry I have two kids I don't see enough. I'm sorry for everything. But do you think I can ever be sorry enough for the parents of the kid I killed?"

It was an unanswerable question, and Mickey Harvey seemed to realize this. He gave an embarrassed smile and moved the conversation to safer ground.

"Hey, tell Mark I go to temple now. Not regular, every week, but I belong to a temple, and I don't miss the High Holidays. My youngest was bar mitzvahed last month. It was a big party. His stepfather paid for it."

She started to apologize yet again. "I'm . . . I'm—"

"Don't. I hear it too much. I *say* it too much. But it doesn't change anything. And you know what? If you find Mark's wife, that won't change anything either. Trust me, it's the one thing no one can fix. Hey, want to see what I'm making?"

Tess recognized the offer as his attempt to behave normally, to ape the superficial style more suitable to an encounter between two strangers. "Sure."

He led her to the back of his workshop. A small bookshelf stood on a dropcloth. Tess didn't recognize the wood—mahogany? Cherry? Something reddish and complicated, with a swirling grain. The design was simple, but she could tell it was a simplicity born of long hours.

"Hand-pegged," Mickey Harvey said, running his fingers lightly over the top. "It's for my son. His grandparents—my parents— bought him a set of *The History of Civilization* for his bar mitzvah, and I'm building this to hold them. He'll have it all his life. He'll give it to his sons, who will pass it on to their sons. I've given him something that no one else can."

"You also gave him life. Don't forget that."

"But I took another child's. You know, that's my biggest fear. That God will take my kid, an eye for an eye. Sometimes I think I should kill myself, just to even the score, keep Benjamin safe."

"I don't think it works that way." Tess was almost frightened for this man, stranger though he was, needful for him to believe in his future.

"But if it did, I would. You have kids?" She shook her head. "Then you can't really understand. Here's the worst thing." He lowered his voice, as if an omniscient God couldn't hear whispers. "If I had to choose between my kid and another kid, if God came to me and said I could have my life to live over—I could choose not to do what I did, but I'd have to give him Benjamin—I wouldn't think twice."

"You mean . . . ?"

"I mean I'd do it all over again, make all the same fucking miserable mistakes to save my kid's life. Oh, sure, I'd try to cheat, find a loophole. That's what we all do when we bargain, whether it's with God or the devil. I'd take the deal, and then I'd try to wiggle out of it. And if I couldn't undo what I did, at the very least I'd stay there. I wouldn't run away again. I'd stay at the scene, take the Breathalyzer. I wasn't drunk, you know. And I wasn't even entirely at fault. I just was worried that I'd blow too high and that would be it for my job. For my fucking *job*. This time I'd help the parents get that little boy out of the car and hold him in my arms."

"I should go." She knew that the words sounded abrupt, even uncaring, but they were true. She should go. The longer Mickey Harvey spoke, the further he seemed to retreat into his own taunting memory. This conversation couldn't be good for him.

"Sure, I understand, you're a working girl. Hey—" He fished into the pocket of his painter's pants, pulled out a card. Tess gave him one of hers in exchange, just to be polite. She doubted Mickey Harvey had anything more to tell her. "If you need any woodworking. My ex is always telling me I have to learn to network. It's funny about exes. They know you, but they're not *invested* in you anymore, so they can be really honest. Know what I mean?"

Tess didn't, but she nodded her head anyway. Agreement was a small enough gift to give to Mickey Harvey, and he seemed grateful for it.

24

"D o you know when I realized I was going to be a thief when I grew up? When I stole the *afikomen*."

Tan and fit, Larry Kirsch had prematurely silver hair and bright blue eyes, which sparkled with . . . well, Tess was still trying to determine what accounted for that glint. Since she had arrived at Kirsch's fragrant cigar store, he had been ladling charm over every word. Sometimes the effect was flirtatious and focused, as if she were the most fascinating creature in the world. But his energy lagged at moments, and his patter became perfunctory, as if he didn't want to put out 100 percent for a woman disinclined to pay forty dollars for a cigar. Then he turned it on again, and she was beguiled—almost. He was trying so hard to make sure she liked him that she didn't think she should.

Plus, Tess couldn't quite shake Mickey Harvey's gloom, not even after two bags of fresh-made Utz chips, one crab and one barbecue. She had read that potato sales were down because of the mania for low-carb diets, and she wanted to help the farmers of the world.

"You're *supposed* to steal the *afikomen*," she said, brushing a fleck of salt from the corner of her mouth. "It's part of the Passover ritual. If every *afikomen* filcher ended up in prison, there wouldn't be any nice Jewish boys left."

"Ah, but I stole the *afikomen* from the kid who stole the *afikomen*. You see, I was the best negotiator among my cousins, and I always got more money for it. I hated seeing Adam and Jody give it back so cheap."

"I've seen your record. You weren't in prison for stealing."

"I stole tens of thousands of dollars from my employer to feed my cocaine habit." He laughed at Tess's arched eyebrows. "I know—cocaine was so *over* by the time I got hooked. A client gave me a little taste, to get me through tax season. By the time April fifteenth arrived, I was a full-fledged addict. Hey, but at least I was ahead of the curve on accounting fraud."

"You served time for possession with intent to distribute."

"Oh, puh-leeze. I wasn't a dealer. I was a *pig*. I planned on snorting every last bit of that myself. Well, maybe selling a little, just so I could make enough profit to buy more. Anyway, my family made restitution for what I stole, so the theft charge was dropped as part of my plea. But they couldn't make the distribution charge go away. You know what my mother said when she found out I had a cocaine habit? 'At least he doesn't drink, like the goyim.' "

"Where are you getting your material—*Portnoy's Complaint*?"

"What does an Irish lass named Monaghan know from Portnoy and *afikomens*? I imagine you reading James Joyce and drinking pints of Guinness in Locust Point bars." He leaned across the counter toward her, making serious eye contact. "I like the freckles, by the way."

Tess smiled enigmatically. She had no intention of telling this garrulous charmer that she was half Jewish. She wasn't convinced

Kirsch had kicked all his bad habits, but she had outgrown her bad-boy jones long ago.

"I hate to dredge up your life in prison—"

"Dredge away. It's some of my best material. In fact, it's the centerpiece of my first-date story. Do you think that's why I'm not getting many second dates?"

She let the pass pass. "I'm curious about the group of Jewish prisoners who met back at Jessup, going back more than ten years ago. One prisoner's daughter ended up marrying one of the volunteers, and now she's missing."

"Whose daughter?"

"Boris Petrovich's."

"Ah, yes. The nubile Natalie. I had first crack at her, you know."

Tess didn't like to show surprise—it was a fatal weakness—but she couldn't help being flustered. "Excuse me?"

"Petrovich showed her photo around our cell block, along with one of a friend. I don't remember the friend so well—she was a little coarse. But Natalie. You don't forget a face like that."

"What do you mean by 'first crack'?"

"Boris was pimping her."

"Bullshit. You can't pimp in prison, not to other prisoners."

"Ah, you're not quite as innovative an entrepreneur as our friend Boris. He had a whole fee schedule. You could get letters from her or photos in a variety of garb—or lack thereof. If you were willing to put more money in his account or slide a few more of your privileges his way, he'd offer to get the girls on your visiting list. The prices went up steeply from there, of course."

"Of course?"

"A hand job from a woman costs a lot more in prison than it does on the street. The old law of supply and demand."

"No way." But even as one part of Tess's mind was trying to knock the story down, the more calculating part was seeing how such an arrangement might work for prisoners who weren't in maximum security. She had been close enough to Boris to touch him—

not that she would—and the guards had been selective about what they noticed. It had taken Boris's sudden movement to get their attention.

"It's not very private, to be sure. And the guards draw the line at visitors going down on their knees. But groping is within bounds."

"Yeah, but he was her *father*. What kind of man would do that to his daughter?"

Kirsch shrugged. "A man who knew his daughter was a whore and figured he deserved a piece of whatever she earned. Once a pimp, always a pimp."

"I was told that Petrovich was a thief, who killed a man in a dispute."

"He did a thriving business in stolen goods, sure. But from what I understand—and I'm good at getting information, I'd be a decent private investigator myself—he killed a pimp who tried to take Natalie and her friend away from him. He didn't care if his daughter turned the occasional trick, but he sure as hell expected her to bring her earnings home every night."

"No way," Tess repeated. It was not that she found the information so unfathomable, more that her mind balked at taking this news back to Mark Rubin. Natalie, a teenage whore. And Lana must be the friend in question. The pool of possible traveling companions had just swelled tenfold, a hundredfold, to all Natalie's former tricks, or even her would-be pimp. No, he was dead, if Kirsch was to be trusted, killed by a father who resented the loss of income, as opposed to the loss of his daughter's innocence.

"Well, I have to admit, she opted out of the prison thing early on, stopped coming around at all. But her friend even married a guy. Boris must have gotten a bundle for that."

"One of the guys in the group?"

"Yep. Famous Amos, the world's biggest Jew. I told my mom about Amos, and she said he couldn't possibly be Jewish. But I think that's because he knew how to fix cars, not because of his size."

I was married once, Lana had told Tess, *for about six months*. No wonder she had found matrimony so dreary. Her groom had been locked up.

"Natalie was last seen in French Lick, Indiana, with a man of medium height and average looks. Dark hair, slender frame."

"Dark hair. Well, that lets me out, unless I was dipping into the Grecian Formula. French Lick, huh? I guess they must be hardcore Larry Bird fans."

Hirsch's unending supply of glib chatter was beginning to wear on Tess. If he was really worried about getting second dates, he should drop the Catskills-style delivery and try a moment or two of simple sincerity.

"Why did you sign up for the men's group anyway?" She couldn't help feeling aggrieved on her uncle's behalf, and Rubin's. They had been trying to do something worthwhile, and the only man who had valued their efforts was Mickey Harvey. Boris Petrovich was pimping, first to his fellow prisoners, then to Mark. The other guys were just passing time. "Everything seems like a big joke to you."

"I admit—at first it was just for the distraction. An Islamic fundamentalist might have signed up for that group, just to vary the routine a little. But I gotta tell you, it helped. Those guys reminded me that I came from a community, and although I had sinned against that community, I could work my way back if I tried."

"The prodigal son."

"No, that's New Testament, your people's gig. The Old Testament isn't quite as big on absolute forgiveness, but I had broken only one commandment. Well, two, because a drug is like a false god. Plus, I did a little coveting on the side."

"What about taking the Lord's name in vain? Keeping the Sabbath?"

"Four, five—the point is, it was good being reminded that I was a Jew. I didn't have a wife, I didn't have kids, and I sure as hell didn't have a career left as an accountant. But I was part of something that was bigger than me, and there was a comfort in that."

"Sounds like you did some twelve-stepping along the way."

"Still do. I catch a meeting once or twice a week. I've got an addictive personality. Then I realized almost *everyone* has an addictive personality. The trick is to peddle legal ones that don't particularly appeal to you. It came down to this or coffee." He held a cigar up to his nose, inhaling its aroma. "Of course, I'm late to a trend again, just like I was with cocaine. Cigar sales aren't what they used to be, and the Internet is kicking my ass. But I'm doing okay."

"Congratulations. And thank you for your time today."

"So . . ." He was back to full-bore-charm mode. "You ever date an ex-con? I may have embraced my heritage, but I've never quite lost the shiksa thing."

Tess didn't have the heart to tell him that she was not the goy of his dreams. "I sorta have a boyfriend."

"Sorta?"

"I mean, I have a boyfriend. He's just away right now, tending to some personal business."

"I don't know. Sounds like a Freudian slip to me, as if you'd be willing to *not* have a boyfriend under the right conditions."

"Yeah, well, sometimes a cigar is just a cigar."

"Not in this shop, sweetheart. Not in this shop."

25

For once Natalie held her ground and insisted on a motel at the top of their price range, which meant extras such as an indoor pool, a free breakfast buffet, and a coffeemaker in the room. After dinner in the restaurant—another meal that Isaac barely touched—she took the children down to the steamy, overheated pool room, letting them swim in T-shirts and underwear until their fingers were shriveled and their lips almost blue. It turned out that the pool's heater was faulty, so while the air was humid and sultry, the water temperature was colder than the Atlantic Ocean in June. But children never mind cold water, and she had to beg them to get out.

Back in the room, she hustled them into hot showers, surprising them afterward with cups of cocoa and hard little chocolate-chip cookies. The twins drank without comment, but Isaac wrinkled his nose.

"It tastes funny," he complained.

"You're just not used to instant," Natalie told him. "Put some more mini marshmallows in it, and it will taste richer."

Their cocoa gone, she tucked them into the bed farthest from the door. Penina was wearing pull-ups now, an utter defeat, but it was only fair to Efraim and Isaac. Natalie had bought another box of the pull-ups today, spending precious dollars at a discount department store not far from the motel. Married to Mark, she had barely noticed the price of anything. Now money seemed to be the only thing she thought about. Well, one of two things she thought about.

Worn out by the swim, lulled by the chocolate, the children fell asleep within minutes. Zeke, lying on the other bed, watching the television with the sound muted, saw that they were out and nodded at her, removing the phone's handset and dropping it in his pocket.

In the car they started out as they always did, giggling a bit, stroking each other's faces, feeling the glad relief of a moment when nothing was expected of them—no childish complaints or tears, no demands, no work to do, no people to deceive. But Zeke quickly moved ahead, urgent, keen to do what they had to do and get back in the room. He unzipped his pants, pushing Natalie's head down with the usual gentle pressure. But this time she slipped her neck from his hand and slid across the unbroken bench of the front seat, straddling him and positioning his hands so he could feel she was naked beneath her skirt.

"C'mon, baby," he said, trying to force her up and off him, but the steering wheel kept her in place. "We agreed. That has to wait until everything is perfect. A beautiful hotel suite, you in a silk gown. Candles, music. It won't be long now. Be patient."

"I don't want to wait anymore. If you insist on perfect, you're never going to have anything. Nothing is ever perfect. Besides, what's the difference between being in my mouth and being in my—" She paused, not wanting to ruin the mood by saying something too crude. "Between my mouth and between *me*?"

He was ready, more than ready. She felt the telltale twitch where she held him, as if Zeke's body were arguing with his head. Natalie began kissing him lightly—mouth, eyelids, ears. When he spoke again, his voice was faint, unconvinced.

"The kids—there's always a chance Isaac will try to make a run for it if we stay out too long. He's always looking for a chance to get away."

"His eyes won't open tonight. I put a little vodka in their cocoa."

"Really?" He put his hand up to her mouth, trying to push her back. She sucked his fingers, but he snatched his hand away and grabbed her chin so she had to look at him. "Where'd you get vodka?"

"At the shopping center, where I bought the cocoa and the pull-ups."

"So you had this all planned."

"I need you, Zeke."

"You have me. Don't you remember anything? Back at Jessup, visiting me? We held hands on the top of the table, not underneath. We held hands and we made our plans, and wasn't that a thousand times better than anything you ever felt before?"

"Yes, but . . . we're together now. There's no reason to wait anymore." She started to weep. "You don't love me. If you loved me, you would make love to me."

"I love you more than anyone has loved you or ever will. I love you so much that I won't let you treat me like one of the men you used to be with, back when you turned tricks in parking lots just so you'd have enough money to buy makeup and go to the movies."

"You always said you didn't mind, that you wouldn't hold that against me."

"I don't. But what we have has to be different."

"It's different, all right. Are you sure you're not a fag? Is that what happened to you in Terre Haute? You decided you like boys?"

He slapped her, and her tears were heavy enough to make her choke. She tried to get out of the car, but he seized her wrist. She wanted to rake her nails down his face, draw blood, show him that she would never again allow such treatment. Yet she was almost grateful for his hold on her because she honestly didn't know what would happen if he let her go. Her arms might go anywhere, strike anything, and there was no doubt in her mind that she could shatter the windows, the windshield, Zeke's face. Her own rages frightened her and she had tried hard, since the children were born, to control them. Zeke had brought them back. She could never be completely in control when Zeke was around.

"Just like my father," she said between hiccups. "Just like my father, the one thing you said you'd never do."

"You mustn't speak to me like that, ever," he said, holding tight to her wrist. "I can't allow that. Look, you're stressed out, it's understandable. You've been a trouper. All I ask is that you be patient for a few more weeks."

"Weeks? How many weeks? What is it that we have to wait for?"

"Just for some details to be worked out. Trust me. Have I ever lied to you?"

The fact was, he had not. Once, just once, he had withheld something from her, but even that had been from love, for love. Zeke had not trusted her with the information about his federal time at first, fearing that Natalie wouldn't allow herself to love him if she knew. But that wasn't really a lie.

"Have I ever wavered in my love for you? Did I ever give up?"

His voice was pitched low now, husky. This was the voice that had come to her in hundreds of arranged phone calls over the year, collect calls made to Lana's number. The complicated plans and timetables that these conversations had required had been as thrilling as a spy movie to Natalie. It got to the point where her blood would race just looking at a phone.

"When we met, you'd already had sex with dozens and dozens of men. Did those men love you?"

Natalie shook her head.

"For the past ten years, you've been married to a man who thinks he loves you, but he loves a person we made up, you and I. Would Mark Rubin love you as you are, if he knew everything about you? Would he forgive what I've forgiven?"

She rubbed her face against his shirt front, saying no and drying her tears at the same time.

"Who loves you?"

"You do."

"Who will always love you?"

"You, Zeke, you."

"Who do you love?" Almost singing it now. "Who do you love?"

"You, Zeke, you."

It was an old refrain, one repeated in letters and telephone calls.

"Did your mother love you?"

"No."

"Your father?"

"No."

"Does anyone else love you as much as I do?"

She broke the ritual. "The children."

Zeke paused. "Yes, the children. The ones you drugged tonight, so you could come out here and crawl all over me. The children love you, Natalie. But do you love them? Really, truly?"

"Of course I do."

"Don't be so quick. Think about what I'm asking. If you had to choose between me and them, who would you choose, Natalie?"

"Don't ask me that. I could never make that choice."

"I won't, Natalie. But Mark will. He'll never let them be with you and me. And he has all that money, which he'll use to hire lawyers and grind you down. In the end you won't have your children, but you and I will be out whatever cash we've managed to put away. Did that even occur to you?"

"They're mine," she said. "They would be lost without me."

"Well, then, I guess you've made your choice. Them over me."

"I didn't *say* that."

"Natalie—I'm going to be honest. I'm not sure I can love Mark's children like a father. I think they'd be better off with him, with their real father."

"They like you," she said. And she believed they would, one day, when they were settled. Isaac would come to see how extraordinary Zeke was, and Penina would stop wetting herself, and the twins would give up the gibberish they now spoke most of the time.

"But I'm not their father, and they're not my children. I want my own children. Did you know that? I want my own babies with you." He reached under her skirt, began moving his hand back and forth. She tried to resist it, but their routine was so perfected, so efficient, that it took no more than a minute for him to finish her.

"Okay," he said, signaling that it was her turn to do the same for him. She bent down, her tears still fresh in her mouth, a pulse pounding in her temple. He needed her.

Wednesday

26

Tess moved her Alden across the water with swift, sure strokes, but rowing could not soothe her this morning. Even as her body found peace in the automatic rhythms, her brain revved, like an engine in overdrive, stuck on one thought. She had promised not to reveal to Rubin anything that Boris Petrovich told her. But she had made no such promises about the men in the group. So where did Larry Kirsch's confidences fit in? Her shell skimmed across the water, and the morning sounds all seemed to coalesce into a refrain of advice: *Call him. Call him. Call him. Tell him. Tell him. Tell him.*

She did the first part, reaching him on his cell when she got off the water at seven, but her resolve crumbled when she heard the eagerness in his voice, the optimism.

"Did you find out anything?"

"Not much," she said. "But the men all spoke so fondly of you, I can't help thinking that Amos would open up more if you came with me to Grantsville." *Open up and tell you that your wife was sort of a whore before she met you, which would keep me from having to inform you of same.*

"Really?" His voice seemed to brighten. "The men liked the group?"

"Really. And this may be a key interview. The one person who keeps coming up, wherever I go, is Lana Wishnia—she was even on your father-in-law's visiting list—and she was married to Amos briefly. Plus, Mickey Harvey said Amos was tight with your father-in-law as well. So I think it's worth the three-hour drive, if you can afford a day away from work."

"I have to make a trip to our storage facility, which is out near Finksburg but sort of en route. Could you be there within an hour?"

"I'll meet you there," Tess promised.

What would she do if Amos didn't conveniently drop the bombshell she needed him to drop? What were the ethics of withholding information from a client, in hopes that someone else would be the bearer of bad news? Tess thought about asking the SnoopSisters, then decided against it. The only problem with the Sisters was that they tended to say what they really thought.

The Robbins & Sons warehouse stood on a frontage road along I-795, just inside Carroll County. The area had probably been farmland as recently as a decade ago, and there were still cornfields to three sides of the plain rectangular building. There was nothing to identify the unmarked structure as the furrier's storage facility, a prudent decision in Tess's opinion. Why advertise the off-season home of hundreds of fur coats? But Tess wondered if she had come to the right place when she noticed that the only car in the lot was a pale green Jaguar, a sporty two-seater. Rubin usually drove a dark blue Cadillac Seville. Yet it was Rubin who emerged from the building, locking a series of dead bolts behind him, then testing the door to make sure the warehouse was secure.

"A Jaguar?" she asked.

"It was my fortieth-birthday gift to myself." He had the good sense to look a little sheepish. "I don't drive it as much as I thought I would, so I figured it could use a nice long spell of highway driving. Sorry to get you up so early, but if we get there by noon, we could be back by four or five—give me a chance to check on the store before closing."

"I've been up since six, putting in an hour on the water." Tess ran her fingers through her hair, still damp and curly from her quick shower.

"On the water?"

"I rowed in college, and I still work out in a single, although I don't compete anymore."

"College crew, very preppy. Have you heard about the crew team at Yeshiva University?"

"I didn't even know they had one."

"Oh, yes, but they were terrible for years. So they finally decided to send their captain to Cambridge, see how the Ivy League schools do it, and it changed everything for them."

"How so?"

"The captain came back and said"—Rubin smacked his forehead with his palm, in the style of a man having an epiphany—"'It's supposed to be *eight* people rowing and *one* person yelling'."

Tess was so unaccustomed to Rubin's making jokes that it took her a bewildered moment to laugh. But he was clearly pleased by her guffaw, belated though it might be.

"A crew-Jew joke! You're in a good mood this morning."

"It's a pretty day, got that nice crisp autumn feel. And it feels good to be doing something. I was wrong not to tell you about Natalie's father, I see that now. I was so wrapped up in the idea that it was a *shanda*, something I must never speak of outside the family. But he didn't tell you anything, did he?"

"No, he didn't."

"So I was crazy, all those years, worrying about nothing. What a waste."

Burdened with the information she was keeping from Rubin, Tess could only nod noncommittally.

The Jaguar drove the way that Tess's greyhound sometimes ran when seized by memories of the track—smooth and fast, with a kind of carefree rhapsody.

"My midlife-crisis car," Rubin said, almost apologetic. "And, of course, I couldn't buy German."

"Of course? Oh, of course. I get to thinking that all cars are the same, mere modes of transportation. But this really is a different ride from my fourteen-year-old Toyota."

"Do you want to try it?"

"No, I'd be too nervous behind the wheel of something whose value exceeds my net worth."

"It's not *that* dear."

"And my net worth isn't that high."

They had already covered over ninety miles, reaching the point where the roads, shaped by the demands of the Appalachians, started to climb and curve. Mark Rubin was relishing the drive as much as the car. In sunglasses, his usual dark suit and tie—shirt immaculate, thick hair gleaming—he had an almost James Bond–like savoir faire, Tess thought. Assuming one could imagine James Bond wearing a yarmulke.

"I have to ask you something," she said.

"'Have to'—that construction actually means a person wants to ask something but knows it's rude."

"Not rude, but naïve perhaps. Anyway, the yarmulke—what's the point?"

"It reminds me that God is always above me."

"You could wear a hat. Besides, if you need a piece of cloth to remind you where God is, how sturdy is your faith?"

"At some point rituals cannot be deconstructed. The acceptance of ritual is part of faith. Why take communion? Why bow to the east in prayer?"

"I don't do any of those things, but at least they can be done in private. A yarmulke—it *announces* you're a Jew."

"So?"

"So did six-pointed stars pinned to jackets, and everyone agrees those were a bad idea."

"One is a choice, the other an attempt to stigmatize."

"But having made the choice, you single yourself out, which can lead people to stigmatize you anyway."

"Single myself out? There are more than a hundred thousand Jews in the Baltimore area. I'm far from alone."

"I mean—the yarmulke tells everyone you're Jewish, which invites everything you do to be viewed through the prism of all sorts of prejudices and judgments." Tess was thinking about how tough he had been in negotiation, the day she had overheard him on the phone. His contact in Montreal probably ascribed Rubin's behavior to his religion—assuming the Montreal supplier wasn't a Jew himself. "Don't you ever want to pass through the world anonymously, responsible for only yourself?"

"Look, Tess, I can take my yarmulke off, but what will that gain me? Do you think that Mark Rubin—seller of furs, resident of Pikesville, owner of a striking yet prominent nose"—he thrummed the tip of said nose with an index finger—"is going to pass? I've never wanted to be anyone but who I am. No offense, but your views on religion are a little warped."

"Warped?"

"Maybe that's too strong a word. But—you'll forgive me a little dime-store psychology—just because you like to have it both ways doesn't mean everyone else wants to play the same game."

"What do you mean?" He had, however accidentally, echoed an accusation made against Tess not long ago, although in a different context.

"You like this game you play, shifting between identities, confusing people. With me, you act like a shiksa naïf. But I bet when it suits you, when you're around more unambiguously goyish types, you play the Jew."

He had scored a bull's-eye, but Tess didn't see any reason to concede his point.

"I'm not *playing* anything. I'm legitimately stranded between two religions."

"Do you believe in God?"

"That's awfully personal."

Rubin laughed. It was the first time Tess had heard *his* laugh, and it was full-bodied, extremely appealing, the kind of laugh that made her want to keep saying funny things.

"Tess, you've asked me about my marriage, my sex life, my wife's convict father, and my finances. I think I'm entitled to ask whether you believe in God."

"Okay, okay. I . . . do."

"Why?"

"I'm not sure I could explain it."

"Maybe there's *your* yarmulke."

"I don't get it."

"Think about it."

Tess might have said something more, but as they crossed the next summit, the horizon turned gray-green and the air changed perceptibly. A sudden drenching rainstorm began moments later, a downpour so complete that visibility was reduced to virtually nothing. The scenario happened to match one of Tess's recurring nightmares, one in which she was driving but could not see—because of weather or simply because her eyes refused to open.

"Pull over," she urged Rubin in a tight, dry voice.

"It's safer to keep going, as long as I can see the taillights of the car ahead."

"Yeah, assuming *he's* still on the road. You could follow him right off the side of the mountain, too."

Rubin did not bother to reply, just drove in grim silence. The freak storm lasted no more than a minute or two, but Tess spent every endless second awaiting a plunge over the side of the highway or the sudden jolt of a runaway truck on the Jaguar's bumper. She would have felt so much better if she were behind the wheel.

The rain ended as abruptly as it began, stopping completely instead of tapering off. Over the next few miles, Tess and Mark passed dozens of cars on the shoulder—cars with crumpled fronts or crushed backs, surrounded by dazed-looking people. At least no one appeared to have been badly injured.

"See?" Mark said.

"See what?"

"They pulled over and ended up having accidents."

"You don't know that. They could have pulled over after the collisions."

"Do you always insist on having the last word?"

Tess opened her mouth, saw the trap he had set for her, and shut it, shaking her head emphatically instead. Rubin's laugh boomed out again, but she could not quite recapture the pleasant mood. The rain had seemed prophetic, a reminder that they had crossed some unseen boundary and all natural laws were now suspended.

Amos Greif lived outside Grantsville on a large farm, a place of several hundred acres judging by the long expanse of barbed-wire fence that fronted the roadway. NO TRESPASSING signs were posted every few feet, and when the Jaguar turned into the long, dirt driveway, two mutts raced it for much of the way, dropping out only because the distance was so great, almost two miles by the odometer.

Tess hummed a few lines from the old *Deliverance* banjo duet.

"Are you sure this guy is Jewish?" she asked Rubin.

"In his own way, yes."

"How did a car thief ever make a living in Grantsville? It's pretty small."

"Amos ran a chop shop out here, dismantling cars stolen from Baltimore and Pittsburgh—and who knows what else. I think he took care of the paperwork, too."

"One-stop shopping. How convenient."

Amos was standing on his porch by the time they reached the top of the hill, probably alerted by the dogs and the Jaguar's noisy approach. He was the biggest man Tess had ever seen—maybe six foot eight and at least three hundred pounds, massive but not fat. He was perhaps the one person who really could attribute his weight to being big-boned. He also looked like he never quite came clean, although not for lack of trying. Perhaps there was just too much of him to wash, and too many places he couldn't see.

Tess and Mark got out of the car but lingered behind the Jaguar's open doors, unsure of their welcome.

"So," Amos said, "the mountain comes to Muhammad."

Tess looked across the roof of the car at Rubin, who seemed equally mystified by the greeting. They had literally come to the mountains, and the man on the porch was far more mountainlike than either of them.

"It's been a long time, Amos. You look well."

This generous description didn't lure Amos forward or even convince him to unfold his huge, muscled arms. "Why are you here?"

"Miss Monaghan is helping me look for my wife and children, who have been missing since before Labor Day. During her investigation she discovered that Natalie had a friend, Lana Wishnia. Tess tells me you were once married to Lana, and that you may have been a confidante of my father-in-law as well. You remember him, Boris Petrovich? I couldn't help thinking—well, hoping—that you knew something, anything, about Natalie's whereabouts. If either one of them told you anything . . ."

Amos just kept staring, assessing them.

"There's money for you," Tess said, "if you know something."

Rubin nodded. "Absolutely. I'd pay dearly for any information that led me to my family."

"Wait here," Amos said, in a tone that made it unthinkable to do anything else. He turned his back on them and disappeared inside the little farmhouse with a slam of the screen door. He hadn't done much to prettify it, but the wood-frame building was well tended.

Tess and Mark were left where they stood, car still idling, its open doors like wings on a green metallic bug. Tess would not be surprised if the Jaguar proved to have magical powers, à la Chitty Chitty Bang Bang, capable of taking them through the sky or across the water. There was no trace in the air of the strange weather they had passed through. The sky was a cloudless blue again, clear enough to see miles in all directions.

"You can see three states from here," Rubin said, "if you know where to look."

Tess didn't even try to make conversation. She was too busy worrying that Amos, not exactly a garrulous sort, wasn't going to let her off the hook. How would she ever tell Rubin what Larry Kirsch had said about Natalie? Perhaps it wasn't even true. She should get at least one more source to verify the information.

"My property's posted," Amos announced, coming back on the porch. "Which means I'm entitled to do this."

He had a shotgun in his arms, and he leveled it at Rubin, taking aim. Even then Tess did not quite believe he meant to shoot them. It was a warning, an order to leave, nothing more. A little over the top, but country people were touchy about property rights.

"A job done is a job done," Amos said, more to himself than them, his finger on the trigger.

Did Rubin scream for Tess to duck? If so, she never heard the warning, falling instinctively to the ground behind the open door before Amos fired and scrambling for her gun, worn on her belt today. She had spent a lot of time working on her marksmanship over the summer, and those hours of practice paid off. She positioned herself and pulled her gun out as automatically as she might hit the snooze button on her alarm clock, albeit with more alertness.

Yet as quickly as she had moved, Rubin had moved faster still, diving into the car from his side, banging open the glove compartment and grabbing a gun. Holding the weapon in his left hand, he reached through the passenger door and pushed Tess's head down with his right, using so much force she almost ate a mouthful of gravel. He then shot his onetime acolyte square in the chest, catching him just as he fired, sending the shotgun blast into the porch roof.

Amos dropped his shotgun, but he continued to stand for several long, agonizing seconds, swaying slightly, as if it took a while for his massive body to transfer the news of his injury to his nervous system. Finally, with a confused yet almost respectful look for Mark Rubin, he fell to the floor of his porch.

Tess and Rubin remained huddled together, listening to each other breathe. After a few seconds, he pulled himself away from her and began brushing dirt and dust from his suit. He approached the porch, his weapon drawn, walking around Amos's huge body, then kneeling down to take his pulse at the neck. Mark's lips moved, and Tess assumed he was reciting a prayer, perhaps a kaddish. Even so, Tess approached the porch with great caution, her own gun in hand.

A thousand questions occurred to her, but she settled for perhaps the least important. "Why in hell do you have that gun?"

"I always carry a gun when I go to the storage facility or transport furs. One of my father's ways of saving money."

"But I mean . . . it's not just any gun." She recognized the pistol from her own recent gun-shopping days, when she had decided to upgrade to the Beretta. "It's a SIG Sauer. A German gun."

"Swiss-German, actually."

"Still, for a man who wouldn't even consider owning a BMW . . ."

"Oh." He shrugged. "They do some things very well."

27

The Garrett County authorities were polite, almost pains-takingly so, to "that girl and that Jew who killed Amos," as Tess overheard one deputy say to another. The tone was innocuous, the meaning clear: They were outsiders who had killed a local. Just their luck, Amos Greif was well liked in his hometown, if only because he kept to himself and paid his property taxes. And if he had come out of prison less than rehabilitated, as a cursory ex-amination of his house seemed to indicate, at least Grantsville was only a staging area for his auto-theft network. Amos Greif was a good neighbor. He left the local cars alone.

Luckily, Tyner knew a Cumberland lawyer willing to safeguard their rights on short notice. Tess had learned through sorry experi-ence that there was no percentage in talking to authorities without a lawyer present, *especially* when she was innocent. The lawyer arrived quickly, and by the time the sun went down over West Virginia, the sheriff had decided to let Tess and Mark Rubin leave, although he reminded them that they would be expected to return for grand jury proceedings. But Tyner's friend said she knew the state's attorney and he was likely to recommend no indictment under the circumstances. Tess and Mark were licensed gun owners on legitimate business, and their stories meshed with the physical evidence at the scene.

"It would have been better," said the lawyer, Gloria Hess, "if you hadn't gone inside his house after you shot him. But I still think you'll both be okay."

She was a tall, striking brunette, gorgeous enough so that even Mark seemed to register the fact, shaking her hand with a faintly dazed look. It occurred to Tess that Tyner's legal contacts all tended to be lookers.

"I had to call 911, and it's hard to get service on my cell out here," Tess told Gloria. "You have to admit, Greif's behavior made more sense after the deputies saw what was in his house. Clearly it wasn't trespassing he was worried about."

The deputies had opened a closed door off the central hallway and discovered a state-of-the-art forger's shop, with a gleaming photocopier and templates for all sorts of documents—temporary tags, titles, driver's licenses. There also were meticulous files, kept in restored oak filing cabinets, showing price lists for certain parts and in-demand vehicles, broken down by region. Another folder yielded voluminous correspondence about firearms, but this appeared to be legal—up to a point. Greif was the registered owner of hundreds of handguns, but the only weapon the deputies turned up was the shotgun he had died holding.

The deputies were impressed by their find, so Tess had pretended to be, too, despite having seen it all, and more. She wished she had thought to shut down Greif's computer—with the flick of a finger, the deputies could have traced her frantic path through it in the minutes before they arrived. She had searched documents for references to Natalie and the children, started and quit all the recent applications. The last thing she did was click on Greif's America Online account.

"What's the use?" Rubin hissed from the door, where he was keeping watch. "You can't get into his e-mail without his password."

"But I can get into his address book." She opened it up and was grateful to discover that Greif had stored only five addresses.

The first four, all Hotmail accounts, meant nothing to her. Tess jotted them down, knowing that a computer-savvy type could discern a lot from mere addresses.

The last address was for Wishnia, Lana, with an AOL user name of SlavicBeautee. And the comment box included the P.O. Box at the Reisterstown mail store where Tess had followed her that first day.

Tess quit the program, scooting out of the room and into the front hallway just moments before the deputies climbed the porch steps and began walking around the considerable corpse left there. Contemplating the lifeless form, Tess had felt nothing, or close to it. Her only regret about Greif's death was that he had taken whatever he knew with him.

"I'm sorry." They were passing the ballpark outside Frederick, home to the Keys, dark this time of year.

"Sorry for what?" Mark said, glancing longingly at the park. "I took Isaac there once. It's a great little stadium."

"I'm sorry you had to kill a man today. You should have let me do it, given that I already have one on my scorecard."

"There really wasn't time to sort it out. I've gotten so used to the fact that you carry a gun that I forgot about it. I suppose we could have done the Alphonse and Gaston thing: 'After you. No, after you. No, I insist, after you.' But we'd both be dead by now."

Tess smiled, feeling through her jeans for the bumpy scar on her knee. She had bruised it when Mark threw her down, and she couldn't help feeling it might burst open once again, exposing the bone. Of all the things she had seen in her life, few had made her queasier than a glimpse of bone inside in her own knee.

"Any idea what he meant, about the mountain coming to Muhammad, or a job done being a job done?"

"I'm not sure *he* knew what he meant. Maybe he had just taken an order for some hard-to-get Jaguar parts. It does seem that the only thing Amos learned in prison was how to run his criminal enterprises with more technological finesse."

"Are you disappointed that he didn't change? You spent all that time visiting Jessup, trying to help these guys, and he goes right back to his old ways."

"I did it as much for myself as for them. That's the nasty little secret about charity. We do it for ourselves."

"Well, sure, if it's just some onetime thing. I read in the newspaper once that the local soup kitchens dread Thanksgiving because all these dilettantes come out of the woodwork, determined to hand out platters of sweet potatoes so they can then go home and watch football while enveloped in a saintly glow. The writer called it 'the one-day philanthropy fix.' But you're not one of those people."

"Still, my motives were largely selfish."

"How so?"

Rubin hesitated. "You've heard me speak of a *shanda*?"

"With Natalie's father, right. It means 'shame.' "

"It's bigger than shame in some ways. I grew up surrounded by relatives who really did evaluate everything on the basis of whether it was good for the Jews or bad for the Jews. Hank Greenberg? Good for the Jews. Michael Milken? Bad for the Jews. We were responsible not just for ourselves but for every Jew, and the bad always outweighed the good. When I . . . became aware of the Jewish men in Maryland's prison system, I felt I should do something. My own father . . ." His voice trailed off.

"Was your father in prison?"

"Oh, God, no. *No.* But there was gossip, ugly gossip, about his business and his money. My stepmother was very well fixed. And, truth be told, my father had a little gonif in him. That means—"

"Thief," Tess said. "I've read everything Philip Roth has ever written."

"Roth. That self-loathing monster, projecting his own problems onto an entire people."

"Read *The Ghost Writer* and *American Pastoral*, then get back to me. What about your father?"

"I told you it was my dad's idea for us to offer lifetime storage to his customers at a discounted rate. What I didn't tell you is that the original building was just an old, crummy warehouse in downtown Baltimore. No climate control, nothing. He figured that most people wouldn't know if their coats had been properly stored, and if one got damaged, he would just replace it and still be ahead financially. It was a gamble, and it paid off. But it was dishonest, taking money from people to put their furs in that nasty old building. When I came on as his partner, I insisted on the new warehouse. It was a big capital expense, but I wanted to make up for all the years my father ripped people off."

"You're not responsible for your dad."

"You're wrong about that. I'm responsible for my dad, and my family. As you pointed out this morning, everywhere I go, people see a Jew, first and foremost. So I have to live an exemplary life."

"Is there an element of shame in the fact that Natalie left you?"

He nodded, his eyes on the road. "Absolutely. If I were a good husband, she never would have gone. Clearly, I failed her in some way."

"Not necessarily."

"Necessarily. I've told you we had no problems, and that was true. But if she left me to keep me from learning something about her . . . well, that's my failure, too. Somehow she came to believe that she couldn't be completely honest with me, that she couldn't trust my love for her."

"Maybe Natalie isn't the person you thought she was. Maybe she's concealing something far worse than you could ever imagine."

"She's the mother of my children. What else matters? We're the adults, we can work out whatever we need to work out. But children are better off when their parents stay together."

They drove for a few more miles in silence. Tess saw an ad for a real-estate agent, one in which two giant hands shook and sealed a deal for a little piece of the American dream.

"You touched me today," she said.

"What?"

"You pushed my head down. Before you—"

"Any Jewish law can be suspended if a person's life is in danger."

"Yeah, but you shook Gloria Hess's hand, too. Didn't hesitate."

He had the good grace to blush. "In business a man has to shake hands sometimes."

"So why did you make such a show of not shaking mine the first time I offered it?"

"You offered it and withdrew it before I could do anything. In that moment . . . well, I didn't think it would be such a bad thing if you were a little off balance."

"You mean you thought it would be good if I felt tentative enough that I didn't ask too many hard questions. What else are you keeping from me, Mark?" Tess realized with a start it was the first time she had used his first name. He had been "Mr. Rubin" to her in conversation, "Rubin" in her head. Nothing like a little justifiable homicide to bring two people closer.

"Nothing. Absolutely nothing. What are you keeping from me?"

"Nothing. Absolutely nothing."

Tess wondered if Mark were lying, too.

The countryside was fading away and the suburbs, with their diffuse, fuzzy lights, came rushing toward them. Mark Rubin was not as delusional as Tess had once thought. He had sought the assistance of a private detective, insisting there were no overt problems in his marriage, convinced that some secret had cost him the life he knew. Almost everything Tess had learned so far supported this original theory. Natalie did have a secret. And her father, used to getting a cut of whatever Natalie made, had tried to blackmail her. Mark Rubin had been stalwart enough not to peek under the lid of that Pandora's box. For a decade, that had granted Natalie a reprieve from her scheming father. But now Boris had a new buyer for his information. If Natalie cared for Mark, would she rationalize that leaving him was the only way to save him?

Then where did the mystery man fit in? And was a desire to protect his criminal enterprises the only reason that Amos Greif had produced that shotgun, clearly ready to kill them both? The mountain had come to Muhammad. Mark was the mountain. Greif had been expecting to see him, only not today, not on his property.

"Lana's the key," Tess said, thinking out loud. "I'm going to follow her tomorrow, see where she leads us."

"Can I come along?"

"You have a business to run. Besides, that's not very professional. You hired me to do this stuff. I don't need anyone riding shotgun." Mark grimaced. "Sorry, poor choice of words. You know, you should . . . see someone."

"I should start dating while I'm still looking for my wife?"

"No, I mean . . . what you did today. It will stay with you in ways you might not expect. Even when there's no choice, when it's you or him, it leaves a mark."

"So you think I should go to counseling?"

"Yes."

"Is that what you did?"

"More or less." Tess had already been in counseling, for unrelated reasons, but she'd been smart enough to realize she needed the therapist's help.

"Well, if you had a God, maybe you could have talked to him and prayed to him. And saved yourself a little money in the process."

"God is great, and God is good," Tess intoned. "But he can't get you prescription drugs."

It was after ten when Tess arrived home, and the dogs were almost hysterical, although she had arranged for a neighbor boy to walk and feed them when she realized she wouldn't be back until late. They were probably scared she had simply left, never to be seen again.

After all, Crow had.

He had been gone less than a month, but even a day was an eternity to Esskay and Miata. Or perhaps they had sussed out, from the tenor of the conversations in the house in the days before he left, that Crow didn't plan on coming back.

Sure, he had left some clothes behind, along with various objects that he would want eventually—CDs, art supplies, a Swiffer. But he wasn't going to come through the door at 2:00 A.M. anymore and slide into bed next to Tess, pirating her warmth. He wasn't around to take over the kitchen, impulsively swept up in his need to make a soufflé or risotto. Crow being Crow, he wasn't the type of boyfriend to wreck a kitchen and leave the mess to his girlfriend. He cleaned up as he went, so there was relatively little to do at the end of one of his meals. When Tess once asked why he was so considerate, he said, "After I've made someone dinner, I don't want her expending all her energy on the kitchen. I want her to focus her goodwill on me." He was, as her friend Whitney had once observed, the perfect postmodern boyfriend.

So why had Tess balked when he suggested that she promote him to perfect postmodern husband?

The proposal, such as it was, had come on a perfect summer night late in August, as they walked the dogs through the deepening dusk. There had been a sudden change in the air, and although the nights were still warm, it was clear the sultry summer was losing its grip. Tess had been meandering along with Miata, so docile and easy to walk, while Crow had been holding on to Esskay, who had a major chip on her bony shoulder when it came to all other living creatures. Squirrels, rabbits, cats, other dogs, fast-moving pieces of paper—Esskay lunged at anything that moved.

"She's like that cartoon character—the little cat—who's always saying, 'Let me at 'em, let me at 'em,' " Tess observed, then felt stupid for having such lowbrow cultural references. Why couldn't she allude to Dickens with the same alacrity with which she cited cartoons?

"She's like you," Crow said.

"That's nice."

"Just an affectionate observation. Actually, you're not quite as thin-skinned as you were when we met. But you used to go at the world that way, always expecting dissent and antagonism."

"And I was right, most of the time."

"Do you think I've been good for you?"

Esskay had dragged Crow from the path, intent on sniffing the base of a tree, so Tess could not see his face just then.

"Probably."

"Do you think we should get married?"

Perhaps it was the fact that Tess could not see his face, or perhaps it was the near dark, which seemed to make everything portentous, so that the consequences of a lie seemed more grave than usual. At any rate, she said what she was thinking, swiftly and regretfully: "No."

Three days of arguing followed, disputes notable only by the universality of the clichés thrown back and forth: *You're afraid to commit. Marriage is just a meaningless legal construct, in which two people agree to pool all their stuff, so they can pay lawyers to split it up seven years later. If it's so meaningless, why not just humor me and do it?*

It would be wrong to say they were relieved when the call came from Charlottesville with the news that Crow's mother had a cancerous lump in her breast. But the family emergency did grant them a reprieve from their own problems. Within a week Crow had called with the glad news that his mother had received the best possible prognosis, but he wanted to stay with his parents for a while, perhaps audit a few courses at UVA. Tess had accepted the decision for the gracious, passive cease-fire she assumed it was.

Was she happy, was she free? The question was not so absurd.

She was free, but miserable. She didn't want to live without Crow, but she didn't want to live with him if that meant being a wife. She wasn't sure she wanted to be anyone's wife. She tried to graft the details of marriage and family onto her life, and they just didn't fit. She imagined herself on surveillance, a fractious baby in a car seat. She saw herself trying to tiptoe out of the house in the morning, en route to her 7:00 A.M. row, only to have a child demanding its due. Unlike a dog, a child would not be content with a quick walk and a biscuit.

But in the end Tess said no because she suspected that Crow had asked for all the wrong reasons. Frightened by her brush with death this past spring, he wanted to protect her, care for her, keep her safe. Which was admirable, lovable even. It was not, however, a good reason to get married. That's what she had been trying to figure out all along, but Crow had run away before she could find the words. Now she was too proud to pick up the phone and ask him to come back, and he was . . . well, who knew what he was? Crow's enthusiasms had always come and gone so quickly. Why should she trust his love for her, when he had a mandolin and a bread machine gathering dust in various cupboards?

So on the night of the day she watched Mark Rubin kill a man, Tess walked her dogs down that same dark path and wondered if she was ever going to get her life right. It was beginning to seem like a Rubik's Cube, in which the colors—love, work, family, self—never lined up.

And unlike the toy she had owned as a child, her life couldn't be pounded into the floor until it was a satisfying pile of multicolored plastic.

Thursday

28

Zeke was distracted when they entered the city limits of New Troy, Ohio, not that the fact would have registered with him even under normal circumstances. The only thing that announced the town was a small sign, the paint faded and battered, with the usual Lions Club and Knights of Columbus insignias fastened to the post. The old state highway continued as rutted and cracked as it had been outside the town's limits, and the scenery was the now-familiar mix of broken-up farms and fast-food places, interspersed with the occasional nondescript warehouse. Even if he had been focusing on the world around him, he wouldn't have noticed New Troy, and it wouldn't have mattered if he had. Later he would remind himself of this fact over and over again. It wasn't his fault. There was nothing he could have done.

As it was, he was barely aware that he was driving, that he was in

Ohio or even on planet Earth. Natalie was haranguing him about the early start, asking what the rush was when they didn't have to work that day, but he just tuned her out. The twins were gibbering in that weird-ass secret language, which usually drove him up a wall, but their noise could have been birdsong this morning. He had been in a fog since eight-thirty last night, after stopping at a library right before closing and checking the e-mail account Lana had set up for him on Hotmail. Under a blank subject heading, Lana had written these words: **Amos is dead.**

It was a punch to the gut, another fucking contingency to roll with, when he'd been doing nothing but rolling since Natalie showed up in Terre Haute with three kids in tow. He wished he could talk it out, share his troubles with someone. Amos dead, everything ruined. But how could he explain to Natalie that the plan to kill Mark was now hopelessly fucked, when Natalie didn't even know there *was* a plan to kill Mark? Not even Lana knew that part. All she had been promised was that she would eventually be repaid for all the favors she had done Zeke over the years.

He had a thousand questions for Lana, but he made it a rule to never send e-mail from the account. He was no Luddite, but the Internet was one of those things that had sprung up while he was inside, and he didn't know how much of a trail it left. He didn't want to call Lana collect either, given that a private detective was already nosing around asking questions about Natalie. If he really needed to talk to her, he could always buy a phone card, use it, and throw it away. But with money tight, he hated to part with even ten miserable dollars.

Amos *dead*. Unthinkable. It was like some huge tree coming down in a storm, or a mountain collapsing. Amos shot to death on his own farm, which seemed even more unlikely. The Garrett County authorities were carrying it as a homicide, Lana had written in her dry, just-the-facts style, but it was expected to be ruled self-defense. A man and a woman had been questioned, and they were quite persuasive in their insistence that Amos had tried to kill them. The sheriff's office wouldn't release the names to Lana—her status as an ex-wife didn't give her that much clout—and the online version of the Cumberland newspaper hadn't posted anything as of last night. So Zeke was left to figure it out on his own. Had Amos panicked, believing that the pair were undercover cops onto his illegal enterprises? But Amos, much as he had hated prison, would have gambled on short time rather than risk big time for killing someone in law enforcement. Plus, he knew his rights. He wouldn't have feared anyone who didn't show him a warrant.

"The speed limit is thirty-five here," Natalie said. "You better slow down."

They had found Lana's name in Amos's papers. Messy and disheveled as he was about his appearance, he had always been meticulous about his affairs. Apparently he kept a folder with all the paperwork pertaining to their brief union. They had stayed friendly, if not friends, because Lana had been gracious enough to claim it was the farm she couldn't live with, not Amos. But even thick-skinned Amos must have known that Lana just couldn't hack sleeping with him. It was one thing to help a guy out in prison, to get so carried away with Zeke and Natalie's romance that she ended up marrying some poor geek so she wouldn't be left behind. Lana was always trying to do what Natalie did, and always getting it a little bit wrong. But it was quite another kettle of fish, as Zeke's father would say, to live with the guy once he got out, especially in godforsaken Grantsville.

Shit, what else was in Amos's papers? Did he keep records of the jobs he did, computer templates for the various things he forged? What if they found copies of the driver's license he had manufactured for Natalie, or the title to this car, or information about the contraband that now sat in a shoe box between Natalie's feet? Even the strictly legal stuff, like the temporary tags, could be a problem if Natalie's real name surfaced anywhere. Then again, it wasn't an open investigation. With Amos dead, there was no real reason to look into his business. That would just be more paperwork for everybody.

Only with Amos gone, who was going to kill Mark? It was another body blow to Zeke's perfect plan. First Natalie shows up, which was bad enough, but with the kids as well, which was a fucking nightmare. Still, Zeke had figured that when Mark was finally killed, he could send Natalie and the kids back with a carefully rehearsed story, one that omitted any mention of him. A runaway wife, even one who claimed to be brutalized in order to get welfare checks, would go home to bury her husband properly. It would have been tricky—the more Natalie had to do, the trickier things got—but it would have worked.

Now Amos was dead, killed just days before he was supposed to kill Mark. Did Boris know anyone that Zeke could use, much less trust? Zeke couldn't risk getting in touch with him, not while he was in prison. Besides, Boris would just want to know when they were going to deposit the money they had been promising him, ever since he threatened to tell Mark about Zeke and Natalie. He couldn't turn to Lana, because she told Natalie everything. The bottom line is that being an outlaw wasn't Lana's gig, despite her association with Boris, her marriage to Amos. She was just a follower. Left to her own devices, Lana would have been content with her dull life, painting fingernails and toes, having a Friday-night splurge at some tacky chain restaurant on Reisterstown Road. Acting as Zeke's intermediary had been the little bit of spice she'd needed. She was the eternal plain girl, the second banana, one of those strange women that always seemed to pop up in the movies, living only to support and bolster the star.

"Do I have to work again today?" Natalie demanded, her voice somehow piercing the fog in his head.

"Got to do your bit at least. We're scraping bottom."

"It's so hard, remembering all those dates. And you know how these women look at you, when you can't say your babies' birthdays bam, bam, bam? Like you're a bad mother, that's how. Last time I forgot, I used the real ones by mistake."

"You have to use the fake ones, Natalie," he said, pretending a patience he didn't feel. "Fake names and fake dates. We've been over this."

"Why? What difference does it make?"

Angry, he began to press on the accelerator, then caught himself. Too late—a motorcycle cop emerged out of the gray, misty morning, red and blue lights flashing. It all came back to Zeke in that moment. He was in New Troy. New Fucking Troy, a speed trap so notorious he had heard about it up in Terre Haute, where an Ohio insurance agent was doing a stretch for his own little money-laundering scheme. The guy was always complaining that what he had done was small-time compared to the shakedown the cops in his hometown had perfected. New Troy, Ohio, an incorporated city that provided no services except a police department that wrote speeding tickets.

"Don't say a word," he told Natalie.

"I *told* you to slow down—" she began, biting off the rest of her sentence when he glared at her.

He wasn't speeding, not really. But okay, no sweat, he'd take the ticket, no matter how bogus. Pay the fine up front, in good American cash, and thank God they had some. No—thank Amos, wherever his soul was wandering. The car's title was clear, the temporary tags clean, Natalie's bogus license untraceable. Even Zeke's license was legal. He had gotten it fair and almost square his first week, through the state-to-state reciprocity program. After all, his Maryland license had lapsed only five years ago.

"You've got a brake light out," the cop said after looking at the registration and license. "That's a two-hundred-dollar fine."

"Really?" He should let it go at that, he knew he should, but it was so goddamn infuriating to be gouged by a yokel cop, a guy that Zeke could rook in almost any other situation. "The funny thing is, I don't even remember hitting the brakes in the last mile or two. I was just driving at a nice steady"—he glanced at the speed limit sign—"thirty-five."

"Yeah, you kept to the legal limit, but you definitely hit your brakes at one point. Right one's working, left one's out." The guy's voice was dry, robotic. "We collect our fines in cash. Two hundred dollars. If you don't have the money, I'll escort you to our lockup, and you can wait there until someone wires it to you."

The amount of money gave Zeke pause. It was most of what they had left. Even fast-food restaurants and cheap motel rooms added up, and this old clunker drank about thirty dollars of gas per day. And there was no guarantee they'd make a nickel today. Still, easier to pay the fine than prolong the encounter or give out any information.

He couldn't have taken more than fifteen seconds to think the problem through, but those fifteen seconds proved disastrous. Natalie, who had never paid a traffic ticket in her life, leaned across Zeke and smiled at the cop. "The brake light was working yesterday, Officer, so perhaps it just wiggled loose while we were driving. If we promise to get it fixed as soon as we can, could you just let us go this time?"

The young cop was charmed, like almost every man who had ever looked into that face. Which was piss-poor luck in this case, because he said, "Well, let's pop the trunk and see if I can fix it for you right now."

Zeke and Natalie knew better than to look at each other then, not that they needed to. It was easy for Zeke to guess what she was thinking. Her: Isaac is in the trunk. How will we explain that? As for him, he hoped she couldn't decipher his thoughts: Stupid bitch, now he wants to open the trunk. Happy now?

Zeke eased himself out of the car, taking his time, praying that inspiration would strike him as he walked the short distance. He was lucky, he supposed, that it wasn't a newfangled car with a trunk that could be popped with a latch by the driver's seat. But what would he do, once he reached the back of the car? How do you explain a kid sleeping in the trunk? That was probably a five-thousand-dollar fine in New Troy, and a trip to family court. He would lie, that was it, pantomime trying to open the trunk, then say the lock was fussy, they hadn't used it for weeks. That's why the luggage was on the roof. Beautiful. No one ever said he couldn't think on his feet.

And if the cop didn't buy it—God knows what Zeke would do if the guy didn't buy it. Had he called in the plates? Had their presence on this road, in this spot, at this time, already been recorded somewhere? Zeke wasn't sure. He thought every cop called in his traffic stops, but maybe this podunk speed trap didn't bother. He tried to remember if he had seen the cop making the call into the radio unit on his shoulder. Had he or hadn't he? It didn't matter. Zeke was going to talk his way out of this, give him two hundred dollars, and get the hell out of Dodge at a perfectly legal thirty-five mph.

He inserted the wrong key in the lock, using the one for the ignition and thanking God that old cars like this still used two keys instead of a universal one. What if Isaac shouted or tried to call attention to himself? But he wouldn't. He would just assume Zeke was taking him out, that it was time for breakfast. He had probably fallen back to sleep in the trunk. Unless—what if the little *pisher* had fiddled with the brake light, hoping for just this occurrence? Oh, fuck him. *Fuck* him.

"Man, this lock is such a pain in the ass. Um, rear. That's why we're not even using the trunk for most of our stuff, because I can't get in here most of the time."

It was going to work, the guy was buying it, Zeke saw that instantly, and relief flooded his body. Once he was out of Natalie's view, the cop's goodwill had evaporated. He just wanted to write up the infraction, get the cash, and let Zeke go. Who knows? Maybe some New Troy cops pocketed the occasional fine. He was almost positive the guy hadn't called in their tags.

"Look, don't mind the missus. The light's clearly out. I'll pay the fine and get it fixed up the road. If you'll just—"

The sharp report of a gunshot made Zeke jump straight up in the air, and he wondered for a moment if the cop had killed him and he just couldn't feel it yet. He waited for the burning pain he was sure would follow, felt his middle to see where the bullet had hit.

But it was the cop who sank to the ground, his bland, white-boy Ohio face registering no emotion at all.

It was only then that Zeke saw Natalie, standing by the car's right rear fender. She had taken the gun from the shoe box at her feet and shot the poor guy through the back. Well, the apple didn't fall far from the tree. Just his luck that Natalie was as impulsive and crazy and, yes, *stupid* as her old man. You try and try to be someone other than your old man, but it's always the same.

He thought she might start screaming, but Natalie surprised him by returning quickly to her seat, subdued and chastened, as if waiting for him to yell at her. Instead he got behind the wheel and did a neat U-turn. They had passed a sign for I-70 not too long before, and the interstate suddenly seemed worth the risk. They would go the opposite direction, east toward Columbus. He'd stop at the first rest area, put the luggage in the trunk, and get Isaac out. Little mud on the tags, just in case, and they might be able to escape notice for a while. But that was a temporary fix. They had to get rid of this car, buy a new one, and they didn't have enough cash on hand to do that. Should they chance going to work, or should they take care of the car first? Car first. He'd have to spring for a phone card now, call Lana, get her to wire them as much cash as possible.

The twins were weeping in the backseat. They had seen everything. Great, just great. Two little witnesses to a capital crime. Another kid in the trunk, doing his damnedest to get them caught at every turn. Amos dead, but Mark still alive. A plan ten years in the making, shattered with two gunshots, one on a Maryland farm, another in an Ohio town that he never should have driven through. Zeke thought of himself in the prison library, reading and taking notes, using his time to devise a foolproof scheme to end up with Mark's wife and Mark's money. Twenty-four hours ago, he was still on target. Now it all seemed impossible. He should abort, dump the whole family out on the side of the road, head for the border, save himself. Fuck, fuck, fuck.

Natalie was murmuring to the twins, telling them that everything would be okay, that the man fell down because he and Zeke were playing a game. Her voice did have a soothing quality, and he found himself getting a grip, reassessing. Car first. In a different car, with three kids in the backseat, no luggage on the roof, they'd be much harder to make. New car, then a new plan.

And if it came down to it, Zeke would drive straight to Baltimore and kill Mark Rubin himself, if only to prove that he was capable of doing what he set out to do.

29

Tess had been parked outside Adrian's for almost two hours—joints beyond stiff, stomach hollow enough to echo—when her cell phone rang.

"Anything?" Mark Rubin asked.

"No. She left her apartment at nine-thirty, came straight to work, and she's been here since."

"You do know Adrian's has a separate entrance for deliveries, right?"

"Yes, I'm aware of that." Tess was cross at being second-guessed. She thought she had gained some ground with Mark yesterday, but his crust must have replenished itself overnight. "I have Lana's car in view, and I'm far enough back so I have sight lines of both entrances. Hey—how do *you* know that Adrian's has a side entrance?"

"Because I'm parked about thirty feet from it."

She shifted her gaze to the right. Yes, there was Rubin's dark blue Cadillac, windows rolled down. He gave her a discreet wave.

"Are you checking up on me?"

"Not exactly." There was actually a note of apology in his voice. "When I woke up this morning, I just couldn't imagine going to work, trying to pretend I had my mind on business. I liked being part of things yesterday. You told me you were going to be watching Lana, so I thought I would, too."

"Watching the detective, huh? Were you outside her apartment, too?" It would be humiliating beyond belief if Mark Rubin had managed to follow her in that huge boat of a Cadillac.

"Actually, I didn't know where she lived, so I just came here and waited. She arrived"—Tess watched him pull out a small pad and read from it—"at nine fifty-five A.M."

"And are you planning to follow us both when she leaves here?"

"Well . . ." His tone told Tess that was exactly what he had intended, although he was beginning to see how silly it was.

"Look, leave your car there and come sit in mine. We'll do this together."

"Mine's nicer."

"Is everything a negotiation with you?"

"Yes."

Tess had to laugh at Mark's honesty on this point. "Well, if we use your car, I get to drive. Following someone is tougher than it looks. But if you'll trust me to take the wheel of your Cadillac, we can use your car."

"Deal."

———

They passed another hour in the Cadillac, and even its wider, plusher seats did little for Tess's various aches. She had heard of tourist-class syndrome, the potentially lethal blood clots that developed on long plane rides. Could there be private-eye syndrome as well?

"This is pretty mind-numbing," Mark admitted, as if reading her thoughts.

"Not to mention other parts."

"You should structure your fee system so you charge more for surveillance."

"I do. At least we have each other for company. Imagine doing it alone."

"Awful. For me anyway. You're more of a loner."

"Where did you get that idea?"

"I don't know." Mark was embarrassed now, as if he had said something unintentionally tactless. "You seem so self-sufficient. Other than your Uncle Donald, I've never heard you talk about your family. You're not married, you mentioned a boyfriend once, but you've never even said his name. When we were . . . delayed in Grantsville yesterday, the only worry you seemed to have was your dogs."

Lord, her life sounded bleak coming from Mark Rubin's mouth.

"How did you sleep last night?" she asked, hoping to change the subject. "Considering the *delay* in Grantsville."

"Fine. I told you, it's not going to be a problem for me."

"Then why use euphemisms? Whoa—manicurist in motion."

Lana barreled out of the front door, her stride rapid, but otherwise displaying none of the self-consciousness of a person who expects to be followed or watched. She was simply in a rush. She jumped into her car and pulled onto Reisterstown Road, heading south. Tess followed, trying to stay two car lengths back, gunning a yellow at one point.

"Shit," she said, catching a flash of light from the corner of her eye. "That intersection had a camera."

"I'll pay the ticket when it comes," Mark said. "Just don't lose her."

Within a matter of miles, the sleek, upscale shops had given way to the more run-down stores in the neighborhood where Vera Peters lived. There were delis, bookstores advertising Judaica, the shell of the old Carvel stand where Mark had claimed to have met Natalie.

"Maybe she's going to see Natalie's mother or someone in her old neighborhood," Tess said, but the words were barely out of her mouth when Lana's car made an abrupt right-hand turn into a small shopping center. She parked outside an off-name convenience store in what appeared to be an old Fotomat store. Tess followed, parking as far from the store as possible.

"Where do you think she's going?" Mark asked, agitated.

"For all we know, she's buying a pack of cigarettes. Although I have to say the transaction seems to be taking an unusual amount of time. She's the only customer in the store, and she's been talking to the guy at the cash register since she went in."

They squinted through the store's dirty window, protected— Tess hoped—by the slant of the sun, which should create a glare on the Cadillac's windshield. Lana and the man were having a spirited back-and-forth. She kept shaking her head and pointing a credit card at him for emphasis. The man seemed unmoved by whatever plea she was making, indicating something on the counter and shrugging as if to say, *What can I do?* An exasperated Lana finally gave him the card, tapped the counter impatiently for another five minutes, then left empty-handed.

"Tough call," Tess said to Mark. "We can follow her, or we can go in there and find out what this was about. He has a sign advertising fax services and wire transfers."

"He won't tell us. No responsible businessman would reveal that kind of information. Let's stay with her."

"The key word is 'responsible.' I'm betting that someone who runs a convenience store called the Royal 7 leans toward the disreputable side."

The man behind the counter was big and burly, probably Mark Rubin's age, but more roughed up by life. Tess found herself fixated on his ears, which were rimmed with dark, furry hair. Between the ears and the eyes, which were green with a yellowish cast, he looked as if he had wandered out of some fantasy novel's dark side. He could be Gollum or at least a golem.

"What?" he asked, before Tess even had a chance to say anything, as if he were in the habit of anticipating trouble.

She thought of various lies to tell. She was from immigration and she suspected that the woman who had just left the store was an illegal alien; what could he tell her about her activities? Or Lana Wishnia was a fugitive and they were bail bondsmen who would give him a cut of their fee if he helped them in any way.

But she just didn't feel like making the effort. Instead Tess let her suede jacket fall open, giving him a glimpse of the gun on her belt, and said, "The woman who was just in here—I need to know what kind of business she transacted."

"You're not police," he said.

"No, but I have friends in the police department, and in the state department of licensing and regs, even in the health department, and I'm sure any one of those agencies could find a beef with your store, whether it's the hot dogs that have been sitting on that grill for the past week or the gas pump that can afford to dispense gas at ten cents below the going rate because it's shorting your customers a few ounces on the gallon."

The man smiled, amused by Tess's bravado. "She wired two thousand dollars via e-mail to a Western Union store in Zanesville, Ohio."

"Which store?"

"Only one I found." He showed Tess the address in a directory. "She said it was going to someone named Wilma Loomis."

"The name mean anything to you?" Tess asked Mark Rubin.

"It sounds as if it should, but . . . no, no, I'm drawing a blank."

"What about Zanesville?"

He shook his head.

Tess turned back to the grinning counterman, whose enjoyment of their discomfiture seemed out of proportion. "What the hell is so funny?'

"There's a server problem. Transfers usually take only fifteen minutes, but this one's going to take at least an hour, maybe two. That's why the girl was so upset. So while you're standing here, Wilma Loomis is still in Zanesville, waiting for the money. Too bad Zanesville is more than an hour's drive from here. But, like Einstein said, it's all about relativity."

"Were you a physics major before you started running an off-brand convenience store?"

The guy smirked. How Tess loathed him. He had no way of knowing how deeply his words cut, how Mark Rubin must yearn to manipulate time. Go back six hours and he could be in Zanesville now, waiting for his family to arrive at the Western Union office, assuming that the transfer was intended for Natalie. Go back six days and he could be sitting at a molded plastic table in McDonald's in French Lick, Indiana, a man's death no longer on his hands. Go back a month and he could refuse to leave for work on a Friday morning, have a chance to dissuade Natalie from this mysterious journey before it began.

"But we *can* play with time and space," Tess said. "In certain parts of the country."

Plucking Rubin's sleeve, she motioned for him to follow her outside, where she quickly dialed Gretchen O'Brien on her cell phone. Tess prayed for a voice, not voice mail. The prayer was answered. Perhaps Mark did have an in with God, because Tess didn't see how she rated.

"Gretchen? Tess. Didn't you just add someone to the network in the central Ohio area?"

"Yeah, east of Columbus. A retired librarian, with amazing on-line research skills. Great at financial stuff—SEC filings, Dun & Bradstreets—"

"I need some more basic legwork. We've got a lead on our missing family, at a Western Union store in Zanesville. They're stuck there for an hour because the server's down."

"But you don't have any paper on them, right? No warrant, no legal way to hold them?"

"No. If she finds them, she should just follow them as discreetly as possible, calling me on my cell to update their location. We'll start heading west on I-70 to get a head start and hope that they're heading east. Meanwhile, tell her the client will pay her hourly rate plus expenses plus a bonus if she has to go beyond eight hours today."

"Okay, but you should know she's not exactly used to this kind of fieldwork."

"She's within an hour of Zanesville, which is all that matters. Just get her on the phone and get her on the road as quickly as possible. She's our only shot."

"Too bad we don't have a Learjet, gassed up and ready to go from some central location."

"Very funny, Gretchen."

"Who's joking? I have big plans for the SnoopSisters. Sky's the limit. I've registered the domain name snoop-sisters.com and I'm looking to get some sort of trademark protection. We're going to be the Starbucks of private investigation. You've got to think big, Tess."

Tess was too busy thinking little, hoping this one precious clue would bring Mark Rubin's children back to him.

———

They stopped at a Dunkin' Donuts on Reisterstown Road before heading to the highway.

"Kosher," Mark explained. "And quick."

"I usually don't have a chocolate frosted for lunch, but sugar and caffeine will be a boon. Zanesville is at least eight hours from here. But if they head east, we could catch a break and overlap them."

"We're due for a break, don't you think?"

"Definitely." Tess, who had taken the first driving shift, was grateful she had a reason to stare straight ahead. She still didn't know whether to tell Mark what Larry Kirsch had said about Natalie's visits to the prison, the "services" she had provided. "Mark"—

the name still felt funny in her mouth, but he didn't correct her—"how much do you know about Natalie's life before you met?"

"How much could there be to know? She was eighteen."

"And she had already decided to embrace Orthodox Judaism *before* she met you?"

"Yes, but she didn't know how to go about it. That was why she sought me out. Her father suggested I could help her find a rabbi who would oversee her education, prepare her for a bat mitzvah."

"How . . . propitious."

"What are you suggesting?"

"Nothing," she lied. "But her father's attempt to blackmail her later—"

"I told you, I was never tempted by Boris's games. Marriages must be based on trust. Whatever Boris wanted to tell me about Natalie was unimportant. She was so young. What could she possibly have done that couldn't be forgiven?"

Tess's thoughts were going somewhere else. If all Boris had on Natalie were his allegations about their own little prison-outreach program, as it were, she could have bluffed her way around that. A few tears, a convincing story, and Mark would have been willing to believe it was all a vile lie. Boris had something more concrete on his daughter—and a potential buyer, as he had told Tess, but one who hadn't paid him yet. *If I don't get my due by the end of the month*, he had said, *I'll put it back on the market*. Why had he been so definite about the date? Something was supposed to happen this month, the same month Natalie had disappeared.

"You should sleep," she told Mark. "We don't know how long we're going to be spelling each other behind the wheel of this car."

"I can't sleep," he said. "I got maybe two hours last night."

"You told me you slept fine last night."

"Two hours *is* fine for me. It's about as much sleep as I've had in the past month."

They had reached the turnoff that had taken them to western Maryland the day before, but the skies were not threatening today.

The countryside's beauty had a mocking edge—the trees crimson and gold, the hills still green. Tess's cell phone rang, and she picked it up, expecting her emergency dog-sitter.

"Tess Monaghan?" The voice was an older woman's, enthusiastic and a little breathless. "This is Mary Eleanor Norris, and I've got 'em in my sights."

30

Isaac noticed the car first because it was a Mini Cooper, a gold one. He loved Mini Coopers. He and his father had watched *The Italian Job*—the real one, not the remake—just last month. His father said he was pretty sure Michael Caine might be Jewish, which surprised Isaac because he didn't know Jews could have English accents. This Mini Cooper wasn't right behind them, but it never lagged more than a few car lengths back. The other cars on the highway whizzed past Zeke, who was driving a very steady fifty-five, staying in the right lane, unusual for him. He didn't drive fast, but he liked to zig and zag, muttering under his breath at the other drivers.

Then again, it was odd to be on such a big highway, which Zeke never seemed to pick. Plus, he had taken Isaac out of the car earlier than usual, and everyone seemed to be acting weird. Whenever

Isaac glanced over his shoulder, the Mini Cooper was there. He twisted his body, so he was looking out the rear window, trying to catch the driver's eye. It was a woman, an old one. She had gray hair, and she used her cell phone from time to time, which shocked Isaac. He didn't think old people did dangerous things like that. He was even more shocked when she lit a cigarette. He didn't know anyone who smoked. Not even Zeke smoked. Paul at his father's store sometimes smelled of tobacco, but that was from a pipe, which wasn't so bad because you didn't do it as much.

The driver noticed Isaac looking at her and pulled into the adjacent lane, keeping at the same pace. She seemed to give Isaac a friendly nod, but he wasn't sure. With a swift glance over his shoulder at Zeke, he began working his hand. She waved back. *No, no, no*, he wanted to scream. *Watch me. Pay attention.* But of course, he mustn't make any noise, mustn't do anything that Zeke would notice.

Too late. "How long has that car been back there, Warren?"

Isaac didn't answer. He never answered to that name.

"Yo, Isaac, my man. The gold Mini Cooper. Has it been with us for a while?"

"I'm not sure," he said.

"Since we left the store?"

"I didn't see it at the store," Isaac said, which was true.

"So how long? Ten minutes? Fifteen?"

"I don't have a watch," Isaac said. "You took it away from me, remember? You threw it away on the second day because it beeped every hour on the hour and you said it made you crazy."

Zeke had done just that, yanking it from Isaac's arm and throwing it out the car window while he drove. *I spent the last ten years of my life living on a schedule*, he had said. *I don't need to be reminded of every hour going by.* Well, duh, school was like that, too, and Isaac never complained.

"I'm probably just paranoid," Zeke said to Isaac's mom. "It's not like the Ohio State Police drive Mini Coopers. Probably just some anxious driver who doesn't want to scratch her precious little toy."

Isaac's mom glanced back. Something bad had happened, but Isaac couldn't figure out what. The twins weren't speaking at all anymore, and his mother had said only a few words to him since Zeke took him out of the trunk, her tone dull and strange. And although the man at the store had given his mother lots of cash—cash, not a check, which was different—they had been given only apples and bananas for lunch. Not that Isaac minded. Fruit was always kosher.

"We're getting close to Wheeling," Zeke said. "Let's see what happens if we exit there."

They left the highway at one of the first entrances to the West Virginia town, and the Mini Cooper followed, much to Isaac's joy. Zeke began driving recklessly, gunning the car through red lights, making sudden turns, but the Mini Cooper was always there, a determined gold bug. Isaac couldn't help rooting for it. He didn't know why the car was following them, but it had to have been sent by his father. He tried to give the driver a little wave, one that Zeke couldn't see, to show that he was on her side.

"Turn around, Isaac," Zeke said.

"But I'm carsick, and this helps."

"Don't be silly. Looking backward makes it worse. Looking forward is what helps."

"No, it really does help him," his mother said, taking his side for once. "I don't know why, but he likes to look out the back when he's sick."

Unable to shake the determined little car, Zeke pulled into a drive-through lane at a Burger King. It was past three, but the line was a long one, moving slowly. The Mini Cooper didn't join the line but parked on the street opposite the restaurant's exit. Car by car, Zeke edged up the line, placing an order for two cheeseburgers and two milk shakes, then finally rounding the corner, out of the Mini Cooper's sight.

"Slide over, Nat," Zeke muttered. "Take the wheel. And when you get the food, just pull over as if you're going to eat it here in the parking lot."

"Why? What—"

"Trust me," he said, and Isaac wished he could say, *No, don't trust him. Please stop trusting him.* But his mother scooted across the seat, taking the wheel, and Zeke ambled away from the car as if he didn't have a care in the world. He headed toward the street, but he didn't walk toward the Mini Cooper. Instead he turned right, strolling away from it.

A few minutes later, as Isaac sat ignoring the cheeseburger his mother had placed in his lap, he saw Zeke walking back, but now he was on the other side of the street. He had left his jacket in the car, so he was in just a T-shirt, but he had taken the baseball cap he always wore, and it was pulled down tight. The woman behind the wheel of the car was talking on her cell phone, glancing at the Plymouth from time to time.

Look behind you, Isaac wanted to scream. *Watch out for that man in the baseball cap.* He thought about trying to get out of the car and running toward her, but he had a twin on either side, so he couldn't move without crawling over one of them, and his mother would probably grab him before he got out. He wondered if he should lean over the seat and start pressing the horn, but that still wouldn't get the woman in the Mini Cooper to look at Zeke. He watched, his stomach flip-flopping, as Zeke suddenly ducked down behind the Mini Cooper. Had he dropped something? He straightened back up a minute later and started walking in the other direction. He disappeared from sight again, and Isaac could tell that his mother was worried. She began to shake, muttering to herself.

"He's going to leave me," she said. "I've ruined everything. He can't stay now."

Isaac thought it would be wonderful if Zeke left, but he couldn't stand to see his mother so upset.

"Mama?"

"What?"

It was one of the first times they had been alone, out of Zeke's earshot, since the trip began. Isaac and his mother used to talk all the time, about all sorts of things. Not the same things he discussed with his father. In fact, Isaac did most of the talking, and his mother listened. But she had seemed so interested in everything he had to say—about school and books and what he had done that day. She didn't know all the things his father knew. She was not a person you would go to if you wanted to find out how something scientific worked or learn about a World War II battle. But she had always been someone Isaac could count on.

"Why don't we live with Daddy anymore?"

"It's hard to explain."

But she had said that before, over and over again, and he wasn't going to settle for that answer anymore.

"Do you love him?"

"Not in the way a woman needs to love her husband."

"Why not?"

"Only God can explain that, Isaac. It's not something people can control, who they love, who they don't."

"But you loved him when you married him, right? You loved him once?"

No answer.

"You have to love people to marry them."

"I suppose."

"Mama—do you love me?"

"Of course I do." These words seemed to rush out of her. "More than anything in the world, Isaac."

"But if you stopped loving Daddy, couldn't you stop loving me, too? Are you going to leave me someday?"

His mother began to cry, sobbing harder than the twins ever did, which was not at all what Isaac wanted. He patted her shoulder, trying to comfort her, begging her to stop. The twins, seeing their mother cry, began to weep, too, wailing like animals who had been hurt.

"Pretty soggy in here," Zeke said, sliding into the passenger seat. "Now, dry off and start driving. She won't follow us."

"How can you be so sure?"

"Just drive, Natalie. Take the highway east, all the way back into—" Zeke paused, looked at Isaac. "Just head east, and I'll tell you how to get where we need to go. I want to buy new wheels— and dump these. We'll park this wreck in a shopping center some- where, take the tags."

"Won't the missing tags just make them notice it sooner?"

"Maybe. But it also means they have to get inside, check the VIN number, which will lead them back to Amos. And that's a dead end these days, you'll pardon the expression."

Isaac glanced over his shoulder, silently rooting for the Mini Cooper. The car started to follow them as they headed up the street, but there was a horrible *whap-whap-whap* noise, and it stopped abruptly, lurching toward the curb.

"I punctured her tires," Zeke said, laughing. "Let her spend the afternoon in Wheeling. We'll be over the state line before she fig- ures it out."

Isaac watched as the Mini Cooper faded from view. He waved, not sure what else to do, then made a thumbs-up sign, so the driver wouldn't feel too bad. She had done her best, but it was so hard to win with Zeke. It was like Battleship. He was going to have to wait for Zeke to make a mistake. But in Battleship, Isaac remembered, it was the littlest boat that was the hardest to find, and that made it the most powerful.

31

The Roy Rogers at the rest stop wasn't kosher, not that it mattered. Mark Rubin had no appetite after Mary Eleanor's last call, in which she confessed she had lost the family in Wheeling.

"She said everyone looked good," Tess said, not for the first time. She was feeling guilty for being able to enjoy food, much less taste it. But she was famished, and the last Roy Rogers in Baltimore had closed its doors months ago, so this meal was a treat for her. "She saw all the kids, especially Isaac, who kept peering over the backseat and waving at her."

"They looked happy?" Mark traced the lines on the place mat on the tray that held his bottle of water. It was a cartoon showing a family's fun-filled day—capped off with a stop for Roy Rogers fried chicken, of course.

"She didn't say *happy*. Just healthy, intact. All present and accounted for."

"And the man?"

"I *told* you." Mark had been asking the same questions again and again. "She described him the same way the McDonald's crew did—tallish, thin but muscular build, dark hair. He was wearing a baseball cap, so she didn't get a good look at his face. Besides, she was staring at the back of his neck most of the time."

Mark didn't look up, just kept tracing the cartoon's family trip, from home to swimming pool to the movies to Roy Rogers and back again.

"Did she say if he was . . . handsome?"

"Mark—"

"She's with him by choice. He left her and the children in the car for ten minutes and walked away, with this midwestern librarian parked across the street from them. All Natalie had to do was drive off, or walk over to the woman and ask for help."

Tess bent over her fries. She had thought that Mark had come to accept the idea that Natalie had left of her own volition and remained away for her own reasons, whatever they might be. Perhaps Tess should not have withheld the information about Natalie's past. But Mark so clearly didn't want to know the worst about his wife. Tess could kill a man, but she still couldn't break bad news to one.

"Mark—we've placed them for the second time in a week. We have a description of the car and the temporary tag numbers. We know they're moving around, probably to escape detection. But they have to light somewhere eventually. Lana's money is only going to tide them over for so long, and she can't have that much socked away, even if she's the best manicurist in the whole Mid-Atlantic region. Plus, they were headed east, closer to us."

"So we should go talk to Lana, demand to know what she knows."

"I'm not a cop. I can't hold a private citizen in a room and interrogate her."

"No, but you can do what you did to the guy at the convenience store."

"Show her my gun and bluff?"

That actually won a halfhearted smile from Mark.

"You could use the same kind of threats. She's a manicurist, right? Threaten to turn her in to the IRS for underreporting her tips if she doesn't talk to you. Or I could run a credit report on her, see if she has any bad debts. A young woman like that tends to get carried away from time to time."

"I don't know, Mark. Her devotion to Natalie seems unshakable. I don't think she's going to fall apart if we find out she was delinquent on a department-store account."

"Then let's go pay her a visit at her place of work. People don't like that. I know I wouldn't be pleased with one of my employees if a private detective and a distraught father came to my shop and started making a lot of noise."

Tess studied Mark Rubin. He was, as always, impeccably dressed, wearing a lightweight gray suit, white shirt, and a silk tie in a conservative pattern of navy and maroon. When they had pulled into the rest stop, he had told Tess he needed to say his evening prayers and walked away from the complex, finding a quiet spot near a copse of trees. He was dignified, a man of what Tess's mother would call good bearing, but his dignity was beginning to fray. She saw the signs of wear in his red-rimmed eyes, in the hair that was at least a week past its normal trim.

"Tomorrow," she said. "I'll go to Lana's salon first thing."

"*We* will go to the salon first thing in the morning."

"In the morning," Tess agreed. "First thing."

"And tonight?"

"Tonight," she said, her voice gentle, "you should do whatever it takes to get some sleep, whether by prayer or pill."

Tess did not take her own advice. In bed, the greyhound all but wrapped around her in a fit of separation anxiety, she began making lists, free-associating. *French Lick*, she wrote, adding the date that

Natalie had been spotted there. *Zanesville. Wheeling.* There was no pattern to discern, geographical or otherwise. The towns just boiled down to three not-big places in the Midwest. Sighing, she checked her e-mail, which included a reminder that the SnoopSisters had their weekly "chat" tonight—or brainstorming session, as Gretchen insisted on calling it. Tess normally skipped the chats, which were held late to accommodate those in the Pacific time zone, but she wanted the others to know how hard the new recruit had worked.

The sisters were already engaged in fast and furious talk, their "voices" falling over each other like dialogue in a Howard Hawks film. Mary Eleanor was not on the log of participants, so Tess waded in, described their newest colleague's valiant efforts, then proclaimed herself stumped. She expected only sympathy, not solutions. But Jessie Ray in Texas piped up.

JR: I have a theory.

TM: Have at me.

JR: What if your runaway wife is using social services?

TM: How can she? She's always moving. She can't settle down somewhere and get AFDC.

SF (that was Susan Friend in Omaha): They don't even call it AFDC anymore, Tess. That went out with the Clinton administration. It's a whole new world of acronyms out there.

GOGO (Gretchen liked the look of her initials squared): More acronyms, but fewer dollars.

JR: True. But some states do have discretionary emergency funds. We're talking tiny amounts—$200 here, $400 there. Enough to check a family in to a cheap motel for a couple of days. Others will cut you a check to buy a used car, if transportation is the thing standing between a woman and a job. The idea is to get a family settled, then start the more onerous paperwork for real services. But you could take the money and split, and they wouldn't do a darn thing about it. No one's going to chase you down and make you take more government aid.

Tess typed: Interesting. But would it leave a paper trail?

JR: Possibly. There's a little-known child-support enforcement program that searches federal databases for deadbeat dads, which are my specialty. It has a lot of flexibility—it can do sophisticated Boolean searches with variables, using suspected aliases in combination with data the applicant is less likely to fake. Downside is, it can take months because it searches millions of records. Veterans, federal employees, anything the feds have access to. But if you know you only want to look at social-services programs in a handful of states, it might go a little faster.

Worth a try, Tess typed, although she doubted Mark Rubin would be placated by something so passive. He didn't want search engines crawling along millions of entries in government databases. He wanted to get in his car and just start driving until he found his family and brought them home.

A virtual door creaked audibly, and the log at the bottom of the screen showed that M'E—Mary Eleanor—had entered the room.

M'E: Hey, gang. I'm the new girl.

TM: All hail Mary Eleanor. She did amazing work today.

The Sisters responded with a variety of hip-hip-hooray emoticons.

M'E: I'm not sure I deserve to be saluted. Gosh, those kids are cute, tho. The one little boy kept giving me a thumbs-up, and doing a sort of Zorro thing, like he was cheering me on. Makes me feel worse for losing them.

TM: Please, no girly self-deprecation here. You tracked them to Wheeling. You told us they were all safe and well. It was—she stopped for a moment, trying to find the right word, one that would be positive but truthful—meaningful to their father, to know his children are well.

She bade the sisters good-bye, her fingers exhausted. The phone rang at almost the precise moment she disconnected from the Internet. It was silly to think the phone's peal was angry and insistent, as if someone had been trying to get through for a while. Yet that's exactly how her caller sounded.

"You missed the appointment with the caterer," Kitty said without preamble. "We waited and waited for you at the Brass Elephant, but you never showed up. I need to know what you think about quail."

"Given the way this country is going, I think anyone can be president."

"*Tesser.*" In thirty-two years Tess's Kitty had never once raised her voice to her niece, or anyone else. Her low, sweet tone was as much a part of her charm as her reddish curls, peachy skin, and perfect figure. Even now she didn't sound exactly loud, but there was an unaccustomed edge to her voice. "This is serious."

"So I'm guessing what was once described as nothing more than a large party where a couple of people happen to get married has turned into a big-ass nightmare of a wedding."

There was a sharp intake of breath on the other end of the phone, and Tess wondered if Kitty was so far gone that she might take offense, or even start crying. Tess was really getting sick of making people cry. To her relief, Kitty laughed instead. A rueful laugh, to be sure, but the laugh of a woman who still had some perspective.

"I'm sorry. PMS."

"You still . . ."

"Tess, please. I'm only forty-five. The thing is, I worry when you don't show up for an appointment, and I can't find you at home or in your office. I should carry your cell phone number, but I never remember it and you don't always answer it. You didn't used to be so hard to find."

"You didn't used to worry about me so much."

"No, not really. But last summer was a . . . bit of a jolt."

Last summer. Kitty made it sound so far away. Tess glanced at the scar on her knee and remembered sitting in the vacant parking lot waiting for an ambulance. If it had been a horror film, the man she had left for dead might have risen again in the endless minutes it took for her 911 call to be answered. But when Tess Monaghan killed a man, she was nothing if not thorough. The cops who arrived at the scene had been almost perverse in their admiration for her work. At least the shooting part. She could tell that the other wound, the one that had been truly defensive, made even the cops queasy.

Kitty had come with Crow to the emergency room at Harborview Hospital. The three had agreed to protect Tess's parents from the full knowledge of what had happened to their daughter in the warehouse. For once Tess had been thankful for the dulled-down newspaper prose, which reduced the most horrific night of her life to a simple construct. *Miss Monaghan followed the suspect to an abandoned warehouse, where she managed to kill him after he inflicted fatal injuries to her associate. A grand jury declined to indict, deciding she acted in self-defense and discharged the full clip only because she was panicky.*

Tess could not fault the newspaper reporter for rendering the event dryly and somewhat inaccurately. She had refused repeated attempts to enlarge the tale, to participate in what the more persistent reporters promised would be empathetic narratives. The only reporter to whom she would have entrusted the full story was her old friend Kevin Feeney. And he, to his eternal credit, wanted no part of it—and not just because it was a conflict of interest to write about a friend. "I don't need to know, Tess," he had said. "If you want to confide in me, I'm here for you. But I don't want the *Blight*'s subscribers to read about the night you almost died while they're chomping on eggs and sausage with their mouths open."

If only Crow could have been spared as well. But he knew everything, and this had made him intent on protecting her in every way. He had started working longer hours at the Point, the bar that Tess's father ran, so Tess wouldn't fret about neglecting her own work. He began speaking of the business degree he hoped to earn, his always-accessible enthusiasm as engaged by the bar and restaurant business as it had once been by music and art. He called her countless times a day and demanded she check in. His marriage proposal, Tess believed, was his last-ditch attempt to protect her from herself. He thought he could keep her safe.

But no one could keep anyone safe in this world. And Tess didn't want a bodyguard. She didn't want people peering at her, faces anxious and voices low, as if she were an invalid or an unpredictable animal. She wanted to be who she used to be, before she'd killed someone. She wanted that mark off her permanent record. But that couldn't be and would never be, so she soldiered on. Let time do its magic act. When people told Tess that time healed, she knew it was true. But she also knew that time could use a little Neosporin in its kit. It left some unsightly scars.

"I really do take fewer chances," Tess told Kitty, thankful that Amos's death would never make the papers this far east. Baltimore, with its two hundred-plus homicides a year, didn't have any attention to spare for other towns' shootings. "I'm much more careful than I was."

"If you say so. How's Crow?" A non sequitur, and yet not. Had Kitty's intuitive brain made the connection?

"Fine."

"He'll be back for the wedding?"

"I'm sure he plans to be." Damn, she shouldn't sound quite that vague, as if she never spoke to him. Luckily, Kitty was too wedding-addled to catch the slip.

"His mother's doing well?"

"Very well. And it's nice for them, being together as a family. *They* like each other."

"Tess, we all like each other."

"Now. More or less. But aren't Uncle Jules and Uncle Lester feuding?"

"I speak only for the Monaghan side. The Weinsteins have to keep track of their own craziness. But you should be grateful to have so many relatives, complicated as they are. Tyner has virtually no family, just a first cousin, and he's a Baltimore bachelor from way back."

"You'd think that euphemism would die out, as society becomes more open-minded about homosexuality."

"Society is becoming more open-minded? What country are you living in, my dear? Today's Baltimore bachelors continue to mingle with all those oh-so-happily married Baltimore husbands, the closeted men with houses in Guilford, society wives, and beautiful children at the city's best schools. Right now I'm trying to figure out if I should invite an old friend, his wife, *and* his boyfriend, who's also a friend of mine. Separate invitations, of course, but still. What's the etiquette?"

"It's hard, isn't it?"

"Planning a wedding?"

"Being human."

"Tesser, is there something you want to tell me?"

"No," she lied.

32

It was well past dusk by the time Lana pulled into the shopping
center outside Martinsburg, West Virginia, and the children
were tired and cranky. The limited wonders of the mall had
ceased to entrance them hours ago, and the twins whined in their
incoherent babble, demanding to know when they might eat dinner,
go to bed, or watch television.

Isaac was quiet, but his stoicism bothered Zeke even more than
the twins' whining. The kid was unnatural. *Be a kid,* he wanted to
shout at him, *loosen up.* He wondered if Isaac had been more boyish
before this began, just as Zeke had been more of a kid before his father's death and his mother's remarriage. If he had known that the
boy existed, would he have even tried to carry this off? For there
was no escaping it: He was going to do to Isaac exactly what had

been done to him, which had never been the plan. Worse, actually. Yet he wasn't a monster, he wasn't a bad guy.

He wasn't, as he kept reminding Natalie, the person who had changed everything by killing a cop.

It was true, he thought, staring idly at the things for sale in the mall. Nothing left to lose was a kind of freedom. Nothing left to lose meant you had everything to gain.

Lana looked grim and unhappy when she finally arrived.

"I don't know what you want me to do," she said. "The money I wired you this morning is all I had. I'm tapped out. I won't be able to pay for the cash advance when my credit-card bill comes due."

"Maybe Amos will leave you something in his will, for old times' sake."

"Don't joke about that." Her voice was sharp and fierce, as if she had actually cared about the guy. "Do you realize who was on his property when he died? Mark. Mark and some woman. So he's dead because of me, because Mark somehow figured out I took Natalie there when she decided to leave."

"Really? Mark was there?" That made no sense. Zeke had chosen Amos for the job because he'd been assured the two had had no contact since Amos left prison. Had Amos lured him there, instead of doing the job when Mark was transporting furs? That had been Zeke's plan, a nice little robbery that made perfect sense. Killing Mark on the farm was stupid beyond belief. "But I thought you said the police told you two people were there. Who was the other one?"

"All I know is that it was a woman."

"*Really.*" The apple sure didn't fall far from the tree. Maybe Mark was as big a dog as his own father, taking up with another woman the moment Natalie disappeared. Maybe before. Wouldn't that be sweet? "Any idea who she is?"

"I don't know for sure, but there was that private detective he hired to find you. She knows about the post-office box, too. I got a certified letter saying I should call someone who knew everything, but I ignored it. There's no law against having a mailbox."

"Good girl." Lana needed a lot of stroking, almost as much as Natalie, if such a thing were possible. "Does she know about me?"

"She didn't when I talked to her. But they found Amos, they went to Amos. Natalie's father may have told."

"No. Boris would never tell. Besides, I wasn't in the stupid group, remember? The last thing I wanted to do in prison was sit and play Passover. I've had my fill of bitter herbs."

Of course, Lana had no idea what he was talking about. She knew even less about Judaism than Natalie had, before Zeke had taken Natalie in hand and taught her what she needed to know to snare Mark.

"What's going on, Zeke? You said something bad had happened, something else, and you needed the money for a car, but I had to come, too—"

He held up a hand. "You don't want to know, Lana. Trust me. But it's bad, really bad. Natalie and I will spend the rest of our lives on the run. That's why we need you to buy the new car, over in Hagerstown. Your name is clean. You can buy a car with the cash you sent us, title it, then give it to us with a notarized note saying we have permission to drive it. No one's going to connect a car purchased in Hagerstown with a car abandoned in West Virginia. This car just takes them back to Amos, who's dead."

"But if they find the car and they do connect it to whatever you've done, then I'll be in the middle of it."

"If you don't know anything, you haven't done anything. Like I said, it will all go back to Amos, and dead men tell no tales."

Only Zeke's father had. Zeke's father had come to him over and over again, insistent as the old ghost in *Hamlet*. As Zeke grew older, he tried to argue with him. The autopsy report said suicide, Pops. *Why would I commit suicide?* Because you burned down the building and killed the watchman, the one you didn't know was there. *Why would I do that?* Because the store was going down the tubes. Your partner went off and grew rich selling furs in suburbia, while you tried to make money selling designer dresses in downtown, six blocks from the department stores that got them first and sold them cheaper. It was good old-fashioned Jewish lightning, Dad. *Yes, but who threw the lightning bolt? Who gained? Who truly gained? I was dead, and my reputation was ruined. Aaron Rubin ended up with everything, and I ended up with nothing. Suicide or homicide? I pulled the trigger, but someone guided my hand.*

"Look," Zeke said, his voice harsh in spite of his best efforts, "you have to convince Natalie to send the goddamn kids back with you. Tonight."

"No. The cops will ask me questions if I show up with the kids, try to give them back to Mark. I don't want to get involved."

"Drive them to Vera's, ring the doorbell, and run. It's about time she met her grandchildren. Besides, it will be nice for Mark to have his kids around."

"Since when do you care about what's nice for Mark?"

Again, he couldn't tell Lana that he wanted the rest of Mark's life, short as it was destined to be, to have a pleasant ending.

"Anyway, Natalie's not going to let those kids go for anything now. Look at her."

Natalie and the children were sitting on the edge of a lackluster fountain. She held Penina in her lap, clutching her so tight that Zeke could see how the fabric of the girl's dress wrinkled beneath her mother's grasping fingers. Efraim was leaning over, trying to fish coins from the murky bottom. Isaac reached out and held his belt so he wouldn't fall in. Something about the almost-unconscious brotherly affection between the two boys made Zeke feel sad, then angry.

He should have had a little brother, a real one. He should have gone to New York and Montreal on buying trips with his father, then had a son to take with him on his. He should have had a nest egg to build his business. Then he wouldn't have pushed so hard and been forced to take shortcuts to stay afloat. He wasn't a bad guy.

He had wanted a legitimate life. He never set out to cheat anyone, much less hurt people. One day you're a guy on the phone making deals that are shady but legal. The next day the cops are coming through the door wanting to know where you got the shipment of Steve Maddens at ten cents on the dollar. And he had no idea his little credit-card scam was a federal offense. The big boys on Wall Street stole billions and gave up 8 percent of their profits. Zeke took the only kind of float anyone would give him and gave up 100 percent of his life for ten years.

"Let's go buy a car, Lana, you and me. I'll drive over to Hagerstown with you, help you pick it out. You can go home from there."

"And when do I get paid back?"

"When I do." He put his hand on her cheek. Natalie was too gone to catch the gesture, which normally would have sent her into spasms of jealousy, but Lana liked it. Lana had always liked him a little more than she should, a fact that had come in handy all these years. "You'll get back every penny, with interest. Just be patient."

———

Natalie awoke in the middle of the night and went into the bathroom, but not because she felt any need. She just couldn't sleep, and she didn't want to lie in the dark listening to all that breathing. She understood why the children could sleep—Isaac had not seen the man fall, the twins did not really understand what happened—they had been told it was all a game. But how could Zeke look so peaceful? How did he sleep so contentedly?

Because Zeke was not a killer. She was. She was her father all over again. And if she were her father all over again, what would her children be?

The light was sickly here, a greenish yellow, and she leaned toward the mirror, touching the lines and shadows in her reflection, as if they were a part of the reflected Natalie but could not be found on her own face. *So beautiful still.* It was not vain to say so, only realistic, a fact. This was her dowry, and it had been sold over and over, with varying results.

What would become of her? Her mother's face bore the sad testimony of what age and a hard life did to a woman. Not even Natalie would always be beautiful. Even if she took good care of herself and didn't smoke, age would come for her. Zeke said he loved her for more than her looks, but she wasn't sure she believed him. After all, she loved Zeke for his.

If she had it to do over again, would she have forgotten Zeke and learned to love, really love, Moshe? He was kind, he was loving, he provided for her. If she had loved him just a little more, she would not be here, and she would not be a killer. But the fact was, he had never stirred anything in her. And while the children had created a powerful bond between them as parents, her feelings for Zeke simply could not be denied.

So here she was, in a motel in West Virginia, with a man who had yet to make love to her in a complete way. All that talk about things being perfect, a honeymoon suite at the Ritz-Carlton, room service and white fluffy robes and Egyptian cotton sheets. Natalie didn't know how to tell him she had already been in the honeymoon suite at the Ritz-Carlton and, while it was all very nice, you didn't get to take the robe home unless you paid for it.

They weren't going to make it. She wasn't sure where they were going or what they were doing, but her heart told her they were doomed. She should have sent the children back with Lana tonight. Zeke had urged, cajoled, wheedled, and finally shouted, shaking her for her refusal to do what he said was best. So he was like her father, too. But she could not bear to give them up. She felt safer with them for some reason. As long as she had her children, she was still a good person, a mother. A woman who loved her children could never be in the wrong.

Disgusted with her, Zeke had gone to Hagerstown with Lana, determined to buy a car before the evening was out. Hagerstown was only an hour away, yet they had been gone five hours, with

Zeke returning in the new car well after midnight. He and Lana were giggling, clearly buzzed from something. Probably Sex on the Beach cocktails, if Natalie remembered Lana's drinking preferences. Strange, she didn't even know what Zeke would drink in a bar, because she had never been in one with him. It seemed unfair that Lana would have an opportunity with Zeke that Natalie had never had, but she was too tired to work up a rage about it. Lana would leave tomorrow morning, after sleeping off her drunk on the floor of the motel room.

But if Zeke had cheated on her and she found out—she would cut it off. Why not? She had killed one man and destroyed another. For Natalie had no doubt that Mark's life was empty without her.

She sank to the toilet seat, cradling her head in her arms, longing to cry but worried that even muffled tears might be overheard. She wouldn't mind if Zeke came to comfort her—he owed her that much—but the children would be upset if they saw her crying for the second time in a day. Since they'd left home, she had been very conscious of being happy, of making everything seem as if it were a wonderful adventure. Even today, when that strange car began to follow them, she had not let the children see how nervous she was.

It was odd, almost a letdown, when she realized that the driver was a woman. Did she want it to be a police officer? Was there some part of her that simply longed for this to be over? No, she had been surprised because she'd expected to see Moshe at the wheel of that car. Every day since she left, Natalie realized, she had expected to see him.

She knew him so well, perhaps better than she would have if she had truly loved him. No one was allowed simply to walk away from Mark Rubin. She had listened to him on calls, haranguing people long past the point of winning an argument, insistent on being heard. His voice ground people beneath it the way Natalie might squash a bug under her shoe. Zeke didn't understand that part of Mark, but it was why Natalie had run, taking the children with her, instead of waiting for Zeke to send for her. She knew Mark Rubin—how thorough he was, how determined he could be about getting his way.

She knew him, she realized, better than she knew the man in the other room.

Friday

33

The manicurist still had the upper hand.

"She didn't come in this morning," the Velvet Frost informed Mark and Tess, frostier than ever after seeing Tess's PI license. "And she didn't call, which is not like Lana, especially with a full day of bookings. We've tried calling her home, and there is no answer. I'm terribly worried about her. Instead of making trouble for her, you might want to wonder if she is in trouble."

Tess decided not to argue about who the troublemaker was in this scenario. "Has she been acting strangely the past few days?"

"She was upset the day before yesterday. When I asked her why, she said someone she knew had died unexpectedly in an accident."

Tess and Mark exchanged a glance, but neither one said anything.

"But she continued to work," the Velvet Frost said. "Then today—no show. Completely out of character."

Mark looked more than discouraged than ever, but Tess immediately saw an opportunity in a missing Lana who wasn't answering her home phone. She called the Owings Mills barracks for the Baltimore County Police Department from Mark's car, identifying herself as a frantic employee from Adrian's, concerned about a missing worker.

"She didn't come to work, and she has a full day of bookings, and she just never, ever does that," Tess told the dispatcher, helping herself to the Velvet Frost's words, if not her tonalities. "And she's been really down lately about the death of someone close to her. I'm worried she might have done something drastic."

"I'm not sure what we can do in this situation," the dispatcher said in the clipped manner of a government employee keen to cut off a request outside the normal parameters.

"Couldn't a patrolman meet us and authorize her landlord to open the apartment, just so we can make sure something hasn't happened?"

"I'm not sure we can do that."

"Why not, if the landlord agrees? Landlords have the right to enter the premises if they think something is amiss."

Tess had to keep laying it on thick, but it was a slow morning in the northwest district, and the dispatcher finally relented.

"Great. We're about two miles away, so we'll meet the patrol cop out there."

———

The cop was everything Tess could have asked for. First of all, he was young, so young that he insisted on calling her "ma'am." Normally, this would have sent her to a mirror, moisturizer in hand, but it was a godsend in this situation. He was even more deferential to Mark Rubin. Only the landlord seemed skeptical of them, and Tess inferred a touch of anti-Semitism in Mr. Hassan's attitude.

With Hassan leading the way, they entered Lana's apartment. It was neat, almost depressingly so, a place that spoke of a lonely existence with few real interests. No books, no art, not even posters.

The only personal touches were two photographs of Natalie, including one with Isaac as a baby. Mark stopped for a moment, transfixed by the images, then shook his head as if reminding himself to keep his focus on the very particular mission he and Tess had devised.

"Hello?" the young cop called, heading deeper into the one-bedroom apartment, opening doors and peering into the bathroom. "There's no odor—" he began, then stopped, as if remembering just in time that his tour group was made up of a distraught coworker and Lana Wishnia's rabbi. For Tess had told him that little lie as well, deciding that it gave them even more credibility.

Tess and Mark played their parts well, tiptoeing around, stealing glances at the things they had agreed ahead of time they must absorb—notes on the kitchen counter, a flashing light on the phone. Using the sleight-of-hand trick Mark had shown Tess at their first meeting, he palmed a key lying in a shallow bowl on the kitchen counter. Perhaps it would open her box at the mail store. When Tess saw that the phone in the bedroom had a built-in answering machine and caller ID, she shot Rubin a look. She then walked out in the hall, dropped her knapsack, bent over to pick it up—and promptly let out a bloodcurdling scream.

"My back. Shit, I threw my back out again. I won't even be able to walk down the steps without someone's help."

The young cop was all sympathy, standing next to her and trying to help her straighten up, while the landlord looked away, indifferent. Tess continued to groan and whimper.

"Why don't I take one side and your friend can take the other, and we'll help you out," the cop suggested.

"Mark can't touch me—as an Orthodox Jew, he's not allowed to touch a woman who's not his wife. He was bending the rules just to be here with me today, unchaperoned. But you can help me, can't you, sir?" Tess appealed to the surly little Hassan, who didn't seem inclined to help anyone. "If you just get me down the steps, I can lie on the ground with my knees to my chest. Five minutes like that, and I should be good enough to get in the car and go home to bed."

"Does this happen a lot, ma'am?"

"Just since I turned thirty," Tess said, and the young cop looked even more sympathetic.

Slowly they righted her, but Tess stayed in her bent-over crouch, hobbling like a crone, a man at either elbow. She called back over her shoulder, "Mark, grab my knapsack, okay? But make sure nothing fell out. I'm afraid some things scattered when I dropped it."

She felt she deserved an Oscar, or at least a Golden Globe, for her oh-so-slow descent down the stairs. Once outside, she allowed the young cop and the sullen landlord to lower her to the grass, where she brought her knees to her chest and hugged tightly. It was a pretty day, and it was pleasant lying on the ground and looking at the sky. Tess had to remind herself to whimper every now and then. By the time Mark Rubin came out with her knapsack, she had almost persuaded herself that she had, in fact, thrown out her back. She eased into the backseat of the Cadillac, holding her knees to her chest, and stayed in that position until they were several blocks away.

"Anything?" she asked Mark.

"Nothing on the answering machine," he said. "But there were long-distance calls logged on the caller ID—Ohio, then West Virginia."

"Did you call the numbers?"

"First I hit the redial button, just to see what number she called last." Tess was impressed. She had not thought of that detail. "A woman with an accent answered, but I couldn't think of anything to ask her, so I hung up."

"An accent? It could have been Natalie's mother. Did you dial the numbers on the caller ID?"

"The Ohio and West Virginia numbers just rang and rang. Pay phones, I guess. We should have stayed with her. She probably would have taken us straight to them."

"Not straight. Based on the geography, the second phone call came only after Mary Eleanor had trailed them to Wheeling. Lana sent them money in Zanesville, but that wasn't good enough for some reason. They need something else from her, something that couldn't be wired."

"Maybe," Mark said, "they're going to send the children back with her. Maybe they think I'll give up if I have the children back."

"Would you?"

"Probably not." He sighed, as if disappointed in himself. "I'd have to see Natalie, just to ask why. And I can't cut her out of our children's lives, whatever she decides to do. She's their mother, after all."

"Do you think she would fight you for custody?"

"If it comes to that, absolutely."

"*If* it comes to that. You still think reconciliation is possible."

"Until I know the cause of the problem, I have to assume it's a problem that can be solved."

Again Tess found herself wondering if the information about Natalie's past could change Mark's view of his wife. *The problem is . . . your wife used to be a whore.* But that didn't explain why she had run away, nor did it shed any light on the identity of the man with her. Natalie was a willing participant in this odyssey, but what was its point, its purpose? If she wanted to be with this other man, why not divorce Mark and take whatever money she could get? Even if his inheritance wasn't marital property, she'd still be better off than she was now.

"Another woman in my network suggested something," Tess said, by way of changing the subject. "A needle-in-the-haystack solution, but it might yield some info. The only thing is, it involves going through government agencies, and you know how slow they are."

Mark actually seemed intrigued. "Ah, but I also know how to grease them so they go a little faster. I've given generously to politicians at every level of government. It's time to call in my favors."

"I never give to politicians," Tess said. "Not that I have any money to give. It's like being shaken down by the Mafia—give me money and I'll take care of you."

"Exactly," Mark said. "Exactly."

Monday

34

It took Mark Rubin less than seventy-two hours to get the results that Jessie Ray said could take several months—and he might have gotten them even faster if the weekend hadn't imposed a rain delay of sorts. By Monday afternoon he and Tess were being welcomed into the office of an undersecretary at the Department of Health and Human Services in Washington, D.C.

I really should work with people who have money more often, Tess thought, looking around the bland office that they hoped would provide their next lead.

"As you know, this program is used primarily to track down deadbeat dads," explained a pouty-lipped blonde in glasses. Without the black horn-rims and the business suit, she would have had no problem passing for a sixteen-year-old cheerleader. Even in conservative attire, she looked more like the sort of bespectacled woman found in a porn film. Tess kept thinking she was going to whip off her glasses, among other things. "But we've been keen to see if it could be applied to welfare fraud as well. Mr. Rubin's case gives us an opportunity to see how clients might abuse the system."

Tess did not literally bite her tongue, but she pressed her lips together until the lower one all but disappeared beneath her front teeth. This was neither the place nor the time to tell the young woman exactly what she thought of the changes in social services and her administration's priorities. By all means, track down those people taking the federal government for a few hundred dollars, while letting rapacious CEOs run free.

"But it's the same old story," the woman continued. "Garbage in, garbage out. That's why I was so pleased"—she cast an almost coquettish glance at Rubin—"to work with someone such as Mr. Rubin, who understood the kind of information we needed. It was the combination of birth dates and aliases that kicked out a pattern. The birth dates alone might have done it, but the names cinched it."

"Names?" Tess asked.

Mark smiled ruefully. "I know my wife well—despite what you've suggested over the past two weeks. She has a singular obsession with the movie star Natalie Wood. Remember Wilma Loomis?"

"The person who picked up the check in Ohio? Sure."

"The formal version threw me. Wilma Dean 'Deanie' Loomis is the full name of the character played by Natalie Wood in *Splendor in the Grass*. Natalie always insisted they looked alike."

Tess remembered her own sense that Natalie Rubin resembled a famous actress. "More Merle Oberon or Gene Tierney, I think."

"Anyway, once I realized she had taken a name from a film, I thought she might give the children names that correlated to Wood's life. I suggested that they try Warren and Robert for the boys, as those were Wood's best-known leading men on-and off-screen."

"How did you know that?"

Mark smiled. "I actually listened to my wife when she chattered. Figuring out Penina's alias was harder. I tried Lana."

"For her friend?"

"No, because it was Wood's sister. I also suggested Maria and Daisy."

"Daisy?"

"From *Inside Daisy Clover*. An odd piece of filmmaking, one of those movies made when Hollywood was in transition, but Natalie—my Natalie—loved it."

"And Daisy was the one that helped us hit!" Miss Horn-Rims almost shouted. "A woman named Wilmadeane—she spelled it wrong—Loomis has been visiting various county social-service offices, inquiring about benefits. She begins to fill out the application but always lacks some crucial piece of paperwork—the children's birth certificates, I'm guessing—and settles for a temporary check to tide her over."

"Doesn't a woman who applies for social services have to provide information about her children's father, so the agency can contact him? I thought there was a big push to make fathers pay."

"There is." The young woman nodded vigorously, a welfare-wonk bobblehead. "But there are loopholes. The woman can decline to provide that information if she says she's a victim of abuse."

"*Abuse!*" Mark Rubin's face flushed wine red. "How could anyone . . . ?"

But Tess was remembering Nancy Porter, the Baltimore County homicide detective who had felt obligated to make the same discreet inquiries, in part because of the insular nature of Baltimore's Orthodox community. Natalie had used the system—and, perhaps, certain cultural biases—quite cleverly. Maybe that explained her route through smaller Midwest towns. She was banking on people's being unfamiliar with the lives of Orthodox Jews and therefore even more inclined to believe her stories about an abusive, vengeful husband who must never know where she was.

"Is there a pattern to the towns or to the route?"

"Not that I can find," Miss Horn-Rims said, in a tone that implied that something she couldn't find didn't exist. "They just zigzagged around Indiana, Illinois, and Ohio."

"But we know they suddenly started heading east in a pretty linear way, driving across Ohio to Wheeling."

"No one ever went to West Virginia to perpetrate welfare fraud," Miss Horn-Rims said. "I could call these county agencies on your behalf to try to get more information, but my guess is she's dropped this scam. The last check was cut in Valparaiso, last Friday. Before that they never went a week without a check."

Which was, Tess calculated, right after they were spotted in French Lick. And just before Amos was killed. The zigzagging had stopped once Amos was dead. Were the two things connected?

"I'm trying to work this out," she said, remembering Amos's state-of-the-art photocopier, the templates for documents. "You say the grants averaged a hundred to two hundred dollars, which she received in the form of a check. So Natalie clearly has a fake ID, or else she couldn't cash the check."

"Right," Miss Horn-Rims agreed. "But the check is issued through the state or the county, so no bank or check-cashing store is going to be too worried about it bouncing. If she has an ID that satisfies welfare workers, she must have one that will meet standards at most banks as well."

"Still, that's not a lot of money. Total it all up. She probably hasn't made a thousand dollars since she left, and that's just not that much money for five people on the move. Her friend Lana couldn't possibly cover them for this long."

"She could be getting off-the-book work or staying in shelters," Miss Horn-Rims said with a blithe shrug, as if food and shelter were simply abstract concepts to be plugged in to her theories and formulas.

"Possibly," Tess said, trying to keep a lid on her partisan animosity. "Meanwhile, could I have a list of the banks and check-cashing stores where Natalie cashed her checks? Maybe someone will re-member her or a telling detail about the man she's traveling with."

"A real man, an able-bodied man," Mark put in, "supports a woman."

The perky Human Services analyst nodded again, mistaking Mark's private bitterness for a larger worldview. "Traditional core values are at the heart of this administration's mission."

"I know," Tess said, pushed past her breaking point, a short trip at the best of times. "Sometimes I can't sleep at night, worrying about welfare fraud. Or whether billionaires are going to qualify for the family tax credit."

Miss Horn-Rims' smooth forehead crinkled. "She means well," Mark said swiftly. "She's just a little agitated. Thank you for all your work on this."

On the street outside the nondescript D.C. office building, Mark offered Tess another life lesson while she scarfed down a hot dog from a street vendor.

"When people are doing you favors, you have to swallow a few things—including your own tongue."

"Is that in the Talmud?"

"If it's not, it should be."

Tess quickly learned that small-town bank tellers don't necessarily remember strangers, not even beautiful ones who resemble Natalie Wood—or Gene Tierney or Merle Oberon—and have three chil-dren in tow. Not in Valparaiso, not in Paoli, not in Mount Carmel. The managers were invariably friendly, smothering her in chatter and irrelevant detail before finding the right teller, but no one seemed to know or remember anything. One teller did recall a dark-haired woman, but he insisted she was traveling with two chil-dren, a boy and a girl. No, he couldn't tell if they were twins. No, he didn't remember anything else.

"It was the seventeenth, a Thursday," Tess said. "Can't you recall anything more?"

The man's voice, already high and effeminate, became shrill. "Look, I'm sorry if I don't remember everything that happened that day. I happened to be held up at gunpoint, and that memory is a little more vivid than cashing some county check."

"I'm sorry," Tess said, understanding the man's testiness. Tellers were sometimes questioned closely after bank robberies, in case they were conspirators in such crimes. "That must have been harrowing."

"Well, I didn't see a gun," he said, mollified. "But you're not supposed to put up any opposition, no matter what. There's a protocol. I guess I should be grateful it's the only one so far this year."

"Really? Is Fort Wayne that dangerous?"

"Oh, the security in our branch is practically nil, but you find that everywhere these days. Did you know bank robbery is actually up, even though the takes are smaller than ever? This joker got four hundred out of my drawer, but he knew enough to make sure I didn't put a dye pack in. Made me count the money out like a withdrawal, telling me all the time that he had a gun and he had an accomplice with a gun inside the bank. I've been on Paxil since, and the side effects are dreadful."

"Side effects," Tess repeated, just to be saying something.

"Dry mouth. Among other things. Anyway, the federal agents spent all of twenty minutes with me—if it doesn't involve some guy in a turban, they're just not interested."

"That's awful," Tess said, unsure how to end the conversation without seeming callous. This man clearly had nothing to tell her, except his own sob story.

"The field agent actually said to me, 'Look, we've had five of these in the past two weeks'—not just in Indiana but in southern Illinois and Ohio, too. It's a new craze, like one of those silly dances that comes along every so often."

"A new craze of bank robberies," Tess repeated. "In southern Illinois and Ohio."

"And Indiana. So I said—"

Through being polite, Tess hung up the phone and asked Mark to read her the number for the Valparaiso bank.

"But you already talked to them."

"I know, but there's something I forgot to ask."

The Valparaiso bank had been robbed the day Natalie cashed her check. So had the Paoli bank. Only the Mount Carmel bank had been spared for some reason.

"That's how they're making it," Tess said. "Natalie gets a social-services check, takes it to the bank. Within an hour or two, it's robbed."

"Natalie's not a robber," Mark said.

"No one's saying she is. But it's three for four, which is a hell of a coincidence. She's casing the places, don't you see? The check gives her cash, but it also gives her a plausible reason to go into the bank and study the layout. That's how they're making it. They're robbing banks with lax security. Bonnie and Clyde, with three kids in tow."

"It's a ridiculous theory."

"Probably," she said, trying to placate him even as her excitement grew. "But I bet it's strong enough to go to federal authorities and persuade them to issue a warrant for Natalie. That means the next time she's spotted, local police can take her in and hold her long enough for you to get there and get your kids back."

"No."

"No?" She had thought her idea sheer genius.

"It's dangerous. The police could give chase, and the children would be in the middle."

"Your children are traveling with a bank robber, who's been risking encounters with the police up to twice a week. They'll be safer if authorities intervene."

"I don't want Natalie to face criminal charges."

"I'm sure she won't, if she agrees to cooperate. But she's clearly not going to turn herself in."

"She's doing this under duress. This man has scared her, forced her to do these things."

"Mark, you yourself pointed out that she didn't get away from him when she had the chance—"

"No." He was yelling now. "No police. And if you go to them, you're violating my confidentiality as a client. Remember the papers you had me sign, the ones drawn up by your lawyer? Those require you to honor my wishes."

"Not when I have evidence of a string of felonies."

"But you don't. This is just some wild idea you cooked up, nothing more."

"It's not as wild as what you're thinking."

He gave her a look that he must have perfected over his years in business, a level, direct gaze that was hard to meet for more than a few seconds.

"Really?" he demanded. "Tell me what I'm thinking, Miss Mind Reader."

"You believe you can turn this to your advantage, that Natalie will have to come back to you if this man is locked up. That you can get her a great lawyer, cut her a deal, and have leverage over her. But if she doesn't want to be with you, then she's never going to stay, Mark. What are you going to do, put her on an even tighter leash when you get her home?"

"I don't know what you're talking about."

"The money, the house, the life you created for her—it was all about control. In your heart of hearts, you were always preparing for the day she might leave you. You tried to make sure she wouldn't have the wherewithal, financially or emotionally. But the fact is, she's chosen another life, with another man. Yes, he's probably a crook, and it's a crappy life, and it makes no sense, but it's what she wants, Mark. You've got to forget about Natalie and focus on your children."

Mark did not speak for several long moments. When he did, his voice was frightening in its controlled anger, its absolute disdain for

Tess and her opinions. "I did not hire you for personal advice. I hired you to find my family. Given the information you've developed today, you might want to go back to the records at Jessup, see if Boris had any contact with someone serving time for armed robbery. That strikes me as the most useful thing you can do."

"Mark—"

"There will be no more talk of warrants or police," he said, holding up a hand. "You work for me. Do as I've told you or you're fired."

35

Two things kept Tess from walking out on Mark Rubin in a fit of pique—the thought of Isaac waving to Mary Eleanor on the highway, and the thought of her bank account waving a frantic SOS in her direction. She had not yet earned out Mark Rubin's generous retainer, but she had spent a large chunk of it. If she wanted to quit on principle, she would have to refund money she didn't have, a principle she abhorred even more.

So she sucked it up and chose the best antidote she could think of to Mark Rubin's cold, high-handed treatment. She invited her WASP-iest friend, Whitney, over for dinner. Whitney was always good company, and she would take Tess's side in this quarrel with her client, which made her even better company. Within an hour of Tess's call, Whitney arrived with Indian takeout from the Ambassador and a bottle of zinfandel.

"The guy at the Wine Source said it was peppery and aggressive, with berry overtones and a strong finish," she said. "Just like me."

"You don't look very fruity," Tess said of her sharp-chinned friend, whose coloring was more easily found in the dairy case—butter-yellow hair, milk-white skin with a bluish undercast.

"Oh, I'm sour as a pickle these days. Everything annoys me. I took my mother to a Barbara Cook concert down at the Kennedy Center, and there was a sign-language interpreter. *At a vocal concert.* Does this mean they're going to start providing audio commentary for the ballet? And I can't speak to the sign language, but the closed-captioning was for shit. Cook was doing Sondheim, and a line from 'Losing My Mind' was transcribed as 'I want to sew.' "

"If I said that," Tess said, "you would know I was losing my mind."

Whitney laughed, expelling a little zinfandel through her nose. "It seemed to annoy Cook, too. Here she is, singing brilliantly, and there's someone blocking her from part of the audience's view, hamming it up."

"How does an interpreter ham it up?"

"Oh, c'mon." Whitney stood, giving Esskay the opportunity she needed to snatch a half-eaten samosa from her plate and bolt. "Damn dogs—they've gotten really nutty since Crow went to Virginia." *Like kids in a divorce,* Tess thought ruefully, but said nothing. She hadn't told Whitney about the breakup either, if only because she didn't want to be castigated for letting go of the perfect postmodern boyfriend. Whitney had always mocked the age difference between Tess and Crow, but she was perverse enough to exalt him now that Tess had lost him. "Anyway, she was trying to upstage Cook, I kid you not. Although I guess it would be downstaging in this case."

Whitney demonstrated, making grandiloquent gestures, opening her arms wide, painting rainbows in an imaginary sky, and finishing up by twirling an index finger next to her ear.

"I don't know sign language either, but I'm dubious about the last one you threw in there."

"I don't mean to sound callous. I'm all for an inclusive society. But a lot of this is just frosting the cannoli." This was Whitney's odd variation on gilding the lily, and Tess still didn't know what it meant after fifteen years of friendship. "I went to a bar mitzvah last week—"

"*You* went to a bar mitzvah?"

"Professional obligation, someone from the Krieger board I'm trying to cultivate. Anyway, they were signing during the half-a-Torah."

"Haftarah."

"Right, what I said. So there's a kid up there reciting a language that ninety-five percent of the people up in the synagogue don't speak or understand, and someone's signing so the deaf people in the audience—of which there were none, I'm pretty sure, although hearing aids were in great evidence—can follow along. But there's already an English translation in the text, so who are they signing for? The illiterates? The blind?"

Tess laughed, knowing Whitney's performance was pure show. She was not as intolerant as she pretended to be. She couldn't be. Whitney played up her hard edges to compensate for life as a professional do-gooder—sitting on her family's board and dispensing gobs of money to worthy causes. Polymath that she was, she had probably learned sign language at some point.

"Were any of those real signs you were making?" Tess asked. "Or were you just faking?"

"Oh, I can say a few basic things. 'I love you. Run away.' " Whitney demonstrated.

"I'd go far with just those two sentences." Strange, Tess wanted to confide in someone, but she couldn't get the words out.

"I also know the alphabet from A"—Whitney cupped her hand—"to Z." She slashed the air.

It was Tess's turn to spit a little wine. "Do that again."

"What?"

"The Z."

Whitney slashed the air.

"Like Zorro."

"Well, duh."

It was one thing to have the action described on a computer screen, quite another to see it. *The one little boy kept doing a sort of Zorro thing.* Mary Eleanor had assumed that Isaac was being supportive in a silly, little-kid kind of way. But what if he had been *spelling?*

———————

Less than an hour later—after consulting the Internet, talking to Mary Eleanor on the phone, then studying the Internet again—Tess was on Mark Rubin's doorstep, an insistent Whitney at her side.

"Don't be surprised if he doesn't shake your hand," Tess muttered after ringing the bell. "He doesn't touch women sometimes, but it's just a mind-fuck."

"I don't touch anybody. I'm a Presbyterian." Alcohol had an interesting effect on Whitney, sharpening the edges it softened in others. Her eyes were bright, her diction crisp, her posture perfect.

"No, I mean—" But Rubin had already answered the bell. He stood, the door only halfway open, as if unsure of whether he wanted to admit Tess to his home.

"I assume you have news." There was a stiff little pause. "Or an apology."

"News."

"And this woman is . . . ?"

"A fearsome buttinsky named Whitney Talbot, but enormously helpful in her own way." Whitney gave him a broad wave as if she were on the deck of an ocean liner and Rubin was on a dock far below. "Does Isaac know American Sign Language?"

"I'm not sure. I think he learned it for a concert at school, but I was working and couldn't go." His voice took on a defensive edge. "It was during the day. If I left work for every concert, my family wouldn't have a roof over its head. But I remember Isaac rehearsing his part around the house."

Whitney poked Tess in the back. "I told you this sign-language thing is completely out of control."

"We think he was trying to send us a message. But it doesn't make sense to us, and I wondered if it meant anything to you."

She handed him the printout, with the American Sign Language alphabet and the variations on which Mary Eleanor had finally decided: Z-E-T-E, Z-E-R-E, and Z-E-K-E.

"Do any of those things mean anything to you?"

Rubin's face was a study. For some reason it reminded Tess of the sky in western Maryland, right before the storm began and the horizon turned green. It was a ghostly, unnatural face.

"The last one. Zeke. It could be . . . I don't see how, but possibly . . ."

"Yes?"

"It's my stepbrother's name."

36

Zeke had taken Natalie and the kids for an early supper outside Charlottesville, hoping that the meal would make up
for the long drive ahead. They had spent the weekend in the
Shenandoahs, acting like any family on a beautiful fall weekend—
driving Skyline Drive, going to the caverns. Zeke had bought the
kids souvenirs, given piggyback rides to Penina and Efraim. Who
could ever associate this picture-perfect family of five with a cop
dying on a roadside back in Ohio? A dead Ohio cop didn't even
make the TV news in Virginia, the old Plymouth was back in the
mall parking lot in West Virginia, and a Taurus with Maryland tags
was nothing extraordinary here. But when Zeke told the family to
pile into the car for dinner, Isaac had gone to stand by the trunk.
Force of habit, Zeke guessed.

"I already told you, no more trunk, buckaroo," he said.

"Oh. I thought you were just giving me time off for the weekend."

"No, we're done with the trunk. You ride in the car from now on."

You think a kid would be grateful, but this one had to challenge everything.

"Why?"

"Well, for one thing, this car doesn't have a luggage rack."

"But we'll need money eventually."

So he had put it together after all. Zeke wasn't sure how much the kid knew, but it was definitely too much. Which only made Zeke more determined to do what he'd decided, to execute the plan he'd plotted in his head while pretending to look at scenery all weekend.

"No, we've got plenty." Which was a stretch, but Zeke decided to live the lie, picking one of the nicer chain restaurants for dinner, a place with menus big as Bibles and apple-cheeked waitresses in provocative little aprons that twitched around their hips when they walked. Every girl in the restaurant moved as if she were a drill-team member, with prancing, pony steps. But Zeke kept his eyes low. It was never good for Natalie to notice him noticing.

But she was absorbed in the twins, sitting between them, an arm around each one, her head lowered as they whispered to her and patted her face. At this point their chatter was almost total gibberish, or so it seemed to Zeke. He wondered if their odd sounds were some sort of bastard Russian, their own Yiddish lite. Natalie nodded and whispered to them as if she understood every word. Isaac, placed with great deliberation between Zeke and the wall, cut his vegetarian omelet into smaller and smaller pieces but didn't put any of it in his mouth that Zeke could see.

"Dunkin' Donuts is kosher," Isaac said. "Some anyway."

"Now that's a healthy way to end the day," Zeke said, trying to sound good-natured. "With a bellyful of sugar and some high-octane coffee."

"I wasn't really talking to you," Isaac said. "I was just observing to myself."

"Observe away, buddy."

Zeke studied Natalie. God, she was beautiful. Women had come easy to him all his life, always good-looking women, too. But the first time he had seen Natalie, he had understood why rich men stole masterpieces they could never display. Some things you owned to impress others, other things you needed only for yourself. From the moment he glimpsed Natalie, waiting in the visiting room for her father, he had to have her. Mark, there to see Zeke, had noticed her, too. Not that he would admit it, the prig. Every man in the room had watched that teenage sylph float across the floor. She gave the impression that she didn't know the clatter she was setting off inside all those men, but that was calculated. Natalie was like a terrorist sitting on a cache of nuclear weapons. She understood exactly how much power she had, and how much damage she could do.

Lucky, she fell just as hard for him as he did for her. He had played to her sense of romance, giving her the one thing that no man ever had, entering willingly into her soap-opera world of love letters and poetry and anguished phone calls.

What do you do when you want a woman like that and you can't be alone with her for a decade? It was one thing to hold on to her while he was in Jessup, but Zeke knew that all bets would be off once he was in Terre Haute. It was too far away, his sentence too long. His solution had been nothing short of genius, if he did say so himself. He stored Natalie in Mark's house, just another beautiful thing in that sterile museum full of paintings and sculptures. It had been too perfect. Orthodox life had required her to dress modestly, to live modestly, not even touching other men. She was hidden in plain sight, locked up in Pikesville waiting for him. And while he had been furious when she showed up on his release day with three little bonuses in tow, he had to admit he was moved by her devotion to them. If only his mother had cared as much. But she had chosen her second husband over her son, time and time again.

Had his mother and Mark's father been having an affair before his father's death? He could believe it of Aaron Rubin—the gonif, the schemer—but not of his mother, never of his mother. It was not so far-fetched to believe that Rubin had coveted his mother all along, even before his own wife had died. Leah Rubenstein had been a prize, a German Jew so proper she was almost a gentile. The two young partners had met her when she came in to buy her first mink, just eighteen. Zeke's father had fallen in love with the shy, proper girl, while the already-betrothed Aaron Rubin had been smitten with her money. And in the end both men got what they wanted. Yakob Rubenstein got love, Aaron Rubin got money.

Jewish women kept their property—but not in death. Zeke's mother had died of breast cancer his senior year in college, and it was then that the boy who was born Nathaniel Ezekiel Rubenstein became just Zeke. What did it say about Aaron Rubin, that every woman who married him died of cancer? Rubin was the sickness. Rubin was evil. Rubin was the one who had convinced Zeke's mother that he would care for her son, so she hadn't felt the need to provide for Zeke in her will. And while Aaron Rubin was ready to share his second wife's largesse with her only son, it turned out he wanted to apply condition upon condition. If Zeke—or Nat, as the family never stopped calling him, despite his insistence that he wanted to be known by his middle name—brought his grades up, if he graduated from Maryland, if he stopped wrapping cars around trees, then he might—might, mind you, might—find a place at Robbins & Sons. The business *his* father had cofounded, the business that was his by all rights.

"Fuck you," Zeke told his stepfather, and struck out on his own, starting his own clothing store. Like father, like son. Right down to the money problems and the subsequent felonies. Zeke chose credit-card fraud. His father tried arson.

People always said that if Zeke's father hadn't died, the gossip would have killed him. Zeke, only five at the time of his suicide, was spared the whispers at first. By the time he was a teenager, however, the neighborhood yentas and yentas-in-training made sure he knew every shameful detail. The division of the business, with the shrewd *macher* Rubin screwing Rubenstein, persuading him to take the downtown real estate and the dress business, while he moved the furs to the suburbs. Then there was the fire at the store, an arson fire that killed a night watchman who should have been on his dinner break, but they never proved that Zeke's father did it. He didn't live long enough to be charged.

To Zeke's way of thinking, his father's death proved only that he was in despair, not that he had arranged that little bolt of Jewish lightning. The fire had wiped him out—the insurance company didn't want to pay because of the arson investigation. Yakob Rubenstein had nowhere to turn, except to his wife's bank accounts, and sweet, pliant Leah didn't want to give him her money. Why did everyone harp on the suspicious fire while ignoring the serendipity of the Widower Rubin marrying the Widow Rubenstein less than six months later? Rubin had screwed his onetime partner, now he screwed his wife. All the while expecting Nathaniel Ezekiel to toe the line, to be a scared little yes-sir boy like his own son, Mark.

If only his own mother had been more like Natalie and put her son first. If only Natalie were more like his mother, willing to abandon her children for the man she loved. One was too weak, the other too strong.

Well, Natalie would need her strength when she learned that her children were dead. It would be hard for weeks, even months—Zeke had no illusions about that. But it was the only solution that made everything work out. He'd give her another baby to make up for the ones she had to lose.

He reviewed the plan in his head, glorying in the details. Zeke would call Mark and propose a deal: All the cash he could raise in one business day in exchange for the children. Once that was done, they would meet—oh, so fitting—in the Robbins & Co. storage facility. He would tell Mark and the children to go into the storage vault, promising to send Natalie to unlock the door in a few hours.

But in a few hours, Zeke and Natalie would be long gone, taking whatever money Mark had given them.

And when Mark and the children were found, suffocated, it would be obvious to everyone what had happened, even Natalie. Mark was so bitter, so warped, that he'd decided to kill her children to get back at her. It happens. Zeke knew a guy at Jessup who did just that, killed two kids to get back at the wife who was divorcing him. Men are capable of anything. So Mark would be dead—which was the plan all along—and Natalie would inherit his money, which was really Zeke's money.

He never wanted to kill the children, truly. He'd been trying to think of a way around it, truth be told. But Penina and Efraim had seen too much, back on the highway in Ohio. Isaac knew too much and talked too much. They would end up hanging their own mother—and Zeke alongside her. Besides, they'd be happy for a few hours. They'd have hope. Before they used up all the oxygen, they'd think they were preparing for a reunion. Even Mark would dare to be hopeful, thinking his life was about to be made whole again, that Natalie was finally coming back.

Horrible yes, but better for Natalie—and Zeke. They would get a fresh start, they would have the life for which they had planned all these years. There weren't supposed to be any children. He thought he had made that clear to Natalie. It wasn't his fault that she had ignored his instructions. No children, ever. He didn't want to be a father to another man's sons, because he knew how impossible that was.

"Everybody settle in," he said, trying to sound cheerful. "We need to make good time." A sign promised that Washington was only sixty miles ahead, which meant Baltimore was a mere one hundred—not even ninety minutes if the highways treated them right. "Good time means we get to the good times that much faster." Zeke's father always said that when they went on their rare trips, usually just long weekends to Ocean City. There was always too much work to do to take longer vacations. He was the one who taught Zeke the traveling song. *"We're hitting the road! (We're hitting the road!) Without a single care! (Without a single care!) 'Cuz we're going, and we'll know where we are when we're there."*

Zeke began singing the song lustily, not minding when the children refused to chime in. This time he sang all the parts himself.

37

B ut I asked you," Tess said, her voice a little whiny even to her
own ears. "I *specifically* asked you about Nathaniel Rubenstein when his name showed up on the list, and you said he
was still in federal prison. You also said he never participated in the
group."

They were in the living room, where Mark had spent a painful
half hour stammering through a family history that made Tess realize how uncomplicated—and, really, how unblighted—her own
family was. Robbins & Sons had started off as a partnership between Aaron Rubin and Yakob Rubenstein, two young friends who
had learned the garment trade from their fathers, both tailors.
There had been no sons, and no wives, when they opened their
store on Lombard Street, but all that was assumed. They soon married, and both had sons the same blessed year. They quarreled, they

went their separate ways. In the same cursed year that Aaron lost his wife to cancer, Leah Rubenstein lost her husband to suicide. The pair married while the boys were in grade school. Everything Mark had told Tess about Nathaniel Rubenstein—the stolen goods accepted to prop up his fledgling business, the credit-card fraud, his refusal to participate in the group—was true.

Mark had just neglected to mention that the man was his stepbrother.

"Besides, he's still in prison, as far as I know. He got two and ten. That adds up to twelve."

"Your arithmetic is great, but your knowledge of corrections is a little sketchy. He probably got credit for the state time. Or he could have been released early for any number of reasons."

Mark held out his hands, almost as if he were a drowning man. "My stepbrother stopped speaking to me years ago, so I wouldn't have any idea if he got out early. I started the group at Jessup for him, but he wanted no part of it, and no part of me. I'm not sure he even knows Boris."

Tess shot a look at Whitney, who was circling the room appraising Mark's art collection. Literally appraising, for Whitney had a complicated formula that identified potential charitable givers according to how much they were willing to spend on the fine arts. *In for a Picasso, in for a pound*, she liked to say.

"Maybe this is the secret Boris has been dangling like bait all these years. He knew there was something between his daughter and your stepbrother."

"What do you mean by that? Besides, it could be a coincidence. Who knows what Isaac was spelling, if anything?"

Given their quarrel earlier in the day, Tess was reluctant to challenge Mark when he went into full denial mode. Whitney, however, had no such limitations.

"Pull your head out of your ass," she said, distracted from the statue she'd been admiring. "Your runaway wife is on the road with your stepbrother. That's not a coincidence. It's a *scheme*."

Mark looked furious for a moment, as if he might throw some-thing or order them out of his home. His hands even balled into fists, then quickly came undone.

"I know," he said, his voice low. "I know. But to what purpose? If Natalie . . . wants to be with him, why couldn't she just tell me? Why run away? Why take the children?"

"I can't forget what Amos said when you showed up on his prop-erty," Tess said. "The mountain had come to Muhammad. A job done was a job done. And then he aimed his rifle at you. Do you think your stepbrother wants you dead?"

"He had no use for me, but he had no anger toward me. Toward my father, on the other hand . . ."

"What about your father?"

"Nat blamed Dad for *everything*. The failure of his father's busi-ness. His father's death, his mother's death. Nat's own failings, in school and work. But Dad gave him every chance. And when Dad died, there was even a small bequest for Nat. That's what he put into his business—and lost, through his own miscalculation. I tried to stand by him, but he made it impossible. The last time I spoke to him was in Jessup, over ten years ago."

"Where you met Natalie."

"Yes, but what does that prove? I told you. I had started the group, and her father was in it. She approached me and said she wanted to embrace Judaism, live an Orthodox life. From there things followed a natural course."

"Maybe it was your stepbrother who suggested she go to you, not her father. Maybe it was his idea that Boris Petrovich join the group in the first place, and that's the information Boris used to blackmail Natalie."

"Why? If Zeke wanted her for himself, why would he send her to me, encourage her to marry me?"

"Because through Natalie," Whitney brayed, like some horrible WASP Cassandra, "he could get all your money one day. Or at least half of it."

Strange, Whitney's directness didn't seem to bother Mark at all.

"I've been over this with Tess," Mark said. "If Natalie divorced me, much of my money wouldn't be considered a marital asset. The bulk of what I have came from my inheritance."

"The bulk of which, you just made clear, came from your stepmother. But if you were dead and the marriage *hadn't* been dissolved," Tess said, "Natalie and the children would get all of it."

They sat in silence. At least Mark and Tess did. Whitney resumed trotting around the house studying Rubin's things. Her sky blue penny loafers clattered on the wood floors, little preppy tap shoes.

"What do you want to do?" Tess asked.

"Kill myself?"

"Seriously."

"I was being fairly serious. I want to scream. I want to talk to my rabbi. I want to go get my gun out of the glove compartment of my car and put it in my mouth. But most of all I want to see Natalie, to ask her what's going on. I don't think she could lie to my face."

"Mark—"

"I know. You're going to say she's been lying to my face for ten years, that she's a coldhearted schemer. But she never told me I was the *only* man she loved, just that she loved me. Isn't it possible for a woman to love two men? Couldn't she have grown to love me in spite of herself? We have three children, this house, a life together. Wouldn't that have to mean something to her?"

Tess pretended these were rhetorical questions. "Mark, I think we have to proceed with the assumption that your life is at risk, that someone's going to make another attempt. Now, I know you're handy with a SIG Sauer, but you should let me arrange some sort of professional security for you."

"A bodyguard?"

"Yes. And I'd like your permission to go to county Homicide, along with the feds, and tell them we believe that your estranged wife wants you dead."

"Only I don't believe that. Nat—Nat and Nat, Nathaniel and Natalie, how cute—may have some dark fantasies and grudges, but he's not given to violence."

"No, but he's willing to delegate. That's what we have to worry about."

Another long silence, only this time the *flap-flap-flap* of Whitney's loafers was interrupted by the phone. Mark went to his study, probably terrified of taking the call within Whitney's hearing. Tess seized the opportunity to grab Whitney and ask her to stop behaving like a human wealth calculator.

"Sorry. Force of habit. Boy, he's got it bad, doesn't he? 'My wife ran off with my brother, and now she wants me dead.' It's almost a country song."

"As sung by Kinky Friedman and the Texas Jewboys. Families and business. I swear, there's nothing more virulent. Mark's stepbrother may have taken it to a new level, but this is what happens in too many family businesses. Makes me glad the Weinstein dynasty went bust before I was born."

"Makes me glad I'm an only child," Whitney said.

Tess didn't point out that there were many people who were grateful the Talbots had decided to procreate only once.

"That was Paul," Mark said, returning to the room. "Another of Mrs. Gordon's famous emergencies. But I've decided you have a point. I'll go spend the night in a hotel, and I'll stay out of the office tomorrow. Only you and Paul will know where I am."

"And the bodyguard?"

"No, not yet. That seems excessive to me. But I'll call you tomorrow and tell you what I want to do, as far as the police are concerned."

"Where will you stay?"

"Harbor Court, if they have a room. Or the Wyndham."

"And you'll carry your cell and check in with me?"

"I'll carry my cell."

Whitney handed Mark her card on the way out. "We're non-secular, but we do good work. Mostly social services with a little symphony stuff thrown in for Mom. I'll send you our most recent report."

She then climbed into Tess's Toyota and fell asleep, in the manner of a hyper child exhausted by her own ceaseless energy.

"How do you know her?" Mark asked with the kind of frightened awe that Whitney often inspired in new acquaintances.

"College," Tess said. "On the Eastern Shore. But she transferred to Yale for languages—and the connections. Whitney was always very canny that way."

"Perhaps I'll send Isaac to the University of Maryland after all."

Tuesday

38

Tess checked in with Mark at 9:00 A.M., and found him at the Wyndham as promised, where his only complaint was restlessness and the lack of a view.

"I don't know what to do with myself when I'm not working," he said. "I need to *do* something."

"Take a walk," Tess said, then corrected herself. "No, you should stay inside. If you're really bored, I'll phone my aunt's store and ask her to messenger over some books, whatever you want. Meanwhile, I'm trying to decide if I should spend the day doing surveillance at your house or tracking down Lana. Maybe she's surfaced back at the salon."

"Do the surveillance," Mark said. "Keep watching for Lana, at least during the day. Then camp out in my home this evening. After all, anyone who knows me wouldn't expect to find me home during the day."

It was a good plan, and Tess felt a little sheepish about her client's being more clearheaded than she was.

"Maybe I should hang out at your work, then, see if any strangers come around."

"No point to that. Paul will be watching. No, go to the beauty salon, then my house."

"Surveillance is tricky on your block. You have the kind of neighbors that are apt to report a strange fourteen-year-old Toyota parked at the curb. And pedestrians are even more suspect in that part of Baltimore."

"What if I give you the security code, so you can open the garage door and enter the house through the kitchen? We keep a spare key beneath a flowerpot on some shelving that has gardening stuff."

"Jesus, Mark. Natalie *knows* that. She could have come in—or sent someone in—at any time."

Mark laughed. "She has her own key, Tess. I didn't change the locks. Who knows? Maybe she'll show up tonight, come right through the front door as if nothing ever happened."

His tone had a light, almost elated edge to it, as if this were the outcome he still hoped for.

"Just stay in your room. I know you can't eat the hotel food, but I'll arrange for someone to bring in a kosher meal."

"I've already made those arrangements for myself. I called the Jewish Museum and asked what catering service they use for their monthly board meetings."

"Great. I'll check in again at noon. Be good."

"Feel free to help yourself to anything in the refrigerator. And the various remote controls for the television and the DVD are in the drawer of the coffee table."

"It's surveillance, not babysitting, Mark." But she wondered just how much food Mark would have in the house, after living on his own for a month, and whether she would find any of it appealing. "If I were to order food—say, a pizza, just for example, or Chinese—is it okay if it's not kosher? Or will I somehow violate your house by bringing in *treyf*?"

"There are paper plates and plastic utensils in the cupboard just to the right of the refrigerator. Use those, take your containers with you, and it should be okay. Although, really, there are some lovely frozen latkes. They thaw in seconds in the microwave."

Hanging out in Mark's house was not unlike the babysitting gigs of Tess's teenage years. Only instead of listening for muffled cries from a child's bedroom, she strained her ears toward any out-of-place sounds on the quiet suburban street. And, just like when she'd been babysitting, she was bored out of her mind in less than thirty minutes.

It had been a long, fruitless day—Lana was still MIA at work and home—and Mark had steadfastly declined to call the police about the possible threat to his life, no matter how Tess coaxed in their phone conversations. "We'll talk about that tomorrow," he insisted over and over.

Uninterested in food, she decided to indulge in another old babysitting habit—unbridled snooping. The house was neat and fairly clean, but there was that indefinable absence, the feel of a missing woman. Everything was just a bit awry, not to mention dusty. After inspecting the bookshelves and the contents of the various medicine cabinets, Tess tried the doors of Natalie's walk-in closet. The clothes, suitable to an Orthodox woman in their style and hues, were clearly expensive. Natalie had dozens of shoes and a shelf of fashionable hats, which she probably needed for synagogue. A built-in safe indicated a cache of fine jewelry. Why hadn't Natalie taken those with her to pawn as necessary? Because she wanted them back, Tess thought. Because whatever's going on is temporary, a contingency. She always meant to get them back. No fur coats, however—could she have sold them to raise money for her escape? Then Tess remembered it was still storage season. Except for excitable types such as the legendary Mrs. Gordon, who had needed her lynx before she headed off to see the fjords.

Only if the famously difficult Mrs. Gordon were on a cruise—how could she have another emergency? A distracted, lost-in-thought Mark had said last night's call was from Paul. Did that mean Mrs. Gordon had located a ship-to-shore telephone at what must be 3:00 A.M. her time and called Paul at home, demanding to have another coat airlifted to the *Norwegian Princess*? Dubious. Extremely dubious.

Adrenaline on alert, Tess called Mark's cell phone and got voice mail for the first time that day. She consulted a Rolodex next to the phone in Mark's study and found a home number for his salesman, Paul Zuravsky.

"Last night? No, Mark and I spoke this morning, and that was it. He told me he was going to be with you all day again."

Tess was too upset to care about the disapproving note in Paul's voice, as if he blamed the freckled shiksa for Mark's taking time away from the business.

"Paul, do you know where Mark was calling from?"

"He must have been on his cell, I think, because the reception was bad. But he didn't mention where he was."

"Did he say anything else about what he planned to do today? Was there anything out of the ordinary about the conversation?"

"No. But something odd happened early this afternoon. The vice president from Mark's bank called, pretty agitated. He wanted to talk to Mark about his decision to close an account. I didn't think anything of it, because Mark's capable of getting in a snit with people, forever moving and closing accounts to get better rates and deals. He's a big believer in the well-timed fit."

Tess remembered how he had terrorized the wholesaler from Montreal. Still, she couldn't see how a bank had managed to enrage him just now. Mark had claimed to be in his hotel room all day. But he had told her to call on the cell.

"Did he take the money out in cash? How much?"

"No idea. Enough to get a vice president to follow up with a phone call."

"That *fucker*," Tess said, and Paul coughed as if shocked, although Tess bet that the Mrs. Gordons of the world used a few choice words when their whims weren't indulged. "He set me up. He made sure I would be occupied all day so he could go behind my back and cut some deal with them. The idiot. They'll take the money and kill him."

"What are you talking about? He's been with you all day—" but she hung up on Paul, too agitated to explain, and dialed the Wyndham's main number.

Mark was registered, but the phone in his room rang unanswered, bouncing her to a voice-mail system in five rings. Fortunately, the valet confirmed that the Cadillac had gone out sometime in the last hour. It helped, Tess realized, being able to describe the driver as a tall, well-dressed man in a yarmulke. That detail tended to stick out in people's minds.

She looked at Mark's phone, realizing too late that she couldn't use the redial trick that Mark had tried at Lana's apartment. But he had caller ID, just as she had advised him. The call that had come in at 9:14 last night was a local one, a 410 number that looked familiar to Tess, although it was listed as "Caller Unknown." She flipped open her cell, looking at the log of calls she had made in the past two weeks, and then the numbers she had stored there since taking Mark's case.

Last night's call had been made from Vera Peters's home phone.

The days were getting shorter, each night falling faster than the one before. Dusk was long past when Tess pulled up at Vera's house, but there was only one light on, somewhere on the first floor.

She banged on the door, making more and more noise, until neighbors began to shout. "They'll be calling the police soon, if you don't answer," Tess screamed into the metal frame of the storm door. The inner door opened slowly, but it was Lana on the other side, not Vera.

"No one here wants to talk to you."

"It's really not about what you or Vera wants at this point," Tess said, shoving past Lana and showing off her gun, although she had no idea what she would do with it here. "If you don't cooperate with me, I'm going to call the police and tell them you're a coconspirator in a long laundry list of crimes."

Lana looked confused and frightened, but her voice remained firm. "No one's here."

"But someone's been here." The telltale trail of a child's detritus snaked through the living room—a strange little rock family with googly eyes, a miniature View-Master stamped "Memories of Skyline Drive," a paperback copy of *From the Mixed-Up Files of Mrs. Basil E. Frankweiler* that looked as if it had been read to death. "They were here. Where are they now, Lana?"

Vera Peters came down the stairs with her heavy tread, tying a bathrobe around her as if she had already been in bed, although the hour was early. "Tell her, Lana. I don't want any trouble. This is not my affair, and it shouldn't be yours."

"But—"

"No more *buts*. Why are you protecting her still? I only let them stay here because they promised to do the right thing by the children. You're not going to get the money they owe you. You're never going to see them again. Didn't you notice? They left the children's things, but they took their own. They're going to leave us here to explain whatever happens. We're better off talking to this nosy one than the police."

"They haven't done anything wrong, except want to be together. There's no crime in that."

"I wouldn't go that far, Lana," Tess said. "They've been pulling welfare-fraud scams and robbing banks throughout the Midwest. And didn't they hire Amos to kill Mark? Wasn't that the plan? To arrange Mark's death by a third party, then let Natalie come home and inherit everything?"

Lana shook her head in adamant disbelief and denial, even as Vera nodded, sad and resigned.

"I believe it. She cares for no one but herself, that one. From the day she was born. She took and took and took, just like her father. I didn't leave him, I left *them*. I was scared to close my eyes living under the same roof with those two criminals."

"Where are Natalie and the children?" Tess asked. "Did they call Mark last night, arrange a meeting? If they end up killing him and you don't help me, you'll be responsible. I'll tell the police you're an accessory."

Lana still didn't answer. Her misplaced loyalty was almost admirable. Tess had seen her all this time as a cold accomplice, but Lana was simply a smitten friend. When Vera turned her back on her own teenage daughter, Lana had been there to play the part of mother, sister, and ardent admirer. Lana had reflected back to Natalie the person she wanted to be—beautiful, worthy, deserving of whatever the world had to offer. She was the nurse to this Romeo and Juliet. Or, given Natalie's frame of reference, the Anita to their Tony and Maria.

"They've gone to make a deal," Vera said. "They're going to sell the children back to that idiot, make him pay for what is legally his."

"Where's the meeting place?"

Vera shrugged, while Lana stared at the floor.

"Lana, get out now. Whatever you've done to help them, I can't believe you would agree to murder."

"They wouldn't—"

"They would. Amos was going to kill Mark, and he would have killed me, too, just because I was there. Amos is dead because of *them*."

Tess was hoping Lana had some residual warmth for the man she had married. Whatever had passed between Lana and Amos, however mercenary it might have been in its origins, there must have been something genuine there. The Velvet Frost had said she was distraught earlier in the week. Lana's name was one of only five in Amos Greif's address book. SlavicBeautee.

"The business," Lana said at last. "But then they're coming back here." She looked at Vera, as if daring her to contradict. "They said they would come back for me and give me my share of the money, pay me back everything I've loaned them and more."

"The business? You mean Robbins & Sons, over on Smith Avenue?"

"No, the place they keep the furs, out in the country."

"How much of a head start do they have?"

"Enough," Lana said, gloating a bit. "You won't catch up to them."

"Only fifteen minutes or so," Vera said. "But those twins can't go long without a bathroom break, especially with Natalie making them drink all that hot chocolate before they went out. So strange, a hot drink on a night as warm as this. But Zeke said they had to drain their cups."

39

Isaac sat as far forward on the seat as his seat belt would allow, fighting his own drowsiness. He didn't understand why he felt so sleepy, not after being stuck in that little house all day with nothing to do but watch television and reread his book. But he couldn't stop yawning, despite his excitement and anticipation. The twins had already nodded off, one slumped on either side of him. The woman they said was his grandmother had chased them around all day, although not in the happy way he thought a grandmother would have. Her only concern had been to keep the twins from touching anything in her house, not that there was anything interesting to touch.

And Lana was there, too, standing by the door while his mother and Zeke shared secrets somewhere else in the house. Isaac guessed that was because they were in Baltimore now and they knew if he got even a chance, he would start running, running, and running until he found a pay phone or a policeman or even a street he knew. He would run all the way to his father's house or store if he had to. But now they said they were taking him to his father, so he didn't have to run. Still, he studied the landscape, determined to figure out where they were.

So far he hadn't even seen anything familiar. He tried to memorize the landmarks that went past. There were the usual stores and restaurants, and now they were on a highway, but it wasn't the baseball highway to Camden Yards or the big highway they took north to New York and south to Washington. Instead they seemed to be heading away from the city. In the middle of this highway, an empty subway car went rattling past, all lit up, but with no one on its blue seats, so it was like a subway car for ghosts. Isaac hoped Zeke wasn't lying. Zeke had promised them their father, but Zeke was mean enough to make a promise and break it. He was, he definitely was.

———

Natalie hadn't wanted to do the cocoa thing tonight, but Zeke had insisted. He said the children would get overstimulated at the reunion, that they would be hard to control once they saw their father again. "This is trickier than it looks," Zeke told Natalie. "We need time, as much as we can get. So you've got to let me take them in, give them to Mark, and go. No drawn-out good-byes. Everybody wins, right?"

"Not me," she had told him. They had been in her old bedroom, which her mother had stripped of every memory after Natalie left with her father, as if Natalie never existed. Vicious old bitch, refusing to fight for her own daughter. Natalie was a better mother by far. "I won't have my children. It doesn't matter how much money Mark gives us if I can't have them."

"If you hadn't killed a police officer, we might have more options," Zeke had said. He had been saying that a lot the past two days, holding it over her head, enjoying it almost too much. Whatever he wanted, it seemed, could be justified by her one mistake. A big mistake, sure, but she hadn't done it for herself, she had done it for him. He was the bank robber, he was the one who would have gone back to prison if they were caught. That had been her only thought at the time, to save Zeke. "You and I need to go somewhere far away and start new lives. We can't do that with the kids. Mark will never let us be. The two of us together have a chance. The five of us—never."

"I don't know. . . ." This was late afternoon, and they had been lying on her bed, the narrow single bed where she had dreamed about the glamorous life she so clearly deserved. Her mother could redecorate all she wanted, but she couldn't erase Natalie from this room. She was in the floorboards, the wallpaper, the dust floating in the air. In this bed, at the age of thirteen or fourteen, Natalie had dreamed about a man like Zeke, and now Zeke was wrapped around her, the fingers of his left hand entwined in her hair, his right index finger tracing the line of her jaw, her eyebrows, the not-yet-visible lines that would bracket her mouth one day, when she was old and sour. No, unthinkable. She would never look like that woman downstairs.

"Trust me. I know what's right for them. And you." He began kissing her deeply, more passionately than he had all these weeks on the road. She assumed it would be the same routine, that he would unzip himself and press her head down to him, then use his hand so she would feel some release, too, their usual teenage courtship. But he began undressing her instead, taking his time, revealing each part of her as if it were a treasure. Strange, but now she was the one who balked, nervous and unready.

"The children . . ."

"Vera and Lana are watching them."

"The door . . ."

"I locked it when we came in here."

"It's not the Ritz." But she was teasing him now, her excitement making her giggly, almost silly.

"Sure it is. Just close your eyes."

But she didn't. She left them open the entire time, so she would remember everything. She was there, she was with him, but she was also hovering above them both, observing. For more than a decade, a third of her life, this man had been the only person who shared her vision of herself, who saw her as something precious and special. She was worried that waiting so long would make it anticlimactic, but it was even better than she had dreamed. She was his now.

She was his now. Pure instinct—and not a little will—had kept Zeke from doing this all these weeks. Abstinence had been a practical decision at first. When she led him back to the motel in Terre Haute, he had assumed he would make love to her and then send her home, instructing her to stay with Mark until he could get settled and send for her. But the three kids sitting on the double bed had pretty much killed that plan—and those desires. Later, when Natalie started crawling over him in the car night after night, he had realized he would enjoy more power over her if he didn't give in right away. He would know when the time was right.

Today had sealed the deal. As drunk on sex as the kids were on their vodka-spiked cocoa, Natalie would wait in the car as instructed, assuming the exchange was going off as planned. The serotonin fumes and pheromones would carry her along, fogging her brain, keeping her from questioning too much. It would be a few days before the call would come, probably from Lana. Such a tragedy—Mark and the children, dead, a vicious act of revenge by a twisted, desperate man. Natalie would return to Baltimore to bury her family. Zeke would show up after a suitable interval, a repentant stepbrother, offering nothing more than his services at the store. The estate might take up to a year to execute, but they didn't have to live in Baltimore during that time. They could go somewhere warm if they sensed the police closing in. Somewhere without extradition, if possible.

He pulled into the parking lot outside the storage facility. Good, there was only one car, a Cadillac, parked there. It would have been more fitting if Zeke could have done this at his father's old store, but of course that was long gone. He wondered what had happened to *its* vault, one of the few things left intact after the fire—and the place his father had chosen to die.

"Wait here just one minute," he said, even as Isaac started to shout, "Daddy's car. That's Daddy's car."

It better be, Zeke thought. But Isaac had given him an idea. "Does it have a code for the locks, Isaac?"

The boy looked at him, suspicious as ever.

"He wants me to have the code, Isaac. I talked to him early today, and he said he was going to leave something in his car for me. If you tell me the code, I'll take you to your father."

"Five-six-one-four," the boy muttered, grudging to the end. Zeke punched the numbers and let himself in, opening the glove compartment. Good old predictable Mark: He had brought the gun with him, but he hadn't taken it inside. The old man had carried a gun whenever he went to the storage facility, and now Mark did it, too. Zeke slipped the SIG Sauer into his waistband and went back for the children. The twins were like little zombies, almost sleep-walking. Isaac moved even more slowly, dragging his feet. But as they reached the door, his eyes focused on the gun at Zeke's waist-band.

"You're a liar," he said. "Daddy's not in there. You probably stole his car just to fool us, and parked it here. I'm not going in there with you."

"No, Zeke, he's in there, waiting for you. Honest."

"Then why did you steal his gun? Why do you steal *everything?*"

And with that the little *pisher* turned and ran, heading down the dark road between the cornfields. It was deserted out here, but who knew what lay over the next hill? Isaac could come back with a farmer carrying a shotgun, or some well-meaning soccer mom.

"Natalie, go get him and bring him back."

"But—"

"Just *go*. Use the car. He's headed away from the highway. He's got no shot of getting far, not out here. We promised Mark three kids for forty thousand dollars. If we don't bring all three, he won't give us anything."

———————

Isaac ran until he felt that his legs and lungs might explode from the effort. Why did his legs feel so heavy? When he saw the headlights burning their beams into the road ahead of him, spotlighting his shadow as if he were a newly restored Peter Pan, he veered into the cornfields. The corn was long gone, but the stalks were still there, dry and crackly, and they whistled as he tried to move between them, announcing his every step. The car stopped and he stopped, but now his breathing was so loud. Could they hear his breathing?

"Isaac." It was his mother's sweetest voice. "Your father really is here. He's waiting for you."

He didn't say anything. It could be a trick.

"I wouldn't lie to you. He's here. This is his storage place, you know that. He's inside, waiting to see you."

Isaac's breath was so noisy in his chest. He had to make it go away, or at least be quieter. He inhaled, tried to hold it as long as possible.

"Isaac, you're going home to live now. You're going back to our house, back to school. Everything will be as you like it."

She was in the corn now. He could hear it crackling around her. He didn't want to say anything, because then she would know where he was. But he had to ask.

"And you, Mama?"

She must have stopped moving, for he no longer heard the rustle of the cornstalks. "What do you mean, Isaac?"

"Are you going home, too?"

She didn't answer.

"You have to tell the truth. You just said you would never lie to me. You said that just the other day."

"Yes, Isaac." She was moving again, getting closer.

"Yes, what?"

"Yes, I told you that. I won't lie to you."

"So tell me."

"Isaac—your father is waiting. Really, truly."

"No, tell me, Mama. What are you going to do? Where are you going to go?"

"I don't know, Isaac. I don't know what I'm going to do. But I know you want to go home."

With that she emerged from the corn, just a few feet from him. He could have turned and run in the other direction, but where would he go, what would he do? This was his choice. He could live in the house he had always known, with his father, or he could live with his mother and Zeke. But maybe his mother would change her mind, if he waited long enough, if he talked to her. Maybe she would love his father again, once she saw him. Or, as time went on, maybe she would miss them so much she would give up Zeke and come back to them.

His mother held out her arms to him, and he went to her, pressing his face into her stomach, smelling all her smells, letting her rub his head.

"You're a good boy, Isaac. I love you so much. Never forget that, okay? Your mother loves you."

"I love you, too, Mama."

She took his hand in hers. "Now let's go see Daddy."

40

T ess couldn't decide if she should be relieved or in despair when she saw that Mark's Cadillac was the only car at the storage facility. *What if I'm too late? What if he's dead inside?* She drew her gun and entered a small anteroom, a makeshift office created by cheap plywood siding, a door in the center. Cautiously, she tried the knob, waiting to see if anyone would respond to that motion.

"Nat?" a voice asked. A man's voice, not unlike Mark's, but definitely not Mark's. Tess backed up and kicked the door, on the off chance that the man had positioned himself behind it, then crossed the threshold with her gun firmly in both hands.

"Put your hands above your head," she told the man, who stood no more than ten feet from her, pacing a narrow corridor with two heavy, vaultlike doors on either side.

The man complied, clasping his hands to the crown of his head, sizing her up as she sized him up. The descriptions of him in the random sightings had always been so vague that Tess had never been able to get a clear picture in her mind. Why hadn't people mentioned how handsome he was? Of course, not everyone might have found him so, but even those who didn't care for this type—tall, lean, with dark skin and light eyes—should have noticed he was a striking man.

But the oddest fact of his appearance, by far, was how strongly he favored Mark. If Tess hadn't known otherwise, she would have taken them for blood relations. The coloring, the features, were all very similar. This one was taller, true, with the kind of body that a disciplined man can sculpt over a long prison sentence. His eyes were a cold, hard blue, whereas Mark's were brown and soft. But there was a resemblance.

"Nathaniel Rubenstein," she said, her gun aimed at his midsection. He kept his hands on his head, making no attempt to reach for the gun tucked into his waistband. She recognized the distinctive grip of Mark's SIG Sauer.

"I prefer to be called Zeke," he said.

"Where's Mark? Is he alive?"

"Well, he's either behind Door Number One or"—he jerked his head toward the other door—"Door Number Two. Are you ready to play Let's Make a Deal?"

"And the children? Are they here, too?"

"You the chick he hired? Lana told me about you." He smiled, sure of his charm even now. Oh, this one had been talking his way out of trouble for most of his life.

"Let him out."

"No can do."

"Excuse me?" She wondered if she could get away with shooting him while his arms were raised.

"I need to keep him there, just for a few hours. Him and the kids. This is a business deal, plain and simple. It doesn't involve you—or wasn't supposed to. I made him promise to leave anyone else out of it, including his private detective, and he was happy to oblige."

"Are they alive?"

"Absolutely. But since you showed up, I need to put you in there, too, for safekeeping. Really, it's just business. Don't take it personally."

"No," Tess said, backing away from him, making sure she was not within reach.

"Well, I guess it's a standoff, then." He flashed her a smile, then started to lower his hands.

"Don't," she said in her sternest voice.

He shrugged, backing up. Tess heard steps in the anteroom and pressed her back against the wall, so she had the best vantage point possible. Natalie appeared, hugging Isaac to one side and cradling a shoe box in the right hand. It was disorienting, seeing the human versions of the people Tess had been seeking, almost like meeting celebrities in the flesh.

"Good girl," Zeke crooned. "You found Isaac. Look, Isaac—I told you that your dad would be here."

He opened the door to his right, revealing Mark Rubin on the floor of a vault crowded with coats, the twins curled up in his lap, clutching him like little orangutans.

"Daddy!" Isaac threw himself at his father. Under different circumstances it would have been a touching reunion.

"Now I really need you to go in there, too," Zeke said to Tess.

"No."

"Do what he says." Natalie had dropped the shoe box to the floor and was now holding a gun on Tess. She didn't look particularly comfortable with it, but she seemed awfully determined.

"Good girl," Zeke said again. "Good, careful Natalie. You always have my back."

"I got nervous when I saw the strange car," she said, tossing her head like a teenager accepting a compliment. "I wasn't sure what was going on, so I thought I should get my gun."

"I'm afraid you're outnumbered," Zeke said to Tess with that same insistent, phony charm. "But it's really not so bad. You'll just be in there an hour or two, and then Lana will come to let you out. That's all. We just need a head start. Oh, and your cell phone. You do have one, right?"

When Tess hesitated, Zeke pointed his gun at Mark and the children. Tess threw him the phone with her left hand, keeping her gun steady in her right.

"I'd be more convinced of your good intentions if I didn't know you're a criminal who's already tried to kill your stepbrother at least once."

"That hurts my feelings, I admit. But at this point I can't really worry about what you think. Mark and the children are safe, as you can see. But if I have to kill you, then I'll have to kill them to keep from having witnesses. So *please*—" Again he gestured toward the vault.

"Let us go," Tess said. "Give us the head start. Mark is more trustworthy than you. He'll give you his word that we'll walk away and wait a day before we tell the cops what happened here."

"Mark lies, too. All Rubins lie. The apple doesn't fall far from the tree." Zeke looked at Natalie. "Right, honey? Like father, like son? Like father, like daughter, too, come to think of it."

Natalie's expression was pained. Did she not want to leave her children? Her husband? But she wouldn't even meet Mark's beseeching gaze.

"We're wasting time," Zeke said. "Please get into the motherfuckin' vault, or I'll kill you, then kill Mark, and take the children with us. How's that for incentive?"

Tess looked at Mark, desperate for guidance, but he was just staring at Natalie, as if she were an apparition, the embodiment of a dream he never really expected to come true. Isaac shook his father's shoulder, and Mark put an arm around his son, but he didn't seem to be focused on the events crashing around him.

"It's death either way, isn't it?" Tess demanded, wanting to force Zeke to state his intentions, in hopes it would jar Mark into action. There were two of them. If Mark rushed Zeke and she went after Natalie, they might have a chance, if only because no mother could be monstrous enough to risk shooting her own children. "You'll shoot us or leave us here to suffocate. Frankly, I'd rather be shot."

"No one's going to suffocate. These vaults are huge. It would take a day for the five of you to use up the oxygen in one, and I plan to send someone here within the hour. You're just being melodramatic."

"Then why," Isaac asked, "did you turn off the fan?"

All the adults turned to the little boy. His face was crumpled and creased, and there was a streak of dirt on one cheek, flaky bits of dry leaves in his dark hair.

"What are you talking about, partner?" Zeke was trying to sound jovial again but not quite pulling it off. "You'd freeze if I left the air on."

"We keep the vault at forty-five degrees," Isaac said, and the plural pronoun just about broke Tess's heart. "That's cold, but not so cold as to make people freeze. But there's a system that makes the air move in and out as well. It's off—I can't hear it humming. You don't want the air to circulate. You want us to die."

"Zeke?" It was Natalie's voice, perplexed yet hopeful, sure he could explain it.

"The little know-it-all is wrong, Nat. It's a cool night. I'm only thinking of them. It doesn't matter if the air is off for a few hours."

"But we're just going to be in here for an hour," Isaac persisted. "You said. And if we got cold, we could wrap ourselves in the coats. So why are you turning off the air?"

"Isaac's right, Natalie." Mark had finally spoken. "There's only one reason to turn the air off."

Her loyalties were still with the other man. "Zeke?"

"We're up against a wall, Natalie. Because of Ohio." He hummed the refrain of Neil Young's "Ohio," mystifying Tess. "We don't have a lot of options. But you have my word. I'll send Lana to get them as soon as we're over the state line."

"I don't know what *Ohio* has to do with this." Natalie's tone was bitter and petulant, the voice of a person who had been reminded once too often of some failing. "I need you to promise me right now that they'll be okay."

"Have I ever lied to you?"

Of course he has, Tess wanted to scream. *He's a liar and a thief, and he's about to become a killer.* But Natalie, after a few seconds of intense thought, just shrugged and motioned Tess into the vault. She didn't take Tess's gun, though. Perhaps it was an act of kindness. The five hostages might prefer to shoot themselves rather than claw for air in the final minutes of their lives.

"Mommy?" Isaac asked, and it was a dozen questions at once. The twins rubbed their eyes, mewling like kittens, but too floppy and boneless to stand.

"I love you all," Natalie said. "Never forget that. I love you more than life itself."

With that she closed the door on them.

Tess waited no more than thirty seconds, then pulled out her second cell phone, the one she carried for outgoing calls only. No signal—the vault was too well built. Foolishly, she had counted on the second phone to save them. If she had known it wouldn't work, she would have thrown herself at Natalie, taken the chance that she could overpower her before Zeke got a shot off. Too bad that Mark Rubin didn't have a little more gonif in him, hadn't tried to get by with a shoddier storage facility. A place as leaky and air-riddled as his father's might have saved their lives.

"Is there any way out?" she asked Mark.

He shook his head. "No, I'm afraid not. It's pretty impenetrable. I used to be proud of that."

"Is there any reason someone—Paul, anyone—might come here before . . . ?" She didn't want to be too explicit about their fate, not in front of the children, although Isaac clearly knew what was going on.

Another sad, mournful shake. "No. I made sure no one would know I was here. I'm sorry."

"Me, too."

She also was sorry that Vera and Lana hadn't stonewalled her longer. If she had been just a few minutes later, Natalie and Zeke would be gone, and she could have been the Rubin family's great rescuer.

"He told me he would give me the children in exchange for whatever cash I could raise. I couldn't imagine . . . I never thought . . . I mean, how could Natalie agree to such a thing?"

"I don't think Natalie knew, until a minute ago, what he had planned. She probably still believes he'll call Lana."

"She never loved me," Mark said. "Everything—all of this—was just a ruse, a game. From the first. Nat played Pygmalion and created my perfect woman, knowing all along he was going to take her back. He enjoyed telling me that tonight. He said I took his bride, not the other way around, which marks me as the true sinner in our family."

"I'm sure Natalie came to love you, in her own way," Tess said. She might as well say what Mark wanted to hear, given their circumstances. "As much as she can love anyone."

She was glad that she had never told Mark Rubin about his wife's past. It didn't matter if Natalie had sold sexual favors to one man, one hundred, or even one thousand. She had chosen Mark's stepbrother over Mark, chosen a man over her children. That was enough pain for a husband to shoulder in the final hours of his life.

"She loves her children," Mark said. "She couldn't fake that."

Tess shrugged. Perhaps Mark was right, but Natalie had left her children to die.

She paced the small area, determined to find a way out. She had no intention of dying, not today. Perhaps it was ridiculous to think she had a say in it, but that was how she felt. A tantrum did not seem out of the question. Let Mark pray, as he seemed to be doing now. Tess wanted to throw herself on the hard floor and beat her fists, drum her feet. Wouldn't someone miss her before their time was up? Could the room really be that airtight? The dogs would know she was gone, perhaps start a mournful cry that would irritate the neighbors, nothing more. Otherwise, there was no one in the world who kept track of her, who checked in with her every day. Even the SnoopSisters wouldn't notice a silence of a day or two.

The door to the vault was suddenly wrenched open. Natalie hugged the jamb as if she were too weak to stand. Her face was as green as her eyes. She still held her gun.

"I don't want the children to see," she said. "But Zeke . . . I'm afraid . . . I think you need to call someone."

Tess, taking no chances, pried the gun from Natalie's fingers before she ran down the hall and out into the air, the wonderful, cool, breathable air of which she had been deprived for no more than five minutes.

She was no coroner, and she didn't want to touch the body she found slumped over the steering wheel, but she was pretty certain that Nathaniel Ezekiel Rubenstein had never seen it coming. He had turned away from Natalie on the dangerous presumption that he had enjoyed the last word.

Death was not instantaneous, but it was close enough. Zeke had felt the shock of the bullet's trajectory, cutting upward through his torso. Natalie, firing a gun for only the second time in her life, hadn't been able to control the kick. He swore he could trace the bullet's exact path, knew which organs it sliced through on the way to his heart, which it missed by a millimeter or two. But it had done its job well enough, ripping through enough arteries and veins to guarantee his demise.

As he hung over the steering wheel, Zeke's last thoughts were for Natalie. They did not follow the seven classic stages, but they were close. Surprise—he never saw it coming, literally and figuratively. Anger—stupid Russian bitch. Amazement—who knew she had it in her? Grudging respect. *She'll tell them I killed the cop, back in Ohio. She'll blame everything on me and get away with it, because of that angel face of hers.*

In the end Zeke had just enough time to lose faith in everything he had ever believed—in his own power and brilliance, in the steadfastness of Natalie's love, in the destiny of the birthright he had been denied. He didn't have time, however, to replace those beliefs with anything else.

November

41

Katherine Frances Monaghan married Tyner Francis Gray at the Enoch Pratt Free Library on November 21. Perhaps it was a bad sign for Baltimore's quality-of-life index that the central branch of the venerable library system rented itself out for weddings to pick up a few extra dollars, but it was the perfect venue for a woman who had devoted her life to the written word. Tess was amazed by the guest list, which had swelled to almost three hundred names and included Baltimore luminaries that she had never known were among Kitty's and Tyner's acquaintances.

"I think I see half of the '66 Orioles pitching staff out there," Tess said, peeking around a set of shelves in the social-sciences wing, where Kitty was making last-minute preparations. "And the entire cast of *Homicide*, first season. How do you know all these people?"

"A bookstore owner isn't much different than a priest or a doctor. I tend to their needs, and I keep their secrets. It builds up a lot of goodwill."

"Why is the former governor here? I'm not even convinced he's literate."

"Politicians are easy. Just give them money and they're your friends for life." Tess remembered that Mark Rubin had given her the same advice. "How do I look?"

Given that Kitty looked beautiful even when she rolled out of bed in the morning, it was to be expected that she would be radiant on her wedding day. But there was something extra, an additional glow, a brighter spark in her eyes. Much to Tess's relief, Kitty had chosen a relatively restrained outfit, a suit in a peach color that had always flattered her. She was the most gorgeous woman in the room, as always, but Tess did well by her black dress, her hair coaxed into an upsweep by the hairdresser Kitty had hired. If the shoes hadn't been so painful, she almost might have enjoyed her glamour-girl alter ego.

"You look great," she told her aunt. Feeling dangerously close to tears, she sought refuge in sarcasm. "But I knew the bride when she used to rock and roll."

"Well, the groom rolls. You'll always have that." Kitty glanced at the large clock high above the atrium. "We'll be starting in two minutes. And in fifteen minutes all these weeks of planning and fretting and me being a basket case will be officially over. Seems kind of silly when you think about it."

"Why did you do it?" Tess asked. "I don't mean the wedding so much as marriage. You're over forty, you and Tyner were already living together, you both have your own money, your own careers. You're clearly not going to start a family—"

"I could always adopt a girl from China," Kitty said, her face full of mischief. "And don't forget that movie director, the one whose wife had twins when she was in her fifties."

"But why *marriage*?"

Kitty answered the question with matter-of-fact, unhurried

calm, as if they were in her store on a slow afternoon, not holding up three hundred people waiting for a wedding. "We take so many unconscious risks in this life—especially you, sweetie—that we might as well take a few conscious ones from time to time."

She smoothed a piece of hair back from Tess's forehead. An hour out from under the beautician's touch, a few stubborn pieces were already asserting themselves. Had her hair always been this unruly, or was it just cranky since it had been shorn before its time? "I wish you had a date for the wedding. It's a shame Crow couldn't make it up from Charlottesville."

"I almost had four dates," Tess said. "But Mark checked the time and realized the sun wouldn't have been down long enough for them to make it here on time from Pikesville. Besides, the catering isn't kosher, and the children would be up past their bed-times. Mark is very strict about their routines—although not as strict as he used to be. He even let the children celebrate Sukkoth late. Isaac said it wasn't fair to have Yom Kippur without having Sukkoth, too."

She had, in fact, helped Mark and the children build the tradi-tional shelter, with Isaac instructing her at great length on the ritu-als of the holiday, a celebration of the harvest.

"We'll make a Jew out of you yet," Mark had joked.

"Maybe a half one," Tess said.

"Can you be a half Jew?" Isaac had asked. "Don't you have to be all or nothing?"

Mark Rubin had treated the question with the utmost serious-ness. Tess was learning this was the way he treated all his children's questions, large and small.

"When it comes to faith, you believe or you don't believe," he had told his son. "But there is a cultural aspect to Judaism, too, and Miss Monaghan is talking about that part of herself. Her mother's family was Jewish, but she wasn't raised to believe anything."

"Yes I was," Tess protested. "I was raised to believe that a good handshake, big tips, and a decent Christmas-card list can grease the wheels of doing business. And that Jews can have crab feasts as long as they have them outdoors."

Mark didn't want to laugh at that bit of sacrilege, not in front of his children, but he did anyway. "Tess doesn't have a religion. But she does believe many things. And she sticks by them, which is more than some religious people can say. She honors her own principles."

"And Mama? Was she a half Jew or a whole one?"

It was as if a cloud had passed over the sun and a bright day had grown chilly and dreary. With just a glance at Mark's face, Tess could tell he was thinking about Natalie, who was being held in a Maryland jail and fighting extradition to Ohio, where she and Zeke had been implicated in the death of a patrolman. Mark could not believe that his wife had killed anyone but Zeke, and Tess saw no reason to argue with him. But a police officer was dead, and Ohio wanted a live suspect to try. Tess, remembering the coded exchange between Zeke and Natalie, had a hunch Ohio was after the right person. But she held her tongue around Mark. People needed to believe what they needed to believe.

"Your mother," Mark said at last, "is a good woman who loves you very much. That was what she believed in—that you were precious and worth making any sacrifice for."

The Rubin Sukkoth table groaned with offerings from throughout Pikesville, and Tess knew that Mark Rubin would remain alone only by his own choice. Still, he had yet to pursue a *get* from Natalie, or even a more mundane Maryland divorce. She hoped he would. Mark Rubin was an awfully attractive man. Not attractive enough to convert for—Tess knew her limitations. But he would make such a good husband for the right woman, once he was through yearning for the woman he couldn't have, the woman no one should really want.

In the Pratt the jazz trio, a group of Peabody students, began playing a light classical piece that Tess knew she should recognize but didn't. *Crow would know*, she thought, the memory almost unbidden. Crow always knew things like that.

"That's your cue," Kitty said, pushing her past the shelf of biographies, and Tess walked the length of carpet that had been put down to create an aisle between the rows of folding chairs. She walked a little more swiftly than she should, although the heels kept her from moving with her usual long stride. At the end of the runner, she greeted Tyner and then turned to watch Kitty walk down the aisle. Because of her dual duties, she did not carry flowers, but she had a tiny velvet bag dangling from a wrist corsage. She would produce the ring from that bag when the time came.

Kitty swept up the aisle on the arm of Tess's father, Patrick, the oldest of her five brothers. The Unitarian minister raced through the service as if he had a train to catch, and it was a little pro forma to Tess's taste, with the usual Shakespearean admonitions—love is not love that seeks to alter, allow no impediments to the love between two true minds, et cetera, et cetera. Kitty had wanted Tess to give a reading, but she had balked. She had no fear of public speaking, but she was terrified of choking up from emotion, and Tyner would never let her live that down.

Fifteen minutes proved to be a generous estimate. The wedding was over in twelve, making way for the grand party Kitty had been promising all fall. Tess followed her aunt down the aisle, finishing the last of her attendant duties—removing the veil and folding it into a sealed plastic wrapper, finding a place to keep Kitty's flowers for the duration of the reception, which was to be held a few blocks northward in yet another library, the Peabody.

"You're in the second car," Kitty said. "You'll find it parked at the curb."

"Really, Kitty, I could have walked it, even in these shoes. Or grabbed a ride with my folks."

"No," she said, reverting back into her adamant-bride mode. "It's very important to me that the wedding party arrive with proper pomp and circumstance. Besides, I want you to open this in the car." She handed Tess a small box from Tiffany's. "It's traditional for the bride to give her maid of honor a gift. Don't lose this."

"I didn't lose the ring, did I?" Actually, she had almost knocked it down the sink in the Pratt washroom before the ceremony, but there didn't seem to be any reason to mention that fact now that the ring was safe on Kitty's left hand.

The Lincoln Town Car was at the curb, as promised. Tess crawled in, inadvertently flashing the guests milling on the sidewalk—she still hadn't gotten the hang of maneuvering in such a sleek skirt—and settled herself in the deep backseat. The car reminded her of Mark's. She'd hate to admit it to anyone, but she had grown rather fond of that Cadillac and had even priced a few used ones on the Internet. A woman who did surveillance for a living deserved a more comfortable ride. Besides, as Uncle Donald said: "It's a write-off, *mamele.*"

Kitty came out and was showered with mesh bags of seed, while Tyner rolled behind her, trying to scowl but failing. He heaved himself into the limousine, a Lincoln Navigator, and Kitty folded his chair with a speedy efficiency that spoke volumes of their ease with each other. If you had to be in a wheelchair, you might as well be with someone who knew how to fold it, Tess thought.

"The Peabody," she told the driver, pulling on the ribbon of the box Kitty had given her. They said good things came in small packages, but Tess couldn't think of anything she wanted that was this tiny. Inside, under layers and layers of tissue, there was only a folded piece of paper. Maybe Kitty and Tyner had bought her the new car she wanted. Or had given her a check to pay for her pain and suffering through this ordeal. Tess was giving them a small wooden chest, courtesy of Mickey Harvey the woodworker. Tess didn't care how old Kitty was. Every bride needed a hope chest.

The paper, folded with almost origami complexity, was a note, nothing more. *I'm not sure what the traditional bride's gift is to the maid of honor,* Kitty had written in her distinctive parochial-school hand, *but I thought I'd give you a nudge.* The inscription was followed by a telephone number that Tess had memorized long ago, a Virginia number she had *not* been calling all these weeks. It was the home telephone for Crow's parents.

So Kitty had known. She had probably figured it out long ago, and she had kept her own counsel, offering Tess chance after chance to confide, but never pushing. Even now she wasn't telling Tess to go back to Crow. She was simply urging her to decide what she wanted, once and for all, to give up this limbo of inaction.

Tess thought of all the things people did in the name of love. She thought of the pain that Natalie and Zeke had caused everyone around them, the literal lives lost because they believed that their love suspended all the usual rules. She thought of Mark, sitting shivah for a marriage that never was rather than expose himself to a world of women who would find him eminently lovable. She thought of Natalie's inextinguishable passion for her children, which had convinced her to do the right thing, albeit in the wrong way.

Wasn't Tess's refusal to do anything simply the other side of Mark Rubin's misguided belief that he could control everything? The fact was, Tess had resented Mark's passionate quest for Natalie because she wanted Crow to pursue her, to fight for her, to engage in some way, any way. Funny—they were so good in a crisis, when they had to bond together, so fragile when it came to day-to-day life. Instead of trying to work out their problems, they had gone to their respective corners to sulk. Crow had a right to such immaturity, but Tess was thirty-three now. She needed to be a bit more adult.

The car arrived at the Peabody Library. The front doors were thrown open, and a beautiful square of yellow light shimmered in the night. The book-filled rooms at the top of the short flight of stairs seemed to hold all that anyone could ask for of life—family, friends, good music, delicious food. Rubik's Cube solved at last, at least on this face. Who knew what the other five sides looked like?

As Tess started to get out of the car, this time remembering to keep her knees together, she realized she must experience the evening not only for herself but also for her virtual clan, the Snoop-Sisters. Susan in Omaha would want to hear about the rare books in the Peabody's stacks. Letha in St. Louis would be curious about the people—what they did and what they wore. Margie Lynn in California would be filled with questions about the menu, while Gretchen would bluntly demand to know the cost of the whole affair. And yes, they also would want to know what happened to Tess in the next moment. For the SnoopSisters had been privy to Tess's secret all these weeks, and they had given her that rarest combination of friendly commiseration—pure empathy and no advice. They deserved to be the first to know what she had decided. Well, maybe the second.

She stopped on the sidewalk, digging her cell phone out of the ridiculously small evening bag Kitty and her mother had insisted she carry. Tess had wanted to use a knapsack—a small one, to be sure, by a name designer—but Kitty assumed she was just trying to sneak her Beretta into the ceremony. This dinky thing barely accommodated her keys, phone, and lipstick. No room for the second phone, the one she used for outgoing calls, so she had to use the one whose number she always safeguarded. But that was okay. Tess didn't mind if this particular person had her number.

An answering machine picked up. "Call me on this phone when you have time to talk. *Please.* No matter how late, no matter how early." Then she climbed the stairs and entered a fragrant room that contained almost—almost—everything she wanted.